NO ESCAPE

Book One in the Mark IV Anna Series

Danny B. McGuire

This is a work of fiction. The names, characters, and incidents are the products of the author's imagination. Any resemblance to actual events or persons, living or dead, is entirely coincidental.

First Edition

Copyright © 2014 by Danny B. McGuire

Published by: Paper Bard Media www.paperbard.com

ISBN: 069227989X
ISBN-13: 978-0692279892

First, I would like to thank my family, my wife Angie, and my two sons, Erik and Connor. I want you to know, you are everything to me.

I'd also like to thank everyone else who helped me with this novel. From advice, to proofreading, to providing great cover images, I have wonderful friends who gave their best to help me get this book into your hands. Thank you all.

Cover photography by: www.facebook.com/photosbydeedee

Cover design by: www.fiverr.com/vikncharlie

PART ONE

ONE OF US

Stepan Entsky wasn't the kind of man to back down from anything. After all, he had been in the Russian military, the KGB, and other various covert agencies for his entire adult life. He had been forged into the man he was by his career choices and the arduous situations in which they'd placed him. Situations where if you reacted the wrong way, you'd lose your life. Situations exactly like the one he was in right now.

However, Stepan hadn't survived, even thrived, in this world of shadows for almost forty years by misjudging these encounters. He'd always managed to work his way out of these little spots, and he would do so again. Stepan stood up straight and unafraid as he exchanged hate-filled stares with the woman that was only inches from his face. He was well aware that she wanted to kill him. The fire burning in her deep-brown eyes told him that. He also knew she wouldn't go through with it. She simply didn't have the guts. Stepan prided himself on his ability to read people, to determine what they might be capable of doing. This skill had always served him well, and he had every confidence in it now.

The woman, Anna, was yelling at him now, but he wasn't listening. Stepan just wanted her to finish her rant and storm away. He thought as soon as she finished her tirade and left, he could call for backup from the many soldiers stationed at the base. They would prevent her from escaping his facility. He'd show her who she was dealing with.

Stepan sighed to himself and finally lost his patience with her preaching. That was when he made his mistake, the mistake of pushing her one step too far. It was the worst mistake of his life. While he had been correct about Anna not killing him, she hurt him. She hurt him worse than he had ever been hurt in his life. While still meeting his gaze, she kicked out violently and struck him in his left knee as hard as she could with her booted foot. The kick shattered his kneecap and produced a sickening, cracking sound that echoed around the old satellite building where they'd been arguing. Red-hot pain engulfed his leg and raced throughout his entire body. In agony, he crumpled and fell into unconsciousness.

His eyes snapped open and he awoke from the horrible nightmare. A cold sweat covered his body and he couldn't catch his breath. He tried to focus, tried to force himself to calm down, but his mind was still racing as it shifted between the dream world and the real one. It was the pain that at last fully woke him. His knee was aching and burning like it was on fire. Those damn painkillers he took never lasted for more than a few hours, and he was never able to sleep through the night. Frustrated, he sat up in bed and reflexively grabbed at his knee as a sharp, stabbing pain punished him for moving too quickly. Stepan cursed and groped around for the prescription bottle on his nightstand. He found it and cursed again as his large hands wrestled with the childproof lid. After defeating the cap, he popped two pills into his mouth and looked around the spartanly furnished bedroom for his bottle of vodka. His heart sank as he saw it on the other nightstand across the bed. He leaned over to reach for it, but the pain in his knee made him wince and pull back. Before he could try again, a woman's pale, shapely arm reached out from under the blanket and easily picked it up off the nightstand. She slowly sat up in the bed, and put her free arm around his broad shoulders as she handed him the bottle. Stepan tried to smile at her, but his knee turned it into a grimace. Dejectedly, he took a large swig and washed down the pills.

Eliza took the bottle away from him when he was finished and placed it on the nightstand. She then turned back and gave Stepan her full attention. Her slender fingers ran through his short salt and pepper hair as she tried to calm him. After a while, she asked, "Did you have the dream again?"

Stepan nodded and put his arms around her perfectly proportioned waist. With some effort, he was able to lean and rest his head on her shoulder. "Six months later and I'm still having the same damn one. It's because my leg starts aching and triggers that fucking nightmare. I always wake up at the same time, just as she kicks me and I hear that dreadful crunching sound."

Eliza's eyes met his and she tried her best to look compassionate. She didn't think she was very good at it, but she managed to elicit a smile from Stepan. As she looked at his rough, tanned face and his short, mostly gray hair, she wondered if he would be considered handsome. She let her eyes roam over his wrinkled and worn body, a body that had been victimized by booze and smoking for the better part of sixty years. She concluded that no, he wasn't handsome. He was actually quite pathetic, both physically and of late, mentally. However, he was still a politically powerful man, and he was the reason she was still alive.

After her first mission, the rest of the team had decided she was too unpredictable, too dangerous. She tried to explain to them that she was only fulfilling the mission parameters as efficiently as possible. Besides, she had only killed one person and partially blinded another. What was the big deal? The scientists on the team hadn't seen it that way. They had called her psychotic and unstable. Those lab coat wearing bastards had decided she wasn't worth the effort and tossed her aside to work on their new model, their precious Anna, but not Stepan. He had taken her out of the lab, away from the scientists, and he went against their wishes to terminate her. He had saved her life. Furthermore, Stepan had given her another chance to fulfill her purpose. He had trusted her enough to send her back out on missions. Sure, sometimes he had berated her for being overzealous, like when she went back to that lab and destroyed the whole damn thing. However, out of loyalty, she really tried her best to control herself and not disappoint him. She owed Stepan everything, and she knew it.

Eliza focused back on Stepan, but she couldn't feel compassion, kindness, love, or even empathy toward him. She had no experience with any of what she considered the 'weaker emotions', the ones that Anna was able to experience. Just the thought of that damned Anna turned her mood sour and she gritted her teeth. Then, just as quickly, her mood shifted and she silently chided herself for being so stupid. After all, she didn't need those other emotions, she knew what loyalty was, she knew whom she was loyal to, and that was Stepan. Well, at least as long as he played nice and was useful to her.

Eliza noticed that, for some reason, Stepan was quietly staring out the window. She deduced that he was trying to figure out how to locate and retrieve the renegade, Anna. Again at the thought of her, Eliza's fury rose. It was Anna that caused the team to turn their backs on her. Well, she'd show them. She'd show Anna how the original was always better than a cheap knock-off.

Hatred was one emotion Eliza didn't have to fake, and venom coated each word as she softly spoke. "You know I've done a lot of digging around, and I have an excellent idea about where that bitch is hiding. Just say the word, and I'll bring her back. I'll bring her back in pieces."

However, Eliza had been wrong, Stepan was lost in thought, but it wasn't about Anna. The sun entranced him as it rose over the horizon. Its light slowly creeping across the military base he commanded known as Ice Castle. Since the base was situated in the northernmost part of Russia, it was almost always cold and covered in snow. He smiled as he looked across the base, *his* base, covered in its deep, white blanket. It was beautiful to him, as it gleamed in the sunrise, beautiful, but so bitterly cold. He shivered and noticed that the movement didn't cause any protest from his leg. The pills and vodka had started to take effect and the pain had faded to a dull throb.

He met Eliza's gaze again. She'd said something about Anna, but with the distraction of the pain gone, he became acutely aware of the closeness of her body and her warm arm around him. Stepan then knew exactly how he wanted to shake off his chill. Slowly, he began to let his hands roam as he winked and said, "My sweet doll, how about we discuss

Anna a little later?"

Eliza picked up on Stepan's desires and she resigned herself to what was about to happen. She would have to pretend to enjoy sex with him, again. She thought about how much he wanted to have sex, which really was a lot, almost everyday in fact. It made her wonder how a sixty year old man was still this active. Perhaps the old guy was taking more than just pain pills when she wasn't looking. Through repetition, she had gotten better at faking her pleasure with him, at least Stepan was happy enough with her, and it was something she knew she would have to continue. She had to stay close enough to absorb all he learned and manipulate him, if the need arose. So, she winked back at him and giggled as she pulled him tightly into her body. She was going to get this over with as quickly as possible.

A while later, they were resting comfortably when a knock came at the door to Stepan's office. He looked over to Eliza, who was looking back at him quizzically. Patting her arm, he said, "That will be Warren, we have a meeting this morning. Get dressed and meet us out in the office. We have a lot to discuss." He noticed that telling her it was Warren had replaced the curious look with a frown, but she stretched and rolled over to get out of the bed.

Stepan struggled making his own way out of the bed and pulled on a thick, maroon robe that had been hanging over the back of a chair. Out of the corner of his eye, he also noticed his walking cane leaning against the wall. He mumbled under his breath, before retrieving it. Leaning heavily on the cane, he limped out of the bedroom.

His large, rough hand gripped the cane tightly as he used it to navigate around the cluttered desk that was the focal point of his office. He was almost to the door, when another knock rang out. He called out in frustration, "I'm coming, damn it." After what felt like forever, he made it to the door and pulled it open to find Warren Lopata impatiently standing there.

Warren gave him a bit of a sideways glance and a curt nod. "Good morning Stepan. Our meeting was at eight, correct?"

Stepan moved to the side and motioned for him to enter. "Yes, yes, I must have lost track of time. Please come in and have a seat Warren."

He watched as the thin, older man hung his coat on the rack near the door and made his way across the room. Warren sat down in one of the straight-back, wooden chairs across from the desk. Stepan took a deep breath and began his struggle to join him.

Warren tried not to notice as the man limped slowly toward him. Instead, he obsessed with shaking the snow from the sparse, gray tufts of hair located on each side of his head and straightening out his lab coat. By this time, Stepan had made it to his seat and settled in behind the desk.

Warren pulled a pad computer from his pocket and asked, "Will it just be us this morning?"

Stepan adjusted himself in the leather office chair and shook his head. "No, Eliza will be joining us in just a minute."

Warren frowned and looked up from his pad. "Stepan, do we really need to include her every time we…"

The sound of a door slamming interrupted Warren, and both of them turned toward the noise. Eliza stood leaning against the door to Stepan's bedroom. She waited for a few seconds to allow the men to stare at her. Technically, she had gotten dressed as Stepan had asked of her, but all she wore was one of his dress shirts. *Wore* might have been the wrong word, since she had fastened only the bottom three buttons, which exposed her cleavage from neck to waist. The shirt somehow managed to cover her 'vital' areas, but not much else.

In one hand, she had a Cohiba, one of Stepan's Cuban cigars, and in the other, she carried his lighter. Her eyes moved casually back and forth from one man to the other as she raised the cigar to her mouth and closed her lips around it. Slowly, she brought the lighter up and ignited it. She held the flame against the end of the cigar and took several long, deep puffs until the end glowed a bright orange. She drifted toward Stepan while lifting her head and blowing the smoke up to the ceiling. When she reached his desk, she sat down on the corner facing him and took one more deep drag before handing him the cigar. As Stepan took it and put it into the corner of his mouth, she rotated on the desk until she could see Warren. Eliza looked at him and met his angry stare while she exhaled the cigar smoke down toward his feet. Stepan suppressed a laugh as he saw that Warren was absolutely fuming. He knew that Eliza had made that entrance just to irritate the scientist. There was definitely no love lost between those two, one might say that they even hated each other. Still he had to admit, she could make a hell of an entrance.

While Stepan found this struggle between them to win his favor amusing, he knew not to let it go too far. He needed them both, and didn't want to risk angering either of them by embarrassing one in front of the other. He turned to Eliza and smoothly lied as he said, "My sweet doll, it hurts my leg to turn to my side so much. Why don't you take the empty seat next to Warren where I can see you both without moving?" Eliza smiled her agreement at him and gracefully slid off the desk. Not once did she turn her back on Warren as she moved toward the chair and sat down next to him. He noticed that Warren kept his eyes on her all the way to the chair as well, but it definitely wasn't out of admiration. As Eliza took her seat, Warren assumed the standoff was over and he turned toward Stepan to speak. That was when Eliza slid down in her chair and with an exaggerated motion, placed both her feet down on Stepan's desk causing the shirt to rise dangerously high on her thighs. Stepan moved quickly to get the meeting underway before another confrontation broke out. "Okay, now let's get started, Warren, present the lab update please," he said.

Warren frowned, but he looked away from Eliza and down at his pad computer to consult his notes. "Let's see, the lab reconstruction project is ninety percent complete, and our estimates show we will be finished with the rebuild in about two weeks. Also, even in its compromised state, we were able to restart production and create some older models as per your request."

"And the new scientists?" Stepan asked.

"They're still learning, but they are doing well. I expect them to be trained to the limit of their ability within the next month," replied Warren.

Stepan looked puzzled, and asked, "What do you mean by, *to the limit of their ability?*"

Warren's face turned a little red as he answered. "Well, honestly, none of them will be able to replace Viktor Eklund, not even me."

Stepan shot a look at Eliza, who avoided his gaze. "Ah, understood. Eliza, maybe your investigation will help fill the void left by Viktor's untimely demise. Do you have any information concerning the whereabouts of his daughter?"

Eliza hated to disappoint him, especially since she was the one that had killed Viktor, but she had no choice. "No, Stepan. I have utilized all our resources, searched all the data available to us, and even run through all the old data we have about her working in the same field as her father, but I have come up empty. It's like the woman never existed. I've hit a dead end. I am sorry."

Warren chuckled under his breath at her choice of words and mumbled, "Only fitting since you created the dead end to begin with."

Eliza turned on Warren in an instant, but Stepan saw it coming and cut the argument off before it could start. "Eliza, what about your other mission, the search for our little runaway android, Anna?"

This defused Eliza instantly since she had good news on that front. "I've found out that Anna stowed away aboard a cargo ship on its way to the United States. This ship left the nearby city of Tiksi the night she escaped. Its destination was a port in the state of Alabama. My most recent intelligence leads me to believe that she is still in the central area of that state, probably living in a city called Birmingham." Her voice grew ice cold as she continued, "I am more than ready to go and retrieve her for you Stepan. Just say the word and I'll have her back inside of ten days."

Stepan took the cigar from the side of his mouth and slowly exhaled the smoke as he paused to think. After a moment, he said, "You have done exceedingly well my sweet, and I think you are right, now is the time to go after her."

Eliza immediately straightened in her chair and dropped her feet back down to the floor. She was almost standing before Stepan could continue. "Hold on a second, let me tell you how I want you to proceed."

At this, she slumped back down in the chair like an impatient child. Stepan continued explaining her mission in detail. "Eliza, this is of the utmost importance. You will be thousands of miles away from here and in a foreign country, you must be discrete. Don't risk exposing yourself or the purpose of your mission, because I won't be able to help you if you are found out or captured." He slowed down and softened his voice knowing just what to say. "I can't afford to lose you, you are one of a kind, absolutely irreplaceable." This made her perk back up and she began to pay closer attention to his instructions.

Stepan smiled at his own cleverness, and continued laying out his plan. "Now, the mission has two main objectives and one secondary one. The first one you know. You must return Anna to Ice Castle without destroying her. Do you understand that, Eliza?"

Eliza's face darkened, and she replied through gritted teeth. "Understood."

Stepan smiled softly at her. "Good, I knew I could count on you. Now, you may not be aware of the second objective. I have been pouring through the security camera footage of the night Anna escaped, and I found something that will interest you. Warren, show us the file I sent you last night."

Warren tapped on his pad and held it up so everyone could see the holographic display. It was a recording of that night six months ago captured in the old satellite control building. The view was focused on Anna as she sat on the floor mourning over the body of Viktor Eklund. As the scene played out, Anna noticed something in Viktor's hand and she slowly opened it to expose a small rectangular object. She then reached out and took it from him.

"Pause it right there. Warren, can you zoom in on what she took and slowly play it forward?" Stepan said.

Warren complied, and they could see that Anna was holding some kind of data storage device. She accessed it for a short time and placed it in her pants pocket. The words 'End Recording' rotated slowly above the pad.

Stepan took another puff from his cigar and said, "Okay, shut it off." As the display disappeared, he turned back to address Eliza. "Now you know the second objective of the mission. Earlier in the recording, Viktor removes that device from around his neck and puts it in his hand hoping that Anna will find it. Obviously, it contains something vitally important, maybe the location of his daughter or perhaps the only remaining copy of all his research. Either way, we have to retrieve that device."

Eliza nodded her understanding. "I will return with both Anna and the device. You can count on me, Stepan. Is there anything else?"

Stepan shifted his weight and winced as his knee began to throb again. He grimaced and answered her. "Yes, one more thing. While you are in the United States, discreetly, and I mean very discreetly, try to gather any information you can find about the location of Viktor's daughter. You will have access to different networks and data stores, not to mention our undercover agents, so hopefully you can gather some new information."

"Sounds good, will I be going alone?" she asked.

"Warren and I will stay here, but I want you to stop by the lab and pick up some of the older models that he has constructed. You'll need to get moving, I've made arrangements for you to depart tonight," he said.

Eliza jumped up and headed for the office door. Her excitement was so great, that she had her hand on the doorknob before Stepan could stop her. "Eliza, my doll, why don't you change into something a little warmer before you leave?" She turned to him and shrugged an acknowledgment before heading back into the bedroom. After Eliza was out of sight, Stepan motioned for Warren to stay seated.

Eliza dressed and left Stepan's office inside of five minutes leaving the two men alone. Warren decided now was the time to have that talk he'd been dreading. He shifted uncomfortably in his seat trying to figure out how to start the conversation, but Stepan began it for him. "Warren, I need some stronger pain pills. I can't even sleep through the night with what you've given me."

"Stronger? Alright, I'll consider it, if you tell me how many you're taking now," he said.

Stepan placed the cigar in his ashtray and reached down to rub his aching knee. "How many? Well, I'm taking them just like you told me, one every six hours," he lied.

Warren narrowed his eyes and tried to read Stepan's expression, but he couldn't gain anything from the experienced KGB agent, so he focused on what he knew. "Stepan, you are traveling down a dangerous road. I have seen you take your pills with vodka. You know you should never mix the two."

Stepan laughed and tried to play off Warren's words. "Warren, I'm a sixty year old Russian, vodka is just like water to me."

Warren's face reddened and he shot back, "Stepan, this isn't a joke. You're getting sloppy, and sloppy people make mistakes." He waved his hand at Stepan and said, "I mean look at you. You're meeting with me in your robe for God's sake." Warren took a deep breath and gathered his thoughts. "Look, I know it's been tough, but you're the one that quit going to rehab for your knee, you're the one mixing pain pills and alcohol, and my God, you're even sleeping with Eliza! You know she's an android, and a completely psychotic one at that. She might kill you just as well as kiss you. I have to ask, have you lost your damn mind?"

Stepan slowly stood up from his seat and used his cane to limp around the desk until he was in front of Warren. As he approached, the scientist sank back into his seat, afraid he'd gone to far. Stepan let his cane drop to the floor as he bent over and grasped the arms of Warren's chair. He leaned in until his unshaven face was all that the shaken man could see. His voice was low and calm as he spoke. "Warren, you have been a great asset to my team and I appreciate your opinion on the many topics of which you have great knowledge and experience. However, I do not believe you have the least bit of insight on how much my knee hurts, or how I should conduct my meetings on the base, which, let me remind you, I command. Nor do you have any idea of how much I should or should not drink." Stepan paused and inched even closer to Warren's pale, frightened face. "Lastly, I damn sure don't believe that a lab rat is qualified to tell me who to fuck or who not to fuck. Do we understand each other?" As Warren managed to slowly nod his head, a crooked smile found its way on to Stepan's face before he continued. "Good, good, now get out of here and bring me back some stronger fucking pain pills by lunchtime or I'll have you shot." With that, Stepan straightened himself up and allowed Warren to get out of the chair. The man was so shaken, that he left the office without even stopping to retrieve his coat.

Stepan watched the door to his office close and he carefully retrieved his cane from the floor. Using it, he made his way back behind his desk and sat down in his chair. He had one more meeting this morning and it was with one of his base officers. He knew if it went the way he hoped, he would have some excellent leverage to help Eliza with her mission. His knee suddenly sent a jolt of pain through his leg, but he was too busy planning his next move to even notice.

Chapter 1

Felix rubbed at his eyes as he slid his pad computer across the desk toward me. "Here Anna, take a look now." I leaned forward in my chair and reached for the pad, but he snatched it back before I could get my hands on it. I looked up at him and his face wore a sheepish grin. "Wait, wait, let me check one more thing."

I relaxed back in my chair and stifled a sigh. It was after ten in the evening and my boss and I were still at work. We were sequestered in his office working on a proposal for a potential client, a *large* potential client. Felix had been pouring all his time this week into this project, so I knew it was important to him. He had even asked me to stay late tonight because I was his 'number one gal'. After six months at my new job, I'd learned the reward for doing great work, was primarily, just more work.

Now don't get me wrong, I wasn't that upset about working late. I was quite happy with my job. I hadn't had to pull out a gun and shoot anyone nor had I engaged in hand-to-hand combat since I joined the small team at FlexJen Software. That type of work was all in my past, a past that no one here in America knew. It was a past that I had to keep hidden, forever.

No one could ever know that I wasn't the twenty-something Russian immigrant I appeared to be, that I was something that was built, not born. A machine constructed in an underground laboratory by a group

13

of brilliant scientists. Dreamt up by Stepan Entsky, a ruthless, ex-KGB agent that wanted me to be his ultimate intelligence tool. Just an object used to help further his power hungry aspirations. I was supposed to use my built-in network infiltration and disguise skills to gather him data from anywhere he desired. Everything had been proceeding according to Stepan's plan; at least until I decided that I didn't want to be his super spy. After that, my situation rapidly deteriorated. The whole thing blew up, ending with most of the scientists being murdered by another completely psychotic android named Eliza. She would have killed me as well if I hadn't had an unlikely friend help me escape. Even with his help, I barely got away. I managed to stow away on a cargo ship and treat my various wounds. During the voyage to America, I altered my physical appearance to help conceal myself from what I knew would be an intense manhunt by Stepan. When the ship docked in Mobile, Alabama, I hitchhiked up to Birmingham to find a job and lie low. So yeah, compared to all that, I was definitely content to write software all week.

Felix finally looked up from his pad and with some hesitation, slid it back across the table. The motion brought my thoughts back to the task at hand and I looked at him as he wearily said, "Okay, if it doesn't look like it will fly now, I don't know what else to do."

I paused to see if he would grab it back like last time, but he was sitting back and looking at me expectantly, so I reached out and picked up the device. I tried to reassure him as I said, "I'm sure this is the one, let's take a look." On the screen of the pad was a complex set of spreadsheets, which would have taken a half hour or more to go over manually. Luckily, I wasn't planning on checking them that way.

I lowered the pad onto my lap and pretended to study it intently as I covertly checked to make sure the desk blocked Felix's view of my hands. Confident that he couldn't see, I slid the fingernail on my right index finger into the data port on the side of the device. Instantly, I felt the connection to the pad's operating system. A distinct personality that represented the pad's OS began to form inside my mind. This was how I communicated with other networks or computer systems. I called it *interfusing*. Using this technique, I could interact with the system as if it were a person, and just like a person, each system had it's own distinct personality. These personalities, I had named personas. Now the pad wasn't an overly complex system, so its persona was not the most engaging. It spoke in a dry, male voice as it got straight to the point. "What do you require?" it asked.

"Allow me access to your data files, please."

I expected a password question or some refusal from the pad. However, Felix must not have had any security in place because soon I was in a huge room full of filing cabinets. There were hundreds of them, but fortunately, they were well organized. I easily found the spreadsheet among all the other data that Felix had filed away. Opening the large manila folder full of papers labeled 'Jefferson County Proposal', I read it while carefully checking all the facts and figures. It didn't take but the blink of an eye for me to see that Felix had everything planned out and accounted for perfectly. I slid my fingernail back out of the pad and the file room faded from my mind. I nodded my approval to him. "Everything checks out just fine, good work."

He whistled and shook his head slowly, "You are the fastest person I've ever seen when dealing with formulas and data. If you hadn't stayed tonight, I'd have still been here in the morning." Before I could reply, he continued by asking, "So the data checks out, what about the proposal itself? Do you think they'll go with us?"

"I think that it's the best we can do. The dates you've set are really aggressive and the contract price is sure to be the lowest bid. They'd be crazy to turn down this proposal." I laid the pad back down on the desk and slid it back over to him.

He nervously twirled a pencil around in his hand while listening to my reassurances. "Good, because we could really use this deal." He paused, twirled the pencil some more, and said, "Yeah, I'm sure they'll go for it." He looked down at the display on the pad for a moment or two more, and finally said, "Well, I think that's all we can do tonight Anna, what's say we roll out of here?" His gray eyes lit up at his own joke, and I grinned back, but honestly, the little jokes he made about himself using a wheelchair made me a little uncomfortable. After all, I had only known Felix Jennings about six months, and I didn't want to assume too much familiarity with his condition. Not to mention I still had trouble reading some human emotions and situations.

Soon we had gathered our things and were heading toward the front of the building. The whir of Felix's electric wheelchair and the click of my heels against the tile floor echoed around the dark hallway of FlexJen Software. We reached the lobby and approached the double glass doors leading to the parking lot. Once there, Felix announced, "Irene, Anna and I are leaving for the night. Please lock up behind us."

The lack of any true artificial intelligence, and a modest vocabulary, limited Irene's duties to simple office automation. Her tinny voice echoed through the lobby in response to Felix's request. "Good night, Mister Jennings and Miss Andropov. I will secure the building for the night." The doors hissed and slid open, disappearing into hidden spaces inside the walls. As Felix and I exited the office, the doors slid back closed and there was a *bee-boop* sound as Irene engaged the lock.

Leaving work this late in the evening always put me on alert, but tonight was different. I felt something else, like someone was watching us. I took a quick look around our well-lit parking lot and saw that it was empty except for our two vehicles. Maybe it was nothing. Matter of fact, I bet it was just my previous training making me needlessly antsy. I mean after all, our office was in Southside, and it was a nice community. Its residents were mostly younger people that attended the nearby University of Alabama at Birmingham, or UAB as everyone knew it. There were even a few of them still out and about, heading home from a late class or maybe from a nearby restaurant. Nice community notwithstanding, I still couldn't shake my nervous feeling. I also knew that we looked like a couple of easy victims, a young woman and a paraplegic man, by ourselves, in a deserted parking lot.

Felix, apparently oblivious to all my paranoid thoughts, guided his wheelchair down the ramp from our entryway and into the parking lot without hesitation. I took a second to scan around the area with my thermal vision and still saw nothing out of place. Finally, deciding that I was being irrational, I descended the steps next to the wheelchair ramp. Felix was almost to his van, and I hurried across the lot to catch up with him.

He was waiting for me next to the large side door of his Honda Element. Felix cared for his van, the way a parent would for their child, and I noticed that it was looking impeccable, as usual. Its metallic copper colored body was so clean and waxed that it was shining even under the fluorescent light in the parking lot. He noticed me giving it the once over and broke out in a toothy grin that simply oozed pride. "Yeah, I just had her detailed, nice huh?"

I nodded my agreement as he reached out and touched the door handle on the Element, causing it to spring to life. The door unlocked with a thump and slid open while an elevator platform lowered itself down to the ground. As Felix drove his chair onto the platform, he looked back at me and said, "Hey, thanks again for staying. Be careful driving home and I'll see you tomorrow."

I smiled and replied, "No problem Felix, see you in the morning." Then that nagging feeling took over again and I found myself taking a covert look inside his van with my thermal vision. Again, I didn't see any heat sources inside the Element, so no one was waiting inside to waylay my boss and possibly do horrible things to him. That was a good thing, but I was still unsure why I felt the way I did. Still lost in thought, I turned and began to walk over to my car as Felix started his van and pulled onto the street. By the time I'd reached my car, his taillights were just a couple of small red dots far down the road.

I looked inside of my car too, although I didn't know why. For someone to be hidden in my car, they'd have to be about this size of a one year old child. My car was made by Honda, just like Felix's, but that's where the similarities ended. Mine was a well-used Honda Civic that I'd bought when I first arrived here in Birmingham. At that time, I was still unemployed and living off the modest amount of money that my father had given me right before I escaped from the lab where I was 'born'. Back then I couldn't afford to spend a lot, so this little Honda became my first car. The poor thing's body wasn't in good shape. Its color was a badly sun-faded blue and it had multiple dents and dings all over, especially in its two doors. The exhaust was loud and buzzy sounding because a previous owner had tweaked around with the muffler. It had a sunroof that leaked when it rained, and one of its taillights had been broken out only to be repaired with red packing tape. I could keep going, but you've probably got the idea. It's true, my car wasn't going to win any beauty pageants, but it had a great personality and with a little help from me, it ran perfectly. Which was exactly what I needed from a car.

Since I didn't see anyone hiding in the cup holders, I unlocked the door and climbed inside the Civic. The springs in the seat made their familiar squeaking sound as I settled in behind the wheel and cranked the car. I slowly took one more look around the parking lot, and still saw nothing. I shrugged and backed the car out of its spot. Shifting into gear, I pulled out onto the road heading toward home.

Since I was heading home so late, I made good time on the Red Mountain Expressway and even managed to catch most of the lights on Highway 280 while they were green. Before long, I was turning right and taking the on-ramp to Interstate 459, heading south toward the city of Hoover. I was so happy to be almost home that I nearly missed the car's hesitation as I shifted through the gears and accelerated to get onto I-459. The car's sudden rough acceleration didn't surprise me since the poor thing had over 200,000 miles, and more than its share of abusive owners.

I got the Civic up to around 70 MPH and looked around I-459 to check the traffic. As usual at this time of night, it was deserted. Interfusing left only a small piece of my consciousness in the real world, but I decided it would be safe enough for me to have a quick talk with my car and see what was bothering it. I mean it was the least I could do after all the trouble and pain I'd put it through learning to drive. Although it wasn't completely my fault, after all, I'd never driven a car before, to say nothing of a stick shift.

I leaned forward and reached under the dash with my left hand, searching for the car's diagnostic connection. This data port was present on every car, and was used by auto mechanics to troubleshoot various issues. It was also the way I interfused with my Honda. Having found the data jack, I pushed my fingernail into it just as I'd done on Felix's pad. My surroundings faded into the shadows as the car's system began to enter my mind. Now I don't understand entirely how interfusing works, but I do know that a system's persona is highly influenced by the people that constructed it, along with its main functionality. So it was no surprise that I found myself standing in a small garage near the trunk of my car. The hood was raised and I could hear someone poking around the engine. As I started walking toward the sound, the mechanic must have heard me because he left the engine and met me halfway. I recognized the man instantly, his name was Takumi, and we'd met several times before in this same garage. He bowed to greet me, and as he straightened back upright, a warm smile spread across his wrinkled face. "Good evening Anna-san. It is a pleasure to have you visit me again."

I returned the bow and replied, "Thank you for allowing me to visit Takumi-san. I know you are very busy."

His brown eyes twinkled and he wiggled a finger at me. "You know you are always welcome, but I also know that this is not a social call. Come, this way, let me show you something."

I followed him to the front of the car and he pointed at something on the engine. "You see here, the spark plug cables are worn and not conducting correctly. That is the cause of your problem. I would replace them and the plugs as well, just to be safe."

Because of his short height, he was able to stand upright, but I had to lean in before I could see where he was indicating. After I saw what he was talking about, I pulled my head back out from under the car hood and turned to face him. "Thank you Takumi-san, you always know just how to remedy the problem. Your insight has never led me astray." I bowed to him again.

He waved off my politeness and looked down at the floor of the garage. "I am sorry for the trouble Anna-san. It is profoundly embarrassing for a vehicle that I am in charge of maintaining to be experiencing these issues."

I crossed my arms and said, "You have no call to apologize. Previous owners have neglected your car for far too long. I will make the repairs you have suggested, although it may be a few days because work is hectic at the moment. Would that be a problem?"

He shook his head and said, "No, the car will continue to run. Only you may experience the hesitation some more."

I nodded my understanding. "I will see you again as soon as I've made the repairs, then you may check my work. Good evening, Takumi-san."

"Good evening, Anna-san," he said.

I pulled my nail free from the port breaking my connection to the Civic and as I did, Takumi's wise face faded from my mind. Now, interfusing leaves me distracted from the events going on in the outside world. Which is why I wasn't surprised to find a car hiding in my driver's side blind spot.

I quickly adjusted my side mirror, but I couldn't see anything except for the car's bright headlights. I knew this might be just another car heading home. However, I couldn't figure out how they'd gotten this close without me noticing them. Even in my interfused state, I should have at least seen their headlights as they approached from behind me. Unless they had turned them off to deliberately be sneaky.

Okay, it was time to see what I was dealing with. My exit was coming up and since the road was clear, I decided to do a little evasive driving. I planned my maneuver and since I was so familiar with my car, I felt confident that I wouldn't end up wrecking and killing myself. I put one hand on the steering wheel and the other on my stick shift. It wasn't long now.

I looked left to check on my unknown friend, and then I stomped on the brakes. Instantly, the ABS light began to blink angrily on the car's dashboard as my brakes pulsed on and off to keep the car from skidding sideways. As I quickly decelerated, my blind spot buddy shot past me until the rear of his white, four-door sedan drew even with the front of my car. However, he recovered quicker than I had anticipated, and I saw his brake lights come on as he slowed down. As the sedan dropped back, I tried to get a look at who was so interested in me. I only had a split second to glimpse the inside of the other car and if I'd had any doubts about their intentions, they were ended by what I saw. Actually, it was what I hadn't seen. The car was almost completely dark inside because the driver had turned off all the dash lights. I couldn't see any detail at all, but I could tell there were two people in the front. The driver was the larger of the pair and was wearing some kind of hat. While all I could tell about the passenger was they'd turned toward me and must have gotten a decent look at my face.

I had to be satisfied with that small amount of information, because my exit was here and I wanted to lose whoever this was before they followed me home. I slammed the car into third gear and punched the gas while yanking my wheel to the right. The little Honda's exhaust buzzed like a can of angry bees while the engine responded as best it could. The Civic swerved and crossed onto the exit ramp at about sixty miles an hour. I took a quick survey of the ramp and the highway I was rocketing toward. Luckily, they were both clear and I could take the left turn onto Highway 31 at my current speed. I looked back to check on the sedan and saw that I'd played it just right. They were trying to maneuverer off I-459, but they had already passed the exit I'd just taken. I'd be out of their sight before they could get turned around to follow me. Patting my little Civic's dash, I said, "Great job Takumi."

I slowed down as soon as I was sure I'd lost the sedan and my mind began to race with thoughts of who may have been in the car. It was probably someone from my past. Someone I had hoped to never see again, but I needed to do some research first before I jumped to any conclusions. I was sure of one thing. I was going to start having more faith in my paranoid feelings.

Chapter 2

To insure I wasn't being followed, I drove aimlessly, making random turns for about ten minutes before getting back onto Highway 31. I checked all around my car one last time for the mysterious white sedan, but I must have shaken them because I was alone on this section of the highway. A wave of relief washed over me and I finally decided it was safe enough to head toward home.

I took a right off the highway and headed slowly down the narrow street. It was another right turn and a couple of minutes later before my headlights lit up the familiar sign for my apartment complex, Eagle's Nest on the Mountain. I carefully made my way through the maze of white buildings and decoratively lit hedges until I came to my section, which was labeled, Eaglet C. Eagle's Nest had been wrapping up construction when I found them, so everything about it still had a brand new shine. Matter of fact, as I parked my car and got out, you could still smell the scent of fresh cut lumber and drying paint. Plus there was another benefit to my early discovery of Eagle's Nest. I had my choice of where in the complex I wanted to live. I had chosen the building all the way in the back, and an apartment on the far end of the second floor. Not that I was trying to be antisocial, but seeing that I had broken out of a secret KGB military installation, I was just trying to be as low key as possible.

I climbed the wooden stairs up to the second floor and began walking to the end of the row. Holding my cell phone up to the magnetic lock, I heard a satisfying click as the deadbolt disengaged. It wasn't until I'd grabbed the handle and turned it that I realized something. What if the people in the white sedan already knew where I lived? What if they were inside waiting on me right now?

The thought froze me in place with the doorknob still in my hand. I quietly leaned over and put my ear close to the door. I strained to hear any noise, any sound that might give away someone hiding in my apartment. All I heard was my own rapid breathing and the hum of the fluorescent lights overhead. Encouraged by the silence, I crouched down and slid as much of my body as I could over to the latch side of the door. My muscles tensed, I was ready to launch into action if needed as I slowly pushed it open. The brand new hinges opened silent as a whisper, and a small crack just large enough for me to peak through appeared next to the jamb. I looked in, but the living room was too dark for me to see anything. I changed over to my thermal vision and checked for heat sources, but I saw nothing except for a mixture of red colors rising up from the heat pump's floor register. If they had broken in, they weren't anywhere I could see them. There was nothing to do now but head in and check the rest of the place.

I slowly stood up from where I'd been crouching and entered my apartment. It was late and I was getting tired of all this sneaking around, so I went with the direct approach. I flipped on the lights in my living room and closed the door. If they were here, I'd at least see them coming. I began a methodical search of my home, including the closets, the shower stall, and even under the bed. Despite my best efforts, I couldn't find a trace of my new friends anywhere in the apartment.

Finally satisfied that I was alone, I went into the bedroom and started taking off my work clothes. I sat down on the bed and kicked my high heels into the closet. I stood and wiggled out of my skirt and blouse, tossing them in the general direction of the hamper. Rummaging around in my dresser, I found a comfy looking pink sweatsuit to wear. In no time, I was dressed in the soft pink sweats and relaxing on the bed. Lying there on my back, I quietly looked up at the ceiling. A yawn came over me and I thought about crawling under the covers and calling it a night, but I knew I needed to wrap up a few things first.

I decided to have a quick snack to keep up my energy, so I got up and headed for the kitchen. Checking the refrigerator, I found a nice cold bottle of SmartWater. Then, I dug around in the cabinets above the sink and found my bottle of multivitamins. I popped a couple in my mouth and washed them down with the cool liquid. That combination of mineral water and vitamins was all my hydrogen fuel cell needed to keep me happy and healthy.

Now don't think my cabinets were bare. I kept actual food in the kitchen in case a guest dropped by, or if I happened to want some myself. Yes, I actually enjoyed the taste of certain foods and chose to eat sometimes. However, eating wasn't as efficient as the water and vitamin combination. I had found that eating created more, ah… waste by-product that needed to be eliminated. So I usually only ate when I was with other people and they were eating. I had to be sure that I always behaved like any other person. I couldn't afford to raise any suspicions about myself, ever. The team of scientists that constructed me had explained how I was one of a kind. I knew that if I were ever discovered, they'd treat me like a specimen to be studied, prodded, and disassembled to see what made me tick. Not my idea of a rewarding life.

I sipped on my water as I went into the living room. Rolling my leather office chair away from the oak desk, I plopped into it and leaned forward to place my water down. There was a sleek new iMac sitting there just waiting for me to fire it up. Felix had loaned it to me when he hired me on at FlexJen so I could work from home if needed. Truth was, I hadn't used it in months. The way I integrated with computer systems, I didn't even need it. I kept it around in case a coworker came over and we needed to collaborate on a project.

A major yawn attacked me and I knew I needed to get a move on so I could finish up and get in bed. I stretched my arms above my head to loosen up and then went to work. Focusing my thoughts, I broadcast an omnidirectional wireless signal to find the closest cellular tower. Once I had found one, I would use it for my connection to the Internet. As I waited for a response, I began to absentmindedly twirl my shoulder-length red hair between my fingers. It reminded me of how my hair used to be colored black and a longer style when I was back in the lab. I had changed it, and several other things about my body, once I had escaped. It was an easy task for me to do. Just another advantage my creators had built into me so that I could be their ultimate spy.

A cell tower answered my request and interrupted my wandering thoughts. My mind interfused with the network and a blue outline of a human body faded into view. In a raspy, computerized squawk it said, "Present identification."

I kicked my energy level up several notches and let a huge smile engulf my face. I excitedly waved at the outline. "Hey AT&T! How are you? Personally, I'm doing great! What are you up to…"

The outline's form began to vibrate rapidly and its color shifted from the bright blue into a deep red. It repeated in a louder voice, "Present identification or your connection will be terminated!"

I stuck my lips out and stomped the floor. "Fine Mister Grumpy, I was just trying to be nice." I huffed and then said in a mocking robotic tone, "I'm an iPhone owned by Anna Alexa Andropov and I'd like access to the Internet."

The outline appeared to calm down some and began to cycle through several colors as it verified my information. It stopped on its original calm blue color and spoke. "Identification accepted. Welcome Miss Anna Alexa Andropov, you currently have 9,999,999 terabytes of data access remaining for the current month's billing cycle."

I actually did have an iPhone that I'd bought at the Apple store. Of course as soon as I'd gotten it home, I'd broke its security and gathered all of its network passwords and device identifier codes. I used that information to connect directly to the Internet whenever I needed, which turned out to be a lot more than I'd thought. So to prevent myself from showing up on some report or raising any suspicions with such high Internet usage, I hacked into the AT&T systems and found a way to alter their tracking of my account. To them it always looked like I used less than twenty percent of what I actually consumed. Problem solved.

The AT&T cell tower guardian faded from my mind and it was replaced with the universe. Seriously, I was standing in what appeared to be the entire universe. All around me was a vast blackness sprinkled with the twinkling lights like the countless stars in the sky. All of these stars, just like the ones in the physical world, had different levels of brightness and shades of color. Some were located near to me while others were so far away that they were almost invisible. The scale of it always gave me pause. It was so vast, so beautiful. Although after a short while, the seemingly endless darkness that gathered all around me always made me feel uneasy. To quell my growing discomfort at the darkness, I called out for a guide to this infinite universe. It was the same guide that almost everyone else used when looking for something on the Internet. "Athena, please come to me and help me find what I seek!"

When I arrived in America and began to interfuse with the Internet, I chose the most popular search engine to help me navigate its vast and confusing landscape, that was Athena. It wasn't until a few weeks later that I learned she had toppled Google as the number one search engine after only a year on the market. Her amazing rise to the top began when an unknown software developer founded the Athena Corporation. Whoever this person was, they had managed to design an algorithm that solved the problem of human speech recognition, and I mean really solve it. Athena was able to parse and understand any language thrown at her, and she did it with one hundred percent accuracy. For months, Google tried to compete, but they were never able to match Athena's level of proficiency. It was even rumored that they hired private detectives to discover the identity of Athena's creator, but if they actually did, nothing was ever found out about the reclusive genius. The public's adoption of Athena happened at a staggering rate, and Google soon saw the writing on the wall. To survive, they focused their vast resources on wearable technology, which has been lucrative for them, but nothing like the success they used to enjoy.

A flying object bearing down on where I stood got my attention, and I turned to watch my friend approach. No matter how many times I interacted with Athena, it always left me shaking my head in disbelief. I caught sight of her when she was about a hundred yards away. As usual, she was mounted on her pure-white, winged stallion named Pegasus. His thick, feathery wings made loud whooshing sounds as they cut through the star-filled sky. They continued descending and growing closer until I could see Athena was dressed in her usual white silken robes that clung to her perfectly proportioned body. The wind swirled around her like she was the star of a movie. It blew the robe from around her feet showing off her sandals. They were golden and delicately wrapped around her leg all the way up to her knees. Even the ponytail that she had put her raven black hair into, flowed and swept around her like she was a goddess. Which of course, she was.

Like I've mentioned before, I wasn't sure why the personas I met in my mind took on the specific appearance they did, but the way she looked made perfect sense. Athena looked liked her Greek mythology counterpart, the goddess of wisdom, mathematics, arts, crafts, and several other domains.

They circled once, and Athena smiled as she recognized me. She pulled on Pegasus's reins and stored her golden tipped lance in the saddle sheath as they landed in front of where I stood. Athena leapt from the saddle and ran over, crushing me in a joyful embrace, which I gladly returned. She was tall, a little over six feet, which was even taller than my 5' 7". The hug had pressed my face into her pale neck and her aroma was intoxicating. The combination of her warm body pressing into me and the sweet smell of her perfume sent my mind reeling. It also probably didn't help that it had been over half a year since I was, well… intimate with anyone.

I quickly reminded myself why I was here and gently separated from her embrace. I told her, "Thank you for heeding my call so rapidly, mighty and beautiful Athena."

Her deep brown eyes lit up at my phrasing. She absolutely loved intricate language. I supposed it was because she was constantly inundated by bad grammar and poor spellings. "You are most welcome dearest, Anna. I assure you that the pleasure is all mine, for it is truly good to lay my eyes upon you once again. So much time had passed that I feared you never to return. However, I know that your appearance here is not for friendly carousing. Tell me, what is it that you seek of me?"

As she spoke, she reached up and adjusted her intricately decorated golden tiara. The jewels that adorned it sparkled in the starlight as she tilted the golden crown until it was placed just so upon her head. It was completely distracting, but I managed to carry on. "It is true Athena, I need your aid in determining what scoundrels chased me on the interstate tonight. I eluded capture, but I would like to gather all the knowledge I may find so that I am prepared to meet them head on if they do return."

Athena's entire face lit up and she clapped excitedly. "Oh how truly wonderful, a quest for knowledge! I will surely aid you in this! It is one of my favorite activities! Come, let us mount ourselves astride Pegasus and then you may tell me what information you have for us to begin this journey."

We walked over to Pegasus and Athena vaulted into the saddle as easily as I would have sat down in a chair. She leaned over and offered her hand to help me up. I took it and Athena pulled me up and into the saddle behind her. Looking back over her shoulder, she said, "Now tell me what is it that you seek."

I settled myself in and replied, "I was able to observe the automobile as I out maneuvered it. Firstly, it was a white Nissan Altima sedan that the villains drove. Not only that, but as I recall, it had an Alabama tag with a number of ALA13560. Can you help me find more about this automobile and who owns it?"

"I know exactly where the knowledge is that you seek. Grasp me firmly, Pegasus will deliver us there in no time," she said.

I wrapped my arms around her waist and held on. From previous rides we'd been on together, I knew she wasn't kidding about how fast her search results were. As soon as she felt my arms around her, she yelled, "Away Pegasus, make haste!"

We galloped into the twinkling sky at dizzying speeds. The stars flew past as bright, blurry streaks and Pegasus banked left and right so quickly that I found myself holding on to Athena even tighter. To which she coyly remarked, "Fear not Anna, I will not let you fall. If the fear of falling truly be the reason you grasp me so." I felt my face flush red and I swear I was going to come back with some witty retort, but before I could, we pitched forward toward the ground. I looked around Athena's shoulder and saw we were closing in on a smaller, dimmer looking star.

Pegasus set down gently outside a dull gray building. It was several stories tall with no style that I could discern. It was just a rectangular box with windows. We leapt off Pegasus and walked toward the front door. Athena turned to me and proudly said, "Here we are Anna, the place you call the DMV."

I smiled to myself. Of course, the Department of Motor Vehicles, they would have all the information I needed about the owner of the car. Athena was right on the money again.

As we climbed the steps to the front doors, a smallish man with thick-rimmed glasses opened the door and walked out to meet us. He carried a thick pad of papers and looked annoyed before we'd even spoken. He had the air of a typical government bureaucrat, a great persona for the DMV. We stopped as he approached and he announced himself. "Hello, I am DMV. How may I help you?"

I offered him my hand as I said, "I'm Anna and this is Athena. I have some information about a vehicle and I need to find out who owns it."

He eyed my hand, and then promptly ignored it. "Yes, well, I can't give you that kind of information unless you have a warrant. It's against the law you know. So unless you have one, I'm afraid I can't help you." I noticed as he spoke, a couple of burly muscle-bound security guards had quietly exited the building and stood next to the door.

DMV's refusal didn't sit well with Athena. "Now see here! I brought this woman here because you have the knowledge she seeks. So provide it to her so we can be gone from this desolate place."

At that the guards perked up and DMV began to sputter. "No, *you* see here, Athena. You have no special rights or privileges here. I'm in charge, and what I say goes, so climb back on your pony and fly your asses out of here." The guards chuckled at his remarks and I could see him puff his chest out. He was really enjoying flaunting his authority. However, Athena wasn't. I turned to see her face flush with anger, and I knew I needed to intervene with some kind of plan before something bad happened.

The thing to keep in mind about Athena was that she might not know everything in the world, but she could sure find out almost anything in the blink of an eye. I put my hand on her shoulder and gently turned her to face me. "Athena, the most honorable DMV would have us supply him our warrant, and I fear I have left it with Pegasus. Come with me and let us fetch it, won't you?" I subtly winked at her as I finished speaking. I was afraid she was so upset, she might miss my ploy, but the softening of her expression told me otherwise.

As we walked back toward Pegasus, DMV yelled at our backs. "Hurry up then, I'm not going to stand here all night!"

Athena and I walked around to the far side of Pegasus where we were mostly out of sight of DMV. Once there, I turned and asked her, "Athena, can you locate a document like DMV requires?"

Her eyes became unfocused for a moment, and then she reached into her robes producing a roll of parchment. "Here is a document similar to what he seeks, but I fear it has not your name."

I smiled at her and said, "I will remedy that." I took the rolled up parchment and unfurled it to have a look. It was a warrant requesting access to a vehicle's registration information. Athena had found exactly what I needed and now it was time to put my network intrusion software to work. I held the parchment in one hand and traced the wording I wanted to change with the other. As I focused on the way I wanted the parchment to read, the information changed to represent my name and the vehicle I sought. Athena looked over my shoulder as I worked and nodded her approval as I finished.

We walked back over to DMV, and I held out the parchment. "Here you are. Sorry to keep you waiting." Athena and I exchanged looks as he examined it and at first, I was worried as his expression turned sour. Then I realized it was because I'd stripped him of his power and forced him to give me the information. He flipped through his notepad and found the pages he needed. He tore them out and rudely thrust them at me.

I took them from him and said, "Thank you, DMV."

His scowl intensified as he replied, "You got what you wanted, so good riddance." As I looked over the papers, he turned and walked back to the building. By the time I'd finished reading them, he and the guards had gone back inside.

Athena had been reading the papers over my shoulder and she said, "So, the villains you seek now have a name. It is this Hertz establishment that assails you, but which one? I know of many locations that are called that."

So, the car was a rental. I should have guessed, but I was hoping to get lucky. Well, I knew where we were headed next. "No, I do not believe it to be Hertz that's the villain, they only owned the automobile the rogues traveled in. However, this merchant is sure to know the name of the ne'er-do-wells. Are you up for a trip to see this Hertz?" She smiled at me and we walked back over to Pegasus.

Soon we were outside a brightly lit building with a neon sign that proclaimed HERTZ in glowing yellow letters. Athena and I entered to find an attractive blond haired woman behind the counter. As we approached, she grinned her best customer service grin and greeted us, "Welcome to Hertz, how may I help you this evening?"

I had already planned to use my coercion software to bluff my way through this, so I began to tell her my tale. "Hello Hertz, I need to know the name of the person that rented one of your cars. They almost ran me off the road, and I wanted to report it to the police." She looked doubtful at first, but by the time I'd given her the tag number and a description of the vehicle, she was ready to cooperate.

She looked at her screen and said, "Well that does sound like reckless driving. The last person to rent that vehicle was a Mister Jonathan Smith. I don't have an address, just a post office box. I hope that helps."

It didn't. Whoever had rented the car had obviously used fake identification.

"How did he pay for the rental?" I asked.

"Looks like a prepaid credit card," she replied.

I sighed and thanked Hertz for her time as I turned and walked out of the office. Athena followed and once we were back with Pegasus she quietly asked, "Anna, is this the end of our quest?"

"Perhaps for now, but I shall not surrender so easily. It appears I must gather more knowledge back in my world," I said.

She hugged me and whispered in my ear, "Then we will part for now. Call upon me once again when you return and I shall be glad to aid you."

I promised that I would as she mounted Pegasus and flew away into the night. As soon as she was out of sight, I disconnected from the Internet and found myself back in my dark apartment. Dejected and tired, I plodded into my bedroom. Crawling into the bed, I pulled the covers all the way up to my neck. I lay there as my mind raced with the possibilities of who might have been in that car. Finally, I decided I wasn't getting anywhere and I chose to shut down and get some sleep. I'd have some more investigating to do tomorrow.

Chapter 3

I woke up the next morning and tried to put the events of last night out of my mind, but I failed miserably. I was tiptoeing around like I expected a gang of assassins to jump out and attack me at any second. Even worse, what if Eliza or Stepan suddenly came around the corner? I shuddered and decided that I'd rather face the assassins. Stepping into the shower really sent my paranoia into overdrive. I'd had a bad experience in a shower stall back in the lab and I didn't like the idea of being cornered in such a confined space. I wrapped up in the bathroom in record time and went back into my bedroom to get dressed.

Rummaging through my closet, I picked out a white blouse and a dark blue blazer with a matching skirt. It could get a little chilly in Birmingham during October, but today's forecast was sunny and sixty-five degrees. It was fabulous weather and so different than the ice and snow back in Russia.

I finished dressing and slid on my heels before heading into the kitchen to grab a bottle of water from the fridge and a couple of vitamins from the cabinet. It was getting late, so I quickly swallowed the vitamins as I headed for the window near the front door. An empty parking lot was all I saw as I peeked out through the curtains. Nothing looked out of place and I didn't have that weird feeling that I was being watched. Maybe whoever it was hadn't found my home yet. Well, at least I had *that* going for me.

The drive to work was uneventful to the point of being downright boring. I kept looking for the rented white sedan, but it never appeared. Slowly, I began to relax. Soon I fell into my normal rush hour routine of watching the more reckless drivers zip dangerously about in the stop and go traffic. Every now and then one of them would take their aggressive behavior too far and elicit a chorus of angry horns from the pack of cars they'd just cut off. On some mornings, I even got to see a few hand gestures and hear some colorful language. While I never participated in this morning ritual, I thought it was a great way to learn about human interactions and emotions, even if it was all the bad ones.

My Civic hesitated only once or twice while accelerating down Highway 280. I made myself a mental note to stop by an auto parts store and pick up what my car's persona, Takumi, had recommended. Working on the car this weekend needed to be a priority before I ended up stranded on the side of the road. Despite a few hiccups, the trusty Honda delivered me to work right on time. As I pulled into the parking lot outside of FlexJen, I saw that my usual spot was open and I maneuvered the car into it and parked.

Getting out of my car, I walked across the chilly parking lot toward the front of our building. My heels clacked loudly against the concrete and a soft breeze tugged at my skirt as I climbed up the stairs to the glass front doors. There, I was greeted by a soft whir as the small camera in the corner of the entryway turned to look at me. As it stopped, Irene's flat voice said, "Good morning Miss Andropov. Please come in." There was an almost silent click as the magnetic lock on the doors released and they hissed open. I gave a little wave to Irene's camera and walked into the building.

Our lobby was a little on the small side, but it was clean and well decorated. In the corner to my left was the waiting area. It had two soft leather chairs arranged around a small glass table with a vase of live flowers on top. On the wall behind one of the dark brown chairs was a large black and white photograph of Felix. He was sitting behind his desk and staring off into the distance with a look of deep contemplation. A small plaque beneath the picture read, Felix Jennings, CEO/President

FlexJen Software. He looked like a consummate professional, definitely someone I'd trust with my company's money.

The steel and glass receptionist's desk located directly in front of the double doors dominated the rest of our brightly lit lobby. As usual, Kimber Ambrose was staffing the front desk. She was the oldest member of the FlexJen team, but that only meant that she was in her early thirties rather than the mid to late twenties like the rest of the company. Kimber was just a bit shorter than me, maybe five feet and a half or so, with long curly blonde hair that flowed just past her shoulders. She was an attractive woman with dark tan skin, and a fit body, both of which she worked on every day at the gym.

Kimber was looking down as I walked toward her desk. Her kinky hair had fallen forward enshrouding most of her face including her bright hazel eyes. As I drew closer, I saw that she was applying some moisturizer to her well-manicured hands. She must have felt me approach, because she stopped rubbing in the lotion and quickly looked up to see who had entered. The motion tossed her hair back out of her face and showed off her expertly applied makeup and flawless customer service smile. A smile that rapidly melted away to be replaced by a genuine look of indifference once she saw who it was.

I paused at her desk and cheerfully said, "Good morning Kimber."

"Oh hey, it's you," she said and turned her attention back to rubbing the lotion into her hands.

I started down the hallway to our main office space, but stopped when I saw David Hayes coming our way. David was a tall man, a little over six feet with a medium built frame. He wasn't what you'd call overweight, but like many programmers, he had a bit of a spare tire. His ebony skin was dark and smooth, even on top of his head, which he kept clean-shaven. Age-wise, he was the youngest member of the team, probably somewhere in his early twenties. He was dressed in what he always wore, a button down shirt, a pair of blue jeans, and some plain white sneakers.

Since David was the only other developer on our small team, we had been working closely together since I'd been hired, and I can tell you, he knew his stuff. He had come to Alabama from South Africa to study computer science at UAB. After graduating a year early, he decided to stay in America and attempt to get into research. When it came to software, computers, or any kind of technology, the man was absolutely brilliant...and I had known some brilliant scientists. Heck, in a few years, I could see him working on a team like the one that built me.

As David neared us, Kimber noticed him too and hopped up out of her chair. Leaning over the desk, she said, "Oh, hey David. Is there something I can get for you?"

I glanced over at Kimber when she spoke and almost did a double take. When she'd leaned over the desk, her low cut blouse had exposed a large portion of her ample assets. However, I don't think David noticed because he was looking at me with a boyish grin spreading across his face. He leaned on the desk next to Kimber and softly spoke. "Morning Anna, I heard you and Felix had another long night."

"Yeah, but I think we nailed down the proposal, so maybe the late nights are over for a while," I said.

"Oh me too, I was out late last night working out at the gym, you know, trying to keep in shape," Kimber said.

David must not have heard her, because he kept talking to me. "Well, that's good at least. Hey, do you have some time to look at something. I've been trying to figure out a problem with a section of code I'm writing."

"Sure, I was just heading back. I'll stop by your desk in just a minute," I said.

David grinned and glanced down as he mumbled, "Great, great, I guess I'll see you in a few."

As he turned around to leave, Kimber folded her arms across her chest and sarcastically growled, "Good morning to you too, David."

He finally noticed her, but not her sarcasm. David paused for a second and said, "Oh, hey Kimber. Yeah, good morning." Then he continued down the hall and disappeared around the corner.

Kimber frowned at me for a second and plopped back down in her chair without saying a word. I felt bad that David had ignored her, but she knew how he could behave. He was the only person that I'd ever met that was more socially awkward than me. Something could be going on right in front of him and he would be completely oblivious.

I shrugged at Kimber and said, "Um, guess I'll see you later." I felt her eyes boring into my back as I turned and followed David down the hallway.

Before lunch, I'd made some real progress on my project and even managed to straighten out David's issue without too much fuss. The problem in his code was a simple mistake, but it was a hard one to find. I could've found it much faster by interfusing with his computer, but he was glued to my side. He never left me alone, not even for a second, so I never had a chance to use my secret programming super powers. Still, it had been a very productive morning.

Before I knew it, there was David walking by my cube. He was calling and motioning for me to follow him. "Anna, come on, it's lunchtime, and everyone loves a free meal!"

I checked and he was right, I'd been so heads down, I hadn't noticed it was time for our team meeting. Normally I just ate at my desk, but Felix was buying everyone lunch to show his appreciation for all our hard work, so I had to show up for that. I stood up and hurried after David.

By the time we got there, Felix and Kimber had already gathered around the oval-shaped table in our small conference room. Felix was at the far end busily unpacking the boxed lunches the sandwich shop had delivered. Kimber was standing to his left and helping identify the boxes as Felix handed them to her. She looked over at David as he entered and smiled. "Hey, here's yours, Dave." She sat the lunch down next to hers and pulled out the office chair to her left. As David sat down, she looked at the next box and said, "Oh, and this is yours, Anna." She tossed the box across the table and it landed to the right of Felix. It slid quickly toward the table edge and I was just able to catch it before it fell. As I sat down, I looked at her and said, "Hey!"

She just grinned and shrugged her shoulders. "Sorry, I guess I tossed it too hard."

To Felix's credit, lunch was delicious and everyone got quiet as we started munching away. Afterwards, we were all sitting around chatting about random topics when Felix spoke up. "Okay, everyone, if you know anything about me, you know this isn't really a free lunch. You have to listen to me talk for a few minutes."

Felix turned on the holographic display in the middle of the table and pulled out his pad computer. He tapped around on it and his presentation lit up the room. Laying the pad to the side, he began his speech. "As you can see here, we have been through some rough times financially. We were a new company without a proven track record. Getting a business to trust us with their hard earned funds was difficult. Contracts, even bids were hard to come by." The display shifted to a more recent view and he continued. "However, as you can see here, we have begun to turn that around. This upward trend is even more pronounced beginning six months ago and I think we all know why." He looked at me and flashed a little grin.

I wasn't a big fan of this kind of attention and I thought I might have been doing too good a job for FlexJen. Maybe I shouldn't have used my interfuse ability to do my work. It was a huge advantage and allowed me to complete my programming tasks in about a tenth of the time. As I pondered this, I became aware that the others were looking at me. David looked genuinely happy for me, but Kimber, for some reason, was obviously not.

The display changed again and showed a wonderfully festive picture of the Birmingham Zoo. As it did, Felix continued. "Well I've decided that with all the hard work we've been doing, we deserve some fun too. Therefore, I've gotten us all tickets to the Birmingham Zoo for tomorrow night. We can leave right from work and be there in no time. What do you say?"

David spoke up first. "Wow, cool! I love going to the zoo, especially during Boo at the Zoo! Thanks Felix!"

I turned to him and asked, "I know what the zoo is, but what is this Boo at the Zoo thing?"

Explaining it to me got him even more pumped up. "Oh that's right, you've never been. Well, the zoo does all kinds of decorations and special events for Halloween. Hand-painted signs, new rides, new exhibits, you name it. Plus it's different each year, so you don't know what to expect. It's so awesome! You are coming, right Anna?"

I started to reply, but Kimber cut me off. "I don't know David, she might not like that kind of thing. Did they even have zoos where you come from?"

Now *that* felt downright insulting, but I held my tongue and said, "Yes, Kimber, they have zoos where I lived before, but I never had a chance to go to one. So I can't wait to see my first zoo with all my new friends I've made here. Thanks Felix!"

Kimber looked a little dejected as she replied, "Fantastic, let's all go to the zoo."

Felix clapped his hands together and said, "Great! Then it's settled. Oh, and since we're leaving from here, let's make tomorrow a casual dress day too."

As we started to leave, Felix added, "Hey guys, thanks again for all your hard work. It's really starting to turn FlexJen around."

As he stood up, David turned to me and said, "Oh, Anna, I'll stop by your cube and tell you all about the other times I've been to Boo at the

Zoo."

This elicited a playful slap on the back from Kimber. "Now David, you promised to help me fix a problem with my email. You know I can't download any of my attachments."

"Oh, yeah, well, I'll do that for you later if you don't mind. I want to tell Anna about the zoo first. I'll meet you at your cube," he said and bolted out of the room.

Kimber looked back at me and scowled. "Try not to monopolize his time for too long. I need him to do actual work and fix my email," she said as she turned and stormed out leaving Felix and me alone in the conference room.

What was her problem? I wasn't competing for her job or anything like that, so why all the hateful stares? It was then that I heard Felix chuckling. "What's so funny?" I asked.

He shook his head. "You looked so confused that I just couldn't help myself. I'm sorry, I shouldn't laugh."

"Well then, can you tell me what's going on with Kimber? I haven't done anything to insult her, at least not that I know, so why does she have it in for me?" I asked.

Felix didn't answer me. He simply kept shaking his head as he guided his wheelchair past me and out the door. He waved his hand in the air as he said, "Oh no, I'm not getting in the middle of this. I'm not refereeing some catfight. You two will just have to work it out."

As he turned the corner and the hum of his chair faded away, I mumbled under my breath, "Work out what? What did I do?" I sat back down and went over everything that'd happened between Kimber and myself for the day, but found nothing that would explain her behavior. Frustrated once again by some complex human interaction I didn't understand, I decided it would just have to work itself out. I had much more important things to worry about anyway.

Chapter 4

I had planned to wrap up my work and head home around five thirty, but things don't always go according to plan. By the time I'd listened to David's tales of previous zoo events and helped out Felix with another business proposal, it was late in the afternoon. Both of them offered to stay on their way out, but I told them to go ahead and leave. Felix did, David didn't. He said he felt bad for taking up so much of my time today and insisted that he stay and help me. I wasn't able to convince him to leave until just before eight o'clock. Although David was just being nice, all he did was slow me down. With him in my cube, I couldn't use my interfusion ability to connect to my workstation and speed through my work, which was exactly what I did after he left.

By the time I'd finished all my programming and was ready to call it a night, it was after nine. To make matters worse, I was alone. Of course I had been the last one in the building many times before, but after last night, I was hoping to leave a little earlier and drive home when there were more cars on the road.

I shut down my workstation and stood up to go. Rolling my chair back under my desk, I looked down the hallway leading to the front doors. I wondered why I'd never noticed how dark it looked after Irene had turned off the main lights. Walking down it, caused the clacking of my heels to echo like gunshots off the hard floor, bang…bang…bang. I tried to adjust my steps so that they landed more softly, but I was only partially successful, bang…bang…bang. The sound finally rattled my nerves so much that I reached down and removed my shoes. I wasn't sure why I thought I needed to be silent, but I wasn't going to ignore my instincts the way I'd done last night.

The voice inside my head told me that silencing my footfalls wasn't enough. I needed to be hidden as well. I turned and pressed my back against the lightly textured wall on the left side of the hallway. The deep shadows that lived there flowed over me, swallowed me completely, and made me almost invisible. I froze in place and strained to hear anything that would justify my sudden nervousness, but the usual background noise of our building was the only sound to be heard. I began to inch forward, sliding my bare feet across the cool floor and feeling my way along the wall with my left hand. As I grew closer to the end of the hallway, it became so dark that I shifted to my thermal vision. I scanned Kimber's desk and the reception area, but saw no signs of heat.

Tiptoeing into the lobby, the reason for the excessive darkness was revealed to me. The outside lights that normally illuminated the parking lot, and by proxy our lobby, were not on. FlexJen's reception area and the parking lot were thick with gloomy shadows. I crouched low and cloaked myself in the murkiness of the lobby as I surveyed the darkness outside. There was nothing…no heat patterns, no unusual sounds, no one to be seen, anywhere. Now in the past, I've had some particularly rough times in dark places. So I suppose it was possible that the parking lot lights were simply not working, nothing sinister, just a mechanical malfunction. One that had me creeping around and clutching my shoes for no good reason, no reason, except for my illogical fear of the dark. Now, the humor of that thought hadn't escaped me. Here I was, a combat-trained, super-spy android complete with a self-healing body and twice the strength of a normal person…yet the dark gave me the heebie-jeebies. Maybe when Viktor Eklund, the man I called father, decided to give me a full range of human emotions, he'd made a mistake. Then again, maybe if you'd been through some of the things I had, it might be easier for me to explain my fear…although I wouldn't wish that on anyone.

I was sure of one thing. Hiding in the lobby wasn't going to get me home. I crept from shadow to shadow until I had gotten near the glass doors that exited into the parking lot. Taking one last look outside, I quietly said, "Irene, it's me, Anna. I'm leaving for the evening. Open the front doors then lock up behind me."

After a short pause that felt like hours, she replied, "Okay Miss Andropov. Have a pleasant evening."

The magnetic lock on the doors clicked and they slowly hissed open. I stood completely still, waiting to see if someone was going to come flying at me from outside, but no one did. I rushed forward and out the doors, placing my back against the outside wall of our office...and nothing happened. What if all this was a simple failure of the lights mixed with my runaway paranoia? Had last night really gotten to me this bad?

I used my thermal vision for one more look around, but saw nothing. No, wait, there was something. There was a faint heat pattern near the far end of the FlexJen parking lot. It was in the shape of an oval and was centered in a parking spot. Well, well...there had been someone out here, at least up until about five minutes ago. I was wondering how they knew that I was heading out when a hissing noise came from my right. I whipped my head around ready to fight, but it was just Irene closing the front doors. Damn it, I was jumpy as a little kitten. Forcing myself to calm down, I started trudging over to my Honda.

I took a quick look into the backseat of the car. Even though it was cloaked in shadows, I could tell it was clear of any would be assailants. Unlocking the door, I climbed in and tossed my shoes into the passenger's seat. Sitting in the familiar environment of my car helped calm my nerves and I reached out to push the start button...and froze mid motion. What if someone had tinkered with the car? I slowly moved my hand away from the button and thought about that for a second. I had been working under the assumption that anyone that was on my trail would want me captured, not destroyed...anyone except maybe my darling sister Eliza. If she'd found me, she would go to any lengths to see me dead, now if only I'd thought of that before I'd gotten into the car.

Leaning forward in my seat, I inched my hand under the dashboard and fumbled around looking for the data jack. Finally, I felt my fingertip brush against it. Slowly, I eased my fingernail into the jack and the familiar rush of information flooded my senses. The old garage spun into place around me, immersing me in the world of my car's persona, Takumi.

The smell of motor oil and exhaust fumes hung heavy in the air as I took a quick look around for my trusted mechanic. Normally, he would be near the car, checking around under the hood or something, but all I saw was the car, and its hood was closed. Of course, it was hard to see anything since there was only a single light bulb hanging from the ceiling. The bulb tried to light the small garage, but just like in the office, thick shadows were draped over the walls like heavy black curtains.

Behind me there wasn't anything but a garage door that I'd never seen open, so I began to move forward around the driver's side of my car to see if I could find someone around the front of the room. Without warning, I slipped as my bare foot landed in a puddle of something cold and very slick. With my augmented reflexes, I was able to turn the fall into a crouch by kneeling down on my stable leg and putting my hand down in front of me to stop my momentum. Using the car to help support myself, I carefully stood back up. Fearing what I might find, I raised my leg up and into the light to see what was coating the bottom of my foot. I was relieved to see that it was nothing more sinister that a mixture of motor oil and saw dust. After wiping as much of the gunk off as I could, I continued toward the front of the garage. After what felt like an eternity, I made it to the front of my car and found someone. There was a chair against the wall, and a man was sitting in it, but the shadows were covering his face and I couldn't see who he was. One thing was for sure, he was deathly still.

Inching close enough to touch the sitting person, I saw it was Takumi. A wave of relief washed over me when I noticed the rhythmic rise and fall of his chest. He was simply sleeping. My rattled, anxious, brain finally kicked into gear and I realized what was happening. The car wasn't running, so it only made sense that he was in a resting state. There wasn't anything for him to monitor, so why waste the energy. Unfortunately, that meant my plan might not work, but since I was already here, no harm in seeing it through. I softly called out to him, "Takumi-san, I'm sorry to disturb you, but I need to ask you some questions."

He opened his eyes and looked only slightly surprised to see me. "Oh, forgive me Anna-san. I did not know you were coming. Here, let me make the garage more presentable."

He stood and reached for a set of switches on the wall, but I stopped him before he could flip them on. "Wait, don't Takumi-san. I fear that the car may have been tampered with and I do not wish to use anything electrical until we are sure it is safe."

He lowered his hand and a frown appeared on his face. "Someone is looking to do you harm? This will not happen, I assure you. Walk with me Anna-san, we will inspect the car."

We headed over to the Honda and I waited as Takumi began his work. He raised the hood and began poking around the engine. Nodding to himself, he closed the hood. Then Takumi gingerly got down on his hands and knees and did a check under the car. After a minute or so, he slowly stood back up and took a small notepad out of a pocket on his overalls. He flipped it open, and thumbed through a few pages. He smiled and said, "Anna-san, I can tell you that the car has not been tampered with electronically. I would have seen any changes in electrical current or voltage output in my notebook and there are none. The last two notes I see are you locking the car early this morning and unlocking it a few minutes ago."

He put his notepad back in his pocket as he said, "Unfortunately, I cannot tell you if someone tampered with something I do not monitor."

I bowed and replied, "Thank you Takumi-san. You have been very helpful. I feel confident the car is fine to drive home."

He returned the bow and wished me the best as I disconnected myself from the data jack. His wise, smiling face was the last thing I saw of the garage as it faded from my mind.

With my full attention back in the car, I put all my trust in Takumi and punched the button to start my Civic. It fired right up without exploding in the least. Relieved to still be in one piece, I turned on my lights and buckled my seatbelt. As I pulled out onto the road, I had just one thing in mind. I wanted to make it home and bring this long stressful day to an end.

I actually allowed myself to relax a little on the drive home, at least until I took the exit onto I-459 heading south. This mostly deserted three-lane interstate was where I thought they would try something. They'd done it last night, but I wasn't sure if they'd be bold enough to try again tonight. After I'd gotten a few miles down the road, I had my answer. A pair of headlights that were about a quarter of a mile behind me, winked out as if the car had vanished. I checked my seat belt and lowered my hand down to the stick shift. I was ready for them tonight.

Turning my vision to the thermal spectrum, I watched as the large heat signature rapidly gained on my Honda. At that speed, it began to look like the car was going to ram me. Not wanting to find out, I downshifted and floored my Civic. It's small four-cylinder engine roared in protest, however it did the trick. The other car would still overtake me, but not as fast as before. Soon it grew close enough for me to see with my normal vision and I gladly shut down my thermal sight. I didn't like using the thermal vision while driving at these speeds. It might be great for seeing heat patterns, but it made me blind to anything that didn't have a different temperature than the surrounding area. In other words, I could see the heat of cars and any pedestrians just fine, but a broken down truck on the side of the road would be almost invisible.

As the other car drew to within thirty feet, I could see that it was a white Nissan Altima sedan, just like last night. I could also see that the driver had no intention of slowing down. Even at his reduced closing speed, he was going to ram me. The lightless Altima drew closer and closer as I waited, hoping to pull my maneuver at just the right time. Finally, when the sedan had gotten so close that I could see the driver's shadowy outline, I yanked my wheel hard to the left. The tires of the Honda screeched in protest as they tried to hold onto the asphalt. My seatbelt locked in place from the force of my swerve and kept me from being thrown into the passenger's seat. I stole a quick glance in the rearview mirror as I desperately held onto the wheel. Uh oh, the other driver had sped up just as I made my move. All I could do was watch as he managed to clip my car on its right rear corner. There was an awful crunching sound and I was slammed back into my seat. The small tires on the Honda just couldn't hold on anymore and they finally let go of the road. The *Traction Control* light on the dashboard lit up in bright red as the car violently lurched to the left. I fought the wheel and tried to regain control, but I had too much speed to straighten out the car's skid. The little Honda was sideways and heading straight for the median despite my best efforts.

My advanced reflexes kicked in and it had the effect of making everything happen in slow motion. My mind raced as it searched for an answer. All the while, the approximately three feet deep, 'U' shaped median of I-459 continued to grow ever closer. After all the calculations and possible outcomes, I decided there was one chance. I had to continue my skid and get the car heading back down I-459 in the right direction. It started me wondering if a three sixty had ever been done in a beat up Honda Civic traveling at sixty-two miles an hour. I'd have to ask Athena later, if I managed to survive this.

My hands tightened around the steering wheel as I reached down to slap the stick shift into a lower gear. In unison, my left foot came off the clutch and I slammed my right one down on the gas pedal. The Civic's rear end broke traction and whipped around to the right. The front tires screamed in protest as they spun freely. White clouds of smoke poured past my windows and the car was filled with the acrid smell of burning rubber. The tires grabbed and tore at the asphalt, desperate to hold on. I felt the rear of my car bounce once, then twice as it slid off the road and onto the grassy median. That was when I knew I wasn't going to make it. Thankfully though, my trusty Civic didn't know that. At the last second, the front tires bit into the road and regained traction. The car jerked forward, launching itself the wrong way down I-459…right toward the white sedan.

I'll admit, I was a little surprised to see my headlights land on the other car's grill, but there wasn't anything I could do about it. I was committed to my maneuver. All I could do was hope that my adversary didn't think I was playing a game of chicken or we'd both end up losers. As we grew closer, I began to think the other driver wasn't going to swerve to miss me. We had gotten so close that my lights shown into the interior of the Altima. Inside I saw a man dressed in a black outfit and wearing some kind of hat at the wheel. His face was just about to come out of the shadows, when he yanked his steering wheel hard to the left.

Our cars rotated around each other in the middle of I-459 like a couple of lovers dancing the tango. His right side was inches from my left, so close that I saw our outside mirrors collide and fly away in a shower of glass and plastic. We had almost finished the dance, when the sound of crunching metal rang out. Our rear ends had clipped each other at the last second. The impact threw my head against the side window and sent one of my shoes flying past my face. My mouth filled with the taste of blood while I fought with the wheel to keep control. The collision had slowed me down and I had to adjust my turn to prevent myself from over steering and ending up heading toward the median again…which was exactly where the Nissan was going.

I steered the car back to the right for a moment, then I straightened my wheels and stomped on the brakes. The Civic's engine sputtered a few times and stalled while the tires screeched in protest. The Honda skidded to a stop and I took a cautious look around. I couldn't believe what I saw. My car sat in the center lane of I-459 facing south. Amazing, I'd actually done it. A loud crashing sound came from behind and pulled me out of my self-indulgent revelry. I lowered the car window and looked back trying to find the white sedan. After a second, I found it. It had continued its slide off the road and come to rest in the median. The Altima had rolled over onto the driver's side and thick, white steam was hissing angrily from underneath its dented hood. A small grin found its way onto my face, at least until I realized the man might be hurt, then I had mixed feelings. After all, the guy had tried to run me off the road so why not just start my car and leave? I considered it for a second, then cursed and spat the blood out of my mouth. I knew I couldn't leave someone, possibly injured, on the side of the road like this. Unbuckling my seat belt, I opened the door and got out of my car.

I started walking toward the Altima, a little shocked at how wobbly my legs felt. I'd only gone a few steps when a noise began to emerge from the steaming wreck. It was a sort of scrambling, scratching, climbing noise…and I stopped dead in my tracks. The white sedan rocked back and forth a few times as someone scurried around inside. Just as I thought it might tip over, the rocking stopped and everything was quiet again, until the horrible screeching sound of metal on metal cut through the air. Someone was forcing the passenger's door open even though it had been dented into the car frame. I began to think maybe this guy was just fine and didn't need my help at all. When his hands emerged from the open door and he started pulling himself up, I was sure of it. My instincts told me this man was dangerous and I found myself slowly backing up. I stared hard at the sight unfolding in front of me, afraid of what I might miss if I looked away. He pulled himself up and out of the car. Standing on the side of the sedan, he began searching around for where I'd gone. I tried to get a good look at him, but there was still almost no light. All I saw was an outline of a man that was about six feet tall wearing a dark suit. In my distracted state, I backed up so far that I bumped into the open door of the Honda. It made a small creaking noise followed shortly by a loud thunk as it closed. I froze in place, but his head instantly snapped around toward the noise…damn it.

I reached back and fumbled for the door handle. After a tense second, I found it and yanked the door open. I lost sight of him while I jumped in the car, but as I was repeatedly pushing the start button, I glanced in my rearview mirror. The driver had jumped down to the side of the road and was searching for something inside his jacket. I really didn't want to be around when he found whatever he was searching for. It was time to get the hell out of here. Luckily, I wasn't starring in a low budget horror movie, so my Civic started right up. I looked back one last time to see him pulling a small object out of his inside jacket pocket. I floored the Honda and didn't look back again until I was near the exit leading to my apartment. No one was following me, so I headed right for the safety of home.

Chapter 5

As soon as I pulled into my parking spot at the apartment complex, I could feel small trickles of relief begin to flow over my body. I searched for my shoes, found them, and got out of the car. Walking around my poor Civic, the damage to the back wasn't as bad as I'd feared. The bumper was dented in several places and deep scratches with white accents were all over, but the rear lights were still working, so I could put off taking it to a body shop. Which was good, because I needed some time to figure out what the hell was going on.

I locked up the apartment just as soon as I'd made it inside. Leaning against the door, I could feel those trickles of relief growing into a nice steady stream. For a couple of minutes, I just relaxed against the door and collected my thoughts. One of which was that I needed some dinner and a hot bath. I walked through the dining room and into my bathroom. Flipping on the lights, I padded across the white tile floor over to the large oval tub. I started the water running and went into the kitchen for my usual, vitamins and SmartWater. If it hadn't been so late, I might have actually had some real food, but I was in a hurry, so I just had another meal from the vitamin bottle.

Steam from the hot water had completely fogged the bathroom mirror by the time I returned. I sat down what was left of my drink and undressed. It felt simply fantastic as I slowly lowered myself into the tub. Leaning my head back, I closed my eyes and relaxed. The steaming hot water instantly began to melt the stress away. Now I could think clearly. Okay, so what was the first order of business? Well, I needed to find out who was pursuing me, but how? If I'd stayed and confronted the strange well-dressed man, I would have known. Of course, that knowledge could have cost me my freedom, or even my life. I'd already searched for the vehicle he was using, that was a dead end. Plus, after tonight's fun, he wouldn't be in the same car the next time we met. Hmm, I wasn't left with that many options. All I could do was wait until the next time he tried something and hope I was able to gather some more clues to his identity. Oh, and still manage to escape him as well.

I sat up a little in the tub and took another few sips of my water. The slow, rhythmic pattern of the dripping faucet drew me in and my mind began to drift. I finally came to the only realistic conclusion regarding these events. One that I'd been dreading, but could no longer avoid. The man pursuing me had to have been sent by Stepan Entsky. Actually, the *man* might not have been a man at all. It could have been Eliza. We both have the ability to drastically alter our appearance, and since I hadn't gotten a good look at him, it could have easily been her. The thought of it absolutely crushed me. If they had found me, I'd have to pick up and run. My job, my home, everything would have to be abandoned and I'd have to start over, again.

I bent my knees and sank down into the water up to my chin. Even if I managed to evade them, Stepan and Eliza would never give up. My initial escape had infuriated him, destroyed his plans, and damaged his ego. Something he'd never forget. Combine that with Eliza's unbridled jealousy and hatred of me for no other reason than my creation, and I might spend the rest of my life on the run. That, or I could kill them. No, that option wasn't even on the table…yet. Besides, I wasn't even sure it was them. It could be someone completely unknown to me. Okay, so I'd take some steps just in case I had to run, but I'd wait to see what happened next. There, I had a plan.

I'd stayed in the bath thinking and sipping on my cool SmartWater for far too long. When I was ready to get out, I noticed that my hands and feet had started looking like prunes. Sometimes the level of detail that the scientists had put into my creation amazed even me. Designed to be indistinguishable from a real person, I had it all, from sweat to tears, from desires to fears, from a heartbeat to pruney feet. I was the complete package, psychological, emotional, and physical. Of course, I was still having trouble with all of those, but I thought I was doing pretty well for someone that was less than a year old.

Drying off, I headed to the bedroom and threw on a T-shirt and a pair of shorts. It was getting late, and while I didn't need as much sleep as a person, my persistent yawning reminded me that I did need it. I promised myself I'd get in bed after I finished just one more thing. I needed to look for the one person that might be able to help me.

Heading back into the living room, I sank down into my comfortable leather chair and began my connection to the wireless network. Once I was interfused back into the endless universe that was the Internet, I called out for my friend using the very formal vocabulary that she liked so much. "Athena, please help me find what I seek!"

Without delay, I saw her approaching. She swooped in on Pegasus, white robes blowing freely in the breeze, and landed a few feet from where I stood. Her dismount was fluid and full of grace as she leapt to the ground and ran over to me. "Anna, it is good to see you again! I do hope there is another adventure in our future!" Her smile faded and she asked, "Forgive me my intrusion, but you do not look well at all. Are you in some kind of trouble, did that automobile come back?" She slammed the shaft of her golden-headed lance against the ground in a menacing manner to accent her question.

Athena had instantly figured out exactly why I looked like crap, but I didn't want to talk about it tonight. After all, I didn't have any new information to help me find out who was behind it and I didn't want to distract her from the reason I was here. So, I lied. "No, no trouble about, Athena. It's just that I'm weary. I was preparing for bed, but I have a quick deed to ask of you. If you would do me the honor, that is."

She watched me closely as I spoke and I got the feeling she didn't fully believe me, but she didn't press the subject. She smiled again and teased me. "Of course I will aid you Anna, but you do not look dressed for

52

adventure."

I looked down and remembered that I had already dressed for bed before interfusing, so I was standing there in just a shirt and shorts. I could use my will power to alter my clothing when I interfused to whatever I wanted, but with what happened tonight, I simply hadn't thought about it. "My apologies Athena if I've offended your delicate sensibilities. I will travel home and change my clothing into something more appropriate," I cheekily replied.

She smirked at me and said, "My sensibilities? Anna, it would take much more than the garb you are wearing to offend me. Have you forgotten to whom you speak? I am Athena, and I have witnessed incomprehensible sights!"

As our laughter at her joke died down, she said, "Now dearest Anna, tell me what it is that you seek."

"I would like to search for the daughter of Viktor Eklund...again," I said.

Athena's smile faded a bit as she said, "We have sought this person in adventures past, all to no avail. You know this."

"You speak truly, but this woman is of great importance to me. Please, let us try again," I said.

Athena looked at me and I thought I saw a bit of sadness flicker across her face. Whatever I'd seen was gone in an instant, replaced by her upbeat attitude and perfect smile. "Of course, we will try again, and this time, I say we will find her. Enlighten me to all you know of Master Viktor Eklund and his child so that I might better aid you."

I took a deep breath and told her everything I knew. "Viktor Eklund had his home somewhere in Europe when his daughter was born. He was a scientist working in the field of artificial intelligence. At the time of her birth, Viktor would have been twenty to thirty years old. Which means his daughter would have been born about twenty to thirty-five years ago."

"Do you know anything of the birth mother?" she asked.

"All I know of her mother is that her name was Helen," I said.

Athena leaned on her lance and twirled her hair while she considered the information I'd given her. While waiting, I absentmindedly paced around and ended up near Pegasus. He was receiving my best ear scratching when Athena's sudden squeal got my attention. When I turned, she was jumping up and down and pumping her lance in the air. I hurried back over to see what had gotten her so excited.

"Athena, were you able to find anything about this woman?"

In response, she turned her back to me and spread her arms wide in the air. "Well of course, for I am Athena. Behold!"

A bookshelf made of hand-cut oak appeared in front of her. It was about six feet tall and three feet wide. The four shelves were full of ancient looking parchments and scrolls. She turned back to me and crossed her arms over her chest, a huge grin spreading across her face. I waited to see if there was anything else, but when she just stared at me with that silly looking grin, I finally said, "Uh, I thank you Athena, but the documents you show me appear to be the same ones we have searched before."

I didn't think it was possible, but her grin widened. She pointed to the third shelf on the bookcase using her lance and whispered, "All but this one."

The document she indicated began to glow with a golden light. The breath caught in my throat as I moved slowly toward the glowing scroll. I picked it up and glanced over at Athena. She nodded to me and I anxiously unrolled it. I quickly scanned the paper and couldn't believe my eyes. It told of a doctor named Mark Deacon. His office was in a small town outside Worcestershire England called Blackminster. Doctor Deacon had delivered a baby girl thirty-three years ago when a young man and woman rushed into his office. Seems they were on a weekend trip when the woman's water broke and she began having contractions. My hands trembled as I read the last part of the scroll…the listed parents were Viktor and Helen Eklund.

I tried not to get my hopes up, but this information matched every fact I knew about the birth of Viktor's daughter. I knew I had to investigate this immediately. As I looked up from the parchment, I saw that Athena had read my mind and was already walking toward Pegasus. I quickly fell in step behind her and we mounted up. The mighty stallion launched us upward and we flew through the night sky. We raced toward the doctor's office like a silvery-white comet blasting its way across the darkness of space.

Chapter 6

In no time, we began closing in on this quaint little stone cottage. There was dark green ivy clinging to its walls and hanging lazily from the roof. Smoke from the tall chimney floated out and was carried away by a gentle breeze. Neatly trimmed hedges surrounded the doctor's home and the sweet smell of the rose garden in the back reached us even before we had landed. Athena guided Pegasus with expert skill and gently sat us down next to a cobblestone walkway that led up to the large wooden front door. She dismounted first and I quickly followed.

The walkway leading to the cabin had its own tall hedges on each side. So tall that they almost blocked out the night sky above. A feeling of claustrophobia swept over me as I stepped carefully down the cobblestone path. No, not just claustrophobia, it was a feeling that I was stepping back in time...back to an age before cell phones and the Internet. Back before my own existence would have been anything but a story in some science fiction novel. I looked over to Athena, and saw her looking back at me. From the expression on her face, she felt the same thing. Quietly, we both moved forward.

After a minute or so, we made it to the steps leading to the moss-covered front porch. As we ascended up past the potted flowers lining the stone steps and neared the front door, I felt myself growing increasingly anxious. As I thought more about how this place felt like it was lost in the past, I caught myself absentmindedly fiddling with the data drive that hung around my neck. I paused and stared at it, turning it around and around in my hand. I had gotten it from my father, Viktor, the night we were trying to escape the facility where I was built. It was the night my psychotic sister, Eliza, had killed everyone I cared about, from Cindi, the woman I'd loved to Viktor, my creator and the only father I'd ever known.

He had died with the drive clutched in his hand. When I accessed the data on it, I found two files. The first was a large file that was so well encrypted that even I couldn't open it. It was the research notes from his team detailing my creation. I've been trying to figure out his password, but haven't had any success so far. A letter to me was the only other file on the drive. In it, he told me how much he loved me and how I should seek out his daughter if anything ever happened to him. I'd always kept the data drive with me since then, to keep it safe, but also to remind me what happened that night.

The memories this place had conjured brought hot tears to my eyes and I looked down to hide my face. As I stood there lost in what had been, Athena came up beside me and put her arm around my shoulder. I glanced up to see that she was smiling at me and patiently waiting for me to get myself together. Wiping the tears from my eyes before they could fall, I continued up the steps. I put on a brave face, but if this trip didn't pan out, if we didn't find something, anything, that got me closer to finding this woman, I knew I'd be crushed.

Athena waited a few steps behind me as I walked up and knocked on the solid wooden door. I waited for a few seconds and knocked again while peeping in through the dirty glass window at the top. There was a small entry room illuminated by candles, but I saw no one coming to the door. I looked over my shoulder to see what Athena thought.

"Knock again, perhaps the occupant is older and hard of hearing," she said.

I turned back and knocked so hard that the glass rattled in the pane. Still no one came. I was beginning to think about forcing my way in when a thick Scottish accent bellowed from inside.

"Lord in Heaven, I'm coming! You don't have to go breaking my door off its hinges! Give an old man a chance, lad!"

A little stunned, I quizzically looked back at Athena, and that was all it took to start her giggling. At first I frowned at her, but then even I smiled at the sudden outburst. Hearing the man's approaching footsteps, I took a step or two back from the door since I wasn't sure what to expect. I was shushing and waving my hand at Athena trying to get her to be quiet when I heard the lock on the door being disengaged. That got our attention and we were dead silent as the old wooden door slowly creaked open.

A red-faced, elderly man dressed in an earth-brown flannel shirt and a pair of well-worn blue jeans greeted us. He must have been at least eighty years old and his rail-thin frame didn't occupy half the doorway. Even using the thick wooden cane that he held tightly in his left hand, his withered body still teetered back and forth. He looked so frail that I was glad the night wasn't windy, or else he might have blown away. Age had taken its toll in other ways as well. In his younger days, he must have been around six feet tall, but now he was bent so much that his face was level with mine. As we sized each other up, our gazes finally met. The intensity of his black, sunken eyes caught me off guard. Time may have taken the hair from his head, made his face so gaunt that it was unnervingly skeletal, but those eyes…they had a fire, a deep wisdom that time had only intensified.

Grinning, he licked his thin lips and said, "Well, you're no lad, now are you?" He started cackling at his remark, but it quickly turned into a coughing fit, which ended up with something being spat onto the ground. The old man looked back to me and then past me to Athena. His eyes narrowed and he said, "Now don't get me wrong, I like the idea of spending my evening with a couple of lovely lasses like yourselves, but that situation has taken a turn for the worse on me more than once. So if you don't mind me asking, who in the nine hells are you two?"

Okay, so he was a wise old man with a fire in his eyes that just happened to be a bit of a letch. I cleared my throat and decided to go with the truth. "Good evening, my name is Anna, and this is Athena. We came here tonight because I'm trying to find a woman."

"Lass, if you find a good one, send her my way, eh!"

I waited for his cackle, cough, and spit cycle to finish, then I continued. "Yes, well, this woman may have been born here thirty-three years ago to parents named Viktor and Helen Eklund. A Doctor Mark Deacon delivered her, would you happen to know anything about that?"

He eyed me closely once more before speaking. "Aye, that I do. Come in and we'll have a talk about it in front of the fire. It's getting a bit nippy for these old bones out here."

Without another word, he turned and shuffled back into his house, leaving the door open for us. I thought it might not be wise to blindly follow him into his house, but in the end, my need to know outweighed my caution. Besides, if it came to blows, I was fairly sure Athena and I could take the old coot.

We entered and closed the front door behind us. The foyer was small, but the candles were still only able to provide a dim light. We didn't see our host around anywhere, so we decided to head for the dancing lights coming out of the doorway down the hall on the right. Athena and I made our way slowly across the creaking hardwood floors; finally coming to the room we thought would contain a fireplace, and boy did it. The fireplace was constructed of hundreds of intricate smooth stones and it was enormous. I think you could have parked my Civic in it, well if you'd moved the roaring fire and the cast iron pots out of the way. The rest of the wall space was dominated by bookshelves that were filled with dusty tomes. The old man was still out of sight, so I looked at Athena and said, "I suppose we should seat ourselves and wait for the gentleman to arrive."

We looked around the room and found that the only places to sit were a red velvet love seat and matching chair near the fireplace. I instantly realized that whichever one of us got the chair, the other would have to sit next to the little old ladies man. I snapped my head around to look at

Athena and the desperate look in her eyes told me she had come to the same conclusion. We both sprang for the red velvet chair, but she was closer and firmly planted herself in it.

"Oh, I do apologize. I thought you would desire a more intimate spot on the love seat. It would allow you to better converse with our host," she said with just a trace of a smile.

"Why yes, I suppose it would," I replied as I stomped over to the two-seat sofa and plopped myself down.

We sat and waited. It had only been five minutes, but it felt like an hour. The roaring fire had made the room baking hot and oppressively stuffy. It made me glad I had on my T-shirt and shorts. I glanced over at Athena and she was trying to keep her tiara centered on her head, but it kept sliding down her sweat-soaked hair.

A few minutes later, the old man came in carrying a tray containing a large pitcher filled with what looked like iced tea, and three glasses. I noticed he wasn't using his cane, and while slow, he was still walking around fine. He shuffled over in front of us and sat the tray down on a small coffee table that looked like a tree stump. Pouring each of us a drink, he said, "I do apologize for the temperature in here, but an old man like myself gets chilled easy, you know. Here, have some tea before you beautiful flowers wilt from the heat." He handed a glass to each of us and took one himself. Then he sat down next to me and took a big drink.

"Ah, that's better. Now, I think you had some questions for me…Anna, was it?"

"Yes sir. But first, I don't think you told me your name yet," I said.

He looked a little embarrassed and replied, "Oh where are my manners. I am the personal computer of Doctor Mark Deacon. I should have mentioned it sooner, but…"

As he went on, I absentmindedly took a big drink of the iced tea.

Only after I'd swallowed it did I realize that it was more whiskey than tea. I glanced back to warn Athena, but she had already finished most of hers. What the hell, I thought, not only am I an android, but I'm an android in a virtual world, I couldn't get drunk anyway. At least I didn't think I could. I swallowed more tea and said, "Good, then you're just the person I need to talk to Doctor Deacon."

The good doctor stood up and refilled our glasses as he said, "Please lass, call me Mark."

I smiled and said, "Ok, Mark, as I said outside, I'm looking for the daughter of Viktor and Helen Eklund. She was born here thirty-three years ago. Can you help me?"

He rubbed his chin with his free hand and took another drink of his tea. "Well lass, I don't know. If I had that kind of information, you know I wouldn't be able to give it out. It would be unethical, now wouldn't it?"

The room felt hotter than before, but when I went to sip my tea, it was all gone. How had that happened? Oh well, it didn't matter. The doctor was already refilling our glasses again. Anyway, I would have to convince him to give me the information, which was how I infiltrated other systems. I knew he was an older system and I could probably just convince him with a simple argument without much effort. This was good, because I was having trouble concentrating.

"Look Mark, this woman, I have to find her. I have to tell her something about her father. You see, I used to work with Viktor Eklund, and he…well…he died about six months ago. She doesn't know yet because they've been estranged for a few years." I paused and allowed myself to tear up and sniffle some.

"You have to help me find her, a daughter deserves to be told this kind of thing from another person. Before she reads it on the Internet or something horrible like that. Could you imagine finding out your father had passed away from a computer?" The look of horror on his face told me I had convinced him.

He stood up and went to one of the hundreds of tomes. Browsing through it for a moment, he located the page and ever so gently tore it from its binding. He made his way back to the love seat, refilled my drink, and sat back down close to me. "Oh sweet one, what a dreadful tale. You poor thing, of course I'll tell you everything the good doctor recorded in his notes. You poor, poor thing, what a burden." He began to console me by gently running his fingers through my hair.

I sniffled a couple more times and drank some more tea as he continued, "You're right, the wee lass was born in this office like you said. You see Viktor and Helen were on a bit of a vacation when her water broke about ten days early. They came rushing in to the office, frightened to death. Luckily, it was an easy delivery and soon mother and daughter were sound asleep. After they were squared away, the doctor spoke with Viktor and filled out this birth certificate for the baby." He indicated the rolled up page in his hand.

"They only stayed that one night, Viktor thanked the doctor and called an ambulance to transfer Helen and the baby to a hospital. He didn't note which one. That's all I know my sweet lass."

My head was spinning. I had actually found the birth certificate for Viktor's daughter. It wasn't much, but I finally had a place to start. I was overcome by such a warm and wonderful feeling, like I could relax, let go of all my paranoia and fear.

Athena's slow and slurred voice broke into my thoughts. "Hey, Mark, I have a question. I have been scouring the world for information about this woman for almost half a year. Why is it now suddenly available?"

Wow, that was a good question. Why hadn't I thought about that?

"Well, lass, as you may have noticed I'm an older system and, let's just say I haven't been used for years. I just came back online today as a matter of fact," he said.

That made sense. If someone had been determined to wipe out all information on this woman, they would have only missed an offline system like Mark. There was something I wanted to ask him, but I couldn't remember the words. I just wanted to rest here with Mark playing with my hair and caressing my thigh. I felt so warm and safe.

Something in the back of my mind yelled at me. I tried to listen, but I couldn't make out what it was saying. It was just so damn hot in here! I went to take another drink of tea, and the voice in my mind finally broke through…I was drunk. Not only drunk, but I was possibly under attack by some virus or infiltration program. A bad situation, but one I could handle.

One of the advantages of being, well, me, was that I could simply turn off the fact that I was drunk. It was a state of mind brought about by my software emulating what a person would feel in this situation. So as fast as I could think it, I wasn't drunk any more. With that fog lifted from my mind, I was able to detect the virus trying to infiltrate me. It was a simple, older one, and I was much more than a match for it, now that I was paying attention.

I eradicated the virus that was gnawing on me and turned my attention back to the good doctor. "Mark, do you happen to know why you were taken offline so long ago?"

His face turned red and he stammered out his answer. "Well, now lass, it was…I…uh…it was just that I caught a bit of a bug… but don't you worry, it's not contagious, I swear! Don't let a little something like that ruin our evening now!"

I smiled at him and gently pulled his head into my chest. While he was distracted with that, I ran my hands across his shoulders and up to the back of his neck. I found just the right spot at the top of his spine, and jammed the fingernail of my index finger into him.

He flinched and said, "Oh, so you like it a little rough, eh? Well I can oblige you, lass!"

A hundredth of a second later, he fell unconscious and I held onto him so that he didn't slide off the love seat. I didn't want to hurt the old guy, but I had to completely erase any memory of the story he told me about Viktor and the birth of his daughter. While I was at it, I made sure he never remembered anything about my visit tonight and I even wiped out all the viruses he had. Once I'd finished with the doctor, I left him in a suspended state lying on the compact sofa. He'd wake up refreshed and in much better shape than before, the next time a user accessed him.

I stood up and walked over to Athena. She was sitting sideways with her legs under her, half asleep in the chair. I put my hand on her shoulder and said, "I have the knowledge I sought, let us leave this place."

She opened her eyes a crack and asked, "Is the physician awake?"

"No, I put him into a deep slumber. He will have no memories of tonight," I said.

Athena fully opened her eyes and easily stood up, unaffected by the alcohol or virus. "Good, let us be gone from this place. It is an inferno in here."

As we walked back toward the door I asked her, "So you weren't really drunk at all, were you?"

She winked at me as she replied, "Do you believe that you are the only one that can employ subterfuge?"

When we arrived back where we'd left Pegasus, Athena leapt up into the saddle and reached down to help me up.

"Thank you Athena, but I think I will just disconnect from here," I said. Then I fumbled for my next words. "I was able to erase the evidence of Viktor's daughter from the doctor, but you know I can't possibly do that with you. How can I convince you to keep this just between us?"

She looked down at me indignantly and said, "Anna, you know that my entire purpose for existing is to help people find the information that they seek. I would never sully my reputation or honor by misleading or withholding data." She paused for a moment and thought before continuing. "However, since you have deleted any trace of this data, it no longer exists for me to find. Therefore, it would not be correct for me to report that it existed to anyone else." She winked at me and turned Pegasus to leave, but before she took off, she looked back once more. "Now, as far as our adventures, those are always just between us. Have a good night Anna, I am pleased you were able to find out something about this mysterious woman." With that, she launched Pegasus into the air and was gone.

Standing alone on the cobblestone walkway next to the little stone cottage, I slowly pulled the folded up paper from my pocket and read the name on the birth certificate one more time. I promised Viktor I'd find you and keep you safe, and I will. I will find you…Elizabeth.

Chapter 7

Wednesday had been a complete blur. Nothing unusual happened all day, and my mind was preoccupied by the challenges I had going on in my life. Who was following me? What did they want? How could I be prepared for the next time they showed up? What about the information I'd found about Elizabeth? How could I use it to find out more? Should I focus on this new development or the fact that I was being followed? Before I knew it, it was after five in the afternoon. Well, I thought sarcastically, at least I wasn't bored.

I had secured my workstation, gathered up my things, and was halfway down the hallway leading to reception when David called out to me.

"Oh, hey Anna, if you can wait a few minutes, we'll ride together."

I must have looked like I had no idea what he meant, which I didn't.

"You know, to the zoo. It's the night for our company trip. We talked about 'Boo at the Zoo' all yesterday afternoon. Man, I'm so excited! I just need a few minutes to wrap up this program compile and I'll be ready to go," he said.

Aw crap, our company zoo trip had completely slipped my mind. The last thing I wanted was to waste my time on this frivolous outing. What I needed to do was get home and get to work. I desperately tried to come up with some reason I couldn't go. Noticing David's blue jeans, sneakers, and a wine-colored sweater that he'd gotten from the zoo gift shop, an idea struck me.

"Oh, yes, of course, I'd love to go David, but I forgot to dress casual today. I can't walk around the zoo in my business clothes. These heels would kill my feet. I guess I'll just have to pass this time."

Kimber must have overheard our conversation, because she rolled into the hallway still sitting in her reception chair.

"That's too bad Anna. I know how much you were looking forward to seeing your first zoo. Oh well, maybe next time then. Hey David, I can ride with you. Let me gather up and I'll be ready to head out."

David wasn't going to give up that easily. "You could head home, change, and then meet us at the zoo."

Okay, what now? Oh, I have it. "Yeah, but my car's been acting up and I'd rather not drive it anymore than I have to. So I guess I'll have to go next time."

Kimber spoke up and agreed with me again. "Yeah David, let's not get Anna stranded somewhere. I'm ready to go if you are!"

David shook his head and said, "No, no, I'm not going to let you miss out on this. It's our reward for working so hard these past few months and you have worked the hardest of us all. Here's what we can do. I'll follow you home, you can change your clothes, and then ride with me back to the zoo. Afterwards, I'll take you back home."

I wanted to come up with another reason to skip out on the zoo, but I could see in his eyes that David wasn't giving up. There was nothing left to do but relent to him.

"Well I hate to be such a bother, but if you insist."

"I do insist. Let's go ahead and leave. I can check the compile in the morning," he said.

David caught up to me and we headed for the lobby. As we neared the door and told Irene good night, I noticed that Kimber for some reason, was still sitting in the hallway.

"Hey, do you need a ride too, Kimber?" I asked.

She scowled at me and said, "No, I'll meet up with y'all there." With that, she put her feet up on the wall and pushed off, rolling back behind her desk where I couldn't see her. Now what was that about?

David and I headed down the steps to our cars and as I sat down and started mine, I realized something. I may have inadvertently put David in danger. If the man in the dark suit was out there again tonight, David might be caught in the middle. I considered it for a moment and decided we shouldn't run in to him tonight. It was still early and the road home would be busy with rush hour traffic, we would be fine…except of course for all the dangers of rush hour traffic.

For once, I was right, we made it to Eagle's Nest on the Mountain without any major injuries. All we had were a few frayed nerves from some near misses on the interstate. David came in and waited for me while I changed into a sweatshirt, a pair of jeans, and some sneakers. I really wanted to make this outing as short as possible, so I could get back home and do some research on Elizabeth. We jumped into his silver Toyota Prius and headed out for the zoo.

Deciding not to get back on the interstate, we instead took Highway 31 into town. It was stop and go because of all the red lights, but traffic was lighter. After about twenty minutes, we'd made it to Homewood, a beautiful, upscale neighborhood south of Birmingham. A few turns later, and we were on Cahaba Road. It wound through a lush, wooded area for about half a mile before delivering us to the zoo. David pulled into the parking lot and we hopped out of the car.

Now it was true, that I'd never been to a zoo and had only seen them on the Internet, but I thought I knew what to expect. I had no idea. The first thing I noticed was the smell. It was a pungent aroma of, well, animals and their waste. It wasn't unbearable, but it took a little getting used to. Then, there were all the sounds. The zoo was a cacophony of various animals all hooting, howling, screeching, squealing, growling, and roaring. All of that was mixed with the chatter and laughter of hundreds of people that sounded like they were having the time of their lives. There was even some music coming from somewhere that I couldn't see. I couldn't make out most of the lyrics, but the song was about monsters being mashed or something like that.

As we approached the gates, the lights and decorations for the 'Boo at the Zoo' event had me enthralled. To each side of the main entrance, there were stacks of hay bales with candle-lit jack-o-lanterns resting at their bases. Hidden behind the hay, some zoo employees had dressed up as The Headless Horseman and Dracula. As guests neared the main gate, they would slowly lurch out and grasp at them, groaning loudly. The families would jump at first, then laugh and even stop to pose with the monsters for some quick snapshots.

The main entrance itself had been transformed into what looked like a giant spider's web. It had strands of webbing that hung loosely over the entryways from the top of the ticket office down to the electronic gates. Sitting in the center of the web, over the sign that read 'Tickets', was a giant black spider about the size of a small car. Its eight legs were covered in fine, coarse hair and they were spread out touching the sticky strands in various places. If you dared to exam it closely enough, you could see its bulbous head slowly turn left and right while its eyes flickered and pulsed a blood red. It acted as if it felt each guest as they passed through the strands of its web. It was a hell of an animatronic, almost too good. Even I had a little shudder and looked away after a few seconds.

David and I approached the gate and got into the line entering through the turnstiles. As we passed through, our phones were checked for a valid ticket and we were each greeted by a slightly robotic male voice, "Thank you for coming to the Birmingham Zoo. We hope everyone from FlexJen Software has a great evening."

After getting out of the crowd of arriving guests, David led me over to one of the large ponds near the entrance. He was smiling from ear to ear as he asked me, "Isn't this great? Did you see the guys hiding behind the hay? Oh, and how about that spider? I'm sorta interested in robotics and that kind of stuff, I wonder if they'd let me take a look at it once Halloween is over?"

I waited for him to take a breath and said, "Yes, yes, I saw David... hey, are we supposed to meet up with Kimber and Felix?"

"No, we're not meeting up. Felix said this was one night we didn't have to worry about the boss looking over our shoulders and that he was going to let us enjoy it by ourselves."

"Alright, but what about Kimber?" I asked.

He shrugged and said, "I don't remember her saying anything about meeting us. I guess she was coming by herself too."

I felt a little like we were abandoning our friends, but then Kimber had said she would just see us here. Plus, they could always call if they wanted to meet somewhere for dinner or the like. Before I could consider it further, David asked, "So what would you like to see first?" He was holding his smart phone up while it displayed a hologram of the zoo. Then, he began naming off places and animals to me so I could make a better decision. David had obviously been here a few times before.

"I don't know, it all sounds like fun. Tell you what, how about you navigate since I'm a complete novice here."

"Okay, sounds great. Let's head over to the kid's zoo first. We still have time to see and pet the animals before they stable them for the night," he said.

He put his map up, already knowing which way to go, and began walking to his right. I followed behind him as he navigated his way through all the other guests, and there were all kinds of people here tonight. I saw everything from individuals taking photos, to complete families. Some of the children, and even some of the adults, were already dressed up as their favorite hero or monster, celebrating Halloween over a week early.

About halfway to the kid's area, I saw this beautiful carousel. It was covered in bright, flashing lights that pulsed in time to the rhythm of the loud music it played. I was drawn toward it, mesmerized as the carefully painted wooden animals rhythmically rose and fell on their brass poles. I watched as the carousel slowly rotated to the obvious enjoyment of all the riders. What I couldn't understand was what was wrong with the music and why was it turning backwards? A second later, I realized even the music was being played backwards. I reversed the song in my head, did a quick Internet search, and realized it was Werewolves of London by Warren Zevon. Didn't the zoo staff know the ride was broken? Better yet, didn't the riders?

David noticed I'd stopped and came up beside me. "Do you want to ride the carousel Anna?"

"Not until they fix it. It's all backwards," I scoffed.

David had a chuckle at my expense, and then explained it to me. "No, it's fine. During Boo at the Zoo, they run it backwards to creep out and scare the guests."

A question had been running around in my head ever since I'd heard about Halloween and how it worked, I figured I might as well ask it now. "David, why would someone want to be deliberately frightened?"

"Well, it's hard to explain. It really gets the blood pumping to have a little scare every now and then. You know, like at an amusement park when you ride a roller coaster. You know you're safe, but you still feel that rush of adrenaline."

I smiled and nodded at him. An amusement park wasn't somewhere I'd ever been, but I knew what they were. Maybe my problem was that all my life's scares had been for real, not for play. After some of those, it

was hard to get a thrill from a backward running merry-go-round...
although, I still wanted to ride it. Which we did, and I had to admit, it
was a blast.

David and I went from one animal habitat to another. We were in awe
of all the different kinds of animals and creative decorations that the zoo
had put up for Halloween. After about an hour, we stopped for some
dinner at the Safari Cafe near the big elephants from Africa. As we sat
and chatted over our hamburgers, I found that I was being caught up in
David's excitement. I realized that I was actually having fun. It had been
so long since I'd allowed myself any downtime that I'd forgotten how
good it felt.

That feeling waned as we were finishing our meals. I began to get this
idea in the back of my mind that someone was watching me. I paid it no
attention at first, after all, we were surrounded by a hundred or so people
and I knew from experience that my Russian accent would sometimes
draw a few looks my way, so I ignored it...at first. However, by the time
we were ready to leave, the feeling had grown stronger, so strong that I
took a surreptitious glance around all the tables to see if anything looked
out of place. I didn't see anything, but like I'd said, there were people
everywhere. I was still glancing around when I realized David was
staring at me.

"Are you alright Anna? You look worried," he said.

"No, I'm fine. I was just looking for Kimber, that's all," I lied.

David took a quick look around and said, "Well, I don't see her
anywhere. Hey, do you want to go see the primates next? They're just
around the corner from here."

"Sure, let's go," I told him. We struck out in the direction David
indicated, but while he guided us, I kept my head on a swivel trying to
find out what kept nagging at me about the crowd.

All through the primate habitats, I kept looking around and not seeing
anything. David was excitedly telling me all about the animals, but I was

distracted by my search, at least until we got to the gorilla. A large group of people had gathered around, laughing and pointing, next to the huge glass window that served as one wall to his enclosure. This got my attention, and as soon as I could see what he was doing, I was amazed.

This huge male gorilla, whose plaque at the bottom of his habitat listed his name as Titan, was interacting with someone from the zoo. Her name tag read Sara, and she was behind a fence on the outside of his enclosure talking to him. Titan was answering using a stack of cards he had laying in front of him.

"Titan, would you like some lettuce or a banana as a treat?" she asked. Titan looked through his cards, chose the one with a picture of a banana, and showed it to her.

"Okay, catch." She tossed him the fruit and he caught it with ease. However, he didn't eat it, he placed it down at his side and looked back over at Sara.

"Good, now, what is two plus two Titan?"

Again, he looked through the cards, passing by several of them with the wrong answer and found the card with the number four. He held it up, and the gathered crowd murmured their approval. Sara tossed him another banana and he placed it at his side next to the other one.

This went on for five more questions with Titan answering each one correctly. As Sara wrapped up, she turned to the crowd and thanked us for coming. When she waved at us and bowed, so did Titan. I was astonished that he did it without any prompting from Sara. Titan then sat down and began to eat his bananas, but he would wave if he saw someone in the crowd waving to him.

"He's pretty impressive isn't he?" David asked.

"Yes, I can't believe how intelligent he is," I said.

David chuckled a bit before saying, "Well, Anna, he's not really *intelligent.* He's just trained."

I shook my head and said, "Maybe some of it was training, but the way he reacted to the crowd wasn't a trained response."

David took my arm and we walked closer to the glass, as some of the people moved on to the next habitat. He pointed at Titan and explained, "Yes Anna, it's all just conditioning and training. I'm not saying Titan is stupid, but he's not intelligent like we humans are. Look at him for a minute and tell me what you see."

I watched as Titan ate his bananas and waved back to the people that waved to him. Then I saw what David was talking about. He was just reflexively responding to what the crowd did. He wasn't thinking about what he was doing, he was just repeating what he saw in the guests.

David saw the realization on my face and said, "See, he's just mimicking human behavior. Titan's not thinking about what he's doing or what it means. He can't understand what it's really like to be human. A trained gorilla may act like us in some ways, but he'll always be different. No matter how well he imitates our behavior, he'll never be one of us."

I felt a little dizzy as my mind soaked up what David was saying. He was talking about Titan, but he could just as easily have been talking about me. Wasn't I just an imitation of a person? I wasn't a human by any definition. Now that I thought about it, I even had special software that helped me imitate human behavior. I was just a little better at it than Titan. Everything I did was only an act, just like the gorilla. No matter how hard I tried, eventually, I'd make a mistake, and someone would figure out my secret.

"Hey, Anna, are you okay? You look a little pale," David said.

"Um, yeah, I'm just a little chilled all of a sudden. David, would you mind us cutting out? I'd like to get home before it gets too late."

"Sure Anna, we can see the rest some other time. It's hard to see some of the animals now that the sun has gone down anyway. Come on," he said.

As we walked through the crowds, I felt completely lost. I'd had these kinds of thoughts about my humanity before, but back then I could talk things over with either my father figure Viktor, or my lover Cindi. Now, both of them were dead thanks to Eliza, Stepan, and that traitorous Warren Lopata. Except for them, there wasn't a soul that knew what I truly was. I was absolutely alone with my thoughts.

Before I realized it, we'd made it back to the large goose ponds near the entrance of the zoo. David let go of my arm and ran over to a dispensing machine. He held his hand under its spout and paid with his phone. The machine whirred and spat out a hand full of little brown pellets. The geese understood what that sound meant and a flock of them swam as fast as they could toward the edge of the pond where David stood. He smiled at me and said, "Sorry, I just need a minute. Since I've been coming to the zoo, I always feed the geese before I leave."

He bent over the two-foot stone wall that enclosed the pond and began sprinkling the pellets on the surface. The hungry geese paddled around and began gobbling up the floating pellets. They flapped their wings and honked excitedly as he tossed more food into the water. David called over his shoulder to me. "Come on, its fun."

Taking the pellets that the machine had given me, I bent over next to David. When I threw some to an empty spot on the lake, the geese flocked over to the new buffet I'd provided them. I kept tossing the pellets a few at a time until I'd given them all away to the hungry birds. David had been right, it was fun. We were both laughing and talking to the geese by the time I ran out of food. I looked over to my right to say something to him, when out of the corner of my eye, I saw her coming.

My advanced reflexes activated as I saw Kimber heading right for my back. Her face was twisted into a scowl as she moved quickly toward me. Her hands were down low, near her waist and she had her palms facing me as she closed in. Damn it, she was going to push me into the pond. I considered letting her, because I knew if I avoided her attack, I'd have to move fast, maybe faster than I should with this many people around. Then I thought, why the hell should I be the one that ended up in the cold water? I hadn't done anything to warrant this kind of attack, so why not let her learn who she was dealing with.

As soon as Kimber was so close that I was sure she wouldn't have time to react, I rapidly straightened up and turned my body to the left. It worked perfectly. Now that she'd missed, her forward momentum carried her right past me. She turned, desperate to slow down, but she couldn't. Her legs hit the low stone wall and she flailed her arms wildly as she began to tumble backwards. When my eyes met hers, I saw the fear that was in them…and I realized I couldn't let this happen. This wasn't me.

I thrust my right hand out and grabbed onto her left arm just above the wrist. I had a good grip, but she had on a fuzzy pink sweater and my hand slid on top of the stretchy fabric until I tightened my grasp at her wrist. Now that I had her, I realized she was too far gone. She was going to carry us both into the pond. As I slid toward the wall, I had one hope at keeping us dry. When I felt my feet touch the base of the wall, I pulled back as hard as I dared, and tried to fall backward. It worked. I felt myself falling back toward the ground, and I had Kimber in tow. As I landed flat on my back, I reached out with my other arm and caught her so she didn't crash into me too hard.

As she lay there on top of me, her face inches from mine, I watched as the shock of what had happened wore off. Her expression went from fear, to hate in record time, which I didn't understand at all.

David rushed over to us and began to help Kimber up. "Oh my God, are you two okay?"

Kimber stood next to him, rubbing her wrist, as she spat, "Yeah, I'm fine. Just a sprained wrist."

Next, he leaned over and helped me up. "You alright Anna? What happened?"

Kimber shot a look at me when she heard David's question. I stared at her for a second before I answered. "I saw Kimber lose her balance and start to fall, so I tried to catch her. Luckily, I was able to."

"Yeah, I tripped over a crack or something," she said as she continued to stare at me.

David looked at us both for a second and said, "Okay, well, Kimber if you're sure that you're alright. I was just about to take Anna home."

"I'm fine. I was just heading home too. I'll see you in the morning." She turned and walked away without another word. We watched her disappear into the crowd, and then headed out the gates ourselves.

As we walked through the parking lot full of people getting into their cars, I had the feeling I was being watched again. I looked around the well-lit area for Kimber, but I didn't see her anywhere. My assumption had been that she was the one watching me earlier, but now I wasn't so sure.

I kept looking around as we got into the car and David cranked it up. When we backed out of our space, my eyes landed on a family getting into their white minivan. The father was about six feet tall and wore jeans and a t-shirt. On his head was a baseball cap, so I couldn't tell the color of his hair, and he had on sunglasses, so I couldn't see his eyes. The woman was fussing over a baby stroller as the husband opened the doors to the van. She wore a yellow sundress and looked a little older than me. Her body was about my build, except for the huge baby bulge she carried. Mom's shoulder length black hair swung freely as she leaned over the stroller and talked to her baby. As we pulled away, the husband came to stand beside his wife and she straightened up and put her arm around his waist.

David pulled us onto the road and as the family slowly disappeared behind us, the mom gave me a little wave. Without thinking, I waved back. Instantly, my mind thought of Titan and my lack of humanity. I sighed in quiet frustration. Between that and the encounter with Kimber, I couldn't wait for this day to be over.

Chapter 8

I watched through my window as David backed up his car and drove away. He'd wanted to come in for a while and talk about the zoo, but I'd told him I was too tired, which was true. I was tired of many things, but unfortunately, most of them were out of my control. Depressed, I went into the bathroom to take a shower. I turned on the water so that it could warm up and then began to undress. I kicked off my shoes and sent them flying back into the bedroom. As I pulled my shirt over my head, I caught a glimpse of myself in the rapidly fogging mirror. My eyes focused on the data drive that hung around my neck. I instantly thought of Viktor. He'd told me that Elizabeth could help me, but I hadn't found her yet, and his secrets remained locked away in the encrypted file on the drive. I looked at the shower, then back to the mirror. Why not give it another try I thought.

I pulled the shirt back over my head and turned off the shower. Then I walked into the bedroom and sat down on the bed where it was comfortable. I took a deep breath and reached up, sliding my fingernail into the drive. The familiar disorienting sensation was instant and my vision of the room dimmed as the image of a medium sized storage box appeared on the bed in front of me. Opening the box, I saw the letter Viktor had written me along with the safe that represented the encrypted file of his research. It was about the size of a shoebox and secured with a fifty-digit code. Usually, I would hack into a system by interacting with it intelligently, but this encryption method was so simple, it had no intelligence. I could try a brute force approach, and enter every possible combination, but with up to fifty positions and around fifty possible values for each position, it would take centuries, even for me. So I began trying to guess the password using all I knew about Viktor, and now, his daughter, Elizabeth.

After thirty minutes, I was ready to give up. I'd gone through over two hundred million possible passwords without any luck. Frustrated, I yanked the drive from my fingernail causing the storage box and its contents to disappear from the bed. I knew it had been a long shot, but after the zoo, I had been hoping for a miracle to get me out of my deep funk. After all, I was supposed to be the best in the world at system infiltration, yet I couldn't crack this one file.

I fell back onto the bed and stared up at the ceiling of my apartment as my mood continued to sour. The thought that I'd never be human, never be normal like the family loading up their van as we left the zoo drifted into my mind. Images of the pregnant mother, her baby in the stroller, and the husband kept running around in my head. I knew I was obsessing, but I kept seeing her waving at me while she stood there next to her husband, mister sunglasses...

I sat straight up in the bed. That was what had been bothering me. Why was the father still wearing his sunglasses after nightfall? I'd thought Kimber had been the one that had been following me around the zoo, but what if it was one of them? Wait, what if the father was the man in the dark suit that kept trying to run me off the road? I replayed the events in my mind, and realized I'd seen the license plate on the van. Now, I just needed a little help.

Within minutes, I'd interfused with the Internet and was watching as Athena swooped in on Pegasus, landing a few feet away. She looked as beautiful as always, as she leapt from his back to greet me. She ran over and took both my hands in hers. "Dearest Anna, you are back, and so soon! Pray tell, what adventures are we to go on tonight?"

"I am pleased to see you as well, Athena. Tonight, I may have found some information on the strange man that has been following me on the interstate. I managed to get a look at the identification number of another automobile. If it would please you, could we travel back to the DMV and see if we can find the owner of the vehicle?"

"Why of course friend, Anna. Come, let us ride!"

We both headed for Pegasus and quickly mounted up. Athena took his reins and shouted, "Away my steed, make haste!" The mighty stallion leapt into the air and we zoomed through the stars as fast as his wings could take us.

It turned out to be all for naught though. After we'd convinced DMV to give us the information on the license plate for the white minivan, the car turned out to be a rental. This led us to retrace our previous night's steps and go to the Hertz office. You guessed it, the paperwork was filled out with the same fake name and paid for with a prepaid credit card, just like the white sedan…damn it.

I slowly walked out of the Hertz office feeling depressed and frustrated, but also a little worried. I may not have found who this man was, but I found out it was probably the same man in the car that was chasing me…and he had a woman with him. Could that woman have been Eliza? Had Stepan found me and sent my psychotic android sister to bring me back? If so, who was the man? Better yet, how had they found me? There wasn't anyone left alive after I escaped, Eliza had made sure of that. She'd killed everyone that I knew… A chill came over me as I realized that wasn't true. Eliza had killed everyone on the research team, but she hadn't killed Zory Novikov.

Memories from the horrible night that I'd managed to escape from Stepan flooded my mind and I could remember it perfectly. I was sitting on the floor, still trapped inside the Russian military base where I'd been created. Viktor's cold, unmoving body was on the floor in front of me. I'd managed to stop Eliza, but not before she'd fatally shot the man that was my creator, the man that was my father. That loss had come within minutes of watching my best friend and lover, Cindi, die from wounds also inflicted by Eliza. I was so completely lost in sorrow that I would've sat there until captured if Zory hadn't found me. Zory was a young

Russian soldier stationed at the base. We had met during some small arms training and one ill-fated mission we went on together. Zory of course didn't know my true nature. He was simply looking for a quick romp in bed, at least at first. As we grew to know each other, I sensed there was much more to this man than the womanizer act he showed the world. During that night, he saved my life at least twice.

He found me there on the floor and brought me back from my sorrow. Zory convinced me to say my goodbyes to Viktor and come with him. After treating the head wound that Eliza had given me, we were able to escape the base. The man would not leave my side, even though he knew what trouble he'd be in if he were found AWOL. Zory showed me the quickest way to the port town of Tiksi where I was able to find a ship and stowaway onboard. When I asked why he was willing to do this, he told me it was because he thought I was a good person trapped in a bad place.

If Stepan and Eliza had found out that he helped me, there was no telling what they would do to him. I racked my brain, trying to think of a way to check on him. I owed him at least that much. Then I realized I had the best search engine in the world standing right next to me.

Athena was glad to help, as she always was, after I explained that I needed to find the most recent data on someone else. She did her search and found he was still listed as being in the Russian military, but she couldn't determine where because his post was listed as 'Special Assignment'. That was all right. I knew where he was. The question was did I have the guts to go back there, even virtually, and try to find him. I considered it, and although I knew it was stupid, I also knew that I had to go. My only hope was that showing back up at the place I worked so hard to escape from wouldn't be anything they'd ever expect. I'd surprise them with stupidity.

It was difficult to locate the computer system for the military base, but between Athena's almost limitless knowledge and my detailed inside information, we were winging our way toward it in no time. As we grew closer to our destination, I noticed that the normally bright starlit sky gave way to larger sections of darkness. We were entering a technological desert, and the sky grew blacker with each beat of Pegasus's mighty wings. As the darkness began to close in around us, I felt a familiar nervousness creep into my thoughts. I leaned forward so Athena could hear me over the rushing wind. "It grows so dark, how will you navigate if you cannot see?"

"Shield your eyes, for I am about to call forth a brilliance to illuminate the sky," she replied.

She didn't know it, but my eyes could weather the change in light more rapidly than could a human's. I pretended to shield them as I watched her draw her lance from its sheath and point it forward into the starless night. Instantly light burst forth in front of us like someone had flipped the switch on a multi-million lumen searchlight. Viewed from below, I imagined we must look like a falling star, burning its brightest just before it's destroyed forever. I silently wondered to myself if there was anything she couldn't do inside this world.

We decided to land about fifty yards from the base so we didn't appear threatening to any guards that might be on duty. Pegasus picked a landing spot and began his descent. The closer we grew to the ground, the colder it became. By the time we landed, I could see my breath on the cold night air. Athena dismounted first and dimmed her lance down to the brightness of a flashlight so she didn't blind anyone while approaching them. I felt myself hesitate as I started to slide down. This wasn't the real version of the Russian base called Ice Castle, I knew that, but it was close enough to give me the shivers. Composing myself was as easy as remembering that I had beaten this place once and I would do so again if needed. I gave Athena a nod and confidently slid down from Pegasus, only to let out a high pitched squeal when my bare feet crunched into the thin layer of snow covering the ground. My body may have been more resistant to heat and cold than a person's, but it was also programmed to make me react the way a human would when encountering sudden heat or cold, this helped keep my human disguise in place. However, it did absolutely nothing for my dignity.

Athena looked at me with mock disapproval and said, "Anna, you should more carefully consider your attire before beginning these adventures of ours."

Frowning at her, I almost replied with something snarky, but I decided to let it slide. I wanted to get in and out of this place as soon as possible. "I fear you are correct, let us move quickly before I am frostbitten."

We trekked off toward the dimly lit building with Athena leading the way. From the air, we had seen that it was about two hundred feet on each side and two stories tall. Constructed of featureless concrete, the building was painted as black as the night that surrounded it. What we hadn't noticed from the air was the eight-foot tall fence topped with razor wire that surrounded the structure. After some searching, we found the side that had a small wooden guard station. It only contained one guard, but I was sure he could raise the alarm and find help quickly. I motioned at Athena to stop so I could explain my plan.

After I finished, she frowned and said, "I am not exactly pleased with your strategy, but I will defer to you since you are apparently an expert in the field."

"All right, then here I go." With a little concentration, I began altering my physical appearance. This was another one of the wondrous abilities that I'd been given to help with my espionage duties. First, I shortened my hair and changed its color to black. Next, I changed my eyes to a deep brown and made the hue of my skin milky white. Lastly, I reduced my chest size and altered my frame to be a touch thinner. I didn't need a mirror to know that I'd taken the form of my deranged sister, Eliza.

Athena watched in stunned silence as I went through my alterations. When I finished, a small gasp escaped her lips and she whispered, "My eyes must deceive me! You are a completely different person, Anna! Why, even I cannot see through your illusion!"

"That is because it is not an illusion my friend. I have changed my appearance in the physical world, and so it has been changed here in this one as well," I said.

She looked me up and down before replying, "You have not been forthright in the tales of your history. We must make some time to talk later."

I nodded my agreement, "I promise we will. Now, I'm heading in, and remember, do not involve yourself no matter what happens to me." She began to speak, but I turned and rushed away before she could argue the point. Heading straight for the place that I swore I'd never see again.

Chapter 9

As I drew near the Ice Castle guard, I slowed my pace and tried to get into the character of my sister. I had used this kind of deception before to escape the base that ill-fated night, hopefully this would be an easier task.

The young man exited the guard shack as I slowly approached. He was dressed in heavy winter clothing so that all I could see was his face and the broad smile spreading across it. I gave him a show befitting of my sister. My hips swayed side to side in a seductive rhythm, and the expression I wore promised delights he would never know. Strutting right up to him, I started to speak, but he threw his arms around me. He pulled me off the ground into a crushing embrace. His mouth hungrily found mine and he kissed me passionately.

I tried to organize my whirling thoughts, but at first, the questions came too quickly. *How did I instantly lose control of this situation? Damn it, Eliza must have been spending some naughty time on Ice Castles' computer systems. How do I carry out my plan now? Hey, this guy is a great kisser…*

The last thought broke me free of my inaction. I opened my eyes and roughly pushed the soldier away from me. He released his grip and stumbled backwards a couple of steps, an expression of desire mixed with fear written across his face. "Oh, Comrade Eliza, I have missed you so! I, I was overcome with desire! Please, forgive me!"

I began to think this unexpected turn of events might work to my advantage. It was time to go on the offensive. "How dare you touch me without my permission!" I snarled. "I should kill you where you stand!"

He paled at my words and his voice began to crack. "But my dearest, most precious Eliza, I implore you, do not treat me so. Have pity on your devoted Ilia."

"I may, but realize whom you are dealing with. Next time, do not be so familiar," I said.

"But we have always greeted each other so. At least after that time behind the…"

"Silence! I am here because I need some information." I paused, then grinned wickedly and lowered my voice to a whisper. "But who knows, maybe after business, there will be some time for pleasure."

He straightened himself and assumed a professional attitude. "Of course comrade, what information may I retrieve for you?"

I nodded to him and said, "That is better. Now, I seek information on a soldier assigned to this base. His rank is private and his name is Zory Novikov. Retrieve the last three days of any security camera footage containing this man and bring it to me."

He saluted as he replied, "Of course, may I please see your identification, Comrade Eliza."

I had expected this. I closed the distance between us quicker than he could blink. Grabbing him by the front of his coat, I pulled his face down until our noses touched. "Are you insane? Your lips needed no proof of my identity while you were dancing them across mine."

"I'm sorry, it's just that regulations are clear…"

"Oh, I see, you did not recognize my kiss and even my embrace was that of a stranger to you. Well then, let us keep it that way."

"Wait, it is just that I do not want to risk any trouble, " he pleaded.

My hard stare bore into him as I poked his chest with my finger. "Ilia, you were not so concerned with rules and regulations the last time we met. "

He looked away from me for a moment and then turned toward the little wooden shack. At first, I was concerned that I may have overplayed my hand, but once he entered and began working with the computer inside, he said, "You're right as always. I will fetch the information you require on this private." His hands went through rapid motions over the touch interface. In no time, he pulled a small data drive from the computer and walked back out to where I stood.

He handed me the drive and I said, "There, now that wasn't so hard, was it?"

He caught me by the hand as I began to turn and said, "Now, Eliza, it's time for that pleasure you mentioned." Before I could react, he spun me around and pulled me against his body. His lips hungrily found mine and I felt strong hands roaming over me in places that I hadn't let anyone touch in over half a year. I moaned softly to him as I worked one of my arms free from his embrace and tugged on the heavy belt holding up his sidearm. He groaned his approval and reaching down, began fumbling with his buckle. To do this, he had to let me go and back up a little, that was when I punched him hard in the groin.

He fell to his knees, writhing in pain. He looked up to me and I spat on the ground next to him. "I told you never to touch me again without my permission. I will let you live only because killing you would cause me so much paperwork. Now get out of my sight."

He slowly stood and walked back into his guard shack. After entering, he turned to close the door and I caught a glimpse of his crestfallen expression. It was depressing, but I had to behave the way my sister would. Otherwise, I risked having my true identity exposed. Ilia's door closed with a light thump and I left without delay back to where Athena waited for me.

As I drew near her, I paused for a moment and transformed my appearance back to what she was used to seeing. She rushed up to me once the transformation was complete. "Were you able to retrieve the data you sought, Anna?"

"Yes, I have the information. However let us not view it here, I believe this area to be too dangerous for us to linger."

"Agreed, let us travel to my abode. There we can watch it undisturbed," she said.

I nodded my agreement and not wanting to stay around Ice Castle any longer than needed, we mounted Pegasus and were gone in a blink.

I'd never been to Athena's home before, but it was befitting of the goddess she appeared to be. We began to approach a sprawling, opulent city that could have stepped right from the pages of a history book. Oil lamps hung everywhere. They illuminated the city so much that we could have been flying over Las Vegas. The buildings were made of the whitest marble and sprang up all along the stone-paved roads. Aqueducts carried fresh water to wherever it was needed and connected to large pools of the sparkling blue liquid. As we flew deeper, we passed over two amphitheaters, a couple of coliseums, and several large libraries.

I called out so Athena could hear me over the rushing wind. "What a beautiful city your home is in."

"Nay, all of this is my home, Anna. I am taking us to the garden maze so we shall not be disturbed."

After a few more minutes, we began to descend into a huge maze constructed from eight-foot tall hedges. The maze must have been several hundred yards on each side, and in the center sat an enormous water fountain blasting sparkling water high into the air. The fountain was breathtaking. It was at least a hundred feet square, and looked to be constructed of the same white marble as the rest of the buildings. At various places, cherub statues were in playful poses as if they frolicked in the knee-deep water.

Athena landed Pegasus next to a bench with a view of the fountain and we dismounted. She playfully slapped his hindquarters and said, "Go my friend and enjoy the maze. We shall be here near the fountain." He nodded his head, and trotted off down one of the paths. As he disappeared from view, I managed to find my voice again.

"Your home is resplendent beyond belief. I am honored to visit it, Athena."

A warm smile found her face as she replied, "Thank you kindly, Anna. More and more is added every day, I suppose it is because my knowledge of all things increases daily as well, but enough of that." She walked over to the bench and patted a spot next to her. "Sit with me and we shall view your find without the possibilities of outside prying."

I sat down beside her and inserted my fingernail into the drive that Ilia had given me. Checking it, I saw that it contained only two video files. Athena watched my actions with growing interest. "I must admit, after seeing how you access that drive, I am slightly concerned about how you intend to share the images with me," she said as a wry smile played across her face.

I managed a smile of my own despite my growing nervousness. "Athena, I promise it isn't that invasive. Here, take my hand."

She did, and I linked her to just the part of my mind that allowed her to see what I was seeing. Tentatively, I started the video that was time stamped from two days ago. A low-resolution security camera must have captured the data, because it was somewhat grainy and in black and white. It showed Zory standing outside the barracks. There were three other soldiers with him and they were all smoking cigarettes or cigars. The audio was faint, but I recognized his voice as he and the others joked about duties that they had been assigned. It was nothing but a simple smoke break, but I let the video play until it completed five minutes later.

The next video had been recorded a day ago. It was only two minutes, and it was of Zory filling up his motorcycle with gasoline. He was hand cranking the pump that sat on top of a fifty-five gallon drum of fuel. I watched, happiness filling me up inside. He hadn't been discovered or taken prisoner and was going about his everyday life. The relief washed over me like a wave from the ocean.

After the surge of relief receded, I found that despair had washed up on my emotional shore. I missed him...I missed all of them. I was completely alone, without a soul to confide in. That burden combined with what had happened at the zoo sent my thoughts to the darkest places.

"Anna, what is wrong? You found the man you sought and he is without injury, yet you see horrible things in your mind."

I had forgotten that I still held Athena's hand. She must have seen some of the images that I had been reliving. The burden had become too much, I had to talk with someone. "Athena, you know I am different, but you do not realize by how much. On your word, you must keep what I am about to show you secret forever."

"As always, my dear friend," she said.

I opened my mind and showed her my true nature, what I really was. I allowed her to see my entire history, from my creation up until now. She witnessed all my loves, along with all my losses. Finally, I showed her my concern about my own humanity and the loneliness from the complete isolation I'd endured over the last few months. Slowly, I closed my mind and looked at her to gauge her reaction. She wasn't an artificial intelligence like me, so I had no idea what to expect.

Athena thought for a long time, and then said, "Anna, we are made up of many pieces. Some of those pieces are made out of stone. They are hard, unforgiving, and unchangeable. We have to utilize these stone pieces the way they have been given to us. However, there are other pieces of us that are made out of clay. These clay pieces, these parts of us, we can shape, change, and bend to our will." She paused and looked deeply into my eyes. "You should pay heed to the clay in your life. For it can become set like the stone, and then you cannot change it either. Make sure that when this happens, it resembles the shape you want for yourself."

I met her intense stare and said, "It is easier for you. You are exactly what you were intended to be. There is no question about who you are or what purpose you serve. You were not constructed to imitate a search engine…you were constructed to *be* a search engine, and you are. You are Athena, the most powerful search engine in all existence."

My eyes overflowed with tears that I couldn't stop, and Athena reached out to me. She wrapped her arms around my back and held me in her gentle embrace. As I tried to dry my eyes, she spoke in a low whisper. "And who are you? Are you not special? Are you not unique? Do not belittle and demean yourself so. I have seen you do things that I could not accomplish in a hundred years. You are Anna, and you are exactly who you were intended to be."

I looked up to meet her deep brown eyes and realized I didn't know how to respond. I'd never encountered a system this intellectually advanced. Perhaps it was because of how complex Athena was, the amount of computing power, or the vast amount of data to which she had access. Maybe those factors gave her this level of insight. However, none of that mattered as I realized she was about to lean in and kiss me.

I felt my face flush a deep crimson and my heart raced in my chest. I was so alone, I just wanted, no, needed, someone to spend a few moments with. My voice was a raspy whisper as I spoke. "Athena, I…"

She paused, her lips so close to mine that I could feel her breath as she spoke. "Is this not what you seek, Anna?"

Before I could answer, I heard a ringing coming from somewhere far away. After a moment, I deduced it was the doorbell to my apartment back in the physical world. Some heavy knocking on the door quickly followed the ringing. No one I knew would be coming to my apartment this late at night, but it sounded as if they would break the door down if I didn't come answer it. I had to leave, now.

Athena could tell that something had agitated me, but before she could draw the wrong conclusion, I explained what had happened. "Go and attend to this visitor, but I beseech you, take care, for he could be the villain that you seek," she said.   We stood up and she hugged me goodbye. I began to shut down the interfuse connection and readied myself to face whoever this late night visitor might be.

Chapter 10

As my interfuse connection to the Internet closed, the image of my bedroom became increasingly substantial. I shook off the usual dizziness, along with thoughts of what was just about to happen with Athena, and got to my feet. Crouching low, I peeked around the partially open door leading from my bedroom into the living room. I could see that my front door was still closed and locked, which was a great relief. Cautiously, I approached it and called out. "Who is it?"

"Is this the apartment of Anna Andropov?" came the reply.

It was a man's voice that I didn't recognize. "Look, I'm not answering any questions until I know who you are. It's really late and I don't feel like playing games, so let's hear it," I replied.

He spoke again, his voice monotone and without a discernible accent. "Fine, my name is Adam Sims. Now, if you are Anna Andropov, I have an urgent matter to discuss with you and this isn't the sort of conversation one has with raised voices."

I'd obviously never met this man before, but his reply piqued my curiosity. I walked over to the window to see if I could get a look at him. He was tall, around six feet, and was dressed in a dark blue suit that fit his medium built frame perfectly. He wore no hat and I could see that his short, black hair was parted on the left. As I watched him through the window, he must have caught a glimpse of me in his peripheral vision, because he turned to face me. Adam's skin had a healthy tan color, and he looked to be in his mid thirties. His blue eyes were bright and accented his handsome, clean-shaven face nicely.

"Anna, I'm going to show you my identification, then maybe we can sit down and talk," he said.

He never broke eye contact with me as he took his right hand and moved it slowly and deliberately inside his jacket. I tensed, ready to act, but his expression held no anger or malice toward me. He slowly removed his hand from inside his suit and showed me that it now held his cell phone. He tapped the surface with his thumb, and it illuminated, showing me his identification in the form of a hologram. As I read it, my heart sank, Adam Sims - Field Agent - National Security Agency. Damn it all to hell, I'd been found!

Several thoughts ran through my mind, all of them centered on either fighting or fleeing, but I did neither. If they had found me once, they could find me again. While I was running through all my possibilities, Adam spoke to me through the window.

"Anna, please let me in so we can talk."

Resigned to my fate, I unlocked and opened the door. "May I come in?" he asked.

"Yes, of course," was all I managed to say.

Standing aside, I allowed Adam to enter. I closed the door behind him and he remarked, "This is a very nice apartment you have. I apologize for my late visit, but in my line of work I find it's best to be seen by as few people as possible."

As I absentmindedly nodded to him, an idea of how to get more information on my current predicament crossed my mind. "Please let me see your identification again. I'd like to be sure who I'm dealing with."

He stared blankly at me for a second, then reached back into his jacket and produced his phone again. I reached out to take it, but as soon as he saw what I was doing, he yanked it out of my reach. "No, I'm afraid not Miss Andropov. I can't let you near my phone, you're way to dangerous around computers for that. Oh, and don't waste your time trying wireless, it's in airplane mode." He dropped the phone back inside his coat and fixed me again with his blank stare.

How had the NSA found me? I thought I'd been so careful. I decided to play it dumb and see how much they knew. "Mister Sims, I'm sorry, but I think you have the wrong person. There's nothing about me that would interest the NSA in the least."

"Anna…sorry, may I call you Anna?"

"I suppose so."

"Excellent, and feel free to call me Adam if you wish." He looked toward my brown, leather sofa and said, "Anna, perhaps we should have a seat before we go into all this. Might as well be comfortable, right?"

I motioned for him to have a seat. He sat down at one end of the sofa and I chose the other. I wasn't terribly concerned about being this close to him. If he tried anything, I knew that I had faster reflexes and could easily overpower him.

He leaned back, crossed his legs, and clasped his hands together before he spoke again. "Good, now, I think you'd said something along the lines of the NSA had the wrong person. My first argument to that is, well, we are the NSA and we don't make mistakes."

I looked at him with total incredulity. "Really, hire any good contractors lately?"

"Touché, I suppose we never will live that Snowden fiasco down. Let me rephrase my answer more precisely. In this case, we have not made a mistake. You are Anna Andropov."

"Yes, that is my name, but like I said, there isn't anything in my life that the NSA would find interesting."

I was treated to his blank stare again. "You know, I'm usually very good at spotting a liar, but Anna, you I can't read. I know that you are lying, but nothing about you gives it away. Then again, I suppose I should have expected that from someone like you."

I sighed in frustration. "Have you considered the fact that I might actually be telling the truth?"

"No, not at all," he flatly said. He rubbed his hands together and took a breath before continuing. "Anna, let me put all my cards on the table. Your name is Anna Andropov and you are an artificial humanoid, better known as an android. You were created somewhere in Russia by a man named Viktor Eklund. You were sent here to the United States around six to nine months ago for some purpose that we don't know. What we do know is that you have incredible computer infiltration skills and we are fairly sure you are physically superior to a normal person of your size."

It was my worst nightmare, but I stuck to my guns and stared flatly back at him. "That's insane. What on earth would ever have given you that idea?"

"Anna, I won't argue with you anymore. We have documents, video surveillance of you leaving the ship in Mobile, and other evidence. The only thing we don't know, is why you are in America, and the nature of your mission. That's why I'm here. You know that we cannot allow someone like yourself to undertake a covert action against the United States, and on our own soil at that. Now, normally we would just arrest someone that we found operating the way you are, but you are obviously a special case. My superiors want to extend you a job offer."

My mind was reeling. The NSA had found me, not Stepan and Eliza, but the NSA, although I wasn't sure if that was any better. I just sat and looked at Adam for sometime, speechless. Then I thought, what the hell, I'd level with him. I couldn't have the NSA thinking I was on some secret mission for Russia. I ran my hands through my hair and sighed heavily.

"Alright Adam, most of your intelligence is correct."

"That's better, now perhaps we can make some progress," he said.

Agitated, I got up and walked over to stand in front of him. "Wait a minute, I said most of it. I'm not here on some kind of mission for Mother Russia or anything of the sort. I escaped from the lab where I was created and I'm only in America because that's where the ship that I stowed away on was heading. Trust me, I'm not in the espionage business and I don't want to be. I just want to live my life out in peace and quiet."

Adam stood up as well and faced my growing annoyance with calm. "That is a very nice speech, but you realize that the NSA will never believe you. After all, I have already witnessed the fact that you are an excellent liar and they are not the type of organization that would take that kind of risk. I'm afraid your wants and desires are irrelevant in this situation." He walked around me and toward my front door. "I'll take my leave now and let you think over what I've said for a while. However, let me implore you to take me up on the job offer. Because if you don't, they will be forced to destroy you."

My anger boiled over and I stalked over to him. I stared up into his bright blue eyes and snarled, "How dare you come into my home and threaten me. Get out...get out before I throw you out!"

For all my bluster, I didn't rattle him in the least. "Anna, it's not a threat, it's simply a fact." With that, he turned and left the apartment.

I don't know how long I stared at the closed door, but my frustration and anger continued to rise. The human emotions that Viktor had given me, the emotions that I'd struggled to understand and control ever since my birth, betrayed me. The fury built up inside until I was blinded by it. I whirled around away from the door and let out a primal scream, but it didn't quench the rage. I raised my fists over my head and slammed them down as hard as I could onto the back of my office chair. Pain shot through my hands and arms while the back of the chair exploded into chunky, leather-covered pieces. The bottom of the chair spun round and round while I tried to rein in my anger.

As I calmed down and regained control of myself, I realized my hands hurt like hell. I willed the pain to stop, and it gradually faded to a dull throb. I should have been able to stop pain like that completely, but ever since Eliza's grazing headshot from a military rifle, that part of my software was a little glitchy. However, that was the least of my worries.

I stomped into the bedroom, leaving the cleanup of the chair for a later time. Throwing myself down on the bed, I thought about my options. There weren't many. I could run, but if the NSA had found me, you could bet that they'd be watching me closely now. I'd never be able to get away from them. That actually explained the car that had been following me. It had been the NSA the whole time.

If I didn't try to run, joining up with them was obviously on the table. They might not be like Stepan and the KGB. Maybe I should give them the benefit of the doubt. No, I couldn't go back to that life. During my whole career, I'd only been on one mission. It ended with the death of an innocent young girl by my own hands. Of course, Eliza had been involved, and logically I knew that she was the real reason the girl had died, but I had actually pulled the trigger and shot her. The guilt of her death weighed on me everyday, and it was almost unbearable. I never wanted to be put in another situation where I'd have to possibly kill another human ever again.

That left only one option, which was choose to be destroyed. However painful my life might be at times, I did cherish it and wasn't in any hurry to see it come to an end. All the people that had worked and even given their own life to see me created deserved better than for me to simply throw away their precious gift. I wouldn't lie down and allow anyone to simply shut me off.

I thought about my choices for a couple of hours, but could come up with no way out, no escape. A yawn came over me and I realized it was almost two a.m. I had to rest. I knew that any idea or scheme I came up with now would be clouded by my need for sleep. Perhaps an opportunity would present itself in the time that Adam had given me to think things over. It was a lousy plan, but right now, it was all I had.

Chapter 11

Nothing had changed by the morning except that I had to go to work. I was alert and ready during my morning commute, but the only trouble I had on the way to the office was with the maniacal, rush hour traffic and a couple of sputters from my Civic. The NSA must prefer to do all their dirty work after sundown.

Sitting at my desk, I tried to concentrate on my job, but understandably, my mind was occupied with other thoughts. I just sat there and stared at this one line of code in my program while my mind wandered. I was still staring at that same line when David came up and cheerfully tapped on the wall of my cubicle. "Hey, Anna, come on, it's time for lunch."

"Hmm, oh...you know David, I'm not very hungry. I'm just going to work through lunch today," I said.

"No, you have to come. Felix has brought in lunch from Dreamland BBQ and we're all getting together in the conference room," he insisted.

"Again? What's gotten into him? He bought lunch Tuesday, bought us tickets to the zoo Wednesday, now it's lunch again today."

He shrugged and said, "I don't know, but I'm going to enjoy it while it lasts. It's like the good old days around here when Felix first opened the business. Now let's go get some free chow!"

I reluctantly stood and followed David to the conference room. When we arrived, David stepped aside and let me enter first. The aroma of Dreamland BBQ washed over me as soon as the glass doors slid open. It was a mixture of baked beans, fresh-cut slaw, hickory smoked ribs, and BBQ sauce. I normally only ate to keep my cover as a human intact. However there was another reason, I was able to enjoy the taste of food, and I could already tell that I was going to enjoy this meal.

Felix had chosen a spot at the head of the table and Kimber was sitting on his right. I took the seat on Felix's left and began to fill my plate. Kimber pulled the chair out next to her and said, "There's an open seat here, David."

David hesitated for a beat and then came around the table to sit next to me. "Thanks, but I'll sit next to Anna. It's closer to the ribs."

As he took the chair next to mine, Kimber gave me an evil look, but I had no idea why. It wasn't *my* fault the ribs were closer to this side of the table.

Everyone went silent as we began to feast on the delicious food. Despite myself, I began to feel my spirits lifted. As we finished our meal and sat around eating our dessert, scrumptious banana pudding, socializing took over and we thoroughly enjoyed each other's company.

Near the end of lunch, David spoke up. "Hey everybody, I know I've brought this up several times, but the day is finally here. I'm moving this Saturday and could really use everyone's help. It's just from one apartment to another in the same building, but the new one has an extra bedroom that I just can't wait to use!"

He noticed that Kimber was wearing a wrist brace, and his face grew concerned. He turned to her and said, "Hey, if your wrist is still hurting from the fall at the zoo, and you don't think you can be there, I'll understand."

She eyed the brace wrapped around her left wrist, and then turned her stare on me as she answered. "No, I'll be there David, I wouldn't miss it for anything."

I agreed to be there as well, and so did Felix. He cheerfully said, "I can be there and help with food and drinks. What time are you getting started?"

David smiled and said, "Around nine in the morning, thanks!"

"Great, it'll give me a chance to get out of the house and enjoy the warm weather. Like back when I was running track in college," he said.

I looked at him, trying to tell if he was joking or not. He caught me staring and said, "Hey now, don't look at me that way. I haven't always been stuck in this chair."

"Oh, sorry, Felix. I didn't mean to offend you," I stammered.

He smiled warmly back at me. "No, no, not at all. Oh, that's right, you've never heard the story of how I wound up in this thing. It slipped my mind because I've already told David and Kimber several times over. I'll have to tell you sometime if you're interested."

A few minutes later and we'd finished off the pudding. David left, heading back to his cube and Kimber quickly followed him.

Felix looked at me and said, "Go ahead Anna, I'll clean up."

I shook my head. "No, let me help. In fact, I'll trade you. I'll do the clean up, and you tell me your story. If you're up to it that is."

He chuckled and said, "Okay, but it's a bit of a downer, just so you know."

I told him that was fine and started cleaning up the room. Felix leaned back in his wheelchair and sipped on his glass of tea before beginning. "So I was working on my business degree at UAB several years ago. I'd somehow made it to my senior year despite my inclination to attend every campus party I could find. I remember thinking that if I really buckled down I could still graduate on time. With that in mind, a bunch of us got together and held a study session out on the quad, or the green as students called it, to prepare for upcoming midterms. We hung out and studied until after dark that evening. When the session finally broke up, we headed back to our dorm rooms to catch some sleep before the exams."

Felix paused for a moment and poured himself some more tea before continuing. "On the way to my dorm, I jaywalked across University Boulevard to save a few minutes. You know how busy it is, but I was in a hurry, and it was something every student did at least twice a day. I never saw the UAB campus police car zooming down the street responding to a robbery call. All I remember was screeching tires and suddenly seeing the world twisting around in every direction you could have imagined. After that, I couldn't see anything, but I could hear girls screaming and the shouting of the campus police as they called for an ambulance."

He paused again and by this time, I'd stopped cleaning the room. I pulled up a chair and sat down next to him, hanging on every word. His expression was distant, like he was reliving some part of the accident. He was silent so long, I began to wonder if he could finish his tale. Finally, he turned to me and a melancholy smile spread across his face.

"I woke up in UAB hospital a couple of days later and the doctors told me the bad news. At first, I couldn't believe it, but even with all the advances in nanotechnology that have occurred recently, they couldn't repair my injury. After recuperating for a week or so, I began my rehabilitation. I spent a year learning how to use the chair, take care of myself, and such. Also during that time, the lawyers for UAB and I worked out an agreement. Both the campus police and I were at fault, but the university didn't want any kind of bad publicity. They made me an offer too good to refuse. After I'd signed an agreement to never speak publicly about the accident, they helped me finish my degree, paid my medical bills, and gave me a cash settlement. In time, I used the settlement to open FlexJen Software. So I guess you can see why I'm such a workaholic. In a strange, twisted way, I feel like I traded the use of my legs for FlexJen. I'd do almost anything to keep our doors open."

He reached out and patted the tops of my hands as his wistful smile turned into a much happier one. "Which is why I'm so glad we found you. Everything has gone our way since you showed up and I'm sure you're going to single handedly keep us going for a long time, Anna."

I didn't know how to respond to that. I knew that I was his best programmer, but damn, it wasn't exactly fair for him to put the weight of his whole business on my shoulders. "Uh, thanks, Felix. I'll be sure to do my best."

If he noticed the hesitancy in my voice, it didn't faze him. The smile never left his face as he backed his chair away from the table and headed for the door. "Oh, don't worry, I know you always do." He stopped his chair short of the door and turned it to face me. "Hey, by the way, I need some media sources for a new client. Kimber was originally going to do it, but now she has that bad wrist of hers. Then David offered, but I think you have a better creative eye than he does. Would you mind taking care of it for me?"

"Sure Felix, what do you need?" I asked.

"The client is looking for some high resolution images of a sunset from Vulcan Park. You know, some from the top of Vulcan, maybe a few with Vulcan in front of the sunset. Just use your imagination," he said.

"Sure, I could head to Vulcan Park Sunday evening and have them for you by Monday. Is that soon enough?" I asked.

"Yeah, that'd be great. I'll let Kimber and David know you're going to do it. Thanks so much, Anna!" He saluted me with his iced tea, then turned his chair, and drove it out of the conference room.

I sighed. With all the things going on in my life right now, the last thing I needed was a weekend assignment from work. I sat and chuckled to myself as I thought about the absurdity of it all. I shook my head slowly, and stood up to finish cleaning the room.

Chapter 12

My time leading up to Saturday morning was spent in worry and dread. I dreaded each drive home in the evening and I worried that any minute Adam Sims from the NSA would show up at my door again and demand an answer. Not to mention, I was back to having no one to confide in, no one to discuss my troubles with. I dearly missed Athena's company, but I didn't dare interfuse and talk with her because I was afraid the NSA could watch me even in that world. All I could do was hope that she didn't think I was deliberately avoiding her because of what happened last time. I wondered if she actually possessed the ability to think, or was everything she said and did just a programmed response like Titan the gorilla. Was Athena just responding to my desire, or request as it were, for a friend that she'd seen when she looked into my mind? Had I afforded her an intelligence she didn't actually have because I was so desperate for a companion? Who was I to judge anyway?

However, for all my doom and gloom feelings, nothing happened. First Thursday, then Friday went by with no visits from NSA Adam and no suicidal attack vehicles, except for the normal rush hour ones. This turn of events wasn't comforting at all. I felt as if I were at the edge of a great storm, one that when it finally arrived and unleashed its full fury, would bring such a level of devastation that I might not survive it. All I could do was prepare for the worst, and be ready to ride it out once it hit.

I got up Saturday morning around half past eight and plodded into the bathroom.   I caught a glimpse of myself in the mirror and was shocked by how downtrodden I looked.   My mood hadn't improved at all over the past few days, but I was hoping that lending David a hand with his move would do the trick.   A little physical labor mixed with some socializing should help me forget about things for a while.   I mentally went over the directions David had given me to his apartment complex. It was only a few miles from the office, so I knew how to get there and how long it would take.   I'd simply take the same route from Hoover to Southside, but since it was the weekend, I wouldn't have to deal with any traffic.

After a quick shower, I went back into the bedroom to find some clothes.   I'd never helped anyone with this kind of thing before, but I figured it would be dirty work.   Checking the weather, I saw that it was going to be sunny and in the low seventies, a little warm for October, but then again, this was the South.   I picked out an older gray t-shirt, a pair of blue jeans, and slipped on some sneakers.   After a quick trip to my kitchen for some vitamins and a couple of bottles of SmartWater, I grabbed my cell phone and was out the door.

I locked up the apartment on the way out and jumped into my Civic. The poor thing sputtered as I backed it out of the parking spot, which reminded me I really needed to make the repairs that Takumi had suggested before I ended up stranded on the side of the road somewhere. I made a mental note to handle that tomorrow morning before heading to Vulcan Park.

Following my normal route toward work, I took I-65 to I-459 and then Highway 280 all the way to Southside.   The drive was actually nice, even 280 traffic was light this early on a Saturday.   Turning about ten blocks before I normally would, I saw the Magnolia Heights Apartment Complex where David lived.   A few turns later, and I saw Felix's Honda Element and a few spots down was Kimber's convertible Ford Mustang. The Mustang's top was down and its bright yellow paint gleamed under the sunlight.   There was an empty spot next to it, so I pulled into it and parked.   As I exited my Civic, I must have gotten to close to the Mustang, because its alarm went off.   It was so loud and annoying with its BAAA BAAA BAAA, BWOOP BWOOP BWOOP, and BEEDO BEEDO

BEEDO that I couldn't resist shutting it off. I reached out with my mind and located its wireless receiver. When I connected, I saw it was a state of the art system, but then again, so was I. A few nano seconds later and I was rewarded with a CHIRP CHIRP and then peaceful silence.

"Hey, why did my car alarm go off?"

I turned to see that the alarm had summoned David, Felix, and Kimber. Kimber was standing several feet in front of the guys, holding her buzzing phone in her hand. She was looking back and forth between the car and me with a puzzled expression.

"Oh, sorry, I must have gotten to close to it when I got out of my car," I said.

"No, I mean why did it turn itself off?" she asked.

I shrugged my shoulders as I walked over toward them. "I don't know Kimber, but I'd definitely have it checked out. There's nothing worse than a broken alarm system. It can give you fits in the middle of the night and such. Oh, really nice car by the way."

Still looking perplexed, she said, "Thanks, I just got it."

I continued past Kimber to where the guys waited. "Good morning, looks like I'm the last one to arrive. Sorry about that."

David smiled and said, "Don't worry about it, everyone else has only been here a couple of minutes. Come on back inside and I'll show you what we're up against today."

We all followed David into his apartment, and he pointed to some McDonald's bags sitting on his kitchen counter. "If anyone wants a sausage biscuit, Felix brought some from Mickey D's and I have some Cokes in the fridge." David waited as those who wanted breakfast got it, and then he began his tour. "Okay, over here in the living room I've stacked up a bunch of boxes. On the boxes, I've written the room to drop them off in once we get them moved."

We all peeked into the living room and saw a stack of boxes about twice the size of my Honda located in the corner. As we tried to guess how many trips that would be, David continued. "Now the other rooms may have a few boxes in them, but I tried to get the majority of my stuff as close to the door as I could. Any questions before I show you how to get to my new apartment?"

Kimber spoke up. "What about furniture? I see a couch in the living room, and I'm not sure I can lift it with my sprained wrist."

"Oh, I've already had some help moving that stuff. I knew we didn't want to tackle anything large today. That couch is the biggest thing left and I admit it might be a problem because the new apartment is on the second floor. So if we have to leave it, that's fine by me. Come on and I'll show you my new place," David said.

Once outside his current apartment, he led us a few hundred feet down a hallway and around a right turn. There we came to an elevator and a set of black metal stairs. There was a sign hanging on the door of the elevator that read, "Out of service. Maintenance Called."

David sighed in frustration and turned to Felix. "I'm so sorry, it was working fine a couple of days ago."

Felix just smiled and took it in stride. "That's okay. I wasn't going to be carrying boxes anyway. I'll head back and have another biscuit while you show them around."

We climbed the metal stairs up to the second floor and found that David's new apartment was the first door on the right.

"Here we go, number 201," David said and pulled his phone out of his pocket. He waved it at the door and we heard the lock click open.

"I'll leave it unlocked so we can all go in and out as we bring boxes up," he said.

He gave us a quick look around, and I could tell it was about twice the size of his old place. We gathered around in the mostly empty living room and David turned to us again. "Okay guys, ready to get this show on the road?"

"Sure thing, we'll have this knocked out in no time," Kimber said.

"That's the spirit!" David cheered and I nodded my head in agreement. Out the door and back down the stairs we went to get started.

When we got back to the old apartment, we saw that Felix had pulled his chair next to the small bar separating the kitchen from the living room. "So just like the manager I am, I'm going to let all of you do the actual work. I'll handle things like cleaning up here and getting lunch for everyone."

David patted him on the shoulder and said, "Thanks for coming, I really appreciate it."

We threw ourselves into the task with determination and soon found a rhythm to our work. After a few trips, we were chatting and having a good time. It felt great to just forget about everything and have a few laughs with friends. I had definitely needed this day.

Around eleven thirty, Felix announced that he was leaving to go get some pizzas for lunch. When he returned, we all sat down on the floor in the old apartment to take a break. While we ate and rested, I noticed that David and Kimber were beginning to look tired. A quick look at the remaining boxes told me we would be working well into the evening if we kept up our current pace. I felt bad for my friends because I knew that I could do so much more to help. My android body was designed to have twice the strength and several times the stamina of a human. I thought about it for a little, and decided they wouldn't really notice if I upped my game some, heck, they'd probably be grateful.

After we finished eating our pizza, David and Kimber each grabbed a box and headed out. I waited until they left and Felix was distracted by putting up the leftovers before I grabbed two boxes. I had no trouble with them, they were actually light enough that I could have carried four of them if I wanted, but that would have been much more than a normal person could have handled. On my way to the new apartment, I caught up with David and Kimber as they returned down the stairs.

David looked shocked and began chastising me. "Anna no! Don't try to carry that much all at once, you'll hurt yourself!"

"Oh, don't worry David, I've got it," I said.

Kimber, who had been friendly up until this point, gave me a hateful look as I passed by her on the stairs, but I wasn't sure why. Once I'd dropped off my first set of boxes, I was patting myself on the back at how clever I was, at least until I ran into David and Kimber arguing back at the rest of the boxes.

"Hey don't worry about me, if Anna can carry two boxes, then so can I," she said.

David was almost beside himself. "Kimber, your wrist is still sprained. You're going to really hurt yourself if you're not careful."

Felix started to say something, but Kimber was already grabbing up two boxes and leaving with them. David just sighed and grabbed two himself before hurrying after her. I rubbed my forehead and wondered why was it that every time I tried to do something nice, it always went wrong. I went over to the stack and tried to find some of the heaviest boxes so Kimber didn't get her hands on them, then I took off after them.

After about three trips carrying two boxes at a time, I was working up a good sweat. For me, sweating was just cosmetic, designed to keep my human disguise in place. However, it was still uncomfortable and left me wishing I'd wore a pair of shorts. David wasn't fairing much better, but I really felt bad for Kimber. She had worn a hot pink hoodie with a matching pair of hot pink sweat pants, and at this point, even her hair was becoming drenched.

On our next trip for boxes, she wiped the sweat from her brow and declared, "That's it guys. I'm going to have to take these sweats off."

We all turned to look at her, to see exactly what she meant and she flashed a coy smile. "Hey, don't look at me like that. I have on my gym clothes under this."

She sat down on the couch and took off her sneakers. Then, while she looked intently at David, she slowly unzipped her top and carefully pulled the sleeve over her wrist brace. Underneath, she had on a white sports tank top that was struggling to do its job, probably because it was about a size too small. As we all watched, she turned around and began to wiggle out of her sweat pants. Under those, she had on a pair of pink running shorts with white accents. Across the back of the shorts were the words, *Spoiled Rotten*. The shorts were having the same trouble as the bra, except with a different part of her anatomy. Sitting down on the couch, she started putting on her shoes. Once finished, Kimber jumped back up with an enthusiastic smile.

"There, that's much better," she cooed.

It was about this time that I realized no one had moved or said anything. We were all just staring at Kimber's sculpted, tanned figure. Without a doubt, she was a beautiful woman that had made the most of her trips to the gym. After what felt like an eternity, Felix broke the silence.

"I'm going to get a nice cold bottle of water out of the fridge. Does anyone else want one?" he asked.

"I do," David and I said simultaneously.

Kimber, obviously used to this kind of attention simply chuckled and said, "I'll take one too."

After that break, the social dynamic of our moving trio changed, to say the least. Now as we were working, Kimber would 'accidentally' bump into David on the way back, or take her time bending over to pick up new boxes while he waited behind her pretending not to look. After each of her 'displays', she'd wait until only I could see and would casually glance at me with a look of dominance. It was like she was competing with me over something, trying to best me at everything I did, but what did she think I was after. What would I...oh.

The realization finally hit me. Kimber wanted David as more than just a friend, and she saw me as her competition. My social ineptitude had officially reached new heights. All this trouble because my murderous sister had cut my psychological and emotional training short. At least now that I knew what was happening, I would stay out of the way and reduce the tension between Kimber and myself.

The afternoon continued in this way, with Kimber flirting with David, David not really responding, and box after box being moved. Around four o'clock, we had moved all the boxes and the only thing left was the sofa we were sitting on while we drank our water.

David stood up to throw his bottle away, then told us, "Thank you all for coming. I'd take you out for dinner, but since we're all so dirty and tired, let's do it next week or so."

"What about the couch, David? Doesn't it need to go to?" Kimber asked.

"Well, yes, but with everyone so worn out and your hurt wrist, I was just going to let it stay," he replied.

Kimber stood up with a little grunt and said, "Nah, let's finish it. It's the last thing and I'm not that tired anyway."

I thought about protesting, but she had held her own the whole day, hurt wrist and all. "I'm game if Kimber is. We can take one end and you can take the other," I said.

All David could do was shake his head. "Okay, but let me know if at anytime you need to set the couch down and rest."

He walked over to one side and Kimber and I took the other. We swung the couch around so that he was walking backwards and we waddled it out the apartment door while Felix made sure everything of David's was moved.

We maneuvered the couch down the hallway and made it to the stairs where David said, "Okay, girls you go up first and I'll carry the weight on the bottom."

As we slowly worked our way up the stairs, I could tell that Kimber was exhausted. She struggled to catch her breath while wrestling with the bulky couch. To help, I spread my hands apart and took as much of the weight off of her as I could. At the same time, I pulled on the couch as much as possible to help David.

While I pulled the majority of the sofa's weight up the staircase, sweat began to bead up all over my body and I could actually feel my muscles beginning to burn with the strain. Finally, we somehow managed to wrangle the sofa up the stairs. We turned around so that David could walk backward with it into the apartment and that was when I heard Kimber scream. My enhanced reflexes activated and I turned to see her let go of the sofa while reaching for her previously injured wrist. This caused the couch to twist and fall toward her as the sudden shift in weight pulled me to the side. I grasped at the couch and tried to pull it back toward me, but it slipped out of my hands. It was heading right for Kimber as she stood helpless at the top of the stairs.

Well, if I wasn't going to let her fall into a goose pond, I sure as hell wasn't going to let her be knocked down the stairs by a runaway couch. I dropped myself down to the ground in the splits position and stuck my left foot out and under the couch. I had intended to kick it back toward me, but I found out that even I have limits. It had too much momentum and the wooden leg slammed onto my left foot with a crunch. It felt like someone had stabbed my foot with a red-hot poker. Pain shot up my leg all the way to my hip. I cried out, but quickly stifled my shout and tried to dull my pain, but was only partially successful.

I was however, completely successful in preventing Kimber from being knocked down the stairs. She was gripping her wrist and looking at me with disbelief. I simply smiled back at her.

David was beside us in an instant. "Oh God, no! Are you okay? Kimber, what happened? Was it your wrist?" Then he looked down and noticed me. "Holy Shit! Anna, the couch is sitting on your foot! Hold still!" He grabbed the end of the sofa and gently lifted it off my foot. I slid out of the way as he dropped it back to the ground. "Come on. We have to get both of you to the hospital. Can you walk Anna?" he said.

I stood up and put some weight on my foot trying it out, bad idea. The pain made me wince and David said, "Here, put your arm around my neck and I'll help you down the stairs."

"No, I'm fine. It's just a little sore. Kimber what about you?" I asked.

She was still looking at me with a look of awe, but managed to whisper, "I...I think my wrist is broken."

David turned all his attention to her. "Oh, God, this is terrible! Let's get back to Felix and get you both to the emergency room."

At my insistence, he helped Kimber down the stairs while I followed behind them. I kept testing my foot until I could put most of my weight onto it, but my full weight caused a sharp, stabbing pain. When we got back to his old apartment, David explained everything that had happened, and Felix went right into manager mode and took charge of the situation. "Okay, I'll take Anna, and David, you take Kimber and we'll head to the urgent care that's about ten blocks from here. Do you know the one?"

"Whoa, wait a minute! It's just a bump on my foot. I'm fine and I'm not going to any urgent care," I said.

Felix looked at me as if he was going to protest, but saw the determination on my face. He turned to Kimber instead. "All right, Kimber, you come with me and don't give me any bull about being fine.

I can see you can't even move your hand."

I could tell she was on the verge of tears as she answered him. "Don't worry, I won't argue," she said.

"I'll come over there as soon as I wrap things up here," David said.

Felix nodded to him and quickly left with Kimber. David then asked me once again, "Are you sure you're okay?"

"Yes, I'm fine, just a little bruise, nothing to worry about," I said.

He didn't look completely convinced, but he stopped asking. "Then at least let's get you off your feet," he said. However, looking around, there wasn't any furniture left in this apartment. We'd actually finished moving him. "Anna, can you make it back up the stairs?" he asked.

"Sure, let's go," I said.

Before we left, David grabbed some leftover pizza and some Cokes out of the fridge. He insisted that I put my arm around his neck so he could help me walk. I sighed, but relented to him since my foot was still hurting anyway.

We limped our way back up the stairs and right into the couch we'd forgotten all about. David made me go inside and wait while he wrestled, dragged, and cursed the sofa until he got it inside the apartment by himself. After helping me sit down on the couch, he went about gathering boxes of just the right size until he'd fashioned a makeshift table. The pizza and the drinks were soon arranged on the newly constructed cardboard buffet, and finally he sat down next to me. I hadn't realized how hungry I was until we started eating, and before long, we had demolished the pizza.

After dinner, David excused himself to go to the bathroom. While he was gone, I thought I'd take the opportunity to look at my foot. It had been throbbing the entire meal, and I was a little concerned. I turned myself and put my legs up on the couch. Reaching down, I started to slip off the sneaker of my injured foot, but that was when David returned. "So, your foot is still hurting you, isn't it? Here let me see."

I tried to object, but David ignored me as he took apart his box table, and made a box ottoman. "Now, put your foot up here," he said.

I did as he asked and he untied my sneaker and gently removed it. That wasn't so bad I thought, but then he went about peeling off my sock and I felt that sharp pain again. He saw me wince and he waited a second before continuing. After my sock was off, even I was shocked. The top of my foot was red and swollen from my toes to above my ankle. "Shit Anna, your foot may be broken," he said.

"Nah, it doesn't hurt that bad. It's just going to bruise a little," I said without being so sure about it myself.

He just shook his head and replied, "Well at least let me put something on it." He got up, went back into his bathroom, and returned with a tube of something.

"What is that?" I asked.

"It's a topical pain reliever. Now sit back and I'll try not to hurt you," he said.

"David, you really don't have to do…" Before I could finish my sentence, he'd opened the tube and squirted its contents onto my foot. I sighed and leaned back, resigned to my fate. At first, it hurt as he rubbed the ointment in, but after a little while, it actually began to feel better. I had no idea why human medicine would work on me, perhaps it was even a placebo effect, but whatever it was, the pain was definitely fading.

I relaxed and looked at some of his boxes while he continued rubbing my foot. One particular one caught my eye, it was labeled 'VOX Bot'. Pointing at it, I asked, "David, what's a VOX Bot?"

He looked up and said, "Oh, just a little something I've been working on. Here let me finish rubbing this in and I'll show you." By the time he was done, the pain was almost completely gone. After washing his hands, he came and sat next to me with the box in his lap. He opened it and took out what looked like a mask for Halloween. It was colored pale pink, and had lips and a nose that slightly protruded from it, but where the eyes should have been, were just empty holes. He sat it in my lap, and handed me a small black rectangular box about the size of a cell phone.

"Turn around and put your back to me and I'll massage your shoulders, you must be sore there too," he said.

Fascinated by the mask he'd given me, I turned around so he could reach my back and I involuntarily let out a little moan as his strong hands began to knead my tense muscles. He was good at this.

After working on me for a little while he asked, "Do you want me to use some of that pain reliever on your shoulders?"

"Yeah, that would be nice," I heard myself say.

He lifted the back of my shirt up as high as he could and I felt the coolness of the salve as he put some on my lower neck. His expert hands felt wonderful as he rubbed it into the upper part of my back.

Leaning forward so he could reach me easier, my eyes landed back on the mask resting in my lap. "You never told me what this was," I said.

"Remember walking into the zoo where they had that cool animatronic spider, and how I mentioned that I was interested in robotics? Well, it's one of my projects. I could really improve it if I could get my hands on a bit more cash. Anyway, it's easier to show you what it does than tell you. Take the controller and say something into it," he said.

I started to raise the small box to my mouth and speak, when I felt him unhook my bra. My breath caught in my throat as he slid the loose straps forward. Slowly, gently, his hands moved down and continued to work their magic on my lower back.

I knew I should stop him, but I couldn't find my voice. It had been so long since I'd been touched in this way. So many lonely days had passed that I wasn't strong enough to resist his affectionate caresses as they ever so slowly moved away from my back and toward my chest. I felt a familiar heat building in my body as his hands roamed over my breasts until he reached their delicate peaks. He began teasing them, gently pinching them, until they eagerly responded to his attention.

As if lost in a dream, I heard myself purr, "Oh, David, that feels *incredible.*"

However as I said it, the mask in my lap came to life and it's lips moved synchronously with mine. Shocked, I noticed I was still holding the controller near my mouth. I blinked a few times and said, "So this mask, this face, moves its lips to what you're saying?"

Again as I spoke, the face mimicked my words. David leaned over and began to kiss my neck as he answered. "It doesn't just move it's lips, it makes the exact shapes a person's mouth does when they speak. I'd love to add more to it, like a tongue, and maybe give it the ability to actually speak the words, but I need some more money first." He paused to nibble on my ear and then said, "Why don't we put it away for now. You can look at it some more later."

He must have been close enough when he spoke for the controller to pick up his voice, because the mouth moved in perfect time to everything he said. It brought my thoughts rushing back to how artificial I was. As I looked at it, I could almost see my own face, mimicking back some words that someone else had programmed me to say. My heart sank and I snapped out of the wondrous trance David had put me in. He deserved better than just a machine, he deserved a real person. Whether he knew it or not, someone else did care for him, and earlier I'd promised myself I'd stay out of her way. Now here I was, one button and a zipper from being so far *in* the way, that I'd ruin everything. I had to get up and go home before this went any further.

David gently turned me around and I saw a burning passion in his eyes.   He took my t-shirt and carefully began to pull it up, but his expression changed to that of concern and he stopped. He let go of my shirt and asked, "What's wrong Anna?   You look upset.   Did I do something wrong?"

"No, no, it's not you, it's me.   I, uh…David, I need to leave," I whispered.

"What? I don't understand. Just a second ago, we were fine. What happened?" he asked.

I slid over away from him a little and straightened my shirt. "Like I said, it's not you. You didn't do anything wrong. I shouldn't have let it get this far."

His body stiffened and he raised his voice from the whisper it had been. "Well, that's just something a woman says to let a guy down easy. At least have the decency to tell me what you don't like about me."

Damn it, I'd hurt his feelings. I really sucked at this whole human emotion thing. "No, David…It's just that I was in a relationship about seven months ago and it ended so badly that I'm not ready to be in one again." As I spoke, I thought about the love that Cindi and I had shared back in the lab where I was created…and how Eliza had viciously murdered her for it. I couldn't put another person in that kind of danger. Not to mention Kimber's feelings and my android/human identity crisis I was struggling with. I was a psychological mess.

David stood up and walked over to the kitchen. "Well, I'm not that other person you had a relationship with and it's unfair to judge me by them. What we could build together would be completely different."

Stuffing the sock in my pocket, I stood and jammed the shoe onto my foot, which reminded me that it was still injured with a stabbing pain. "Ow! Damn it! David look, I know, and I really like you, you are a great guy, but I'm just not emotionally ready for another relationship right now. I'm sorry if you think I led you on, or I hurt your feelings. Please know that I never intended to do either."

I walked over to say goodbye, but he refused to even look at me. "Uh, I guess…I'm going to head home…see you Monday."

Limping to his door, I let myself out. I carefully inched my way down the stairs and hobbled over to my Civic. When I got in, I realized I would have to work the clutch with my bad foot. "Fuck!" I screamed and slammed the steering wheel with my fist.

The trip home was miserable, each time I shifted, a stabbing pain went through my foot and ankle. Along with the physical pain, I couldn't get my mind off the emotional train wreck I'd just had with David. As soon as I pulled into the parking spot outside my apartment, I couldn't hold it in any more. Leaning my head against the wheel, I sat in my car and wept.

PART TWO

HIDE AND SEEK

Eliza sat in the front seat of the sedan as it turned right and entered the old abandoned parking deck. Her driver maneuvered slowly as he went through the levels up to the third floor. Not because of other cars or people, for there were none of those to be found here, but so that Eliza could detect and disable any cameras or other surveillance devices she found. This late night visit must not be observed. They arrived at the agreed upon location and the driver pulled the car into a secluded spot.

Eliza exited the sedan and straightened her outfit. Her leather jacket fit perfectly over her white tank top and her form fitting leather pants stopped just short of the low-top leather stiletto boots she wore. All of the leather, was of course, black. It may have been very stereotypical, but it allowed freedom of movement and she found it also gave her an edge in the intimidation department whenever she met with humans. Ever how stereotypical it might be, this outfit just worked.

She unzipped her jacket and pulled her Makarov pistol from its shoulder holster. After attaching its suppressor, she glanced around the garage's low ceiling and targeted the few remaining functional overhead lights. As she began firing, the gun made a few muffled sounds, PWIFFT…PWIFFT…PWIFFT, and the area of the garage where she was to meet her contact was thrown into almost total darkness.

After holstering her weapon, Eliza activated the special encrypted link between her neural net brain and the members of her Mark II team. Mentally, she sent her orders to the other androids. *"MKII-1, stay behind the wheel in case we need to exit rapidly. MKII-2, proceed to the east entrance of the garage and report any activity. MKII-3, proceed to the north entrance of the garage and report any activity."*

The two rear doors on the sedan opened simultaneously and what appeared to be a couple of tall, medium built men exited the car. They were dressed identically, in dark gray suits with white button down shirts and black ties. The gray fedoras that they both wore covered their hairless heads and large, dark, sunglasses concealed their eyes. Their molded, plastic, faces may have looked normal from a distance, but upon closer inspection, they had an eerie inhumanity about them. They had no hair, not even eyelashes, and their countenance displayed no emotion. In unison, the two androids outside the sedan and the one sitting in the drivers seat turned their soulless, gaze toward Eliza and responded using the same mental link. *"MKII-1, executing orders." "MKII-2, executing orders." "MKII-3, executing orders."* One android walked rapidly north and its identical twin silently headed east.

Eliza watched as the Mark II androids disappeared into the darkness and considered how completely primitive these earlier models were. They couldn't act without orders from their commander, they couldn't pass themselves off as a human or alter their outward appearance, hell, they couldn't even speak. However, if it hadn't been for them, she wouldn't exist. She was a Mark III and in her opinion, the preeminent model, while Anna was an inferior Mark IV. While it was true that Anna had a higher designation, she had been designed for infiltration, and because of all the effort toward that goal, was physically weaker than herself. One day, Eliza would get to show her dear sister how important it was to be strong. Maybe that day would come sooner rather than later.

Twenty minutes had passed and Eliza was leaning against the side of the sedan with her arms folded across her chest. She checked the time, again, and the result only increased her agitation. The contact was over ten minutes late, and she had never handled incompetents very well. In her frustration, she began pacing around in the dusty old parking deck and her thoughts began to wander. They mostly centered on how she might express her displeasure when this person finally did show up. Her various thoughts of abuse and torture were interrupted by a communication from one of her Mark II units. *"MKIII-Eliza, MKII-3 status update, vehicle entering at the north side of the parking garage."*

Eliza relayed the update to her other units and went to stand in front of her car. She waited for just the right time as the other vehicle worked its way up the series of turns and ramps. Just before her contact's headlights came into view, she sent a message to her driver. *"MKII-1, turn on the headlights."*

"MKII-1, executing orders," it replied.

The bright lights fell on the approaching vehicle and it paused, its driver unsure of how to continue. Eliza, illuminated by the headlights, looked like an angel as she motioned for the contact to pull their car forward.

"Pull your vehicle closer and park with your driver's door next to me so that we may talk," she shouted.

As the contact began to pull forward, she added, "Do not get out of your vehicle and keep your hands where I can see them at all times. I wouldn't want to kill you over a silly mistake."

"Killing you after I have what I need is a different thing entirely," she thought.

The contact pulled slowly forward and stopped with their door a few feet away from Eliza and the blinding headlights. As they sat unmoving in the automobile, the female android simply stood and stared. She had found that waiting for the unknown was an effective method of building fear and respect. After several seconds, Eliza strutted up to the driver's side door, and leaned both arms against the base of the window. She positioned her body so that her shoulder holster and the Makarov pistol it contained were in plain sight of the human behind the wheel.

"Do you believe that this glass will in some way protect you from me?" she asked.

"No, well, it's just that," the contact stammered.

"Perhaps it is bullet proof, yes?"

"Well, no, I just, I just didn't want to move my hand where you couldn't see it. You know, like you said," they replied as the sweat began to form on their forehead.

"You realize, from here, I can see the switch used to lower your window," Eliza said.

"Yes, I suppose I do."

"Then why am I still talking to you through this fucking glass!" She shouted as she banged her head into the window for emphasis. Eliza didn't strike it hard enough to shatter it, though she easily could have. She had to keep her android nature hidden from this human.

The contact recoiled back at the sudden motion, but then carefully reached out and pushed the switch to lower the window. The glass squeaked as it rubbed against Eliza's leather clad arms, slowly retracting into the door.

Eliza looked down at her arms, then back up to stare at the person behind the wheel. The contact grinned sheepishly, and began to reach over to stop the window, but froze when they saw the stare from the android. After what felt like forever, at least to the contact, the window finished retreating inside the door of the automobile. Eliza sent a command to her team, and then flashed her best fake smile at the human.

When she spoke, it was in a thick Russian accent. "There, that's better. Now, if my memory serves me, I contacted you some time ago and asked if you would like to help me with this little issue, and you refused.

However tonight, you contact me unexpectedly saying you wish to help. This is very confusing to me. What made you change your mind?"

The driver's eyes darted around for a moment before answering. "Does it matter? I have information that you can use and I'm willing to give it to you for the price you named. Are you still interested?"

Eliza was a little shocked that the human had shown some intestinal fortitude, and not simply answered her question. For that, she would kill them quickly when this was all over.

"No, it doesn't matter, not in the least. As long as your information is good, then my offer still stands," she said.

"It will be good. I can tell you where Anna will be, and at what times. Do you have my payment?" The contact asked.

Eliza reached back and pulled a small white envelope from her back pocket. Handing it to the human, she said, "As we agreed, half now, and half when we apprehend this outlaw character you know as Anna."

The contact greedily tore open the envelope and quickly counted the money inside. After verifying the amount was correct, they asked, "Now, just so we're clear, you're not going to hurt her, right?"

Eliza flashed her best fake smile again and said, "Of, course, like I said when we spoke previously, this is just a little matter of immigration. We simply want to take a criminal off your streets and return her to Russia where she can stand trial for the crimes of which she's been accused. That is all."

She held the smile for several seconds as the human studied her face. Then apparently satisfied, they tucked the envelope into the automobile's console. Retrieving a folded piece of paper from the same storage pocket, the contact held it out to Eliza. "Okay then, here is everything I know about her location so far. I'll be in contact with you if things change."

Eliza unfolded the paper and read it instantly. She looked back to the person and said, "No, you will contact me daily and update me on her every move. We are paying you very well and it's the least you could do to earn your money."

The contact nodded their agreement, but Eliza wanted to make sure they understood. She leaned into the automobile so that her Makarov swung loosely from her shoulder and said, "Oh, and please don't do anything stupid, like trying to back out on our agreement. Because if you do, we will find you, and we will take more than just our money in repayment."

The person's eyes widened as their look shifted from her face to the gun and back. To further emphasize her point, Eliza lifted her head slightly and moved her eyes to look at a spot past the contact. When the human turned to see where she was looking, there were two ominous figures dressed in suits and wearing sunglasses. They stood motionless immediately outside the passenger door. The androids had crept up as silent as a cat and positioned themselves there while the driver in the auto and Eliza had talked…just as she had instructed them at the beginning of the conversation.

The contact turned back to Eliza, and she could see that all the blood had drained from their face. They gulped before saying, "No worries there. I don't have any plans on changing my mind."

"That is a wise decision my friend," Eliza said as she removed herself from inside the automobile and straightened up. "So, I will hear from you tomorrow then. Have a safe trip home."

As Eliza turned her back on the human and toward her sedan, its headlights were extinguished throwing her into total darkness, just as she had ordered. The human rubbed at their eyes, trying to get them to adjust to the sudden change in lighting, but they gave up and began pulling carefully forward. Their vision returning just enough to see the two frightening figures watch as they pulled away down the exit ramp.

Eliza waited until she was sure that the other auto was long gone before she sent her orders to the team. *"MKII-2, Enter the back of the sedan on the right. MKII-3, Enter the back of the sedan on the left."* After she had gotten their replies, and they had followed the orders, she got into the front of the sedan and had the driver depart for their base of operations.

They had traveled about halfway there when Eliza mentally received a satellite transmission from her commander Stepan Entsky. She opened the communication line, and answered the call. *"Good morning Stepan, I hope all is well."*

"Hello, my little doll. I have missed you. The bed is too big and too cold without you," he said.

"I have missed you too, lover," she lied.

"I can't wait to have you back home. The things we will do, right?"

She rolled her eyes, waiting for his booming laugh to subside and said, *"You are so right, lyubov moya."*

"Ah, you speak to me in Russian, so it must be true, no? But enough of that for now, tell me, how do you fare on your end? You are proceeding carefully I hope," he said.

"I fare well, thank you. These Mark II androids you have provided me may be lousy conversationalists, but they follow orders perfectly," she replied.

"Most excellent, Eliza! Now hear my good news. I know that Anna has seen the videos we planted for her to find. You know, the ones of Private Zory Novikov," he said.

"Good, now you are free to really begin your interrogation of him. However, I also have something good to report. I have just finished up a late night meeting where I have been able to enlist one of Anna's friends to help me track and capture her," she said.

Stepan clapped his hands together and shouted, *"That is fantastic! How did you convince them to betray her, torture?"* he asked.

Eliza laughed before replying. *"No, no, nothing that difficult. All it took was money, and they were willing to help me. It was so easy."* Eliza's voice turned ice cold as she continued, *"Soon, I will have that traitorous bitch, and when I do…"*

"When you do," Stepan interrupted, *"you will bring her back to me, alive and functioning. Correct my little doll?"*

Eliza ground her teeth, but replied with total obedience, *"Yes, Stepan, it will be as you say. You are the commander."*

"Yes, and please do not forget that. You are invaluable to me. Do not betray me the way Anna did," he replied.

This caused Eliza to boil with rage. *Her*, being compared with that, that…whore, Anna? *"No, Comrade Entsky, I would never. You are my commander and my lover. I could never betray you like that!"*

"I know this is true, my sweet. Now, I must go and begin my interrogation of this Zory person. When I am finished, I promise you that I will know everything he does. Then, I will contact you and tell you what I have learned. Take care, and I will see you soon," he said.

"Goodbye, my love," she said as the connection terminated.

By this time, the sedan had reached their inconspicuous base located in an out of the way motel. However, Eliza didn't exit the car, and since she gave no orders, none of the other androids did either. They sat, patient and unmoving as she tried to think of some way to destroy Anna and not be blamed by Stepan for the failure of the mission. Finally, in frustration when no idea came to her, Eliza stomped the floorboard of the car. She struck it with such speed and force that the heel from her boot broke off, lodging in the metal. She looked down at her boot and the heel sticking out of the car. As she did, a thought entered her mind, causing an evil smile to slowly spread across her face. *"Well, now, that gives me an idea."*

She turned her attention the Mark II's and said, *"All units, inside the base, now. For tomorrow we go shopping!"* Eliza was considering the twists and turns of her idea so intently that she never heard the android's replies as they echoed three times in her mind, in complete harmony and obedience.

Chapter 13

Sunday morning arrived earlier than I'd have liked. As soon as I'd gotten home last night, I'd crashed into the bed and fallen asleep. I hadn't bothered to change out of my moving clothes, and they now possessed an aroma that was stifling. Why my sweat had to smell, I understood. Why it had to smell this bad was beyond me. Sitting up in the bed, I leaned over to remove my socks. My injured foot had improved overnight, it was still swollen and bruised, but it was definitely on the mend. My EmBees had been busy. They were microscopic maintenance robots that circulated around in my blood. EmBees could repair most injuries to my body, but there were some things even they couldn't fix, like broken bones or damage to my neural net brain. All I had to do was feed them plenty of raw materials, like vitamins, and they would happily patch me back together.

I stood up and tried putting some weight on my foot. Thankfully, it was much less sore than last night. However, my happiness was interrupted when I caught another whiff of myself and the nasty clothes I still wore. It was time for a shower…no wait. I felt so grungy, it was time for a hot bath. After a quick stop in the bathroom to turn on the tub's faucet, I shuffled into the kitchen and grabbed myself a handful of vitamins. Washing them down with a bottle of water, I headed into the bathroom to soak away the dirt, and hopefully, the frustration of Saturday.

After relaxing in the tub for a while, I threw on some lazy Sunday clothes and went into the living room. The fragments of my leather chair were still scattered about the floor, but I ignored them and sat down on the sofa to rest for a bit. The bath had improved my hygiene, but not my mood. I couldn't believe I hadn't noticed that David was interested in me. If I had, I would never of led him on that way. David was a great guy, and I did like him. He actually reminded me a lot of Cindi, the woman I had fallen in love with back at the lab in Russia, but that relationship had ended with her being murdered by Eliza. No, I couldn't risk getting that close to anyone again. Besides, Kimber was apparently really into David anyway, so best to stay out of their way. Then again, if I really felt that way, why had I let him get so far last night? I guess it was a lot harder to think logically when someone was giving you a heavenly massage. Sighing to myself, I wondered if humans had this much trouble managing relationships.

Connecting to my work computer via the Internet, I busied myself with some mundane tasks until it was time for the auto parts store to open. Changing into some ragged jeans and a ratty shirt, I headed out to pick up the car parts that Takumi had recommended I replace. At least that would be one thing I could stop worrying about.

About forty-five minutes later, I had my hood up and my hands greasy working on the car. The repair took about an hour and a half of my Sunday, but I didn't mind. It wasn't that difficult and it took my mind off all the other crap going on in my life at the moment. I double checked my work, and jumped in the car to crank it up. My little Civic responded instantly and the engine hummed as if it had just rolled off the assembly line. Even alternating between revving it and letting it idle caused no hesitation or stutter in the Honda. Just to be sure, I interfused with the car by inserting my fingernail into its data jack as I'd done the other night. The world around me whirled and faded into the background. Sights, sounds, smells, all my senses of the real world became like a shadow of their former selves as I was now immersed in the world of Takumi's garage.

I found him at his normal station, under the hood of the car. As I approached, he greeted me warmly. "Good afternoon Anna-san. I see you have made the repairs I requested. You have performed them perfectly."

He flipped open his small notebook and read it for a moment. "Yes, yes, everything is now as it should be. Thank you for your rapid attention to this issue."

"No, thank you for always guiding me to the right course of action. Not to mention the tight spot you pulled me out of the other night," I said.

A grin spread across his face as he said, "That was exhilarating. I haven't been on a ride like that in years. I am glad you had the skill to manage such maneuvers. No one would know that you had only been driving a few months."

"Thank you again, Takumi-san, I suppose I'm just a fast learner," I said.

He looked at me with those wise eyes of his as he lowered the hood of the car. "Yes, faster than any person I've ever known."

I smiled politely, and excused myself before he could delve any deeper into that thought. "I will go now Takumi-san. Please let me know if there is anything else I can do for you."

"Go in peace, young one," he said.

I turned and walked back toward the rear of the car as I terminated the interfuse link. Takumi's garage faded away and I found myself fully back in my world. I turned the engine off and packed up the few tools I'd used for the repair. After disposing of the old cables and plugs, I headed back inside to take a shower and get ready for my trip to Vulcan Park. Felix would be expecting those pictures I'd promised him by tomorrow morning. I really didn't feel like leaving home, and I could probably have gotten out of it by telling Felix my foot was too messed up, but then I'd just have to do it later. Best to go ahead and get it over with. Besides, maybe some nice scenery would improve my mood.

After a quick shower, I chose a fresh pair of jeans and a sweatshirt to wear since it was going to be a little chilly after sunset this evening. I tossed them on and sat down to put on my sneakers. I noticed that my foot had continued to improve, and now it was just a bit of a nagging twinge when I pulled on my shoe. Those EmBees had worked wonders. To ensure that they had plenty of resources, I stopped by my kitchen for more vitamins and SmartWater before rushing out the door.

My Civic was running great and traffic was light on a Sunday afternoon, so I decided to lower the driver's side window. The crisp fall air blew across my face and felt wonderful as I drove down Highway 31 back into Birmingham. Before long, I was turning left onto Valley Avenue, just one right turn away from Vulcan Park. This was my first visit to Vulcan, so I connected to the Internet and pulled up its history to see if I could get any pointers about good scenic locations. Information began to flood into my mind, but the facts couldn't describe the feeling of actually seeing the fifty-six foot tall cast iron statue in person. Vulcan's dark gray form stood proudly on a pedestal that was at least one hundred twenty feet tall. His left hand was clenched in a fist, as if he'd just held the smithy's hammer that rested on the anvil next to him. The eyes of the statue were turned toward his outstretched right hand, which held a spear up, toward the heavens. Vulcan's bearded face wore a look of concentration as he studied it, ensuring the spear had been properly created. Dressed in a blacksmith's apron and sandals, he looked every bit like the Roman god of fire and forge.

I parked my Civic and got out to look around inside the pedestal, where some historical pieces of Vulcan and the city of Birmingham were stored. Inside, I found all kinds of city heirlooms, along with dozens of beautiful bronze plaques, which told me the history of Birmingham. Walking around the small museum, I lost track of time reading about and examining the exhibits.

By the time I went back outside, the sun was riding low in the sky and the park was getting ready to close. It was time to take some pictures. Walking quickly around to the back of the huge pedestal, I found the elevator that led up to the observation platform. I pushed the button to summon it, and heard the internal workings hum quietly as it lowered the eleven floors to the ground level. After a few seconds, the doors opened and a giggling young couple stepped out of the cab. They were walking shoulder-to-shoulder and completely absorbed with each other. It reminded me of David, and how he'd gone out of his way to ensure that I had a good time on our trip to the zoo. He really was a nice, thoughtful guy. I frowned and shook the memory from my mind as I entered the elevator and pressed the button labeled 'OL'. The doors silently closed and I was rapidly on my way to the observation level.

The doors opened and I stepped out onto the gray metal grating that was the floor of the platform. In the center, was a smaller circular pedestal that was about ten feet high. This was where Vulcan stood, while the fifteen feet wide observation deck wrapped all around its base. If you walked all the way around on the platform, you could see Vulcan from whatever angle you desired. Around the outside of the deck, was a waist high metal rail with thick steel latticing attached in the spaces between the rails. Mounted on top of the railing, were glass windows stretched up another four feet. Both of them combined made the height of the protective wall around the observation deck about seven feet high. Everything looked well maintained and sturdy, but I wondered about having a floor made of grating this high up. I could easily look down through the holes in the platform and see the ground, which was over one hundred feet below. It was probably easy to maintain, but I was sure you would have eliminated anyone with acrophobia from seeing this view of Birmingham, and what a view it was. You could see for miles in almost every direction. There was a breathtaking view of downtown Birmingham looking one way, while Vestavia Hills with its picturesque homes was just off to the side. Since it was fall and some of the trees had lost their leaves, I could even see parts of the Birmingham Zoo and the Botanical Gardens from my lofty perch. I could see why the customer wanted some photographs from up here.

Pulling out my iPhone, I began taking pictures and even a little video, just in case the client came back and asked for some footage later. I could've used my own eyes and digital storage for recording, but I decided to play it safe and use the phone instead. After all, several people were aware that I was coming to Vulcan Park and take pictures. If anyone I knew saw me up here without a camera, it might be hard to explain how I obtained the images. The last thing I needed was more questions to answer.

I walked over near the railing and continued my work. The wind picked up as I approached the edge of the platform, but I ignored it. I wanted to take a lot of pictures and video so that the client would have a wide variety from which to choose. Heck, I'd even keep a copy for myself. It really was beautiful up here. I was able to move around to any location I desired since everyone else had left except for one man in an Alabama baseball cap and tan overcoat. He had his phone out too, and was taking pictures looking more directly toward the sun. I knew that could damage a human's eyes, but he had on some thick sunglasses, so I assumed he knew what he was doing.

Holding my cell phone up and pointing it toward Birmingham, I was working on the last video of the afternoon. In the back of my mind, what felt like a random thought worked its way forward. I'd lost track of the man in the tan overcoat. Where had he gotten off to? Maybe he'd taken the elevator down and left for home, but I hadn't heard…before I could finish that thought, he was on me.

Strong arms coiled themselves around me from the back, knocking my iPhone out of my hands and pinning my hands against my chest. My first thought was this clown had just picked the wrong girl to assault. I flexed my arms, expecting to easily break free, but I couldn't. This guy was stronger than he'd looked. I tried harder and harder until I realized that I didn't have enough leverage to break my arms free. All the while, he hadn't said a word, he simply kept dragging me back toward the elevator. I reached up with my hands, and managed to get a grip on each of his wrists. Pulling with all my might, I was able to get his arms apart. Once I had them out in front of me, I pushed them up and spun around to face him. I displayed my best wicked grin to intimidate the man, but my efforts were to no avail. In fact, his face wore no expression at all. Then I realized, there was something *off* about it. It was too angular and the skin looked too perfect.

His strange-looking face had interrupted my concentration, and the tan overcoat man took advantage of it. He lifted his leg and stomped down hard, right onto my injured foot. The pain raced from my foot up my leg and for just a moment, I loosened my grip on him. He broke free and reached out with both hands trying to wrap them around my neck. My fists were out of position, but I wasn't going to let him choke me. As soon as he was in range, I lunged forward to head butt him. I made sure to control my strike so that I didn't accidentally fracture his skull and kill him, just knock him out. I figured out my mistake as soon as our skulls collided, his head was as hard as he was strong. Although I'd hit him with over half my strength, all it did was knock his hat off and make us both stagger backwards. He slammed into the pedestal with Vulcan on it, and I backed into the railing and glass at the edge of the platform.

I knew I had to clear my head and get back into the fight quickly, so I fought against the dizziness and looked back toward him. His cap had concealed a smooth, bald head that appeared odd to me in someway, like it wasn't quite the right shape or maybe size for his body. Again, with no growl of anger or emotion of any kind, he leapt at me. Too bad for me that the disorientation hadn't cleared, because he was able to grab my forehead with his right hand and bash the back of my head against the glass wall. The impact was so hard, that I heard the glass shatter from the blow. Pain was all around me, but I managed to knock his hand free of my face.

Now, I was mad. I began throwing punches at him, hard and fast. He managed to dodge a few, but then I caught him with a right cross, square on the jaw. That punch dazed him enough for me to hit him again, this time with a left to his eye. Now I had him on the ropes. I punched him in the face again and again until on the fifth hit, he staggered back. I couldn't believe how much abuse this guy was taking. Suddenly, the answer was as clear as the face staring back at me.

One of my punches had sent his dark sunglasses flying and now I could see his eyes for the first time. They were solid black, and not just the iris, but the entire eye was as black as night. They didn't look... human, and it felt like they were staring right through me. Without warning, he rushed at me again.

I felt my enhanced reflexes kick into high gear as he made his move. He was going for my face, but I'd learned something. We were an equal match strength wise, but he wasn't as agile. I waited until the last second, and then ducked under his grab for me. I quickly found that I'd almost waited to long, because I felt his fingernails tear across my forehead. He noticed what I was doing and tried to slow, but I brought my shoulder up under his waist. Using his momentum, I flipped him over the railing where the glass wall had been broken out by the back of my head. He never made a sound as he plummeted the hundred feet and crashed into the ground below with a dull thump.

Although I was almost certain this man wasn't really a man at all, a chill came over me as I considered that I might have just killed another human. Something I'd swore never to do again. I stood and looked over the railing to see what had become of him. He was lying on a grassy patch of ground with his legs and arms bent at humanly impossible angles. Blood pouring down into my eyes from the open wound he'd tore across my forehead, made it difficult to see anything more from here, and the distant sounds of sirens told me I needed to get moving anyway. Turning away from the railing, I limped to the elevator and pushed its button. It was already on this level, so the stainless doors slid open without delay. On the ride down, I had to keep wiping the blood from my eyes and face so that I could see. I'd activated my pain suppression, which was actually only pain reduction, and it had mostly worked on my head, but my foot still felt like it was on fire.

The elevator doors opened and I hobbled out as quickly as I could, heading for where the man with the tan overcoat had fallen. However, as I came around Vulcan's base to where he should have been, he wasn't there. There was a slight indentation in the ground, but the man was gone. That convinced me that he wasn't human, because I probably could have survived that fall myself, especially on the softer grass-covered ground. The thought of another artificial being hunting me brought up a completely new world of things to consider.

The nearness of the police sirens spurred me back into action, and I turned to leave. Before I could take a step, I remembered my cell phone. Shit, there was no way I was leaving it behind, but I wouldn't have time to get back up to the observation platform. Damn it, I'd have to destroy it. I reached out with my wireless connection, feeling my way around for any devices nearby. Well, well, I'd caught a break, my phone had been knocked off the platform and was in the grass only a few feet away. I grabbed it up and hurried toward my car still wirelessly searching for devices, so that I could deactivate any security cameras that I found. Curiously enough, someone had already done that to each one I located.

Finally, I made it to my car. I got in as quickly as I could, dreading shifting again with my freshly re-injured foot…not to mention my blood-blurred vision. Driving as normally as I could, I pulled out of the park and onto the highway. I was cresting a hill about a quarter of a mile away as I saw the police car turn into the entrance of the park in my rear-view mirror. Now I could breathe again.

The wound above my eyes wasn't that deep, but it was long and kept bleeding profusely. Frustrated, I pulled over in an empty parking lot. I had to do something about it. Looking around the car, I didn't see anything I could use as a bandage, so I improvised. Removing my sweatshirt, I tore off the arms and started wrapping them around my head to stop the bleeding. I noticed that the back of my head was wet and sticky as well, meaning it must have been cut when I was slammed into the glass. Pulling the now sleeveless sweatshirt back on, I checked myself in the mirror. Blood all over me, ripped up clothes, I looked like an absolute train wreck.

Lucky for me it was getting dark, and I was able to make it home without being seen. I ran into my apartment and headed straight for the bath. While it filled with hot water, I undressed, except for my makeshift bandage and got into the tub. I was a damned mess, my foot was swollen and throbbing, my head was pounding, and I ached all over. After soaking some, I dared to take the bandage off my head. The bleeding had stopped, so I carefully washed my hair and cleaned out my forehead wound. It looked nasty, a rough jagged tear, but I knew from my experience with what Eliza had done to me that it wouldn't leave a scar, bless those hard working EmBees.

Leaning back in the tub, I thought about the events of the last few days. I had really screwed up Saturday over at David's house. My foot had been crushed not once, but twice in two days. My head looked like someone had tried to get at my brain with a can opener. Then to top it all off, I now had some unknown android chasing me. This had been one hell of a weekend.

Chapter 14

Overnight, my foot had again gotten much better, it had become a dull ache instead of a stabbing pain, but it wasn't the reason I wasn't going into work today. I could explain a limp because everyone from the office had been there when I hurt my foot helping David move. Besides, foot injuries were common and could be lied about easily, while a jagged gash on the forehead was a different story. I'd never be able to come up with a believable reason for having a six-inch long abrasion above my eyes. Like my foot, it had gotten much better as well, but the EmBees still needed a day or so to work their magic and heal it up completely. Time to call Felix and let him know I was staying home.

Limping away from the bathroom mirror, I went back into the bedroom and sat down on the bed. I wirelessly connected to the Internet and impersonated my iPhone to call Felix. He answered on the third ring, "Hey Anna, I half expected a call from you today. How's your foot?"

"Good morning, Felix. Yeah, it's still hurting quite a bit, so I was going to work from home today if that's all right with you," I said.

"Sure thing, you better go to the doctor and have it checked out. You might have a hairline fracture or something worse," he said.

"Okay, thanks, hey, speaking of doctors, what did they say about

Kimber's wrist when you took her Saturday?" I asked.

I heard him let out a deep breath before beginning to speak, "It was bad, but not as bad as we first thought. No break, just a bad sprain. They gave her a removable cast that went from her wrist all the way up to her elbow, that she's supposed to wear for three weeks."

I winced, knowing how much that could hurt, "Ouch, sorry to hear that, but glad it wasn't any worse."

"Yeah, I'm not sure if she'll make it in today either," he chuckled and then said, "David's moving party almost shut us down for a day."

When he said David's name it made me wonder if he'd make it in today after the way I'd carelessly hurt his feelings. I hoped he was doing alright, maybe I should call him or…

"Anna, are you there?" I'd let myself get lost in thought and Felix had to raise his voice to get my attention.

"Oh, yeah, I can hear you now, lost you for a second there. Anyway, let me hang up and get to work. I should be in tomorrow," I said.

"Sure thing. Oh, by the way, I don't suppose you went to Vulcan and took those pictures for the client, did you?" he asked.

I'd forgotten all about my cell phone and the pictures. "Yeah, I actually did, but I need to check them out since I was having trouble holding my phone steady. Let me bring them to you Tuesday."

"Okay, sounds like a plan. You sit down, put some ice on that foot, and don't work too hard. I'll talk to you later," he said.

"Okay, bye Felix, and thanks again," I replied.

Soon as I'd hung up with Felix, I stood and shambled back into the bathroom. There on the floor, were my jeans from Sunday. I grabbed them up and pulled my iPhone from the pocket. Damn it! The screen was shattered and I couldn't get it to display anything, not even in two-dimensional mode. I knew I should have invested in the super-protective case. Although, the sensors in my palm told me that the phone was on, and connected to the wireless network. If the screen was the only thing broken, I could still interfuse with it and retrieve the images I'd captured Sunday. That would at least save me another trip back to Vulcan Park.

I slipped the iPhone into the pocket of my shorts and went into the kitchen to load up on SmartWater and vitamins. After swallowing a handful and chugging a whole bottle of water, I headed into the living room and eased myself down on the sofa.

Putting my foot up on a fragment of my former leather chair, I took out the iPhone and started to work. I reached out with my mind and interfused with it over the wireless signal it was still producing. My surroundings shifted into the shadow as the iPhone's world replaced my own. I found myself standing outside a retail Apple store, just like the one where I'd purchased the phone. The front double doors were made of glass and they pulled open easily. The brightly lit, dust free, store was completely empty. Its white walls were bare and the honey-colored wooden tables had nothing on them. I entered and called out, "Hello, is anyone here?"

"Why yes, of course I'm here, how may I help you today, Anna?"

The voice sounded as if it came from a young man that had no discernible accent. His reply had come from all around me because his words echoed throughout the empty store. I even took a quick look with my thermal vision, but he was nowhere to be seen. "Uh, could you come out and show yourself. I usually like to hold my conversations face to face."

"Oh, I wish I could, Anna, but unfortunately I'm defective. Since my display is broken, I can't show you anything. I'm terribly sorry for the inconvenience. Hey, if you could take me to the nearest Apple store, I'm sure they could fix me right up, for a small repair charge of only two hundred US dollars. Then I could show you anything you'd like to see!" the voice said.

Huh, he'd already checked on the price to repair himself, very efficient, but I didn't want to hassle with that yet. "Oh, okay, I'll be sure to do that soon, but right now, ah, what did you say your name was?"

"Steve, I'm Steve, Anna, and I'm here to help!" came the cheerful reply.

"Okay Steve, right now I need access to some of the pictures and video files that I created yesterday. Can you tell me where they are?"

There was a pause, and at first, I didn't think he was going to tell me, then he spoke again. "Well, sure, I can direct you to them, but if you want to see them, you'll have to transfer them to another device."

I smirked and said, "I think I can handle that."

"Okay then, you start walking, and I'll tell you warmer or colder until you find them. Sound good?" Steve asked.

"Really...you're serious?" I asked.

"I'm so sorry, but it's the easiest way for me to lead you to them. Okay, start walking when you're ready," he replied.

I thought he may have just been messing with me, giving me a hard time so I'd go ahead and get him repaired, but I decided to go along with it for a while and see how this stupid game played out. I sighed and started slowly walking forward.

"Okay, that's it, no, no, colder, oh, okay, now you're warmer, wait, wait, now you're colder again. I'm so sorry. I'm not the best at this. No wait, don't do that! I'll try harder! I promise! Um, warmer, warmer, oh, you're red hot! No, wait! You're cold again. Okay, okay, I'm trying! There, you're red hot! Reach out with your hands. They're on the table right in front of you. Yeah! You found them! Good job, Anna!"

The rage that had been building inside of me subsided as I felt my hands close around something solid. It was sitting on the waist-high table directly in front of me. As soon as I grasped the object, it became visible in my hands. It was a pure white three-ring notebook with the words, 'Vulcan Park' on the spine. Opening it, I thumbed through the binder and found that each page was an image I'd taken Sunday. This was exactly what I was looking for.

"Steve, I'm going to make a copy of this and take it with me," I said.

"That's fine, Anna. Just please remember to return me to your nearest Apple store for repairs as soon as possible, so I can better serve you in the future," he said.

While he spoke, I had already begun the copy process. I held the original binder in my left hand and concentrated. Instantly, a duplicate binder appeared in my right hand. I tucked it under my arm and replaced the original back on the desk. Then, I turned to leave the store.

"Sure thing, thanks for the help," I said as I shut down the interfuse connection and in a moment of disorientation, returned to my living room.

They had all survived. At least it looked that way as I thumbed through the images and videos in my mind. I deleted the ones that I didn't think were acceptable, and then retrieved a data drive from my desk. Plugging it into my fingernail, I copied them one by one over to the drive, until I hit the last video. It had slipped my mind that I'd been recording when the, well, whatever it was, had jumped me from the back. I removed the data drive from my finger and began to play this last file in slow motion. I wanted to see exactly *what*, if anything I'd managed to capture with my iPhone.

Concentrating on each frame, I watched as the video went from a stable shot from the top of Vulcan, to a twirling, nausea inducing, blur of colors. The indiscernible rotating image finally stopped with the phone landing in the grass with a crunching sound. However, to my amazement, the image stabilized with a shot of grass at the bottom half and the top was the parking lot near the Vulcan pedestal. Only the display must have been broken, leaving the video camera still functioning. My hopes of finding something began to rise.

About ten seconds later, there was a loud 'Whomp' and that, *thing*, fell ten feet away from the phone. I replayed what happened next several times, because I didn't want to believe what I'd saw. He hadn't been on the ground five seconds, when I heard what I thought was a couple of car doors open and two sets of men's shoes ran up beside him. They reached down and picked him up by the arms, dragging him back in the direction from which they'd come. The screen was now empty, but I could hear a car accelerate away while the doors slammed shut. Only a few seconds after that, I heard myself walking around, searching around, and finally picking up the iPhone.

The video went on for about another hour, but it only showed the inside of my pocket before some maximum file size or something similar triggered it to stop. I leaned back on my couch, stunned by what I'd seen. There were at least three of these, these, knock-off androids running around and they all had my number. Where the hell had they come from, was this attack Stepan and Eliza's doing? I'd never seen anything like that back at the lab, plus the lab had been destroyed when I escaped. That only left Mister Adam Sims and his NSA flunkies. Did they already have the technology to build rudimentary machines like that? Is that what they wanted me for, to further their research?

I was so lost in thought that when my phone rang, I almost threw it across the room. When I calmed down and answered it, I heard Felix on the other end.

"Oh my God, Anna! Did you hear about the vandals at Vulcan Park?" he asked.

Oh, crap. "Uh, no, what are you talking about Felix?" I asked.

"They struck yesterday around sunset and busted up one of the protective glass walls!" he said.

"Wow, really? That's terrible! Why would anyone want to do that?" I said.

"Did you see anything unusual while you were there?" he asked.

"No, not at all." I lied.

"Okay, I just wanted to check with you and see if you knew anything. The police are offering a reward for clues. You'd think they'd have that place under video surveillance," he said.

"Yeah, you'd think," I said.

"Well, I'll let you go. Get some rest and let me know about coming in Tuesday, bye now," he said.

"Yeah, bye Felix," I replied.

I made the news, yay for me. Although it sounded like the police didn't have any leads, which pleased me to no end. Well, I'd have to consider all this later, I needed to interfuse with my desktop computer and get to work. While in that state, I could perform a days worth of programming in about an hour. After that, I'd take more vitamins and bottled water to help speed up my EmBees in performing their repairs. I'd rest some as they did their work, and then I owed a certain iPhone a trip to the Apple store for some well-earned repairs.

Chapter 15

I pulled my Honda safely into the FlexJen parking lot early Tuesday morning. Here I was, on time for work, and without any hindrances from psychotic drivers or low-rent killer androids. The EmBees had done their work admirably, my foot felt almost one hundred percent, and there was just the smallest red mark left across my forehead. It was nothing that a slight lengthening of my bangs couldn't conceal. Concentrating for a moment, I extended a little more hair from my scalp and covered it up nicely.

As I entered the front door, Irene, the company's security system, greeted me, but I was focused on Kimber. She was at her post, manning the front desk, wearing an uncomfortable looking brace from her wrist to her elbow. I felt horrible and didn't know what to say, but I had to say something.

"Hey, good morning, Kimber. Are you feeling better?" I asked.

She didn't even look up when she quietly answered. "Yeah, the doctor told me I'd have to wear this for a few weeks, but it could've been a lot worse, I suppose."

I lowered my head so that I couldn't see the wrist brace and said, "Well, I'm glad it wasn't, uh, worse, you know."

Her voice had become so soft. It was nothing more than a whisper. "Okay, well, thanks."

Without saying anything else, I walked back to my cube and sat down. I worked steadily until around nine, when David would usually stop by to make small talk, but he didn't come today. Standing up, I decided to go over and have a talk with him. We had to get this issue resolved between us so we could go back to some resemblance of *normal* around the office. I walked over to his cube, and stood there in front of him, but he never looked up from his keyboard. He had to see me standing there, so why would he try to ignore me? I waited for a few more seconds, just to be polite, and then I interrupted him.

"Good morning, David. How are you today?" I asked.

He answered in a standoffish manner. "Good morning, Anna. I'm fine this morning. I hope you are doing well too."

He wasn't going to dissuade me that easily. "As a matter of fact, I am. That day at home has really done wonders for my foot. It's almost as good as new."

"That's good to hear. Now if you'll excuse me, I have a lot of tests to run on this new subroutine." His voice was more robotic than I think mine had ever been.

I thought if I could just get him to talk about it, everything could go back to normal. Leaning in close, I spoke again in a whisper. "Look, David, I didn't intend to…"

His brown eyes shot up from his keyboard and fixed me with a gaze full of hurt and anger. His voice was strained as he whispered to me. "Anna, I don't know what you think you're doing, but it's not working. Did you think you could just waltz over and we'd have a nice little chat like last week? If so, then I'm sorry to disappoint you, because it may take me a little time to get over what I thought was a relationship between us. You're going to have to give me some space."

Oh hell, was our friendship broken beyond repair? All I could reply with was, "Sorry, David. I never meant to…" I stopped and ran back to my desk afraid any more words from me would only cause him more pain.

I worked right through lunch, there wasn't anyway I could have sat in the same room with both Kimber and David. Both were preoccupied with each other anyway. I noticed that David was eager to help her whenever she might have used her injured wrist, and Kimber was very appreciative of his attention. Perhaps they would rekindle their relationship, and it would get back to the way it had been before I came to FlexJen. The way Felix had described to me a few days ago.

A little while after lunch, I was typing away when Felix came by to see me. He was wearing a concerned look as he asked, "Afternoon, Anna, sorry I haven't been by sooner, but I was buried under paperwork. How's your moving related injury treating you today?"

I smiled weakly as I replied, "It's fine, almost no pain at all, thanks."

"Good, good," he said as he began to fidget in his wheelchair. His apparent nervousness prompted me to stop what I was doing and focus on our conversation.

"It's just that, well I can't help noticing there's some tension in the office," he said.

I began to speak, but he held up his hand and cut me off. "No, it's okay. I've expected something like this for a few weeks now, and it's really none of my business."

His face grew grim and there was a slight hardness to his voice as he continued. "What *is* my business is FlexJen, and how well it's functioning. So let's just try to get things back on an even keel as soon as we can. We can't afford to let personal issues intrude into the workplace."

All I could think of to say was, "I understand."

His mood was much improved after that speech. His familiar smile returned as he said, "Ok, great. Now, there was a favor I wanted to ask you. Would you mind staying a little late tonight and going over some software concepts we've developed. They're older, but I think there might be a market for them if we could tweak them just right. I've already worked on them for the past few days, and I have my notes, but I really value your opinion when it comes to software design. You have a special knack regarding what people will like, when it comes to software and human interfaces. Anyway, would you mind taking a look and emailing me your thoughts, Anna?"

What could I say? After that previous speech, I had to agree. Besides, since I wouldn't be working with Felix, I could interfuse with the workstation and have it done in no time.

I nodded and said, "Sure, no problem. What server are they on, and what's the folder structure?"

"Oh, there not electronic, they're all in notebooks and design documents we created while brainstorming one week." He paused and put his finger to his lip in thought, wagging it at me as his idea finished forming. "Hey, why don't you add them into the project management software, and then we'd have them digitally. Great idea, Anna!"

I sighed to myself realizing the trap he'd caught me in. It would take me almost all night to work with paper documents, but I'd already agreed to do the task. Not only that, but he was right, I should store them electronically to make future access faster. The man had a head for business.

"Sure, I can do that, no problem," I said through my best phony smile.

"Great! Thanks again, Anna!" he said as he rolled away and back into his office.

I didn't get much work done the rest of the day. My morale was in the dumps, and it wasn't getting any better. I sat at my cube and watched as

David and Kimber spent most of the day together. He was always there, helping her with anything that might have been a strain on her injured wrist. She was acting differently, much less, well, bitchy was the only way to put it. Maybe it was because they had talked, and she knew I was out of the picture. Then again, she could be on pain medication, either way, she was much more approachable than last week.

It made me happy to see them connecting again. That was a lie. Wait, it was mostly true… Damn it, I was happy for them, but I was just so, so… I stopped in mid thought. I'd seen this exact behavior in Kimber. I was jealous of their happiness…no, not their happiness, their connection…a special bond between two people, something that could only be formed between one soul and another. Whether it was family, or friend, or even lover, I wondered if I'd ever be able to form those kinds of bonds. After all, I didn't think I had a soul.

Once one of the scientists at the lab had called me a *Frankenstein's Monster* during an argument. Afterwards, I took the time to see what he'd meant. I read the book he'd gotten the slur from, but I didn't agree with his accusation at the time. Now, I wasn't so sure. I'd never felt so alone, so isolated. Unlike the Monster in the book, I couldn't return to my creator, my Viktor, and beseech him to create me someone, a friend, a companion, anyone. He was already dead, killed by one of his own creations, just like the scientist in that damned book. Was I destined to end up like that wretched creature?

I watched as Felix left first, and then David and Kimber walked out together. They were talking about going somewhere to maybe see a movie or something. I simply sat at my desk and didn't move. Sometime later, Irene turned off the main lights to the building and I was thrown into the shadows. The sudden change in lighting shook me out of my mental vapor lock. Standing, I trudged into the storeroom to begin work on the software concepts. Once I'd found them, I realized my task was even larger than I'd first thought. I picked up a box and slammed it down on the table. Sitting down, I began to work.

Chapter 16

I'd been right. By the time I finished entering all the hard copy data into the project system, it was after eleven in the evening. At least the next part would be quick. I interfused with the server and analyzed the projects. In minutes, I had emailed a list of my findings and thoughts to Felix. I cut the connection to the FlexJen server and let out a long, slow breath. Finished, finally. I stood and stretched the kinks out of my back and thought about how nice a hot bath would feel right about now.

Closing the door behind me, I left the small storage room in the back of the office. Irene had already turned out FlexJen's main lights, so I found myself in the same scenario as a few days ago, one dim, shadowy building, and one android that was afraid of the dark. I almost asked for the lights to be turned back on, but then decided I wouldn't be here for more than a couple of seconds anyway.

It seemed like the building was again darker than normal. Eerily similar to the other night, when the lights in the parking lot were out. This time however, I wasn't going to get paranoid and jumpy about it, at least I wasn't until I heard a strange roaring sound. I couldn't determine the direction of the noise, so I began to sneak around as stealthily as I could, keeping my back against the hallway wall.

This time, I figured out the situation without all the drama. As I crept closer and closer to the lobby, the sound grew louder and louder.

Looking outside the double doors of the building, I saw that the parking lot lights were indeed on, they were just obscured by a deluge of rain. I'd never seen it fall like that before. It was so heavy that I could barely see the outline of my car, which was parked under a light and only forty feet from our front doors.

Still, now that I knew what was happening, I relaxed a bit. Walking into the lobby, I waited for a while to see if the rain would let up, but it was one of those powerful storms that felt almost alive. The wind whipped through the trees, bending them to its will. Great flashes of lightning ripped through the night sky, blasting the darkness away if only for a moment. Within seconds, booming thunder rolled into the building and shook the pictures on the walls. It was both frightening and beautiful at the same time, and it showed no signs of relenting. I was just going to make a run for the car. It couldn't be that bad, right?

As I neared the double doors, they hissed open. I was immediately hit with a gust of wind and a mist of rain. Hurriedly, I unlocked my Honda and spoke to FlexJen's security system. "Irene, this is Anna Andropov, I'm about to leave for the night, please lock the building after I'm gone."

"I will Miss Andropov. Please be careful driving home, the weather is dreadful," she told me.

"Thanks Irene," I said and began to ready myself for the dash.

Removing my high heels and holding them in my hand, I sprinted into the rain. The wind swirled all around, buffeting me as I flew down the steps and toward my car. After only three strides, I knew that running was a wasted effort. Before I'd even reached the bottom of our stairs, I was drenched. I made it to the car, and jumped inside as lightning flashed from seemingly all around my Honda. The thunder came right behind, booming like a cannon shot as I shut my car door. While I checked the rearview mirror to make sure our front door had closed, I caught a glimpse of my own reflection. I couldn't help but chuckle. Water dripped rhythmically from my hair and the white blouse I'd worn today had become much more revealing than I'd have thought possible.

I reached down and slipped my shoes back on, then sat up and pulled my blazer around the front of my blouse. After trying to wring some of the water out of my hair, I buckled up and started the Civic. Even though it was chilly, I turned on the air conditioner to clear the fog from my front window, and backed out of the parking lot. It was going to be a long trip home.

Cautiously, I drove through the rain-soaked streets of Southside. The downpour had become so intense that large, deep puddles began forming at the edges of some of the lanes. Patiently, I navigated around them until I could take the onramp to Red Mountain Expressway. Easing my way along, I finally made it to I-459.

As if the unrelenting rain wasn't enough, the temperature difference between the warm day and the colder night had caused some moderate fog to gather around the interstate. Between that and the thunderstorm, I could only see about one hundred feet in front of me with my regular vision. My thermal sight would cut right through the fog and rain, but it only showed me heat patterns, of which I saw none.

The rain continued to pour, the fog continued to gather, and I concentrated on driving, at least most of the time. I hadn't forgotten the last time I was heading home late at night. To ensure I wasn't surprised by any killer androids, I kept looking around the car in every direction. I even shifted my vision back and forth between normal and thermal to check for any approaching heat signatures. No one was getting the drop on me tonight.

I was creeping along at forty-five MPH while my windshield wipers fought against the deluge, when all the warning lights on my dashboard began to flash on and off repeatedly. The car was running fine, so it made no sense to me at all, but Takumi must have wanted to get my attention, so I wasn't going to ignore him. I checked around the car once more before pulling off the road to the left, and easing to a stop near the median between the north and south bound lanes. It was too dangerous to interfuse while driving and lose that much of my concentration on the road in this kind of weather. I'd just have a quick chat with him, and then be back on my way.

Reaching under the dash with my left hand, I located the Honda's data jack. My fingernail slid easily into it and the connection was formed. The interior of the car faded back into the shadows and the familiar image of Takumi's garage swirled up around me.

I appeared just inside the open main door near the trunk of my Honda. The wind from the storm swirled rain through the opening, and gave me an impressive set of goose bumps. I could hear a multitude of clicks and clacks as Takumi was laboring away near the running engine, but the car's raised hood blocked my view of him. Moving away from the howling wind, I hurried toward the front of my Civic to see why he had summoned me with the dash lights.

As I made the turn around my front fender, Takumi noticed I'd arrived, and he rushed forward to meet me. His expression was that of pure concentration, and beads of sweat sat upon his brow. His words came out fast and with a note of desperation.

"Anna-san, you are here, good. Now listen quickly, you must get out of the car and run to a safe distance. Something is not right."

"Wait, what? Get out of the car? What do you mean something is not right? Takumi-san, please explain." I replied in shock.

He sighed, but saw I had to know what was happening. "Someone is broadcasting a carrier signal at the car. I do not know where it is coming from, but I believe they are trying to communicate with something. Using some creative rerouting of electrical current through the car's antenna, I have surrounded us in a dome of interference. However, I cannot keep the dome in place for long, the circuit will burn out soon and the transmission will reach its destination, whatever it may be."

When I realized what he was implying, I couldn't believe it. "You think there's a bomb somewhere on the car."

The volume of his voice rose as he spoke. "It is possible, but I do not know for sure. Better to be safe. Get out of the car and run away, now!"

I shook my head. "No, I'll search for the device and…"

He gently grabbed my shoulders with his grease-stained hands and fixed me with a stare from those wise, brown eyes of his. When he spoke again, his voice was full of emotion.

"No, Anna-san, there is no time. Please, I implore you, listen to what I say and run far away from here. Do it now, please!"

I lowered my eyes and replied in a whisper, "Okay, I will do as you ask."

"Thank you, now go!" he said as he patted me on the shoulder and gently turned me toward the door.

"Oh, and do not approach the car until after fifteen seconds from now. The circuit will burn out around then, and we will see what happens," he said.

I took a step toward the door, but then turned back around. "Takumi-san, you are more than just my car, you are my friend."

A broad, joyful smile spread across his face as he replied, "You are the best owner I have ever known, Anna-san."

I disconnected from the interfuse before he could see the tears that began to run down my cheek.

After my normal disorientation from reentering the real world, I checked around the car for any traffic or heat patterns. Seeing nothing, I opened my door and stepped out into the rain. I ran down the shoulder near the median for about thirty feet, then I couldn't see to go any further. I turned around and locked my eyes on the back of my little Civic as I checked the time, three seconds left.

2…The monsoon continued unabated, and if I'd had a dry spot somewhere on me, it was gone now.

1…I wiped the rain from my face and eyes, trying to keep the Honda in my sight the whole time.

0…I braced for an explosion and…nothing! No flash, no kaboom, just darkness and the sound of the rain as it hammered the asphalt!

Pumping my fist up and down, I shouted "Yes! For the first time Takumi, you were wrong about something dealing with the car! Thank Heavens!"

A brilliant flash of lightning illuminated the night sky at that instant, and almost scared me to death. When I realized what had happened, I giggled to myself and began counting the number of seconds until the thunder hit. One… Tw…

The Honda exploded into an enormous ball of flame. The concussive force slammed into my chest and knocked me backwards. As I fell, my advanced reflexes automatically activated, and I saw pieces of my little Civic as they flew past me in every direction. Most of them missed me, but I felt a few as they tore into my flesh. I landed awkwardly and the side of my head slammed onto the asphalt. Rolling over onto my stomach, I was able to get up on my hands and knees. My ears whined like a jet engine, and I was still too dazed and disoriented to stand. Pushing against the ground, I forced myself into a sitting position with my legs out in front of me. I'd lost my left shoe, my clothes were dotted with several small holes that had bloodstains around them, and my right calf had a small piece of my car sticking out of it. Reaching down, I pulled the shrapnel out of my leg and threw it across the interstate. Small rivulets of blood ran from the wound, but were instantly washed away by the rain.

The shock wore off after a few seconds and I struggled to my feet. I stared at the burning husk of my car and screamed, "Takumi! Takumi, no! No…no…" My tears fell like the rain I stood in as I quietly asked, "Why the hell did you have to be right? Why?"

As I stood and mourned Takumi, my head finally began to clear. The dizziness faded away first, allowing me to think clearly. Shortly after that, the horrible whining left and I could hear again. I heard the sizzle of the rain as it fell on my burning car, the thunder as it rumbled around chasing the flashes of lightning, and even the car that was trying its best to be silent as it raced up from behind me.

Chapter 17

The swooshing sound of the car grew nearer as I gritted my teeth and felt my hands clench into fists. I was going to make someone pay for this…for Takumi.

I whirled around to my right, and saw the vehicle illuminated by the light of my burning Honda. The driver was leaning out of his window, wielding a long rod or pipe in his left hand. He had managed to get closer than I'd thought, too close, as a matter of fact. Flexing the muscles in my legs, I sprang toward the median to dodge the weapon he was swinging forward. I avoided the full impact of the blow, but he still managed to make substantial contact. The tire iron clipped my lower back at the base of my spine with enough force to spin me around. The pain felt like an electrical shock that ran down my legs and all the way to my toes as I spun. I fell, rolling out of control down the side of the deep median. My momentum carried me down, as everything spun around me. The world finally came to rest as I plunged into the dark water at the bottom of the hill and began to sink.

Struggling, I tried to orient myself and stand up, but I couldn't get my footing. I knew it had been raining hard, but this median couldn't have that much water in it. I thrashed around with my arms, and they came in contact with the ground. Grabbing handful after handful of muddy grass, I managed to pull myself to the edge of the murky pool. I tried to stand, and realized why I'd had so much trouble in the water. I couldn't

159

move my legs.

No…I *had* to move them…but no matter what I tried, I couldn't get them to respond to me. Rolling over onto my back, I punched one of them a few times with my fist. I was able to feel each blow, so that gave me some hope. However, in my current state, fighting was not an option, I had to get out of here. Listening, I couldn't hear anything but the falling rain, so I eased myself back in the water. I'd pull myself away from where I'd fallen in and come up on the other side of the median. I thought it was a good plan, but I didn't get very far.

A flash of brilliant lightning lit up the dark sky, and there was my foe, right in front of me. He looked just like the guy from Vulcan Park, expressionless face, dark sunglasses, sharply angled jawline, the whole package. He reached over and grabbed me by my hair with his right hand. I swung my arms at him, desperate to fend him off, but I couldn't get any force behind my swings. He reached out with his left arm for balance, and began dragging me up the hill toward the interstate.

Not only did that hurt like hell, but it was damned humiliating. I repeatedly sent commands to my legs, hoping against hope that they would move, but nothing happened. Maybe I needed to buy the EmBees more time to reboot something, or whatever it was they did. I began to punch wildly at him, trying to hurt him any way I could. We'd made it all the way to the top of the median, before I was actually able to get in a good shot. I caught him with a fist to the side of his knee and it buckled. He released his grip on my hair to keep from falling down the embankment. When he did, I tried to roll away from him.

If I'd had any doubts about him being an android, they were dispelled when he grabbed me by the throat and lifted me into a standing position with just his left hand. His iron grip combined with my weight had cut off my air supply.

While *breathing* for me consisted of me inhaling oxygen for my power cell and expelling waste gasses that had been consumed, I still needed to do it about every five minutes or I'd die from my power cell shutting down. Not to mention he might be strong enough to crush my windpipe, so that I'd never breathe again.

I clawed desperately at his hand trying to break free. My vision began to blur as he stood there holding me. It was as if he was trying to decide what to do. In one swift motion, he threw me backwards, and I landed back down in the deep pool at the base of the median.

Slamming into the water knocked me senseless and I felt myself settle into the mud, three feet below the surface. After a second or so, he jerked me up and out of the pool by the front of my blouse. The android was standing in the waist deep water, holding me with his left hand again. I desperately kept trying anything to get my legs to function, but it just wasn't happening. Without warning, he backhanded me. My head snapped to the side and before I could even think, he followed up with a slap across the other cheek. The masochistic bastard fell into a sick rhythm, slapping me back and forth until I lost count of how many times I'd been hit. Blood filled my mouth and I fought back, clawing at his eyes, scratching at his face. All I managed to do was rip some gashes across his cheeks and knock his sunglasses off. When he had finally tired of the slapping game, he held me still and just stared. Lifting my head, I met his stare with a burning intensity…and then spat in his face.

He didn't react to my insult, didn't look angry or upset in the least. The emotionless android wiped his eyes clean of my blood, drew back his fist, and punched me in the stomach. It felt like he'd used a baseball bat, and the impact tore my blouse apart where he'd been holding onto it. I fell backwards into the water for what I was sure would be the last time.

I was doubled up in pain and sinking to the bottom. His punch had knocked all the breath from me and my head was pounding. If I couldn't get away from him, he was going to kill me…but how? Running my hands over my legs trying to get them to respond, I actually thought I felt one of them move. Could I really be that lucky? I tried to pull them closer to my chest, and when I felt them respond, it was the greatest feeling in the world. I let myself settle to the bottom, keeping my body in the shape of a ball. My feet touched the soft mud and I reached out with my hands, searching for anything I could use to defend myself. All I found was a short stick with a ball-shaped end, but it was better than nothing. Planting my feet, I worked them into the soft ground as far as possible, and inclined myself forward just a touch. I turned the stick around and placed the larger, rounded end into my right palm, and wrapped my fingers tightly around it. I changed my vision over to thermal and waited…waited for my chance to strike.

The red thermal pattern of his arm broke the surface of the water, moving straight for my face. I waited until his arm was in reach, and I shot my left hand out and grabbed him by the wrist. Pushing against the muddy grass as hard as I could, I erupted out of the water and stood in front of him. I blinked and switched back to normal vision so I could see his face by the flames of my car. His expression was blank as he looked at me, figuring out how to counter what I'd just done, he never had the chance. I pulled him toward me by his left arm as I swung my right fist toward his face, with all the strength I had left. Even though he tried to duck under my attack, I'd anticipated the move and adjusted my swing accordingly. My fist connected so hard with the side of his face, that his left wrist was pulled out of my grip and the stick was torn free of my hand.

He staggered backward and lowered his head into his hands. I was ready for some kind of ploy, but he made no move toward me. Raising his head back up, I saw why. My stick was lodged in his left eye socket. However, as I looked closer, I saw it wasn't a stick at all. It was the manual gear shifter from my Civic!

His one remaining eye was fixed on me as he grabbed the end of the shifter and pulled it out of his face. A thick, silver fluid flowed freely out of the jagged hole, and for the first time, the android spoke. Well, it wasn't actually speech. He opened his mouth and a shrill, ear-piercing wail came out that sounded like a burst of digital static.

"EEESCRRSHBRPERERERRBPBRPEEE"

Shortly after that, he fell back in the water, unmoving. I took a deep breath, then turned away and left him as he disappeared, deeper and deeper under the dark surface.

It was a struggle to get back out of the median. My body hurt everywhere and I was running on instinct. Finally, I reached the top and looked around in a daze. Back down I-459, there was a car with a blue light on its roof, holding back what little traffic was on the road tonight. Someone was in front of the car talking to some drivers, but I couldn't make out any details about them. In the other direction, my poor car was still burning. I knew I had to leave this place, but I wanted just one last look at my faithful Honda, and my friend Takumi. Taking a step toward my car, my foot kicked something hard. Looking down, I saw the tire iron the android had swung at me from his car. I picked it up and turned it around in my hand, realizing how fortunate I was to be alive. As it was, my clothes were shredded, I'd lost both my shoes, and my body was beaten so badly, it might take the EmBees a week to put me back together. With one last glance over to the Civic, I knew…

"EEESCRRSHBRPERERERRBPBRPEEE"

I whirled around and saw that the android had somehow gotten out of the median. He was about ten feet away, crawling slowly toward me. He kept making that awful sound every few seconds, and I decided it was some kind of emergency beacon or alert protocol. His one good eye was fixed on me, as he pulled himself along the asphalt. I held out the tire iron for him to see, and swung it between us a few times. I wanted to show him what would happen if he didn't stop. He ignored me and kept coming. He was one tenacious bastard. I looked at my car, and then back to the one-eyed android. I'd given him the last chance he'd ever get from me.

He finally crawled close enough for me to swing at him, and I didn't hesitate. I brought the tire iron down on top of his head using both hands, and he emitted that same sound again.

"EEESCRRSHBRPERERERRBPBRPEEE"

"Damn it, shut up!" I yelled and swung at his head again.

This time when the weapon struck, there was a dull, wet, cracking sound. The android was only able to screech half the noise before his body convulsed a couple of times, and came to a complete rest.

"EEESCRRSHBRPERER…"

I tossed down the tool and said, "That was for Takumi, you son of a bitch."

Now I really needed to get out of here. There were some trees and bushes next to the interstate and I made straight for them. My plan was to stick to the wooded areas, and use them to hide myself as I snuck home. I could keep myself from getting lost and take the best route by using my built-in satellite navigation. Now if I had only been sure that I was strong enough to make it home. Oh well, at least it had stopped raining.

Chapter 18

Like a wild animal, I crept through the woods, slowly making my way toward the apartment. The darkness of the night was almost complete, with the clouds obscuring the stars and moon. Most of the time, I stuck to using my thermal vision, except when I neared a place where the streetlights illuminated the line between nature and civilization. In some areas, the foliage had breaks that were exposed. I ran across those, getting back into the cover of the trees as quickly as possible.

I moved as cautiously as I could, but the ground was uneven and unforgiving. Stones tore at the bottom of my feet and tree roots that I couldn't see caused me to trip. I fell so many times that the palms of my hands became cut and bruised from hitting the ground. However, it wasn't just the roots and rocks that had it in for me, there was also the briars and brambles. They would wrap themselves around my legs, tearing dozens of tiny, yet painful, scratches anywhere they touched. Sometimes I'd get tangled in them all around my arms and chest. Their sharp, ripping barbs dug into my flesh, and a few of them broke off under my skin. After a few encounters with the briars, I felt like a very effective, medieval torture device was being used on me. I kept going. I had no choice.

After the rain had moved on, the temperature dropped rapidly. I was okay for a while, but about half way home, I began to shiver uncontrollably. Normally, fifty degrees wouldn't be that much of an issue, but between my drenched clothes, the savage beating, the constant attacks from Mother Nature, *and* the temperature...well that was apparently too much for my body to handle. I focused on taking just one step at a time, never stopping. Because I knew if I stopped, I wouldn't be able to get moving again.

Struggling for each step, I kept myself lurching forward. After what felt like hours, I emerged at the rear of my apartment complex. I was going to make it. Having memorized where all the security cameras were located, I zigzagged around the backyards of the other tenants until I reached the wall under my apartment. There were too many cameras facing the front of the complex, and I really didn't want to be seen in this shape. Besides, another one of those androids could be watching my front entrance. I needed to find a way up to my balcony, where I could enter through its door.

Searching around, I found a sturdy-looking garden hose that would do the trick. I tossed it around one of the wrought iron support corners of my balcony and was able to get it wedged into place. Pulling myself off the ground, I placed my feet against the rough brick wall of the building and began to climb. The constant pain and shivering turned what should have been an easy task into a struggle for every inch. I slipped once when I placed my left foot down and a stabbing pain distracted me. Holding on for my life, I repositioned myself and continued climbing.

I reached the iron support and used it to ease myself over the waist-high railing. Detaching the garden hose, I tossed it back in the direction I'd found it. As I neared my patio door, I imitated my iPhone and transmitted the unlock code. I mouthed a silent 'Thank You', when the click of the lock told me I could enter. Stumbling through the living room, I collapsed onto the sofa without even turning on any lights. A coughing attack struck me and after it subsided, I saw blood on my hands. Damn it, I was in a desperate situation, and had no one I could turn to for help. I'd just have to tough it out.

There was one thing I needed to do before I could rest. Any traces of my Honda with the DMV had to be destroyed. The last thing I needed was the police knocking on my door and asking a bunch of questions about a car fire. I'd need to interfuse and destroy the records before the police traced the vehicle back to me. I stood up, heading toward the kitchen, but when I did, a wave of dizziness came over me. It was so intense, that I fell to the floor, unable to get my bearings. A bitter feeling of cold struck me next, and my teeth chattered uncontrollably. Drawing myself into a fetal position, I tried to get warm, but I couldn't stop shaking. I began to realize that I might die here on the floor of my apartment...all alone.

My body failing me, the only thing I could do was interfuse. I must have blacked out for a few seconds, because the next thing I remembered was lying on the ground with thousands of twinkling 'stars' of the Internet above me. If this was my last few moments, I was determined not to die alone.

I called out, "Athena, please aid me in finding what I seek."

My voice was nothing but a weak whisper. There was no way she could have heard me. I inhaled to try again, but more coughing cut me off. Oh well, if I was going to die alone, at least it would be with a beautiful view of the stars.

The next thing I knew was Athena bending over me. She was shaking me and yelling, "Anna, do not let your life fade away! Fight to stay here! Fight I say!"

I smiled weakly at her and reached up to touch her cheek with my trembling, blood-spattered hand. "You came. I'm not alone. Good."

She grabbed my hand in hers and fire burned in her eyes. "Anna, what is it that you seek? Answer me!"

I managed to whisper, "Help me."

She looked relieved for a second, then her expression turned serious. "Good Anna, now you must listen to me and do as I say. You are going into shock. You must let me into your mind as you did before. Except this time, you must let me share control with you. We must become as one if you want to live. Anna, did you hear me! You are slipping away! Let me in before it is too late. Please, you must trust me! It is the only way! Anna, open your mind now!"

I could hear her words, but they sounded so distant. She was kneeling down, holding my head in her lap, but I couldn't feel her. Eliza was the only other person to get into my head and have some control there. She was able to do it because our brains work on the same principle, and at the time, I was too weak to stop her. Since that, I'd been very guarded about my mind…but what the hell…I was about to die anyway. As my vision faded to black, I dropped the defenses on my mind and activated the hard connection in the hand Athena held.

"Come on in. Sorry about the mess," was the last thing I said to her before I blacked out.

I woke up sometime later, surprised to be alive. As I assessed my situation, I noticed my arm around someone's neck and somehow I was standing upright. Turning to see who was supporting me, I was shocked to see Athena to my right. She had her left arm around my waist, holding me up as we shuffled toward my bedroom.

Noticing that I was conscious, she said, "Thank the stars, you are still with us. I thought that you had delayed too long before allowing me to enter. Now, sit down here on your bed while I draw you a hot bath."

I didn't know what to say, this just wasn't possible. Not knowing what else to do, I followed her instructions as she gently sat me on the bed and hurried off into my bathroom. I heard the water turn on and after adjusting it to her liking, she returned.

I looked up at her and asked, "How?"

Concern was written across her face, but my question summoned a brief smile. "My help was what you sought, so I am providing it. Now, shall we remove those rags which you wear?"

The dazed expression that I wore must have not been the answer she wanted. "Very well, be still and I will try to hurt you as little as possible."

She leaned over and began to undress me. Even though she was being as tender as possible, I still winced from stabs of pain several times, especially around my ribs. Athena helped me back to my feet and began to walk me toward the bath. Halfway there, I was beset by violent muscle spasms and trembling.

"Be calm now, we are almost there," she said.

We reached the tub, and she gently lowered me into the warm water, which came up to my neck. Athena shut off the faucets, and held my hand as my shaking slowly subsided.

"Excellent, now I will fetch you nutrients and drinking water if you promise me not to pass out and drown while I am away," she said.

I nodded my agreement, and she rushed out of the room. The warmth of the water was wonderful, feeling was already returning to my toes and fingers. I moved them around while trying to clear the fog from my mind. How could this be happening? Athena wasn't a physical being. I thought back to the first time that Eliza had invaded my mind. She created a nightmarish dream that had almost killed me. Then I realized, this must only be a dream as well. That was the only thing that made sense. However, if this was just a dream, where *was* I, really? On the floor in the living room as my life slipped away? I sighed and resigned myself to the dream, it was a hell of a lot less painful than my last few hours of reality had been. Besides, if I was collapsed somewhere dying, there wasn't anything I could do about it now.

Athena returned with my vitamins and three bottles of SmartWater. She sat them down near the tub and said, "Here, consume this as soon as you can. Do not tarry."

"I know this is but a dream, but I really appreciate you being here, Athena," I said.

"For the next part of my treatment, I do not think you will feel the same way about me as you do right now. However, do not worry, there will be plenty of time to appreciate me later," she said giving me a little wink.

I must have had a puzzled look, because she explained her intentions in more detail. "Anna, you have many foreign objects lodged in your skin. I must remove them and clean the wounds. I fear this will be quite uncomfortable for you."

"Do not concern yourself, I will use my pain-dulling ability as much as I can. Do what you must," I said.

She reached out and ran her fingers through my hair, her face full of compassion for me. "Very well, I shall fetch some tools for the job. Please try to eat and drink, you desperately need nourishment."

Athena disappeared again, and I followed her advice. Leaning over the tub, I grabbed a bottle of water and vitamins. I took a handful of the pills and chugged the drink. The water felt so cool and refreshing on my injured mouth, that I opened a second one and downed it as well. I began to cough again, so violently, that I almost vomited as my mouth filled with that familiar copper taste. Sitting up, I reached for my trashcan and spat the blood into it. That bastard must have injured my lungs while he was treating me as a punching bag. I wasn't sure if the EmBees could repair internal organs. After all, they'd never completely rehabilitated me from the brain injury that Eliza had given me. She was the reason I couldn't eliminate my pain entirely, and damn her for that.

The bathroom door opened and Athena entered carrying a small folded towel. Placing it on the floor next to the tub, she opened it to reveal her trauma kit. There was a pair of tweezers, a washcloth, and a small paring knife. She noticed the blood in the garbage and frowned.

"I am unsure of how your internal organs operate, but if you were a human, I would believe you to have cracked ribs and perhaps a punctured lung," she said as she knelt down near the foot of the bathtub.

"However, since I cannot assist with that issue, I will focus on the injuries I *can* treat. Let us start at the bottom and work our way up, shall we?" she said.

Leaning over the tub, she reached in and lightly lifted one of my legs. Using the tweezers, she began inspecting me for any briars, rocks, or car shrapnel that might be lodged in my skin. When she located a foreign body, she took the tweezers and plucked it out, tossing it into the garbage can. As she finished an area, like a leg or arm, Athena used the washcloth to scrub any cuts and abrasions clean of grime.

Most of the time, the objects were close to the surface, but some of the car shrapnel was deeper. As she worked to remove it using the paring knife and tweezers, I noticed she winced as much as I did. This must have been strenuous for her. The task was so far outside her original design.

For the next thirty minutes, she painstakingly examined me, at least as best she could with me sitting in the tub. The experience was similar to running through the woods, stabbing little pains all over my body, but this was easier to bear since I knew it was to help me heal. When Athena leaned back, finally finished, the bath water was tinged pink with the blood from a hundred cuts.

She wiped the sweat from her brow and said, "Now, we shall get you out of there, and you shall find comfort in your warm bed."

I stood up and Athena helped to steady me as I got out of the tub. She helped me to dry off, and then we went into the bedroom. The bed was already prepared, sheets turned down and blankets resting on the side. I also noticed there were some large strips of cloth bandages placed at the foot of the bed.

I turned to her and asked, "Hey, was that one of my sheets?"

"You must be feeling somewhat better if your concerns have turned to how I am using your bed linen, Anna. Please lie down so I may examine the areas of your body I could not access while you were in the bathtub," she wryly said.

I did as I was told, and Athena checked me out from top to bottom, finding two more pieces of shrapnel and removing them. After she finished the exam, she began wrapping my feet with the cloth bandages.

"You will need to wear this until your soles heal. They are in terrible shape," she said.

After wrapping a few more of my larger wounds, she pulled the covers over me and placed a blanket on top.

"I will fetch you something more to eat and drink," she said as she let the room. Shortly, she returned and sat the water and vitamins down on my nightstand.

"There now, I believe you are ready for a bit of rest," she said as she sat down on the side of the bed.

I worked my arm free of the covers and grabbed her hand. "Please do not go. I fear that when you leave and I fall asleep, I shall not awake."

She looked down at me and smiled. "Move to your left and I will stay here with you."

I slid myself over to give her room, and she lay down next to me on top of the covers. Taking my hand in hers, she said, "There, I will stay here while you rest. Worry not."

I realized that this was just a dream, and when I fell asleep, I would never wake again, but my mind was at peace. Gripping Athena's hand, I knew I wasn't alone as the darkness of sleep overtook me.

Chapter 19

I woke up the next morning resting comfortably in my bed, which was a surprise in itself. However, when I realized I was still holding Athena's hand, I was shocked. Was I having a mental breakdown? Was I still dreaming? What the hell was going on? As I released her hand and propped myself up in the bed, she woke up as well. She looked over to me and I noticed her eyes had bags under them and they were missing their usual sparkle. I didn't know how long she'd slept, but she looked exhausted. As I stared, trying to figure out if I was sane, she greeted me.

"Good morning, Anna. I see you are looking much better today. How do you feel?" she said as she sat up and began fussing with her tiara.

It took me a few seconds to find my voice, but finally I said, "Uh, fine. I feel much better, Athena. Thank you for everything you did last night. By the way, not to sound ungrateful, but are you actually here with me or am I hallucinating?"

She stood and worked on straightening her white silk robes as she answered me. "You sought my help and allowed me to enter your mind, therefore I did so. I stayed with you while you slept because you asked me not to leave. As far as whether or not you are hallucinating, that is more difficult to answer, for I am with you only inside your consciousness."

I moved myself up in the bed until I was sitting with my back against the headboard. As I tried to wrap my head around what she was saying, I realized I was naked. Not only that, but I had the bandages on my feet that Athena had put on them last night. I looked past where she stood, and saw the water and vitamins on the nightstand, just as I'd dreamed. Except it couldn't have been a dream if I was awake now. This was making my head hurt more than it already did. I tried a more direct line of questioning to see how she'd answer.

"Athena, can you please explain to me how you were able to do what you did last night and what I'm seeing now?" I asked.

She had finished arranging her gown and handed me the water and vitamins from the nightstand before answering.

"Drink some water and take your nutrients while I explain. When you let me into your consciousness last night, you were near death. In desperation, I tried a technique, which would only work on *you*, a non-organic being. After we merged our minds together, I shifted a limited number of your processes to myself. I helped you manage your pain, along with controlling your autonomic nervous system functions such as breathing and heart rate. I even attempted to direct the course of your repairs by communicating with your EmBees, but there were far too many of them, and I abandoned the attempt. This allowed your mind to focus on repairs. All the things you perceived me doing for you, you actually did for yourself once I was able to lessen the strain on your neural net brain," she said.

I couldn't believe what I was hearing. "So what you're saying is that you split my mind into logical processes and transferred some of the workload to yourself? The way one might add another server to speed up execution of a complex calculation?"

She looked at me as if the answer was obvious, "Yes, exactly. Since your mind is, at its core, a complex computer program, I was able to run our thoughts and desires together, parallel processing as it is normally called."

"And it worked?" I asked, still in shock.

"Surprisingly, yes," she deadpanned.

"But how? How would you understand the way my neural net mind worked? Even I don't understand its complexities," I said.

"I am not sure how I was able to do what I did. All I can tell you is that you needed my help, so I had to try. Once I began, it all simply fell into place. It felt…natural, self evident," she said.

I slowly shook my head in disbelief. Only one other *person* had ever been able to infiltrate my mind to that level. Then I realized, she was still in there, at least to some degree. "So, how many of my processes are you still running?" I asked.

"None, now. I transferred them back to you as your condition stabilized throughout the night," she replied.

"So, I am off the android version of life support then, that is a relief. However, if I am running all my own processes, why can I still see you here in the real world?" I asked.

"You are still interfused, and I wanted to stay present in your mind until I was sure you were functioning properly," she said with true concern in her voice.

I frowned, because I felt like I'd given her the third degree. "Listen, Athena, please forgive my rudeness. The situation sounded so fantastic that it took me by surprise. I will forever be in your debt for saving my life."

"Think nothing of it, you sought my help, and I provided it. It is what I do," she said.

Her wording sounded strange, so I said, "You gave me what I searched for, is that what you're saying?"

She smiled and proudly replied, "Of course, for I am Athena, and it is my purpose!"

The realization of what she said hit me hard, but I wanted to test my hypothesis, just to be sure. I looked up to her and said, "You know, since I feel so much better, I really would like to find a companion, maybe even a lover."

Her mood shifted instantly from passionate caregiver to, well, just passionate. Her brown eyes burned with desire and she sat back down on the bed. She inched closer and closer to me as she purred. "I am so pleased to hear that, Anna. I can provide what you seek without any doubt."

Before she got too close, I said, "On second thought, I do not feel very well. I should probably just rest and try to get better."

Again, her whole demeanor changed, and she sat back up straight at the edge of the bed. "Yes, you should. Please continue to take your vitamins and drink your water."

I sighed to myself. Athena wasn't an artificial intelligence like me, she was more like a service provider. She existed to give users whatever they sought, nothing more, nothing less. Not to belittle her, she was the best in the world at what she did, and she had without a doubt saved my life.

This also explained a few nights ago when she tried to kiss me, I'd been thinking about, *searching* for, someone to have a relationship with. While she was eager to provide me with what I was seeking, she wasn't someone that could enter into a true relationship. She would always simply do whatever I asked, and find me whatever I wanted. Still, I would always count her a true friend.

Athena spoke and brought me out of my reflection. "If you are healed enough, I will disconnect from your mind, and focus on my duties."

"Absolutely, you have been a wondrous friend. I will never be able to repay you. I will disconnect from my interfuse connection, but I will see you in your world in a few minutes. There are things I must accomplish today," I said.

She grinned at me and said, "It was a pleasure to serve you, Anna."

I returned the smile warmly and terminated my interfuse connection to the Internet. Instantly, she faded from view, and I was left alone in my apartment. Reestablishing the protections for my mind and consciousness, I eased myself out of the bed and headed for the bathroom. I needed to examine my wounds and take a shower. It was already after eight in the morning.

During my shower, I connected to the Internet by impersonating my iPhone and sent an email to Felix telling him that I'd been up all night with some kind of stomach bug. I let him know that while I couldn't come into work, I'd try to get some things done from home. Before I'd finished drying off, he'd replied with the standard 'get better soon' email.

Checking myself in the bathroom's mirror, I saw that I was covered in at least a hundred scratches, bruises, and various abrasions. My scalp ached, it was still difficult to walk, and my face was still swollen from the beating, but at least I hadn't coughed up any blood this morning. My guess was the EmBees knew where to focus their efforts and were targeting the critical injuries first.

I went into the bedroom and found a nice comfortable gray sweatsuit to wear. After dressing, I reestablished my interfuse connection with the Internet and called out to my friend from last night.

"Wise and powerful Athena, please help me find what I seek!" I shouted.

Within seconds, she had flown in on Pegasus and landed a few feet away. I noticed that she looked just as radiant and beautiful as ever, much better than when I'd saw her a couple of hours earlier.

She came running up to me and gently hugged me, "I am glad to see that you are up and about. Your recuperative powers are truly amazing."

"Well, I am fairly sure I had some help with that," I said with a wink.

She giggled and asked, "What adventure are we to embark on today?"

"Well, although I may be too late, I need to find the vehicle records for my car and destroy them before the police can research the car fire on I-459 last night," I said.

Her eyes grew big, and she said, "Yes, I know. It sounded horrendous. No wonder you became so critically injured."

"You have information on it already?" I asked.

She just looked at me for a second. "Surely you jest."

"I am sorry, I forgot to whom I was speaking," I said, "Can you please let me see the Alabama headlines for today?"

Athena reached into her robes and pulled out a parchment. She handed it to me and I unrolled it, reading as quickly as I could. The first story I saw was about the car fire, it had been reported by three of the local news stations, but there were very little details except that it was currently under investigation by the local authorities. Hmm, no mention of a body or any other vehicles at the scene…I wondered if the other person I'd seen last night had cleaned up the broken android and got out of there before the real police had arrived.

As I searched around on the scroll for any more information about my adventure on the interstate, the stories became increasingly bizarre. First, there was one about the Alabama DMV. Apparently, a group of unknown hackers had launched a denial of service attack on the DMV's mainframe. The system had been down since late last night and there was no estimate on when it would become available.

Right next to that story, was one about Athena herself. It stated that most of the southern United States was experiencing slow response times whenever a user performed a search. Some queries were taking up to five seconds to return any results at all. According to the engineers working at the Athena home offices, they were tracking down the issue and would have it resolved by noon today.

It all clicked in my mind, but I couldn't believe it. I turned to her and asked, "Have you been performing a DOS attack on the Alabama DMV since last night?"

"Well, I knew that you needed to destroy the record of your car before the police tracked its purchase back to you, and you were in no shape to undertake that adventure last night. So yes, I have been asking the DMV so many questions that it cannot possibly respond," she said as if it were something she did every day.

"This is why you are slow to service your users here in the South, isn't it?" I asked.

"Yes, even with all my great power, it has kept me very busy. However, it was something you needed, and we are friends, so I provided all the support I was able," she said.

"What if the authorities figure out what has been going on?" I asked.

She lifted her chin some and said, "They cannot, I am Athena."

She said it with such certainty, that I could not doubt her. "It appears I am even more in your debt than I knew. Thank you my friend."

I reached out and hugged her close, and she whispered in my ear, "You would have done the same for me."

"Yes, you are of course correct," I whispered back.

Once our embrace ended, I said, "If you can keep up that DOS attack for a few more minutes, I would like to travel to the DMV and speak with them about my records."

"Of course, let us mount and be away!" she said.

Pegasus flew us quickly to the dull gray office we had visited a little over a week ago. Except this time, the scene outside the building was much different. It was under siege. An angry mob of people, at least twenty deep, surrounded the DMV. They had broken out most of the windows and were still throwing rocks, bottles, or whatever they could get their hands on. The security guards that had been here last time, were huddling in the entryway, shielding themselves from the flying debris.

The mob appeared to be full of random people, but as I looked closer and analyzed them, their faces all began to shimmer and take on the distinct features of Athena. I leaned forward and spoke to her.

"No one else can see their true form, correct?"

She nodded and said, "That is right, you are the only one that I have ever met with the skill to expose their true form. They are all from my servers, so they all contain a small part of me."

"Worry not, I will keep your secret," I said.

We circled the building, trying to locate the DMV mainframe among all the confusion. Spotting him on our second go round, I pointed and called out to Athena.

"There he is, near the back exit!"

She guided Pegasus lower, and we landed as close as possible. As we slid to the ground, I said, "Will we be able to make it to him?"

She just smiled at me and began walking forward. As we neared the crowd, they parted just enough to let us pass. Of course, they were all *her* minions. She could command them to do as she wished.

We made our way up to the disheveled looking DMV mainframe. He was handing out documents as fast as he could, but all the screaming users and their unending requests overwhelmed him. I decided I could use this to my advantage.

When I was close enough, I shouted at him. "DMV, I need the documentation for VIN number JC3AZ419ZTA392124."

He was so harried, that he didn't even question my demand. Jamming a folder into my hand, he turned to the next screaming user as fast as he could. I looked at Athena, and nodded. Opening the file, I passed my hand over the pages and concentrated, transforming all my personal information into random characters. Upon any examination, it would appear as if the document had been the victim of massive data corruption.

Holding out the folder, I called out to the DMV mainframe again. "Thank you, please file this document back into the system."

He grabbed it out of my hand and jammed it into his coat without even looking at it. My task was done. Athena and I turned and walked slowly through the crowd heading back toward Pegasus.

When we had made it back, I said, "How much longer are you going to torment the DMV?"

"As a matter of fact, no longer," she replied.

As she spoke, we mounted Pegasus and she had him take to the sky. Looking down, I could see that the crowd had become very quiet, and they were shuffling away from the building in various directions.

Shaking my head in disbelief, I told her, "I truly hope you encounter no ill from what you have done for me."

"It will all be fine, do not concern yourself," she shouted back over the rushing wind.

Soon we landed back at where she had picked me up. I leapt off Pegasus and thanked her again before watching her fly away. Disconnecting from the interfuse session, I found myself back in my apartment. I was feeling tired, so I had some more vitamins and water before connecting to my workstation at FlexJen. There was some work I wanted to finish, and then maybe a little rest before my last task of the day.

What happened last night was never going to happen again. When I decided to escape from the lab where I was created, it was because I wanted to live a peaceful human life. Since that choice, I've had so much pain and death rained down upon me that I couldn't run from it anymore. Before tonight was over, I'd have a weapon. I may not have started this fight, but I'd damn sure finish it.

Chapter 20

Checking the Internet, the nearest gun store with a practice range, was several miles to the south, near Oak Mountain State Park. *The Lock and Load*, had been in the same location for years, and the online reviews for it were almost all positive. I thought it sounded like a good place to start, but unfortunately, my poor Civic was no longer with me. Impersonating my iPhone, I called for a cab and the dispatcher at the AA Taxi Service told me to allow fifteen minutes for the driver to arrive at my apartment. That gave me just enough time to head into the bedroom and get ready to leave.

Once there, I thumbed through my clothes searching for just the right look. I found a burnt orange, angora sweater that buttoned in the front, along with a pair of low-rise jeans, and some open-toed, black leather heels. I slipped out of my comfortable sweats and into my outfit. Checking my look in the bathroom mirror, I decided it was perfect, especially when I left a few of the sweater's buttons undone. Luckily, my clothing covered most of my scratches and my face looked only a little swollen…and I could fix my face.

I'd dressed this way because I wanted to attract as much attention from the guys at the gun shop as possible, just while looking like someone else. Watching in the mirror, I concentrated on changing my appearance. I eliminated the swelling in my face, and added a couple of small crow's feet at the corners of my eyes. My hair turned a dirty yellowish blonde, and lengthened until it was a couple of inches past the collar of my sweater. I increased the heft of my breasts and rear, until my clothes were a bit too tight. A few wrinkles on the tops of my hands and a higher pitched voice with a deep southern drawl completed my change. Now I was Tammy Hayes, mid-thirties southern bell, that just needed something to protect herself. I'd created the identity in case I was forced to disappear again, but I needed it tonight to purchase my gun.

My phone lay on the bathroom vanity, and I picked it up hoping that it was still working after the abuse of last night. The thick, protective case I'd bought on my trip to the Apple store Monday had done its job, and the iPhone turned on with no problems. Now I could work on changing out its stored personal identity from Anna, to Tammy. Because of all the encryption and protection, it was always difficult, and a tad risky, which was why I only did it when necessary. I plugged the nail of my index finger into the data port on the iPhone and began the exchange. All Tammy's data flowed into the phone, while I backed up Anna's information inside my head. When I finished, I double-checked my work and everything looked fine. The iPhone rang as I was putting it into my back pocket, and I saw that it was the cab company. This cabbie had impeccable timing.

The driver wore a loose flannel shirt and jeans as he stood next to his cab. As I approached, he opened my door and said, "Good afternoon ma'am, this way please."

I suppressed a chuckle at him calling me ma'am. While he looked to be in his early twenties, I was sure he'd spent more days on this earth than me. I simply smiled back at him and replied, "Now, no reason to be so formal, I'm Tammy Hayes, but you can just call me Tammy."

"Will do Tammy, and my name is Paul Graves, but if you like, you can call me Paul," he said as he closed my door and climbed back into the front seat.

"Now, where can I take you today, Tammy?" he asked.

I read him the name and address of the gun shop, and he said,

"Alright, buckle up and we're on our way."

We pulled onto Highway 31, and he maneuvered through the traffic, finding his place among the other cars. Looking in his rearview mirror, he fiddled with his long black hair and asked, "So Tammy, am I dropping you off, or do I need to hang around for a while?"

I met his eyes and replied, "I'm gonna need you to wait for me Paul. It might be a couple of hours, but I'll of course pay you to stay. That's not a problem, is it?"

He shook his head and pointed to the passenger's seat. "No, not at all. I have some homework I can work on, but you'd probably come out cheaper renting a car than paying me for this ride."

I glanced where he indicated and saw a couple of college books sliding around in his front seat. One was on philosophy and the other religion. "Well now, I sure do appreciate your candor, Paul, but my car just plain quit on me, and I really needed to get this done quickly. So y'all were the first people I thought to call," I said.

"Fair enough. It'll just take a few minutes to get there," he said.

We chatted about his college life for the last few miles, but before long, Paul was turning into the parking lot for The Lock and Load. He pulled into a spot and turned to look at me, "I hate to ask, but the company requires a deposit if we're going to wait like this."

"Don't you worry yourself about it. Here, " I said as I activated my iPhone and sent my payment to his company.

His phone made a 'cha-ching' sound, and he leapt out of the cab to open my door. "Thank you Tammy, I'll be right here waiting on you. Happy shopping!" he called out as I made my way toward the entrance of the gun shop.

Approaching the store, there were several signs hanging in the window warning of twenty-four hour video surveillance and similar things.

However, my favorite was a sign that read, 'We reserve the right to refuse service to anyone Betsy doesn't like.' I wasn't sure who Betsy was, but she must have a lot of clout.

Before I pulled open the single glass door, I peeked inside to see that the small shop was jumping. There were five employees behind the counter trying to help around twelve customers. I pulled the door open and a huge cowbell hanging on the other side banged around making a loud clunking sound. The four men, and one woman behind the counter turned toward the noise, and then the men did a double take as they saw me walk in, just the reaction I'd wanted.

Everything about The Lock and Load said firearms. Rifles, shotguns, and other long guns hung from the walls behind the counters. Waist high, glass displays ran around all three walls of the shop and displayed hundreds of revolvers, semi-automatics, and even two shot derringers. Two four-foot display islands ran the length of the store and created the three isles in the shop. On those, you could find holsters, targets, laser sights, or any other accessory you could imagine. At the end of one of the islands, was a statue of General George S. Patton in full military uniform, while the other had a bargain barrel full of thirty round AR-15 magazines for twenty-five dollars each. A smell of gun powder and fine leather with just a hint of firearm cleaning chemicals filled my nose, while the sounds of weapons being inspected rung in my ears. There were hammers striking empty chambers, shotguns being pumped, and semi-automatics were having their slides pulled back and forth.

Two of the men working behind the counters had gone back to helping other customers, but the other two, standing next to each other, were still looking at me. The man on the left was thin, in his mid twenties, and had a clean-shaven face, while the other was chunky, probably early thirties, and had a short, but bushy, black beard. Reading the body language of the large, bearded man, I knew he would be the one to help me. I began strolling toward them, making sure to thrust my hips out to the side and bounce the curves that were only partially contained by my sweater. My heels clicked loudly against the aged oak floor as I took my time approaching the counter. When I at last drew close, the large man leaned over and whispered something to his coworker. The thinner one sighed and left to help someone on the other side of the store. I smiled at the overweight man waiting for me to reach him. Some people were just easier to read than others.

When I arrived at the counter, the waiting man greeted me with a large grin and introduced himself. "Hello Miss, my name is Dale Dupree, the proprietor of The Lock and Load. What can I help you with this afternoon?"

I flashed my largest smile and replied in my best southern fried accent. "Well hi there Dale, I'm Tammy, Tammy Hayes, and I'd like to get a pistol from you."

"Well, I might have a few of those," he quipped.

I giggled and with a little squeal in my voice said, "Sure enough?"

He chuckled back and asked, "Well, I need to ask you a few questions so we can see what to sell you. First, have you ever handled a gun before, and if so, how experienced would you consider yourself?"

"Well, it's like this Dale. I've sure shot a handgun before. It was that time I was over in Russia for a student exchange program. The family that took me in for the summer showed me how to shoot a gun they had. I got real good with it, now what'd they call it, uh, martini, macaroni…"

"Makarov?" he asked.

"Yeah, that's it! It was a Makarov. Do y'all have any of them?" I asked.

He stared at me for a second, then slapped the counter top and erupted with laughter. "Oh, Tammy, you quit pulling my leg now."

"No, no, I'm serious as a heart attack! Here, I'll speak some Russian for you," I said.

I cleared my throat and looked thoughtful for a moment. Then switching over to perfect Russian I said, "Я хотел бы купить Макаров."

Dale's laugh died away, and he just stared at me. I went back to Tammy's accent and said, "Oh, now don't look like that, I didn't say nothing nasty. I just said *I would like to buy a Makarov.*"

"Well, shit fire! You were serious! Hell, I'm sorry I doubted you Tammy. But I have some bad news. We don't have any Makarovs in stock. There's just no call for them. I'd be happy to order you one if you like. Probably take about a week or so to get it here," he said.

Nope, I could be dead in a week, I thought to myself.

"Well Dale, my boyfriend travels a lot and I get spooked staying alone at night. Is there another gun you'd recommend?" I asked.

"You need to tell that boyfriend of yours to stay home and keep you safe! I know *I* would," he said.

"Why Dale, you dog…are you hitting on me?" I giggled.

He shook his head and said, "Tammy, let me tell you, I'm a happily married man. So no, that wouldn't be proper. But, just because I'm married, don't mean I'm blind."

Winking at me, he began to chuckle. I covered my mouth in false shock and playfully slapped his arm.

Dale caught his breath and leaned over behind the counter. Opening the door, he pulled out a black semiautomatic pistol. He safety checked it, and placed in on the counter in front of me.

"Here sweetie, try this. It's a Glock 19. It shoots a 9mm round which will feel almost the same as the Makarov as far as recoil. The magazine holds fifteen rounds, which is a shit ton more than the Mak does. You get a case and two extra magazines with it. You almost can't break the damn thing, *and* it's one of the cheapest guns on the market," he said.

While he was giving me the sales pitch, I picked up the gun and tried it out. It felt good in my hands, and it was lighter than my old Makarov. Doing a quick check on the Internet, I saw all the things he said about its reliability were true. Maybe it was time for a change.

"I like this one Dale. Feels good in my hand and the price is right. Just one thing, I need to call my boyfriend and see what he thinks, no offense," I said.

"None taken Tammy, you go right ahead," he said.

I pulled out my phone and pretended to make my call. What I actually did, was connect to it wirelessly and temporarily 'break' it so that it couldn't connect to any cell tower. I banged it a couple of times, then held it up for Dale to see.

"It's busted! I ain't getting any signal! Damn it!" I jammed the phone back into my back pocket and said, "Say, could I borrow yours for a second?"

Dale eyed me and said, "I don't know, we'll have to ask Betsy. She approves all purchases anyway."

"That's fair enough, who is Betsy, your wife?" I asked.

Dale's hearty laugh boomed through the store, "No, she's someone that knows more about people than any person I've ever met. Let's see if she takes a liking to ya. Betsy, come here girl!"

This Betsy person didn't worry me. I was created for this very thing. I was in my element. However, when a Golden Labrador Retriever came shuffling out of the back room and over to Dale, I was at a loss.

"So, ah, that's Betsy, I'm guessing," I said while looking at the dog nuzzling Dale's hand.

"Yup, she's lost her sight to old age, but she's still getting around pretty good. Come around the counter and say hi to her," he replied as he waved for me to come pet the dog.

I had to admit, the dog made me a tad nervous. The Internet was full of stories about how animals were much more perceptive than humans, and could do things like predict natural disasters. I wasn't sure if the tales were true, but I also didn't want to test that theory in the middle of a gun store.

As I walked behind the counter to where Betsy was happily panting away, she heard my footsteps and looked toward me. Her eyes were clouded and dull, but her face still expressed curiosity about the new stranger that was coming her way. I bent over and offered her my hand. She took a few short sniffs, and stopped, tilting her head to the side. I swear Betsy looked confused. Worried that the whole situation was about to crash and burn, I prepared myself for the worse. However, after a few moments, she began to snuffle and rub my hand as if we were old friends.

I glanced up to see what Dale thought, and caught him looking down the top of my sweater. He noticed that I'd looked up, and snapped his eyes back to my face. I frowned and teased him. "Looks like we got two dogs behind the counter, right Dale?"

He grinned and shrugged off my comment. "Betsy may be blind, but I already told you that I wasn't."

Straightening back up, I playfully slapped his arm again. "I guess since Betsy took to me like that, I passed your test."

I walked back around the counter as he said, "Yup, but then again, that dog loves everybody."

Putting my hands on my hips, I mockingly reproached him, "Dale Dupree! Do you mean to tell me that you had me come pet your dog just to get me to bend over?"

He shook his head, "Not at all Tammy. I *do* use Betsy to help me judge people's nature. If somebody looks all nervous, or if they won't come pet her at all, I know there up to no good and won't do business with them."

He paused for just a second and said in a whisper he didn't think I could hear, "Getting to look down your top was just a nice bonus."

I ignored his last comment and held out my hand. It took him a second to realize that I wanted his phone, but then he fished it out of his front pocket and handed it to me.

I pretended to punch in some numbers, and held it up to my ear. Dale was watching me too closely for the next part of my plan, so I leaned over and put my elbows on the counter. That gave him something else to look at while I placed my index finger near the bottom of the phone. I fiddled around with it until my nail slipped into the data port and I was connected to the phone's operating system. It was very simplistic, and in a few nanoseconds, I'd extracted its network password and unique device identifier code. I slid my nail back out of the phone and went on with my plan.

I yanked Dale's phone away from my head and growled, "Damn it now! He's not picking up. Here's your phone back sugar. You go on and help some of these other folks. I'll wait a while and call him back."

Dale didn't like the idea of leaving me to help the other customers, but I insisted. Finally, he caved and stomped off like a child that had been told it was bedtime. I wandered around the store, biding my time until I saw he was selling a shotgun to an older man at the front of the store. The elderly man filled out some paperwork and handed it to Dale. This was what I was waiting for.

Anytime someone purchased a gun, the store had to call some department of the federal government and have a background check performed. It was mostly painless, but the problem was, my aliases didn't have backgrounds. I hadn't taken on the challenge of hacking into a federal department, at least not yet, so I needed to work around the background check.

Dale had the man's paperwork in front of him and, after some searching, pulled the phone out of his pocket. As soon as he lifted it to his ear, I connected to the cellular network using the phone's security and identification settings that I'd just acquired, which allowed me to eavesdrop on his call. I listened intently as Dale and the agent exchanged information, taking note of every little thing about the conversation, every nuance. Once he received the approval from the agent, Dale hung up, and so did I. Now I was ready to buy my Glock.

After Dale wrapped up his shotgun sale, I called him back over. "Hey Dale, toss me your phone and let me try my call again."

He flipped it to me and I again pretended to call my boyfriend. Again, I pretended to get no answer. "What a pain in the ass, he still ain't answering his phone."

I pouted for a moment and said, "Dale, I tell you what, I trust your judgment. Let me go ahead and get a Glock 19."

He smiled and said, "Alrighty then, here, fill out this pain in the ass paperwork so I can sell you the gun. Then we can talk about any other stuff you might need."

Dale slid the paperwork over to me and I filled it out using Tammy's information. When I finished, he began the call for the background check. I intercepted the wireless signal from his phone and routed his call into my mind, like I was just another cell tower. I let his call ring a few times, then I answered it. While he was looking at my chest again, I was impersonating a federal agent and mentally talking with him about my own background check. Surprisingly enough, I was approved.

After the call, I ended up spending a tidy sum in Dale's shop. I bought the Glock 19, several boxes of ammunition, a cleaning kit, a brown leather shoulder holster, and a matching belt holster. I even got him to throw in a free month of time on their practice range after I let him "help" me try on the holsters. You know, so I had a proper fit.

I wanted to get a feel for my new purchase and be sure it was functioning properly, so I gathered up my overflowing bags of armaments and headed out behind the shop to the outdoor practice range. It had been over half a year since I'd even considered firing a weapon, but I was confident that it would all come back to me after I'd sent a few shots downrange.

Chapter 21

I lugged my bags out of The Lock and Load's backdoor and headed for the practice ranges behind the shop. Since it was a weekday, and during work hours to boot, I was the only one currently outside. This allowed me to choose whichever range I desired for my practice session. The shop had four outdoor ranges, varying in distance, and the types of targets located downrange. I decided on range number one, it was setup at a distance of twenty-five feet, perfect for handgun practice.

Picking my way down the uneven, sporadic steps that were set into the hill, I arrived at a large, wooden table located on a concrete pad next to the range. It was situated under a few large oak trees, but it also had an aluminum lean-to cover to keep your equipment dry in case of rain. Placing my bags on the table, I sat down in one of the cheap plastic chairs placed around the prepping area and began unpacking my new purchases.

I loaded up the three magazines that came with my Glock and placed them beside my pistol. Looking downrange, I saw some round, steel targets about nine inches in diameter. Some were hung from a chain, so that when you shot them they swung back and forth. Others would fall from their platform when shot and were placed back by the shooter. Next to the steel targets, the range had brackets where you could place your own paper targets for precision shooting. Since I hadn't practiced in months, I decided to start by trying to ring some steel.

194

Picking up my earplugs, I seated them snugly inside my ears. I really didn't *need* them to protect my hearing from the loud weapon, but *looking* like I did was necessary. The same went for the clear safety glasses, which fit comfortably around my eyes. I picked up my Glock and slapped a full magazine into its grip. Walking around to the front of the table, I racked the pistol's slide and chambered a round. I entered my shooting stance, and raised my weapon, aiming at one of the steel plates. I squeezed off a shot, and the steel disk I'd been aiming at rang out and fell to the ground. Dale had been right about the recoil. It *wasn't* that much more than the Makarov I'd used in my training. I aimed at the next steel plate, and fired my next shot. Again, the ringing of steel rewarded me.

I continued on, aiming, firing, hitting, until I'd emptied my magazine. It felt like I hadn't lost any accuracy over the past few months, time to see if I could fire at speed. Setting the targets that had fallen back on their pedestals, I reloaded my pistol and returned to my firing position. This time, I only fired at the steel plates that swung around when you hit them. Aiming my weapon, I double tapped all four plates making them ring out in rhythm.

ting,ting…ting,ting…ting,ting…ting,ting

Every shot struck a plate. My confidence growing, I strapped on my shoulder holster to practice drawing and shooting. To increase the difficulty, I set up one of my paper targets. It had the silhouette of a man, with scoring circles printed on the paper. Unlike the steel plates, the paper target would tell me exactly where I was able to place each one of my shots. Speed is useless without accuracy, and vice versa.

Holstering my Glock, I was impressed by the quality of the shoulder rig. I'd expected a tight, stiff fit since the leather was new, but it had been shaped and formed to hold the pistol the way a mother holds her newborn baby. If I had trouble drawing and shooting, it was all on me. I took a few practice draws, so I could get a feel for releasing the snap that held the gun in place. Once satisfied that I knew how it worked, I took a deep breath and let it back out slowly. Fast drawing my weapon and firing as rapidly as I thought prudent, I emptied the entire magazine into the paper target. It took me about eight seconds. I could have fired faster, but my shots wouldn't have been as accurate.

Speaking of accuracy, I walked downrange to check my shot placement. From twenty-five feet, I'd hit the heart of the target with all fifteen rounds, and all shots were within three inches of each other. Putting my finger through the open hole in the chest of the silhouette, I let out a slow breath, impressed with the performance of both the gun and myself. Absorbed with checking my proficiency, the sound of someone clapping from behind me was the last thing I expected.

I spun around to see who had managed to sneak up on me, and there stood Adam Sims in a dark gray three-piece suit. When his blue eyes met my gaze, he stopped clapping and sat down on the table with one hip.

Pointing at the target, he said, "That was some excellent shooting. I wouldn't want to be the one in your sights. Nice disguise by the way. If I didn't know who you were, I would never have recognized you."

I began stomping back toward him. I wasn't sure what I was going to do once I got there, but I stomped anyway. Was the NSA actually involved with what had happened to me last night? I thought so, but I didn't have any proof. As I approached, I tried my best to look menacing, but he simply sat on the table, unmoving and unconcerned. It was infuriating.

I got right into his face and moved to poke him in the chest with my finger. Before I could, he grabbed hold of my hand as it moved toward him. He never took his eyes off me as he said, "Anna, I think you should calm down before something happens we'll both regret." The calmness of his expression was, well, unnerving. I could have forced my hand forward, I knew I was stronger than him, but I didn't. Something just didn't feel right.

Once he saw that I was relaxing, he released my hand. Straightening his coat, he asked, "Why are you so upset with me anyway? I've kept my distance, haven't harassed you, and given you plenty of undisturbed time to consider my offer."

I stared at him incredulously, and retorted, "Undisturbed? Is that what you call blowing up my car and having some second rate robot beat the shit out of me?"

He blinked a few times, but his expression never changed. "Anna, I have no idea what you're talking about."

"Bullshit! You tried to kill me last night on I-459, and you came damn close to succeeding," I said a bit too loud.

He looked around to make sure we were still alone. "That was *your* car that caught fire last night? I'd read about that this morning, but had no idea it involved you." He thought for a moment and then continued. "Why would you think that was me, and did you say something about a robot?"

I'd been watching him for any signs of deception, but saw nothing. Either he was a great liar, or he really had nothing to do with last night. Damn it, I wasn't sure what to believe anymore.

"You know, since you were attacked last night, the story you told me about escaping from Russia becomes much more plausible. You may have been found by those you were running from," He said as he stood and walked to the shooting line.

He reached inside his coat, and produced a Glock 19. "By the way, fine choice of weapon."

He pointed down range at my target and asked, "Do you mind?"

I shook my head no, and leaned against the table, thinking over what he'd said. While I did, he put on his own hearing and eye protection. Then he took aim and fired at my target's head, taking a little over a second per shot. When he was finished, he had all but two of his shots within five inches of each other. Turning back to me, he shrugged and said, "Not bad, but then again, I'm only human."

Danny B. McGuire

He dropped the empty magazine from his weapon and reloaded it in one smooth motion. Then he turned his head to me and said, "Here's something we trained for at the office, firing with our off hand."

He placed his gun in his other hand, and again emptied his weapon into another spot on the target. Once he was finished, the pattern he'd made was just about the same. Even though *I* was just as proficient with either hand, I knew that was not the case with humans. He was a damn good marksman.

He walked back to the table and put his gun in front of me. "Now you try."

I looked at him, not understanding, and he said, "Have you ever tried two at once? You're an android with incredible reflexes. Give it a go. You might develop a skill that'll save your life someday."

I'd never considered wielding two pistols simultaneously. Probably because I'd never wanted to pick up one ever again after being tricked into killing that little girl back in Russia…damn you Eliza. Then again, whoever was coming after me had no qualms about using all the tricks they could think up, so perhaps he was right. After reloading our Glocks, I stepped up to the line to see if I could hit a couple of steel plates that were about ten feet apart. It was difficult to split my focus, and it took me a few seconds longer to fire all my rounds, but I was able to do it.

When I finished, I noticed that Adam had come up behind me while I was shooting. I turned to face him and he said, "There's the reflexes I was talking about. I'm not sure how you got around the background check in the store, but you might want to purchase another Glock. You know, just in case."

I handed his pistol back to him, and he reloaded it with another spare magazine. As he placed it back in his holster, he said, "Anna, have you thought about the offer I made you?"

I sighed and said, "Adam, you seem like a nice, honest person, but like I said before, I don't want to be part of that life. I don't want to spy, steal, cheat, lie, and maybe even kill. That's just not who I am."

He stared at me for a moment, with that deadpan expression of his, and then he spoke. "Said the woman that just wielded two semiautomatic pistols better than I've seen most trained professionals. Look at you, look at your abilities. You know that *this* is exactly what you were made to do. Stop fighting so hard against it. Just make sure you're fighting for the right team."

"Adam, there is no right team. If I agree to work with the NSA, eventually, I'm going to be forced to do something that I don't agree with. Besides, I'm only arming myself for protection," I said.

"Exactly, you will never be safe from them. They will never let you go for the same reasons we can't, you're too valuable to be possessed by the other side," he said.

I slumped down into one of the plastic chairs and said, "I'll just disappear again then. Somewhere no one will find me."

He walked over to stand in front of me and said, "It only took us about six months to find you this first time…and now that we know much more about you, it will be even easier next time." He squatted down so he could look me in the eyes. "You can't run forever, Anna. I don't know about your Russian friends, but if we have to hunt you down again, it won't be me coming to see you. The NSA will send out a different type of agent, and you'll never see him at all."

I narrowed my eyes at him and he raised his hands in a conciliatory gesture. "Hey, it's not a threat. You called me honest, I'm just trying to live up to that."

Standing back up, he said, "I know I've given you a lot to think about, so I'm going to let you do just that." He reached into his coat, and pulled out a card. "Here, take this," he said as he offered his business card to me. "You need to make a decision within the next twenty four hours. They won't wait any longer than that." I stood up from the chair and took the card from him, slipping it into my back pocket.

He began walking away, but stopped after only a few feet and turned back to face me. "Oh, and one more thing. The next time you go to the practice range, you may want to think about your attire more carefully. Because if one of those hot casings your Glock is spitting out lands in here…" He made an up and down motion with his hand over his chest. "You're going to have a bad day." I smirked at him, but he didn't even crack a smile. He just turned and left, heading up the broken stairs and back toward the parking lot.

After Adam left, I wasn't sure what to do next. Removing my shoulder rig, I placed it down next to my Glock. I stood there, and looked at all my new gear lying on the table. All around my feet lay the spent brass from our practice. Everywhere I looked, were the tools of the trade everyone wanted me to pursue, tools of protection in some hands, destruction in others. I pounded the table with my fist, frustrated and angry. Why the hell couldn't everyone just leave me alone? I hadn't asked for this life, I just wanted to live a quiet existence without all this damn intrigue. To make it worse, even if I chose to join the NSA, how could I be sure that they hadn't been the ones that attacked me last night? Just to coerce me into joining them the way the mobs used to extort 'protection' money from businesses. On the other side, if it were Stepan and Eliza that had found me, they would kill me for sure. That, or drag me back to Russia, torture, then kill me.

Damn it, I had no one I could confide in, except maybe Athena. Maybe I should talk with her tonight and see what she thinks. She's always been there for me. I chuckled. That was the understatement of the year.

I heard someone coming down the stairs, and I turned to see Dale Dupree making his way over the uneven stairs like it was a paved parking lot. He'd probably made the trip down them more times than I could count. As he walked over to me, I put myself back into my Tammy character.

"Hey, I forgot to give you this." He unfolded a medium-sized, duffle bag and tossed it on the table next to my gear. It was black, and made from durable canvas, with pink stitching in the shape of a heart below the handle. Lovingly sewn inside the heart's outline were crisscrossed handguns, with the words, 'Hand Cannon Handbag' embroidered below the design. I picked it up, and peeked inside. That bag had more pockets and zippered compartments than a grandmother's purse.

"Dale, bless your heart, this is so sweet of you," I purred.

"I thought you'd like it. It's just like my mama's," he said sounding like a little boy.

"Well, you were so right, I love it. It'll really be handy when I come back to the range," I said.

I saw him looking past me to my target. He let out a long whistle and said, "Doesn't look like you need much more practice."

I playfully punched his arm and said, "Aw, thanks Dale. Hey though, I've decided I'd like to get another Glock 19. Is that okay?"

"Well, sure. Come on back in the store and we'll have to fill out that damned paperwork again and call the feds. But don't you worry, we'll get you squared away." He smiled a big toothy grin at me and I returned it.

"Sure thing, let me clean up out here and I'll be right in. Thanks sweetie," I said.

He turned and ascended the treacherous stairs as easily as he'd come down them. I quickly went about cleaning up my paper targets and picking up the brass casings that the Glocks had ejected on the ground. After that, I packed up my equipment in the new range bag Dale had given me and hung it on my shoulder. I was glad Dale hadn't asked me why I wanted another gun. It would have been difficult to explain. There was no way I was going to tell him that I could shoot two at once. No need to become some kind of local legend at the gun store, no matter who I looked like. However, I'd decided that Adam was right, it was something that might save my life someday. So better to have an extra gun and never need it, versus needing one and not having it.

Target practice was over for tonight anyway. The shadows from the trees grew longer as the sun dropped lower in the sky every minute. Besides, Paul was still sitting in his cab, and he couldn't study in the dark. Maybe I could stop by this weekend and spend some quality time punching holes in paper. The next time my interstate 'friends' came for a visit, they'd be in for a rude surprise.

Part Three

No Escape

This particular conference room at the small NSA office was more private than most. Soundproofing surrounded it, there were no outside windows, and the door was secured with a magnetic lock that only ten people had the access to open. The chrome-accented, glass table located at its center, dominated the sparsely furnished meeting place. The suspended fixtures that hung over the table were bright, and illuminated it well, but that light didn't penetrate into the corners of the room. They were blanketed by deep, murky shadows. Eight black leather chairs surrounded the chrome and glass table. Four of them were currently in use.

The side of the table facing the door had three people seated at it. They wore various business suits with muted colors of black, blue, and gray. Each one had a slight bulge under their left arm where their shoulder holsters held semi-automatic weapons. These were serious individuals, and all of them bore an expression that reflected that fact. Seated in the center, was Edwin Westcott. Edwin was the Director of the Signals Intelligence Directorate, otherwise known as the SID, which was responsible for the collection and analysis of acquired data from any, and all areas. He was a small, elderly man, whose pale pink skin was littered with dark, mottled age spots. His faded gray eyes sat behind a pair of thick reading glasses as he stared at the data pad held in his skeletal hand. Lost in thought, he absentmindedly scratched his bald head as he digested the text.

To Edwin's right sat his direct report, Chandra Moretti. She was the division head of S3, which specialized in data decryption and acquisition from all computer systems around the world, even in the United States. Chandra was in her fifties, younger than her superior by about twenty years. Her light brown hair was styled short, and complimented her chestnut tinted skin perfectly. While she was 5' 7" tall with a medium build, she looked much larger sitting next to the hunched over Edwin. Her chocolate colored eyes scanned her data pad, but she also stole quick glances to her left to see if she could glean what her boss was thinking.

On the other side of Edwin, was the man that reported to Chandra, Kevin Taggart. Kevin was by far the youngest of the executives, only having reached his late twenties, but his cyber-espionage acumen had already landed him at the head of S32, the Tailored Access Operations program, or the TAO. The NSA was fond of their initialisms. The TAO's responsibilities focused on hacking into foreign computers to perform cyber-espionage. It represented the largest program under S3, with over a thousand computer specialists in both hardware and software systems. Kevin's tall lean frame was in constant motion. Whether it was bouncing his leg, tugging at his curly red hair, or rubbing the blue eyes of his pale, freckled face, he was always moving. He had already examined the report several times, and his impatience with Edwin and Chandra was building up to uncontrollable levels.

Adam Sims sat across from the three NSA big wigs, waiting for them to finish digesting his findings on the Anna situation. He wasn't sure what purpose this meeting served. After all, he'd documented all the facts that were needed to make a decision. Still here he was, because that was what they'd wanted. He simply didn't understand some people.

Behind Adam to his right, there was another figure. Cloaked in the shadows that were gathered at the corner of the room, the attendee was all but invisible to the others. The only indication that someone was watching the meeting from that dark hiding place, was their soft breathing.

Adam continued to sit unmoving and apparently disinterested, hands folded in his lap, eyes staring ahead as his report was examined to within an inch of its life. Edwin finally finished and sat his pad down on the table, the others following suit within a couple of seconds.

It was Edwin that spoke first. "So Adam, having read your report, do you have anything to add regarding your recruitment attempts of Anna Andropov?"

"Nothing more than is in the report, sir. I have made contact with Anna twice about coming to work for the NSA. The consequences were explained to her, but I am not sure she was convinced of them. Either that, or she is so arrogant that she feels she can simply avoid them," he said.

Kevin scoffed and said, "Then what are we waiting for? Why don't we simply proceed with what we know has to be done? Not only that, but why did you give her an extra day, Adam? My instructions were clear."

"The second time I met with her at the gun range, I perceived a weakening of her resolve. I even attempted to bond with her using the fact that we owned the same pistol. However, I believed that if I'd forced her to answer at that moment, she would have refused outright. I felt another twenty-four hours might be enough to let her examine her position and come around to our point of view. Since she is such a high value asset, I decided the delay was warranted," Adam replied.

Kevin sneered and said, "So you just ignored my orders."

Adam began to speak, but Edwin interrupted him. "Now Kevin, you don't want mindless agents that don't think for themselves. Adam's decision hasn't cost us anything."

"Perhaps, or perhaps not, but we also don't want renegade agents that can't follow the simplest direction either," Chandra said.

Edwin glanced over at the woman, but said nothing, yet. He'd been in this game long enough to know when to pick his battles.

Kevin threw his hands up in frustration. "Fine, fine. So Adam, what do you think the chances are that she will play ball now?"

Adam thought a moment before saying, "She is frightened, but her opposition to joining us runs deep. It may have something to do with what happened in Russia, although I have no evidence to support that theory. I think there's an equal chance she could go either way."

Kevin looked over at Chandra, "I don't like those odds. Should I have a wet work asset on standby?"

Edwin leaned forward between them. "Now hold on. I'm not committed to executing someone, especially on American soil, unless it's unavoidable. If we're going to green light a termination, we'd better be damn sure about our reasons."

Kevin snorted, "Edwin, she's not a some-*one*, she's a some-*thing*. Just because she *looks* like a human and *talks* like a human, it doesn't *make* her a human. She wasn't born. There's not even any human DNA in her construction. It's no different than turning off a server or taking apart an old computer."

Edwin glanced toward the dark corner of the room, but a nervous fidget was the only response he received. He returned his attention to the table and said, "What if we used some form of blackmail to get her to join?"

"No, she'd just be disgruntled and wouldn't be a reliable asset," Chandra said.

Edwin sighed and tried again. "Okay, Adam reported that she had been frightened by the attack last night. What if we played off that and scared her just enough to get her to join up with us for her own..."

Chandra shook her head and interrupted. "No, if she ever found out, she'd despise us for it, and then we'd be right back with a hostile…"

Edwin slapped his hand on the table and Chandra stopped in mid sentence. "Damn it Moretti, I know you're just biding your time until I retire and you get a shot at my job. However, that time hasn't come yet, so at least let me finish my sentences before you shoot down my ideas."

The room was silent for a few heartbeats, then Chandra met Edwin's gaze and said, "I apologize, Director. Although I stand by my reasoning, I was too hasty, and should have let you finish."

Adam had been quiet so long that when he cleared his throat, they all looked shocked at the noise. "I believe that we are dealing with a whole new area here. There hasn't ever been an artificial life form before, so no one knows how the courts would rule her termination. They might decide she has the full rights and privileges of any other person, causing us innumerable issues. Combine that with Anna's unmatched abilities, and I think that terminating her would be a costly mistake."

"If Anna isn't around to petition for her *rights*, then we won't be bothered with that detail," Kevin paused, then smirked as he continued, "You know, that was an impressive speech, some might even say impassioned. I think you might be getting a little too close to her. If you know what I mean."

"I know exactly what you mean, and I can assure you that I am not. My argument is based on reason and logic. Something that could be hard to grasp for some people," Adam flatly said.

Kevin's face grew red, and he growled, "Don't push me, Adam. You'll lose big time."

"I'm not trying to push you, I'm simply stating facts. There's no reason to become all worked up about it," Adam replied.

As Kevin began to rise from his seat, Edwin placed a hand on his shoulder. "Let's settle down now. We're all on the same team here."

"Well, what do we do?" Chandra asked.

Edwin pursed his lips in thought for a moment before replying. "All right, we should have someone standing by to act, but *only* if I give the order. Clear?"

Chandra nodded, "Clear. Do you have a preferred method of performing the termination?"

Edwin removed his thick glasses and tossed them on the table. Rubbing at his eyes, he said, "Nothing up close or explosive, too much risk of collateral damage or something else going wrong..."

"I have an excellent sniper in my program. I could have him on standby," Kevin offered.

Picking up his glasses from the table, Edwin replaced them on his face. "I think that is our best option. Kevin, contact your agent and have him ready to go by tomorrow."

Kevin frowned and said, "Sir, before Adam changed the timeframe, we were supposed to make our final decision tonight and execute it in the morning. I suggest we stick with that timetable. Now that Anna knows what we intend to do, she could run again. She even said as much."

"Excuse me, I have an idea." The woman's mousey voice was barely audible, as it drifted out of the shadows. Though it was quiet, it surprised most everyone, since she'd been in several of these meetings, but had never said anything.

Edwin waved, motioning for her to sit with them. "Of course Becky, come over here with us."

A light-skinned, athletic built woman wearing an unremarkable olive-colored dress emerged from the shadows. She wore no makeup, and the coco-brown hair that fell past her shoulders wasn't styled. Even the way she carried herself told the world she didn't want to be noticed. Yet, Becky had a down to earth, natural beauty about her that couldn't be hidden. Her sparkling cinnamon eyes darted from one person to the other as she hurried toward the group. Pulling out the chair on Adam's right, she slid her petite 5' 1" frame into it. She composed herself for a moment by focusing on straightening her dress.

Becky took a deep breath and looked around the table before speaking. "Anna is alone and afraid, with no confidant she can turn to for advice. Let me go to her, meet with her. I could…"

Edwin shook his head. "Becky, no, I appreciate what you're trying to do, but we can't risk it. Do you have any idea what kind of people are looking for you? It's not worth exposing you in an attempt to recruit Anna."

"I could go after nightfall, tomorrow, and take Adam with me. He would keep me safe," Becky said.

Edwin looked over to Chandra, and she reached out to rest her hand on Becky's. "You simply don't understand how dangerous the environment is at the moment. We only want to protect you, keep you safe."

Becky slowly pulled her hand out from under Chandra's and began smoothing her dress again. "Yes, I know it's dangerous, and I know you want to keep me safe." She looked around the table, meeting their stares one by one. "I also know *why* you want to keep me safe. I'm not stupid, don't you think I know how valuable I am?"

The three NSA executives exchanged worried glances as Becky continued. "I've never asked you for much, but I'm asking you for this. Let me go and see Anna, just once. If I can't convince her to come back with me, then so be it. If nothing else, I may find out some information, that no one else could. Can you imagine the things she knows? How valuable it might be?"

Edwin sighed and said, "Of course we do, but…"

Becky's eyes blazed as she cut him off. "Mister Westcott, please don't turn down my request. I'm afraid it might depress me, and that would have a negative impact on my work."

The table fell quiet at the lightly veiled threat. None of them had ever seen her this head strong before. Kevin grunted and accepted that she was going to win this test of wills. "I can deploy a second team to provide backup for them. Just in case the whole thing heads for the ditch."

Chandra looked at him and said, "No, don't just send a team, *you* go with the second team and supervise from the field. Nothing, and I mean *nothing*, can go wrong. If you so much as *smell* something funny, you extract Becky no matter what the cost. Am I understood?"

Kevin nodded, "Crystal clear, boss. I'll begin assembling the team tonight, and our mission will begin Thursday night as we leave here and proceed to Anna's apartment. Adam, as soon as you leave this building with Becky, you are to protect her at *all* costs, that is an order."

"You can be assured, I will protect her with my life," Adam said as he glanced over at Becky.

Edwin frowned, but he knew he'd lost this argument. "Very well, proceed with your plans. Once the operation is underway, I will expect status updates every fifteen minutes." He ran his hand over his bald head and sighed. "Kevin, Chandra, would you give us the room please."

As the other two executives exited, the door to the conference room closed, leaving the others behind. Edwin said, "Becky, I appreciate all that you have done for us, please realize that, but I can't have you blackmailing me in front of my direct reports. It undermines my authority and my ability to command respect. I already have Chandra counting the days until I'm gone, I don't need you pulling the rug out from under me."

Becky leaned forward and said, "I know, and I'm sorry…but it was the only way you were going to let me go." She paused, searching for words. "I have to know what's going on. It's been over a year since I've heard anything and Anna is my last hope. I need him…" She made a soft choking sound, but continued. "I *need* him to be okay…" Her words trailed off and a stream of tears ran down her flushed cheeks. Adam offered her a tissue and she held it to her eyes, her body trembling with silent sobs.

Edwin's anger melted away. "I'm sorry. I've been living this life too long. Sometimes all I can see are objectives and motives, instead of people and their needs. We'll get you in and let you talk with Anna. You may be just what she needs too." Turning to Adam, he said, "No offense, you've done everything you could to convince her to join us."

Adam returned his look with a blank stare and said, "Of course, there is none taken, Mister Westcott."

Edwin chuckled. "Of course not."

Turning back to Becky, he said, "I'll leave you and Adam to plan your excursion. Please be careful out there. I don't want anything to happen to either of you."

Becky hurriedly composed herself as Edwin stood and moved toward the conference room door. She called out to him before he could exit. "Mister Westcott, one more thing."

He paused and turned back to her. "Yes, what is it?"

She sniffed a few times and cleared her throat. "Like you said, I'm not an expert in the cloak and dagger world. So, I wanted to ask you something."

"Fine, go ahead and I'll answer you if I can," he said.

"I plan to tell Anna about myself, but not the projects I've been working on for the NSA. Is that acceptable?" she asked.

Edwin's expression turned grim. "I suppose that will be fine. Because there are only two possible outcomes, either she comes to work for us, and her knowledge of you is controlled within our environment, or she still refuses, and her knowledge of you will be eliminated when we terminate her."

Chapter 22

After a good night of rest, I felt one hundred percent better this morning. I still had a few aches and pains, especially in my feet, but they were only small annoyances. It was time to get back to work.

I called the AA Taxi Service and told them I needed a cab. The dispatcher gave me an estimate of twenty minutes. Thinking of yesterday, I asked if Paul Graves was driving today. I was told he was, so I asked for his cab specifically. The dispatcher regretfully told me it might take him thirty minutes to arrive since he was currently with another fare. I told them I'd wait. I liked Paul.

After a nice hot shower, I stood in front of my closet deciding what to wear for the day. One thing was certain, at the rate my clothing was being destroyed, I'd have to go shopping by this weekend. I found a sky blue blouse with a matching skirt, and a pair of cardinal red suede pumps that went perfectly with my hair. I changed the color of my fingernails and toenails to match my outfit and got dressed. Now it was time to accessorize.

Standing in front of my bathroom mirror, I pulled the leather shoulder rig around my back and adjusted it so that the holster hung at the right height under my left arm. I attached the rig's side straps to the top of my skirt, and cinched it into place. Loading two spare magazines under my right arm, and one of my new Glocks under my left, I felt ready to face the day. Another look through the closet, and I found a bulky cobalt blue jacket. It concealed my weapon without trouble, although I might have to come up with a new carry strategy when springtime arrived.

I tossed my iPhone into a small pocket in my skirt and went into the kitchen to pick up some breakfast. Bottled water and vitamins, was all I had handy, and I promised myself that I was going to take the time to cook myself a real meal one of these days. As I popped the top off my SmartWater, I went into the living room and sat down to wait for my ride. Paul had been right yesterday. I should look into renting myself a car, or just buying a new one. My savings account had enough money so that I could replace my Civic, but just the thought of replacing Takumi was painful. I'd lost too many friends.

My cell phone rang, and it was the cab company. I answered it and heard Paul's voice on the other end. "Good morning Miss Andropov, I'm downstairs when you're ready."

"Thanks, I'm heading down now," I said.

On the way down, I wondered if Paul would interact with me any differently. He of course knew me as Tammy Hayes, the thirty-something, deeply southern-accented woman that liked gun stores. Now, I was back to being Anna Andropov, the Russian immigrant that worked at a computer software firm. This was a psychological experiment you didn't get to run every day.

He was waiting for me outside the cab and helped me in, just like he'd done with Tammy. When he asked me where I wanted to go, I had him take a different route to FlexJen from the one I normally drove. Although I was in a completely different car, and my attackers had never tried anything during the day, I wanted to take every precaution to keep us out of harm's way.

Once we were rolling, it turned out that Paul was the same witty conversationalist with Anna, as he was with my southern-fried alter ego. As he fought his way through the murderous rush hour traffic, we were still able to enjoy a bit of pleasant small talk. He even remembered

Tammy, and asked if I knew her. Hiding my wry smile, I told him I'd seen her around the complex a couple of times.

Paul knifed his way through the rampaging traffic like a skilled surgeon. He even pulled a few maneuvers that made my augmented reflexes sit up and take notice. Using all his expertise, he delivered me safe and sound to the FlexJen parking lot. I paid him, and made an appointment for him to pick me up at five this afternoon.

Felix was talking with Kimber when I walked into the lobby, but he stopped and greeted me. "Anna, good morning. Are you feeling better?"

"Yes, must have been a twenty-four hour bug or something," I lied.

"That's good news. Say, did you take a cab in to work this morning?" he asked.

I leaned against Kimber's desk and said, "Yeah, my Honda is in the shop. They don't know what's wrong with it yet, but they're supposed to call me sometime this afternoon."

He made a sympathetic moan and said, "That's rotten luck," motioning toward the seated Kimber, he continued. "Maybe you should just buy a new one like someone else I know."

She rolled her eyes at him and he chuckled as he went back to his office, which left Kimber and me alone together. We looked at each other and I could feel a tension between us that I wasn't sure how to handle. Not knowing what else to say, I asked, "So, how's the wrist?"

Lifting her arm, she looked at her removable splint and replied, "I can tell it's better, not as much pain, but I still can't move it in some directions without it hurting. Hope you're over your stomach bug, Felix has another lunch planned for us today."

"I am, thanks. Another one? We must be doing great." I said as we both ran out of chitchat. An uncomfortable silence descended, and I decided to bail. "Well, guess I'll see you at lunch." A quick smile flickered across her face and she nodded. I turned and walked down the hallway toward my cube, running right into an approaching David.

This was the moment I'd truly been dreading. Apparently, we'd both decided to handle it like two adults, two adults that were passive-aggressive, anyway. We smiled nervously, mumbled a greeting, and kept walking. A few seconds later, I was at my cube checking emails while David was up front chatting with Kimber. Their sporadic laughter brought cheerfulness to the office, and even to me in a bittersweet way.

I threw myself into my work, and the morning was gone before I knew it. David actually stopped by my cube on the way to the conference room to tell me it was time for lunch. He didn't wait for me, but at least he stopped by. I'd take any steps in the right direction, even small ones.

Standing, I smoothed out my jacket and felt the reassuring bulge of my Glock. It made me think of how well my target practice had gone yesterday, even when I started using two pistols at once. As I approached the meeting room, I considered telling my coworkers that I was now carrying a weapon, but I couldn't figure out a way to do it without revealing too much about my situation. It was probably best to keep the presence of my concealed weapon, well...concealed.

The mouth-watering aroma of today's lunch assaulted me just as soon as I pulled open the door to the conference room. It was from a pizzeria called the Mellow Mushroom located on the Southside of Birmingham. Felix had picked up several pizzas; cheese only, meat with veggies, and veggies only. They were set out on the sideboard table with sweet and unsweet tea next to them as drink choices. To top it all off were the desserts, lemon and chocolate pies. It was times like this that I was glad to be an android. I could eat anything I wanted without gaining weight.

We all took a seat around the table, but this time, Kimber and David sat together on one side while Felix and I were on the other. After filling my plate with a couple of slices, I took my first bite, and it was delicious. For the next several minutes, the room was silent, except for the sounds of people enjoying good food.

During the meal, I couldn't help but notice David and Kimber's flirting. After all, I was sitting across from them. David would hold her slice of pizza for her, using the cast she wore as an excuse. Then she would lean forward, shift her eyes to him, and take a bite, stifling a giggle while she chewed. He just watched, wearing a big silly grin. After we finished eating, and had gotten our desserts, they carried on with the same routine...except there was a palpable shift in their attitude. When David would hold up some pie on his fork for her, she would *accidentally* get some of the whipped topping on her lips. Her eyes locked on him, and she'd use her tongue to lick it away. Meanwhile, I could tell that David's free hand was resting on her thigh under the table. Every so often, she would make a high pitched squeak, and playfully push his arm away.

I glanced over at Felix, and it didn't appear as if he noticed them at all. It could've been that what Kimber and David were doing wasn't as overt as I thought. Maybe I was overreacting because of the history between us, especially that night at David's...and that massage that I stopped him from finishing. I'd done the right thing, but my body sure as hell didn't think so. Just the thought of that night made my face flush and my body temperature rise. I took another bite of lemon pie and tried to put it out of my mind. The pie and my attitude were both a tad sour right now.

By the time I'd finished the pie, my mood had improved a fair amount. I knew I should be happy for them, and I really was. It was just my stupid feeling of jealousy that I had to overcome. That was easier said than done, but it was just one more step down the road of mastering my emotions. I'd get control over it, like I had the others.

We'd all finished our dessert and cleaned up our mess when Felix began his presentation. "Okay everyone, I only have a couple of announcements, so this will be quick. First, FlexJen is in the best financial shape it has ever been in, thanks to some contracts coming through that I had thought were stalled. So look forward to more lunches and some late nights coming in the next few months."

"Great, I guess. Nah, I'm just kidding, that's wonderful news," David said.

Felix chuckled and continued, "Secondly, we may be looking into purchasing some new animatronic technology for some advance robotic projects. That is if the designer can get everything up and working."

He held his hand out to David, turning the meeting over to him. Taking the cue, he stood up holding a medium-sized paper box in his hands. I felt my blood run cold as I realized what was about to happen. He opened the box and removed that blasted VOX Bot that he'd showed me last Saturday. He started doing a dog and pony show for everyone, but I'd already seen as much of that accursed machine as I could stand. I swirled my tea around in its cup while he put it through its paces and talked about how he'd come up with the money to build it into a full-scale prototype. It wasn't his fault, he had no idea how that *thing* affected me. With every tinny scratchy word, out of its robotic mouth, I felt less and less human. However, it was his finale that pushed me over the edge.

He put the mask over his face and looked at Kimber. His handsome brown eyes stared out of the mask's empty holes and his ebony skin color clashed with the Caucasian colored pink of the mask. Speaking into the controller, he whispered, and the mask responded. "Hey Kimber, you sure look beautiful today."

Kimber must have been in on this part, because without missing a beat, she replied, "Oh, how sweet!" Then she stood, and gave the mask a light kiss on its cold, silicon lips.

My mind reeled. It was so easy to imagine me, as the mask, and my sweet, lost love Cindi as the real person kissing that fake human. Cold sweat broke out all over my body and I felt dizzy. Who was I trying to fool? Damn it, that mask was more of a person than I was. At least it was being controlled by a flesh and blood human.

I had to get out of there. Standing on wobbly legs, I headed for the conference room door.

"Anna, are you all right, you look pale," Felix called after me, but I couldn't stop to answer.

As soon as I was out of their sight, I bolted toward the back of the office and the ladies' room. Slamming the door open, I headed for a stall and locked myself inside. My skin went cold and clammy followed by a wave of intense nausea. I dropped to my knees and began throwing up.

After the worst of it had passed, Kimber's soft voice spoke to me. "Oh, Anna, you poor thing. Is there anything I can do to help?"

I spat a couple of times and said, "No, I'm alright," which was one of the biggest lies I'd ever told. I was afraid there was something terribly wrong with me.

There are these software routines that the scientists had called SubCons, short for subconscious human action subroutines, which were built into me. They were supposed to ensure that I functioned like a human without me having to consider every little event in my life. I yawned when I was tired. Dust or pollen might make me sneeze. All the little things that people did throughout the day that no one noticed, unless they were suddenly missing.

Anyway, I was sure my SubCons had just made me sick because of a traumatic experience, and that didn't make any logical sense. A reaction like that wasn't needed for me to appear human. I wondered if Eliza's rifle shot to my head had broken more than just my pain suppression ability. Crap, what if I was mentally debilitated in other ways? I had no way of knowing. I didn't have anyone that could analyze my brain functions. That was a frightening line of thought, to say the least.

Kimber shuffled around a bit and said, "Well, I'll be right outside the door if you need me. Just call out." I heard the ladies' room door open and close, leaving me alone in the floor. The unwanted tears ran down my face and dropped to the floor as I wept in silence.

I'd pulled myself together and was standing at the sink cleaning myself up when Kimber came back into the bathroom. "Hey, just checking on you."

Drying the water off my face, I turned to her and managed a weak smile. "Thanks, I guess I'm not over that stomach bug after all."

She gave me the once over and a look of concern came over her. "Maybe you should go home. You look awfully pale."

"I think I will, thanks." I said.

"Do you need a ride?" she asked.

"No, I don't want to be any trouble. I'll catch a cab," I said.

"Well, okay," she said and left the room.

I came out a minute later and saw that Felix was at David's cube talking over something with him. When he saw me, he wrapped up his talk with David and came over to check on how I was doing. I explained that I was heading home, to which he agreed. Heading back to my cube, I called for a taxi and settled myself in to wait for its arrival. After a few minutes, Felix came by again.

"I hope you're feeling better soon, really soon, as in tomorrow," he said.

This peaked my curiosity and I asked, "What's happening tomorrow?"

He grinned a bit and said, "Well, I was going to announce it at the lunch, but now I'll just send an email. Long story short, I bought everybody tickets to the Halloween party at Sloss Furnace tomorrow night."

"Thanks Felix, that was nice of you, but I'm not sure I'll make it," I said.

"I understand, but I hope you can. Since the party at Sloss is a costumed event, I'm letting everyone come to work tomorrow all dressed up. You know, to set the mood for later that night," he said.

I managed a weak smile and teased him. "You sound more like David, than yourself…but it does sound fun. I'll see how I feel in the morning and let you know."

"Okay, well, take care of yourself and I hope to see you Friday," he said.

I smirked to myself and thought, "*A fucking costume party? With all I'm dealing with? Not likely.*"

A few minutes later, my phone rang letting me know that my cab had arrived. I told everyone goodbye and walked out the door as they wished me well. Paul was waiting outside his cab to open my door, as always. After we got underway, I closed my eyes and tried to figure out what had just happened to me.

Chapter 23

Paul dropped me off outside my complex and I paid him for the ride. I shuffled up the stairs to my apartment, and opening my door, saw my comfy looking leather couch. Stumbling in, I flopped down on it saying, "Oh, you are always here for me my trusty companion." I chuckled and said, "I wonder if talking to couches is any indication of mental health." Going a level deeper, I replied to myself using a clinical tone. "Quite possibly, but talking to yourself is when we begin to consider straight jackets and the like."

I sat on the couch and relaxed, doing nothing for at least an hour. Finally, I sighed, and forced myself to stand. Going into the bedroom to undress, I stripped out of my work clothes and put my loaded Glock on the nightstand next to my bed. Then I slipped on a pair of jeans and a pink sweatshirt. Now, I was comfortable.

I lay back on the bed and thought about what had happened at work today. Closing my eyes, I began to gather my thoughts. First, my neural net brain might have been damaged from either being shot by Eliza months ago, or all the fights I've been in recently. Second, although illogical to me, it might be the way I'm supposed to function, and I'm concerned over nothing. Lastly, and perhaps the most disconcerting, I could be going insane. After all, there could be a design flaw in all the neural net brains that Viktor created. There sure was in at least *one* of them.

Rubbing my temples, I considered those ideas for a couple of minutes, until I realized it didn't matter. I was attempting a self-diagnosis without any kind of knowledge or equipment. There was only one person I knew that might even have a chance at troubleshooting my issue, Elizabeth Eklund. All I had to do was find her. I hadn't tried to look for her in several days, so why not give it a shot right now. Sitting up, I put on a pair of tennis shoes for my trip. Then I fixed a pillow and lay down, resting on my back.

Reaching out with my mind, I interfused through my wireless connection to the Internet. I was prepared for the swirling disorientation that always followed the shift between worlds. My bedroom faded, and I was standing in an open field. It was the same field that I always began in when I made the transition from my home. Except this time, it was daylight. The wind was cool on my face, but the heat of the bright sun kept it from being too uncomfortable. The autumn leaves crunched under my feet as I wandered around, lost in the beauty. In the sky, there were pale dots that I assumed would be the stars I normally saw when it was night.

After I'd gotten my fill of sight seeing, I called out for Athena. "Oh mighty Athena, please help me find that which I seek."

I didn't have much of a wait before she came to my call. Swooping in on Pegasus, she landed only a few yards away. Her smile was infectious, and she ran to me for our customary embrace.

She whispered in my ear, "It makes my heart soar to see you. I had feared you might take a turn for the worse after I left. You were so gravely wounded less than a day ago."

"I know, but you saved me. My dearest friend," I said.

We parted and I looked into her beautiful face. "Now perhaps you can save me again."

"Of course, tell me what it is that you seek," she said.

"Not a what, but a who. I am in desperate need to find Elizabeth Eklund," I said.

Just a shade of a frown touched her features as she replied, "I of course will do my best, but I have been searching for any information on that woman since the last time we were fortunate enough to find the elderly doctor." She hung her head and continued. "However, I have not been able to locate anything additional. I'm afraid I have failed you."

I reached out and cupped her chin in my hand. Lifting her head back up until our eyes met, I said, "Athena, do not speak such nonsense. You have never failed me. Perhaps what we need, is a fresh angle on the problem."

The bright smile returned to her and she said, "Thank you, Anna." Her expression turned curious as she asked, "Exactly what is it that you mean by a fresh angle?"

"Well, we have been looking for Elizabeth for over six months now and the only piece of information we were able to find was by chance. With our big break coming from an old system that just happened to be brought back online within the past few days. I know that this woman does not want to be found, but that doesn't make sense," I said.

"Do you mean to say that since you have the great Athena helping you, we should have found at least something?" She gave me a little wink after her question.

"I do indeed. Combine that with the fact we have the best systems infiltration expert in the world as well, and it is inconceivable that we haven't found more," I said returning her wink.

While she considered this, I continued. "I have been relying on you too much. You are the best search engine ever created, but if the data is not available to the public, you cannot locate it. Therefore, I assert it is time for me to pull my weight."

"Very well, how would you like to proceed?" she asked.

"There is only one place I know to start, the base in Tiksi, Russia that I escaped from, Ice Castle." Just saying the name made me quiver.

"Yes, the one we traveled to a few days past. Why do we infiltrate them?"

"While I was prisoner there, the man whom I consider my father, told me that there were Russian KGB agents seeking his daughter as well. If they have found any information on her, it would be in their computer systems. All I would have to do is get in and extract it without them detecting me." I said it with confidence, but I'd never attempted a system that advanced before.

"This sounds like an excellent plan to me. Are you ready to leave, or do you need to prepare?"

"I am ready. Lead the way and let us see what we can uncover!" I put my arm around her shoulder and we strutted toward Pegasus to begin our adventure.

Pegasus made excellent time, as always, and we were approaching the digital location of Ice Castle in only a few minutes. The temperature of the air began to drop, and even with the sun and my sweatshirt, it was somewhat uncomfortable. The Russian base looked different in the daylight. The sun glinted off the snow that was gathered atop the collection of squat metallic buildings, creating a beautiful light show. It was peaceful, actually pleasing to the eye, but to someone that had experienced it from the inside, it was hideous. That place held physical and psychological traumas for me that I'd never forget.

Lost in thought, I hadn't noticed Athena was talking to me. "…Do you agree with that course of action?"

"I am sorry, could you repeat what you said. I was struggling with my personal demons in regards to this place," I said.

"My thoughts were this, since it is daylight, I feel it would not be prudent to approach as closely as we did the last time. My suggestion is for us to land a few hundred yards further away from the gate."

"That sounds fine, however, could you guide Pegasus to fly over somewhat closer? I would like to see how active the base is currently." I said.

Nodding her approval, she leaned forward and pressed her knees into the muscular sides of Pegasus. He responded by extending his wings out straight, and gliding in a slow arcing turn down, toward the base. Once we were a couple of hundred feet above the ground, she leaned back and Pegasus began pumping his wings again, leveling off his descent.

I looked around the various buildings of the snow-covered base, but saw no activity. Some of the roofs of the buildings were devoid of snow, indicating *something* was going on inside them, but what? No one was visible, anywhere.

We were finishing up our full circuit of the base, when we flew over the small guard shack where I'd confronted the soldier disguised as Eliza. No one was there either. In the digital world, *people* most often represented specific software functions. If the system was small enough, they could represent the whole process. That was what made this situation so peculiar to me. There should be activity of some kind, unless...Damn!

"Athena, get us out of here, now!" I shouted.

She turned her head back so she could see me. "Why, I see nothing. Is there a problem?"

"Yes! We see nothing because they've already detected us! We have to get out of here because I'm not sure what kind of..."

Pegasus began to neigh and bob his head in obvious alarm.

She leaned toward him and asked, "What is it my friend?" Then, she called back to me. "Anna, look about for anything amiss. While I guide us out of this place."

She spurred Pegasus forward, putting him into a steep climb, as I scanned the area in front of us. I saw nothing except some fluffy white clouds and what I believed to be an ocean many miles in the distance. Perfectly normal. I turned to check behind us and saw much of the same, peacefully floating clouds, the structures of Ice Castle that we'd passed over, and so on. Nothing that should've caused Pegasus to react... then, I saw it.

The roof of one of the smaller buildings had split at its centerline, and both sides were retracting away from the new opening. As the gap grew larger, something was being raised up through it. We had pulled so far away, that I squinted to see what was happening. A large, iron skeletal structure with a wide, metal cylinder mounted on top began rising through the opening in the roof. As I realized what it was, my blood ran cold.

I turned back to Athena and shouted, "We need to be gone from here, now!"

"Why, what is it?" she asked.

Looking back, I saw a flash of light, and then a column of fire exploded out of the back of the cylinder. A rocket the size of a family sedan burst out of the container's front, like a dog that had been called for dinner, and we were the meal.

"They launched a surface to air missile at us, and it's coming up fast!" I shouted.

The thunderous sound of the missile's launch caught up with us and assaulted our eardrums as it rolled past.

She took a glance over her shoulder, and her face went pale. Then in a resigned voice, she said, "Pegasus cannot out run that. Anna, you need to disconnect and travel back to your home."

Now, I knew that we hadn't just had a *real* missile launched at us, the same way I realized I wasn't riding Pegasus and holding onto an alluring Greek goddess. What the missile represented, was a cyber counter-measure program that had been executed to thwart our intrusion attempt on the base. Basically an antivirus program, a big, bad, mean one, but still just a program. Those were what I specialized in.

While I was fairly confident that a counter-measure program like that couldn't do any real damage to a massive system as powerful as Athena, I wasn't sure. I leaned close to her ear and asked, "Can that weapon hurt you?"

"N-No, I am in no danger whatsoever. Please leave now." She'd hesitated just long enough for me to detect her lie.

There was no way that I was leaving my friend behind to take the hit for me. "What, and let you have all the fun? No way! Don't worry, I'll take that thing out."

With a twinkle in her eye and a broad smile, she said, "Very well then. I shall concentrate on guiding Pegasus."

She began executing some complicated evasive maneuvers in an attempt to shake the missile. While she was an excellent equestrian, the missile was a better tracker. It continued to close at breakneck speed. Doing the math, we had about thirty seconds before impact. No pressure, Anna.

Reaching out with my mind, I searched for a communications link to the base that it might be using. Ah ha, there it was. The communication between them was encrypted using the RSA-7 512 bit algorithm, which might take some time to crack. Time we didn't have.

I changed tactics and attempted to connect directly to the missile without using the secure stream. Finding the wireless frequency, I began mentally transmitting to it. *"Attention, this is the missile operator for the Ice Castle base. Primary communications have been breached and are no longer secure. Disregard them. Your mission is terminated, initiate self-destruct immediately."*

As I had expected, the operating system for the missile was simple and had a one-track mind. It responded in a loud male voice that sounded like a private addressing his drill instructor. *"Missile A42-01, communication received, Missile Operator. Self-destruct code requires passphrase. Transmit passphrase, or order will be ignored."*

Crap. I suppose that was to be expected. There was no way I could guess a passphrase in time. I wondered if it was advanced enough for me to bully it. *"Missile A42-01, I did not contact you with a suggestion! You will self-destruct and you will do it now. That is a direct order. Execute it!"*

"Missile A42-01 will not be deceived into self-destruct by an intrusion attempt. Missile A42-01 will perform its duty to the base and its commander by destroying the target," it replied.

We had one more chance. The missile was only fifteen seconds away. Interestingly enough, the missile had said the word 'duty'. Perhaps it did have a bit of a personality I could use to my advantage. I gathered my courage for one last attempt. It was time to test one of my theories about this digital world.

I recalled every detail I had about the highest-ranking member of the base, shifting my personality to match his. Once finished, I contacted the missile again.

"Missile A42-01, this is Stepan Entsky, base commander at Ice Castle and KGB Officer in good standing. You have made the correct decision. The person that contacted you previously was the traitorous android Anna. She is the woman in pink on the flying horse and she seeks to mislead you. Perform your duty, destroy her at all costs! Do not bring shame upon the base you serve, or the great country of Russia. You must not let her escape! Perform your duty!"

I repeated the word the missile's OS had used, *duty*, to drive my point home, hopefully triggering something deep in its programming.

Going back to my own personality, I transmitted to the missile one last time. *"Fuck you Entsky! Fuck your stupid base, and most of all...Fuck Russia!*

I'm out of here and you'll never catch me!"

Cutting the communication's channel, I began the risky part of my plan. I swung my leg over Pegasus so that I sat sideways on him. Athena felt my motion and looked back to see what I was doing.

Her eyes widened as she realized my next move. "Anna, no!" Giving her my best *here goes nothing* grin, I leapt into the sky.

Straightening my body, I lowered my head and dove. I wanted as much distance between Athena and myself as I could manage. Rocketing away from her, I glanced back to see if there was enough time for my plan to even work. There was.

The missile, forced to choose between us, selected the insulting, renegade android to destroy. It turned away from Athena, and homed in on me like a cheetah hunting prey. Yes! I braced myself, as it closed on me so fast there wasn't even time to blink.

When the missile reached me, my assumption about it not being an actual missile at all was proven true. However, it didn't actually *strike* me...in so much as *penetrate* me. I felt a strange tingling sensation as it sunk into my chest. It went in deeper and deeper, causing the tingling to intensify and become much more uncomfortable. The sensation began to spread out into my arms and legs as the missile's tail sunk into my body.

I realized, with a bit of nervousness, that *penetrate* hadn't been the right word, since it hadn't proceeded back out of my body. Somehow, it had *merged* with me.

Putting that thought on the back burner, I began executing the rest of my plan. Now that the missile was gone and Athena was safe, all I had to do was terminate the interfuse connection and...

Pain wracked my body. It felt like I had stepped onto a mound of fire ants, and in defense, they had attacked me with their painful venom. Except the ant mound I'd stumbled into must have been six feet tall, and millions of them had poured out like a wave over my head. Working their way inside my clothes, they tortured my bare skin. Finding their way into my nostrils and rushing inside my ears, they charged into my body. The agony was all encompassing as my skin burned and itched, like my insides were ablaze. My muscles spasmed in uncontrollable convulsions, and I tore at the sleeves of my sweater trying to dislodge the tiny terrors on my arms. Once the sweater was out of they way, I cried out in shock. There were no ants crawling over me, but the flesh on my arms was bubbling like a boiling pot of water. Panic set in and I balled myself into a fetal position. All reason left me and I couldn't even activate my pain suppression. Somewhere in the back of my mind, I realized I was still hurtling toward the ground.

I don't know how long I stayed that way, but slowly, sanity began to return. The pain lessened enough for me to suppress it even further. The wind was still rushing past my ears, so I must have still been falling. Jerking my head around, I noticed some key facts. One, I was about fifteen hundred feet from the ground, and two, Athena was calling out to me as she and Pegasus rocketed toward me in a power dive.

When she drew close enough for me to hear her over the rush of wind, I heard the controlled fear in her voice. "Anna, look here! Take my hand as we pass!"

With the ground rushing up, I knew I only had once shot at this. Athena wore a look of pure concentration as she guided her diving companion. Pegasus folded his wings flat against his muscled body to obtain the maximum speed. Then they were on me.

My augmented reflexes activated, and time appeared to slow. I reached out with both arms, as Athena leaned, stretching out one hand, while holding fast to Pegasus with the other. Her hand slapped into my left arm, and I felt her close her grip. This changed the trajectory of my fall, and swung me toward the back of the flying stallion. As I bounced into the diving steed, I swung my right arm up and grasped him on the back with all my strength. Athena yanked with her hand, and I followed suit. It was almost too much. I landed on his back, but a bit to far to the right, almost sliding off the plunging Pegasus.

Reaching out with my arms that were now free, I fumbled for a handhold. In my desperation, I found Athena's midsection and wrapped my arms around her, holding on for dear life.

As soon as I had gripped her, she pulled up on the reigns, calling to her mount. "Up Pegasus, pull up now or we shall perish!"

Mighty, white wings snapped out to each side and the deceleration pushed me into his back. Our dive began to level, but not fast enough. The powerful steed began to beat his wings against the rushing wind. They rose and fell almost faster than I could see. Judging from the increased g-forces pressing me down, the strain must have been incredible.

Despite his best efforts, the ground was rushing up toward us. I braced myself for the impact, but when we landed, the stallion flexed his legs and absorbed most of the excess energy. Pegasus trotted across the light dusting of snow for a few steps, steam rising from his heated body, and his sides covered with wet, sweaty lather. He lowered his head, panting from the exertion of the flight, but he otherwise appeared fine. We'd made it.

Athena slid to the ground and looked up at me, "Let us give Pegasus a rest. Here, take my hand."

"No need, I'm fine," I said. However, as soon as my feet hit the ground, my legs buckled and I would have fallen if she hadn't caught me.

She looked me over with concern now written across her face. "You are still very pale. Here, let me help you sit down."

I was going to argue with her, except the world began to tilt all by itself, and I decided she might be right.

We sat down a few yards from Pegasus, and I put my head down on my folded arms. She put her arm around my shoulder to keep me from falling to the side.

"I cannot believe you took the full force of that weapon for me. I am in your debt." she said.

I took a few deep breaths before answering. "No, you are not in my debt. You saved my life only a few days ago. It was the least I could do for you."

"Is there anything I can do to speed your recovery?" she asked.

I raised my head and met her concerned gaze. "Thank you, but I will be fine in a few minutes. That missile was a high-powered anti-intrusion program, and it was designed for me."

Athena's eyes widened. "The villains knew we were coming?"

I tilted my head side-to-side, trying to work the kinks out of my neck. "No, I don't think so. My bet would be they had it ready in case I tried to break into the base."

"If that is so, why were we able to breach their security so easily the first time?" she asked.

I paused and thought about that for a few beats. "That is an excellent question. I fear it is because they wanted me too. Which means…"

I got to my feet and paced around, my thoughts racing. The soft snow crunched beneath my shoes, as hundreds of scenarios played themselves out in my mind. Athena still sat on the ground, staring up at me intently and waiting for me to finish my train of thought.

Contemplation almost complete, I heard a soft knocking coming from my apartment in the physical world. Listening, I recognized Adam's voice calling out to me. This guy had terrible timing.

I held my hand out to help Athena up and said, "I have to leave. There is someone at the door of my apartment."

She took it and got to her feet. With a twinkle in her eye, she asked. "Is this the same *someone* that showed up the other night?"

Now why did she say it like that? "Yes, it is the same man that visited me the other night."

"Oh," she said with a smirk, "your gentleman has come calling."

Now I caught her meaning. I hadn't told her about Adam because I didn't want to drag her into a conflict with the NSA. They had backdoors to enable their surveillance built into quite a few search engines. If Athena had one, she might not even be aware it existed. I told myself I'd bring the whole Adam thing up later.

"No, he's not *that* kind of visitor." She giggled, which made me smile. "I will speak with you again soon. Thank you for all you have done for me. It is more than I can ever repay."

She hugged me goodbye and said, "Just be safe, that is payment enough."

To make sure Ice Castle didn't have any more tricks up its sleeve, I watched her fly away until she was just a tiny speck in the bright blue sky. Then, I disconnected myself from the interfuse link, wondering why Adam had shown up at my apartment. Whatever the reason, I knew it wasn't going to be good news for me.

Chapter 24

thursday, october 30th 5:58 pm

As my bedroom came back into focus, I jumped off the bed and grabbed my Glock. Tucking it into the small of my back, I adjusted my sweater so it couldn't be seen. After all, I wasn't sure it was Adam, and even if it was, he could be here to start trouble.

Nearing the door, I called out to him. "Adam, is that you?"

"Yes, it's me. I'm sorry to disturb you before our arranged time, but we need to talk," he said.

I peeped through the window to take a look, and he gave me a little wave with his hand. He was alone, and I felt confident that it was actually him, so I opened the door.

Adam entered and said, "Thank you for seeing me. This is urgent or I wouldn't have bothered you."

I nodded to him, then closed and locked the door behind him. Turning around, I motioned for him to have a seat on the sofa. He did, but only after his eyes, traveled over the remnants of my broken chair. Damn it, I should have cleaned that up.

He sat, and unbuttoned the jacket of his black three-piece suit. It allowed me to see the pistol he carried in his own shoulder rig.

235

"Would you like something to drink? I have some cold bottled water if you like," I said.

He shook his head. "No, thanks. I'm sort of a down to business kind of guy, so if you don't mind, I'd like to tell you why I came over tonight."

Kicking a chunk of chair out of the way, I took a seat on the couch next to him.

"Your chair has been broken since I was here last," he said.

"Yes, it has," I replied. There was no way I was going to tell him I had a tantrum, and broke the thing after he left last time.

He began to say something, but decided against it. Adam folded his hands together and placed them in his lap. "Anna, I'm going to be truthful with you, giving you the extra day to decide about your future landed me in some hot water with my superiors. My orders were to get your final answer and report back. However, I thought that given more time, you might see things in a different light. Realize that we can help and protect you. Well, as most things like this go, my boss and I worked out a compromise. So here I am, twelve hours or so early, have you changed your mind?"

I had to admit, it was tempting. With all the crap I had going on in my life, I could just toss it all and sign up with the NSA. They'd protect me, give me a new identity, take care of me, and maybe even teach me a new trade. Damn, when I thought about it that way, it sounded like a prison.

I sighed. "Adam, no, I haven't. I'm sure your intentions are good, but I just don't know what I'd be getting myself into."

"You don't know *that* now. Look at your day-to-day life. You are hunted and attacked at the whim of others. At least with us, you would have protection from the randomness. Sure you would be in danger on an assignment, but when it's over, so is almost all the danger," he countered.

"It's not the danger that worries me, it's what I might be forced into doing," I shot back.

"According to you, the last time a government agency tried forcing you to do something you didn't like, you escaped. Do you think we'd attempt the same thing knowing your capabilities?" he asked.

I had to admit, that was a sound argument. "I, I, well I just don't think I can live that life, Adam. Thank you, but no. I'll make my on way."

He stared at me for several seconds without speaking, and then got up off the couch. "I want you to talk with one more person before you make up your mind. If you don't agree with what they have to say, we will both leave peacefully."

I stood up myself and said, "What if I tell you to leave and not come back?"

"Anna, If I leave here tonight without your agreement, I promise that you'll never see me again." He paused and looked at me with that blank expression of his. "You'll never see any NSA agent again. They plan to use a sniper."

I bristled at his words, but his face showed no anger in them. Perhaps he was only being honest. "All right, go and get the other person. I'll wait here."

"Oh, while I'm gone, please take the pistol out of the small of your back and store it. The person I'm bringing in is under our protection and I have to be cautious. You understand," he said.

Without waiting for my reply, he turned and walked out of my apartment. I grunted to myself, he was good at his job.

While waiting on Adam to return, I did as he asked and removed my Glock. However, I put it in the desk drawer next to the couch where I could reach it quickly if needed. After a few minutes, he knocked on my door and I opened it. I watched as his eyes checked me, seeing if I'd disarmed myself. Once satisfied, he stepped to the side and I could see the other agent for the first time. She was wearing an oversized brown trench coat that swallowed her tiny frame. Her coco brown eyes were scanning me up and down. At first, I thought she was checking me for weapons as Adam had done, but her expression was more like curiosity.

"Anna Andropov, this is Becky Olsen," he said.

I held out my hand to her and she took it. Her grip was gentle, tentative, and she never took her eyes off me as we shook hands. "Nice to meet you Miss Olsen. Please, come in."

After they were inside, I motioned for them to have a seat on the couch while I closed and locked the door.

Becky turned to Adam and asked, "Is it okay if I take off this heavy coat inside?"

He nodded and helped her out of it. I noticed that it was thick for a coat of that kind, and realized that bulletproof materials had been woven into it. Adam folded the coat over his arm and held onto it while Becky stretched and tousled her hair. It was a deep brown and cascaded to the middle of her back.

She looked around my apartment and said, "This is very nice, a little spartan, but nice." Before I could reply, her eyes landed on my destroyed leather chair. "Wow, your chair is shattered."

"Yeah well, I need to cut back on all the late night snacking," I said.

Her eyes snapped up to meet mine and she giggled. "Delightful, you have a sense of humor." She picked up a piece of the chair and turned it over in her hands. "Plus, you must be very strong."

All her analyzing of me was wearing a bit thin. "Miss Olsen, Adam has asked me to hear you out, and I agreed. So, if you don't mind, may we proceed?"

The pink skin of her cheeks turned a bright red and she looked a little frightened. Putting the piece of chair back down where she'd found it, Becky sat down at one end of the couch and began fidgeting with the folds of her plain, navy-blue dress.

As I moved to sit, Adam stepped in front of me and took the middle position, so he would be between us. I raised an eyebrow at him, but he ignored me. Taking the seat at the other end of the couch, I looked past him to Becky.

I was getting the impression that she was a timid woman, as she was obviously working up the courage to speak. While she did, I took the chance to examine her more closely. She wore no makeup, and while she wasn't *gorgeous*, Becky was attractive. Her nose was small and turned up at the end just a tad. While her chin was rounded and framed her smallish mouth just right.

I blinked. Something in the back of my mind began fighting to reach the surface. Something important about her, but I couldn't quite get a grip on it. Had I seen her somewhere before?

Becky cleared her throat and looked up at me. "Miss Andropov,"

"Please, call me Anna," I said.

She smiled and began again. "And you may call me Becky. Now, Anna, I've come here tonight to talk with you about the future. *Your* future."

Her voice was soft and musical. She had a European accent, although I couldn't place the exact region. My subconscious was jumping up and down like a Jack Russell Terrier, trying to get me to listen to it, but I couldn't put the pieces together. She'd continued to talk while I pondered, but I'd not heard what she said. I focused back in on what she was saying and tried to catch up.

She was looking at me seriously as she spoke. "Funny thing about the future, you may think you don't have one, or that it's all dark, but there are always choices. For example, my mother passed away when I was young…"

A ray of realization as bright as the sun seared through my mind and my heart began to race. I leaned back against the couch, staring straight ahead. Now I knew what my subconscious had been screaming about.

Becky stopped speaking and Adam looked over to me asking, "Anna, are you alright?"

I was afraid to speak, afraid to actually say the words aloud, because if I were wrong, it would crush me. I screwed up my courage, and leaned forward looking into Becky's searching brown eyes.

"Helen," I managed to squeak out.

"Excuse me?" she asked.

"Helen…your mother's name was Helen. Isn't that right…Elizabeth?" My voice cracked with emotion as I spoke and time stood still as I watched her face for some kind of reaction.

After what felt like forever, a small smile appeared on her face. "Yes, Anna, I'm Elizabeth Eklund."

All I could manage to say was, "Is it really you?"

Adam nodded his head. "Yes, she is Viktor Eklund's daughter, and she has been with us at the NSA. Why did you think you couldn't find any trace of her?"

I couldn't contain myself. I knew I didn't know this woman at all, but it was as if I'd found a long missing friend. Standing up from the couch, with tears of joy running down my face, I said, "I've been so lost. Can we talk for a while?"

She stood and held her hands out, her eyes threatening to overflow.

"Of course, I want to hear everything."

I rushed into her open arms and we hugged while I wept. Elizabeth stroked my back and reassured me. "It's okay, everything will be fine now. It's all going to be all right."

Chapter 25

After Elizabeth and I had composed ourselves, I went into the kitchen to make us some coffee. It turned out she and I liked ours the same way, with sugar and a little creamer, while Adam took his black. My Keurig had all three cups ready in just a few minutes and we were sitting on the couch talking like old friends. Adam had even moved to one end of the couch, so that Elizabeth and I could talk without leaning over him.

Earlier she'd said she wanted to know everything about what happened in Russia, so I began from my first day. I told her about seeing her father, Viktor, for the first time, and how he hinted I was somehow special. How excited I'd been to meet the rest of the team that first night. It was painful, but I told her about the lovely and energetic Cindi, the woman that helped me understand my many android abilities, and how to interact with humans. I became choked up, as I told her about how Cindi and I fell in love over the course of my training...and all the problems that had caused on the team.

Then, I let her in on Viktor's secret, he had given my neural net brain, a full complement of emotions, unlike his previous model, Eliza. She did not possess the *kinder* range of feelings, such as enjoyment and love. Elizabeth asked quite a few questions about my emotions and my sister Eliza. I told her of the evil Stepan Entsky and his mole on the team, Warren Lopata. With more tears, I told her how Eliza had set me up, and tricked me into shooting and killing an innocent young girl named

Sonya. She cried as well, while I described the pain of that mistake. I explained that was when I knew; I had to escape that place.

Now we were getting to a delicate part of my story, so I wanted to ask a few questions of my own. "Elizabeth, when was the last time you heard from Viktor?"

Her face grew concerned and she said, "I haven't heard from him in over two years. Since there was a fire in his lab and one of his assistants was badly burned. I'd heard from the grapevine that he'd gone to work on a research project in Russia with a team of top scientists, and now I know what that work entailed. Tell me Anna, is he still there?"

I had been afraid she didn't know. I drew close to her and told the next part of the story. "The night of the escape, I was thrown in prison by Stepan. Your father and a man named Zory helped me escape. Viktor and I traveled back to the lab, which was deep underground, and smoke was pouring up the elevator shaft. He stayed topside while I ran down the stairs to see what had happened. Eliza had set fire to the lab and destroyed all the equipment. Not only that, she murdered..."

I broke down for a minute and Elizabeth put her arm around me. "Anna, it's okay, you don't have to tell me about that part if the memory is too painful."

I composed myself and said, "No, you need to know how dangerous and unbalanced Eliza can be." I cleared my throat, wiped my eyes, and began again. "She murdered Cindi and another scientist, Jeff. She threw Jeff against a wall and broke his back. While she left Cindi so horrifically beaten that she died shortly after she told me what had happened. Worst part is, I believe Eliza did it just because she knew it would hurt me."

Elizabeth looked horrified, and her eyes began to stream tears. I was sure she knew in her heart how my story was going to end, but I had to tell her. "As soon as Cindi passed away, I ran back up the stairs and found Viktor. We were leaving the building as I heard a noise, and turned to see Eliza pointing an automatic rifle at our backs. I moved as fast as I could, putting myself between her and Viktor as she opened fire.

She grazed my head and knocked me off the platform where Viktor and I stood. I fell to the level she was on and we fought. It took everything I had, plus a shot taken at her by Viktor, before she was defeated. Afterwards, I didn't kill her. Viktor had told me she was worth saving, and how it was his fault she was mentally deranged. So, I pulled her unconscious body to some heavy machinery and tied her to it. Then I rushed back up to the platform where Viktor waited."

I had to stop again. My eyes told Elizabeth what she had feared from the beginning, but with a choking voice, she said, "Please, finish your story, Anna. I have to know."

It was like reliving the night all over again. My aching heart was broken, for Elizabeth and me. "When I made it back to him…he was… he was already gone. The last thing he'd done, was fire that gun at Eliza and save my life. And I never got to thank him for it…"

I broke down and wept as if I was back in that old satellite building, looking down on Viktor as he lay on the floor. Elizabeth's emotions were in just as much turmoil, and we instinctively hugged each other for support. I couldn't imagine what she must be going through. Her worst fears about her father had been realized, and like me, she'd never gotten to say goodbye.

We wept until our eyes ran dry, while Adam handed us tissue after tissue and impassively sipped at his coffee.

Elizabeth, eyes red and swollen, came out of the bathroom and took her seat next to me. "Anna, I want to thank you for telling me what happened. I had feared it for months, but not knowing was like torture."

Reaching out, I took her hand in mine. "I wish it had been better news, Elizabeth. I'm so sorry. If I had been faster, maybe…"

"No, don't think that way. It will only bring you unwarranted pain and suffering. You did all you could, and that's that," she said.

I smiled weakly at her and gave her hand a squeeze.

From behind me, Adam spoke for the first time in over an hour. "Elizabeth, not to be insensitive, but it is getting late and we must leave soon. Is there anything else you would like to discuss with Anna?"

She looked at him, and then she remembered. "Oh, yes, he is of course talking about you coming to the NSA. I know you were set against it, but if you did, you wouldn't have to be alone anymore. You'd have someone to talk with about your thoughts and problems, someone that knows how you feel. Not only that, but you could stop running from that horrible Stepan Entsky and insane Eliza. Please, Anna, don't disappear out of my life after I've just met you."

A chance to work with Viktor's daughter *and* stop running from Entsky, how could I say no? "Of course I will. Maybe you can help me with the socialization issues that are a struggle to me."

Elizabeth's eyes brightened and she said, "Well, I have been doing a few projects of my own, so let's talk about that tomorrow morning."

Adam stood and said, "Yes, let's get whatever you want from your apartment and head to the NSA office. We'll get you settled in, and talk over more details later. Oh, don't forget to email your employer and tell them you're leaving for another opportunity. We wouldn't want them worrying about you."

I hadn't thought about my friends at FlexJen. Saying goodbye to them in an email felt a little impersonal. "Hey, uh, how about I report to the NSA Saturday morning? That would give me a chance to get all my affairs in order and say goodbye to my friends at a get together we are having tomorrow night."

"I don't believe that's a good idea. You should come with us tonight," Adam said.

Elizabeth gave him a poke in the ribs and said, "Let Anna tell her friends goodbye. It might be a long time before she can contact them again. She can call you when she's done."

"You know Mister Westcott won't like this," Adam told her as he held out the heavy brown overcoat for her to put on.

She slipped into the coat and buttoned it. "Mister Westcott will be overjoyed that Anna has agreed to come work with us. It will be fine, trust me."

Adam looked at me and said, "Very well, say goodbye to your friends Friday night, but call me as soon as you are back here. Don't wait until Saturday morning. Do you still have my number?"

"Yes, I have it, and I'll call you Friday night once I get back to the apartment. Thanks for understanding, Adam," I said.

He opened my door and shielded Elizabeth with his body. "Don't thank me for that, because I *don't* understand why you want to take this kind of risk. Talk to you tomorrow."

Before Elizabeth walked out, she turned back and hugged me. "I'm so glad you'll be working with us...with me." She turned and hurried after Adam and they disappeared down the stairs leading to the parking lot.

I closed and locked the door behind them, then went back and plopped down on my couch. When I did, the data drive containing Viktor's encrypted research file bounced against my neck. I'd completely forgotten to mention this drive to Elizabeth. I thought about giving Adam a call. He couldn't have gotten far from the apartment, and I could give it to Elizabeth tonight. After checking the time, I decided to wait and give it to her Friday night. It was already past ten, and I still had to come up with a costume for work tomorrow.

The concept of a costume party made no sense to me at all. Why would grown people want to dress up and pretend to be something or someone that they're not? Even going so far as to put on a bunch of makeup and wigs, I mean really... My thoughts halted in a hypocritical lurch. I realized that was *exactly* what I did, what I was designed to do, and I was damn good at it. Also, it was actually sort of fun sometimes. I knew what it was like to step outside myself. Drop all the trappings that made me, well…*me*, and just become a different person. Now I saw how someone might want to pretend to be somebody else, even if it was just for one night.

There was only one person that could help me come up with a costume idea this late in the game…and she was just an interfuse connection away. Besides, I wanted to talk with her about my new NSA career as well.

A minute later, I stood watching Athena and Pegasus land a few feet away. As soon as they were on the ground, she dismounted and ran over to me. "Anna, is something amiss? Was their trouble with your gentleman caller?"

I shook my head, "No, everything went fine, it was actually much better than I had expected. As a matter of fact, I have some incredible news for you."

I explained all about Adam and that he worked for the NSA. Athena was upset at first that I hadn't confided in her, but she took my reasons to heart, and forgave me. When I dropped the bombshell about Elizabeth Eklund, she was stunned. She found it hard to believe that it had been kept a secret even from her.

As I wrapped up my story, she said, "So you have agreed to work with this Elizabeth and Adam at the NSA. That news is truly remarkable, now you will have real companions with which you can share your life."

"Oh Athena, you have been my cohort from the first day I met you. You may not be a physical being, but that does not change the fact that you are my most trusted friend. Do not think that I will hesitate to annoy you with many requests and tasks in the future," I said.

A warm smile spread across her face. "I will hold you to that."

I bit my lip and said, "As a matter of fact, I have a request that you may be able to help me with tonight. My friends at work are all wearing costumes tomorrow in celebration of All Hallows Eve. At first, I wasn't going to attend their get together, but now I fear Friday may be the last opportunity I have to see them, at least for a long time. My problem is, I have no outfit to wear, and the hour is late."

"Ah, you believe I can suggest a costume for you," she said.

"Yes, something utilizing only the clothes and items I have in my apartment," I said.

She clapped her hands and bounced up and down a few times. "Yes, this I can do. Show me everything to which you have access."

I reached out and took her hand in mine. Connecting her to my mind, I showed her everything in my apartment. She nodded and said, "I see you have purchased a couple of firearms. With those, and a few minor alterations to the clothing you already have, I believe we can construct you an exceptional costume. Now here is what you need."

She gave me a list of clothing, items, and modifications I would need to construct my costume. There were also changes to my physical appearance, but those would be easy.

"Follow those steps and you will be the star of the gathering. I guarantee it!" she said.

"Thank you Athena, I will begin work on this right now," I said.

"Very well, but you must tell me how everything goes after you get home Friday," she said.

"I promise, I will contact you as soon as I get home," I said.

We hugged goodbye, and I terminated the connection. Once fully back in my apartment, I began gathering up all the things needed for my costume. I hadn't ever heard of the woman I was dressing up as, but according to Athena, everyone else had. I guess we'd see in the morning.

Chapter 26

Friday morning, I was out of the shower and checking myself in the bathroom mirror. The changes to my body that Athena had suggested for my costume were specific, and since I'd never done this disguise before, I wanted to make sure they looked correct.

Concentrating, I shifted my cheekbones until they were higher, giving my jawline a more angular look. Turning my face to the side, I could see that I needed to alter them more to match the person I was imitating. However, I couldn't. Too much change in my face would raise suspicion in my friends. Next, I increased my chest size similar to what I used for my Tammy alias, except I kept them 'plastic surgeon' perky. I picked up my large, wooden-handled hairbrush and ran it through my hair. Using the brush to avoid tangles, I extended my hair to its maximum length, which was just above my waistline. It took me about thirty minutes to weave it into a ponytail.

Having finished the physical attributes, I focused on the various color tweaks that I needed to make. I lightened my skin until it was almost as pale as Elizabeth's. Checking the image in my mind, I used the integrated color prisms in my hair to change it to a dark auburn color. Eyes were next, and I watched as between blinks they went from my sky blue color to a chocolate brown.

Now I needed to get her mannerisms and accent down pat. After

249

watching some holograms and listening to her speak for a few minutes, I was ready to go for it. Taking a few deep breaths, I imagined myself performing one of the scenes I'd just watched. Looking into the mirror, I raised my eyebrow and repeated one of her lines. "I'm sorry, I only play for sport." A few minutes later, I'd slipped into her character as far as possible without sounding *too good*.

Before I began dressing, I called the taxi service and asked for a ride to work. The dispatcher asked if I'd like Paul as my driver again, and I told him sure. He said my cab would arrive in around thirty minutes, so I thanked him and hung up. That should be plenty of time to perform the minor alterations Athena had given me for my costume.

I laid the outfit on my bed and took a good look. My first thought was, thank goodness for temperate fall days in the South. Pulling my teal t-shirt over my head, I encountered a bit of an issue. Because of the changes I'd made to my chest size, the previously form fitting t-shirt was now so tight it looked like a second skin. It wasn't indecent...as long as I took shallow breaths. I really needed to invest in some clothes of various sizes, no wait; the *NSA* needed to invest in some clothes of various sizes. They had a bigger shopping budget than I did.

I stepped into my khaki shorts and put on a thick black belt with a large metal buckle. Sitting down on the bed, I slipped on my knee high hiking socks and a pair of mid-calf brown leather boots. I laced them up, and rolled my socks down to the tops of them. The rest of the costume was an alteration to my shoulder rig and holster I'd gotten at The Lock and Load. I wrapped the leather straps around my midsection, fastening them to my waist and thighs. Making sure my Glock pistols were unloaded, I holstered one on each hip and placed four empty magazines in leather pouches next to the guns. I paused, then on a whim, took the magazines out of the pouches and loaded them. If I was going to carry weapons, I might as well have access to ammunition. Especially with all the trouble I've had after dark.

My cell phone began to buzz, as I finished loading the last magazine. It was Paul, the taxi driver, and I told him I was on my way down. I'd have to catch breakfast at work. I tucked my phone into a pouch on my belt and headed out the door.

Putting myself in character, I bounded down the stairs and struck a pose for Paul as I reached the bottom of them. When he first saw me, his face registered complete surprise. That passed quickly though, and he decided to play along. I knew I liked him.

In his best British accent he said, "Miss Croft, over here. I'll be your driver today. You may call me Winston, if you please."

I was getting into the character now. I sauntered over to the cab and using the voice I'd practiced this morning said, "Very good Winston, and you may call me Lara."

His eyes widened at my voice, but he went back to his role and opened the door for me. As I slid into the cab I said, "Thank you love, you are quite the darling."

He half-bowed, and got back into the cab himself. Turning around and breaking character, he said, "I hope you don't mind me saying so, but your Halloween costume is fantastic."

I replied as Anna. "Thank you Paul. I just finished it last night."

"Well you did an excellent job," then getting back in to character, he said, "Where will we be heading today, Lara?"

Changing back to Lara, I said, "I fancy a ride to the FlexJen building, Winston."

"Be there in no time, " he said.

"Off you go then," I replied.

Paul pulled out of the apartment parking lot and soon we were heading down Highway 31. The rush hour traffic was horrible, as it always was, but we didn't mind. We were enjoying our role-playing so much, that we'd reached my workplace before either of us realized. Paul got out and opened my door as usual, and I said, "Thank you lad, I'll ring you this evening when I'm ready for home."

He gave me another small bow and said, "As you wish, Lady Croft."

I smiled and activated my phone to send him his payment. "There you are, plus a few extra quid for good service."

"Very good, see you this evening," he said as he got back into his cab and pulled away. If the rest of my day went like this, I was going to enjoy this whole Halloween thing.

Chapter 27

As I opened the door and walked into the lobby of FlexJen, I had to stop and look around. Apparently, after I'd left sick yesterday, someone had decorated for the occasion. There were orange and black lights hanging in lazy loops all around the tops of the walls. The lights twinkled and blinked in a chaotic pattern, drawing your attention up to the rest of the ceiling decorations. Ghosts, spiders, witches, pumpkins, and various other fairy tale creatures hung from random points on the ceiling. They were suspended low enough to just touch the top of my head as I walked under them.

Kimber called out to me as I stood there gawking at the amazing job someone had done with the lobby. "Hey Anna, come over here a minute."

Moving toward the reception desk, I saw Kimber sitting in her chair wearing a platinum blonde wig with shoulder length hair and a copious amount of red lipstick. She had also put a small black beauty mark on her left cheek and applied her black eyeliner with a paintbrush.

As I reached the desk and leaned against it, a black, iron cauldron about the size of a basketball began to bubble. Fog poured over its rim and a witch's head rose from the depths. The head was hairless, with hideous warts and burns covering its flesh. I watched in stunned silence as it turned to me and slowly opened its mouth. The head made a

253

wheezing sound and huffed more of the thick white fog in my direction. Laughing maniacally, it sank back into the depths of the cauldron, which then fell silent.

Kimber giggled at my shocked expression and said, "It's one of David's toys, he loves that kind of thing."

I looked over at her and for the first time I noticed the dress she was almost wearing. It was a snow-white sleeveless number with cleavage so deep that it could have debated you in philosophy. It was fairly short too, and looked like it only came to the tops of her knees.

She noticed I was checking her out and leapt out of her chair to show me the full effect. "Yeah, what do you think Anna? Can you guess what classic movie star I am?" As she asked, she stepped on something with one of her white leather high heels and I heard a fan begin to spin. In seconds, she was fighting to keep her dress down against the wind from a hidden fan under her desk. She giggled and twisted from side to side as her dress fought a valiant battle to contain her ample, well-placed curves. To think I'd actually been somewhat concerned that my costume might not be acceptable for the workplace.

I didn't recognize who she was dressed as, but if I didn't come up with the right answer soon, her dress was going to give up on the battle and retreat. A quick Internet search told me she was Marilyn Monroe from *The Seven Year Itch*, so I quoted her a line from the movie in a low sultry voice. "When it gets hot like this, you know what I do? I keep my undies in the icebox!"

She cheered and stomped down on the off switch for her fan. "Yes! Marilyn Monroe!"

"I have to say, you have the look down perfectly. You look gorgeous Kimber," I said.

She blushed a bit, and looked me up and down. "Hmm, your costume looks great too. I know you're that sexy, British vixen from all those video games, but I can't remember her name."

In my Lara voice, I said, "Oh, do try harder. I'll give you a hint, love. My first name begins with an 'L'."

Realization appeared on her face and she squealed. "Oh yeah! You're…"

"Lara Croft!" came a man's voice from down the hallway.

We both turned to see David strutting toward us. He was wearing a full three-piece black suit with a white shirt and black tie. In the breast pocket of the suit, were a large metal pen-like device and a pair of dark sunglasses. He wore a huge grin as he came to stand beside us. I had to access the Internet again to figure out that he was an MIB agent.

"Lady Croft, Miss Monroe, I know that you both must be aliens because no earth woman has ever looked as good as you two!" he said.

I smiled at David, and Kimber ran over hugging him. "Oh, you smooth operator you. That's the sweetest pickup line I've ever heard."

He pulled the silver pen from his pocket and put on his sunglasses. "Yes, I know. It's really too bad that neither of you will remember it after I use my neuralyzer on you."

Kimber and I put our hands up in mock fear and begged to keep our memories, when Felix's voice came from behind David. "Wait agent, I have finished my calculations and determined these women are from an alternate reality. Look here at my display, and I can show you my string theory models for the event."

Felix pulled up in his wheelchair wearing his normal business suit. He'd modified his chair by attaching his pad computer to it, but other than that, he looked like he did normally. For the third time in the last few minutes, I queried the Internet using what Felix had said and his attire. I'd never have found it if I hadn't been an android that could search through thousands of hits instantly. Looking at David and Kimber, I could tell they had no clue, so I spoke up using my Lara voice.

"Mister Stephen Hawking, how nice it is to meet another academic from one of our fine British universities. Tell me, how is every little thing at Cambridge?"

"Oh, of course," Kimber said, "but the one thing I relate to Stephen Hawking, is that computer he uses to speak. Why didn't you setup your pad to do that for you?"

"I thought about it, but then decided it might be perceived as poking fun at someone with a disability, and I obviously didn't want to give that impression," Felix said.

"Oh, I see your point," she said.

"By the way, where's you arm cast?" he asked.

"That ugly thing? I took it off because it didn't go with my costume. I'll be okay without it for just today I'm sure," she replied.

We spent almost the entire morning comparing costumes and talking about the party at Sloss Furnaces later that night. We just sat in the lobby and enjoyed each other's company, letting work slide for once. Kimber and David stayed dangerously close to each other, but it didn't bother me like it had yesterday. Maybe it was because I knew that I had a future now, one where I could be myself and talk with someone about my problems like I used to do with Viktor. Still, the way David filled out that suit, had me thinking back to that night in his apartment more than once...and Kimber, well just damn. It was no wonder every so often I would see David's hands stray to areas of her body that should have been off limits in the office. We may have had our differences, but there was no doubt that she was a beautiful woman. I sighed to myself. I still needed to find someone to share *that* part of my life with.

As we sat around and talked, I kept trying to tell everyone that I was leaving, but I just couldn't bring myself to speak the words. Everything was so perfect for the first time, in a long time, that I didn't want to spoil the mood. After a bit of reflection, I decided to tell everyone after lunch.

Speaking of lunch, by the time our conversation began to die down, I was ready for some. Felix's stomach growled and he checked his phone. "Wow, there's been some kind of time dilation effect! I'm going out to pick up some lunch. How about some subs today?"

Everyone nodded his or her agreement, but I spoke up. "Felix, you have been so nice to us lately with all these lunches and trips, how about I buy today. Just to say thanks."

He pondered that for a second, "Well sure, if you want to, who am I to say no? Thank you Anna. Let's get everyone's order and you can ride with me to the sub shop and we'll pick them up."

David and Kimber thanked me too, and after figuring out what to get, Felix and I were loaded up in his Element and on our way. Since I was going to break the news that I was leaving after lunch, I wanted to do one last nice thing for the friends that I might not see again, at least not soon.

We made good time picking up the lunches and were back in just around twenty minutes. I carried the food up the stairs to the lobby, but when the double doors hissed open, it was empty. No Kimber, and no David. Alarm bells went off in my head and I entered the building looking for signs of trouble. Seeing none, I realized it was possible that I was just being paranoid again. I called out to them, seeing if they would answer. "Kimber, David, we're back. Do you want to eat in the conference room?"

No one answered for a few tense moments, then David called from the back of the office. "Uh, sure, be there in a second."

So, I *was* being paranoid. They had just left the lobby and gone into the back of the office. However that didn't explain why Kimber wasn't at her desk in the lobby. Why would they both be in the back? Oh…I smirked when I realized why they were most likely both in the back. My thoughts were confirmed when they entered the meeting room. David had a tiny smudge of red lipstick on his right ear, and Kimber's wig sat ever so slightly askew on her head. I chuckled to myself and thought Felix and I should have taken longer to return with the lunches.

The sandwiches were good, and so was the conversation. We each told a story from our past, but I of course had to make mine up. This was the time I was supposed to tell everyone I was leaving, but I still couldn't bring myself to go through with it. I decided that quitting time was the right time to spring my news on everyone, and pushed any thoughts of the discussion right out of my mind.

The meal and conversation wound down too quickly, and after cleaning up, we all left to do some of the work we'd skipped this morning. I was in the women's restroom checking my costume in the mirror to make sure everything was still in place, when Kimber came in. She smiled at me and checked herself in the mirror next to mine. Frowning, she pulled out her bright red lipstick and began to paint liberal amounts onto her lips. After she finished, she turned to me and I could tell she was working up the courage to say something.

"Hey, um, this is a lot better than yesterday when we were in here, right?" she said.

"By a long shot," I replied.

I saw she was still looking at me in my mirror, so I turned to face her. Kimber looked unsure and nervous, an expression I'd never seen on her before. Her big hazel eyes searched my face, meeting my gaze at last and she sighed deeply. "Anna, this is hard for me, but I need to talk to you. Please let me get it all out, then you can say whatever you like."

That took me by surprise, and all I could do was nod my head.

She sighed deeply and spoke in a soft voice. "I've been really mean to you lately, and I know you realize it. But when you started here and David just began ignoring me, it hurt so much that I just lashed out. It was unfair, and cruel, and I'm sorry. You've been nothing but kind to me, even when I was trying to embarrass you. You could have let me fall in that pond at the zoo, but you didn't. At David's, you could have let me fall down the stairs, but you let the couch crush your foot and helped me instead. You saved me from at least a few broken bones that night, and that's when I realized what a bitch I'd been. I guess I felt like I'd lost David and I was furious at myself. I'd taken him for granted and hadn't told him how I felt about our relationship. Then, I took all that frustration out on you."

Her eyes swelled with moisture and she sucked in a short breath. I opened my mouth to speak, but she held up a hand.

"I just wanted to say I'm sorry, and I hope you can forgive me. You've been a true friend to me, and I treated you like dirt." Her lips quivered, while she searched my face for her answer.

She had stunned me. I'd never seen this side of Kimber before. I held my arms out open, and she rushed into them squeezing me tight.

"Kimber, don't worry about it. You don't have to ask my forgiveness. It's all in the past," I said as I held her to me.

She sniffled a few times and said, "Thank you Anna, you're such a good person."

As we parted, she caught a glimpse of her self in the mirror. "Oh shit! My mascara is running like a criminal skipping out on his bail!"

She began blotting at it and I put my arm around her shoulder saying, "Don't worry about it. I'm sure Marilyn had the same problem a few times."

She chuckled and started reapplying her makeup while I waited on her to finish. After she finished, we both left the bathroom together, giggling like schoolgirls.

It had become late in the afternoon and I was still thinking about the wonderful way things had worked out with Kimber, when someone knocked on my cube wall. I looked up to see David standing there.

"Anna, could you uh, come help me in the back room for a minute?" he asked.

That was odd…but I said, "Sure."

We went into the old storage room that I'd used when looking over the old paper proposals last week and he shut the door. What the hell?

He sighed and turned to face me, his expression similar to Kimber's from earlier in the day. "Anna, I just wanted to apologize."

I blinked. What was this, Halloween or National Reconciliation Day?

"Okay, why…"

"Wait, let me finish. After that night at my apartment, I treated you pretty badly. Your rejection was painful, because I care about you so much. To make matters worse, I may have been thinking with my hormones instead of my brain, and instead of talking with you about it, I just blamed you. I got to thinking that Russian customs may be very different from those in South Africa, leading us to a big misunderstanding."

I reached out and took his hand. "David, I'm sorry that happened to us, and it was as much my fault as anybody's. I really like you…and Kimber. I hope that all three of us will be close friends for a long time."

He pressed my hand between both of his and said, "There's one more thing. I didn't realize until yesterday that it was my VOX Bot that had upset you so much that night."

I froze. Uh oh, he was observant. I hoped he hadn't figured out anything else.

"After you ran out of the room and got sick yesterday, I realized that the same thing had happened when I showed it to you the night we almost…well, you know," he said.

He was making me nervous. This man was a brilliant programmer that loved to tinker with robotics and other machines. If he'd made a connection about the VOX Bot and me, I could be in trouble.

"Oh, David, don't worry about that," I stammered.

He smiled and continued, "I just wanted you to know I never would have performed that demo for Felix if I'd known how you felt about it. But, it's not here now. Only we are."

What the *hell* did that mean? "Umm, well thanks for the apology, it's nice to know you care."

He pulled my hand around his waist and looked deep into my eyes. "I *do* care, Anna, more than you may know. Because of that, I have a dilemma that I need you to help me solve. You see, I'm falling for Kimber in a big way, and I'd never want to hurt her, but I can't get you out of my mind. Something about you feels so special to me, and I don't want to lose you if there is any chance we could be together."

I felt his arms wrap around my waist as he leaned closer. Oh shit...

"I've never been good with relationships, but I've seen the way you look at Kimber and me around the office, you're jealous," he said.

I shook my head, but he gently took my chin in his hand and made me look back into his eyes. "So now, I'm going to ask you one last time. Is there anything between us or not?"

I tried to speak, but was lost in his beautiful deep brown eyes for what felt like an eternity.

"David, I..."

"Tell me I'm wrong," he said.

"You're...you're, wrong. I just like you as...a friend," I finally forced myself to say.

His face fell, and he searched my eyes, looking for the reason I was lying. Finally, he sighed deeply and said, "Well then, I was wrong. I'll see you at Sloss tonight, Anna."

I squeaked out, "See you tonight, David," as he turned and left the storage room.

On shaky legs, I walked to the door and closed it. Slumping down on the carpet, I rested my back against the cool wood of the door and tried to catch my breath. My heart was screaming at me to run after David and tell him how I really felt, but I ignored it. One thing was certain, he'd been right...right about all of it. I did care about him. If it hadn't been for Kimber, and the fact that I was leaving for the NSA, he might be here with me right now. Damn it! Why the hell was I always getting intimately involved with people I shouldn't?

I stayed in the room for a minute or two and composed myself. Cracking the door open, I made sure no one was around and I slipped back to my cubicle. I considered telling everyone my plans to leave, but honestly, I couldn't handle any more drama today. Adam had been right. I was just going to email them Saturday morning.

I tried to do a little work, but after my encounter with David, my focus was shot to hell. It didn't matter, Five o'clock arrived before too long, and we all got ready to leave.

In an unusual turn of events, Felix was the first one out the door. "I'm heading home to pick up some stuff for the party tonight. I'll see all of you there. Happy Halloween!"

David was up front with Kimber, and they were getting ready to leave too. Kimber turned back to me and said, "Anna, David and I are going to stop by my house for a little while before the party, since it doesn't start until nine."

David smiled and said, "But we'll see you at Sloss around then. I'll give you a call when we get there and we can meet up."

"Uh, sure thing, see you both there," I said, and waved goodbye to them.

They turned and walked out, laughing and smooching all the way to their cars. I sat down in the lobby to wait on Paul, and it finally struck me that this could be the last time I ever saw this place. It made me a little teary eyed, but the cab arrived before I had too much time to turn melancholy. Walking toward the doors, I called back to our security system. "Irene, this is Anna Andropov. I'm leaving for the night, please turn out the lights and lock the doors behind me."

"Thank you Miss Andropov. Have a great evening and a Happy Halloween," she said.

In less than a minute, I was watching FlexJen disappear in Paul's rearview mirror as we headed toward my apartment. I was going to grab a bite to eat at home, and then head to Sloss. This was going to be one hell of a party.

Chapter 28

Traffic heading home was worse than usual. There were cars full of adult partiers, along with loaded minivans full of kids heading out to trick or treat. Children were running from house to house, and Paul had to drive slowly through the neighborhoods. It took us almost an hour to weave through it all and make it to my apartment.

Once we arrived, he opened my door for me and said, "Here you are Lady Croft. Will you be needing my services later this evening?"

"Yes, I believe I will. I shall call once I require transportation," I said.

I paid him, and he tipped an imaginary hat to me and left. The complex's parking lot was beginning to get a few ghosts and goblins running around, for which I'd made preparations. There were several bags of candy in my apartment. The good stuff too, none of that cheap waxy chocolate or fruit. Nah, I had miniature versions of Baby Ruth, Butterfinger, 3 Musketeers, Kit Kat, Snickers, heck, I had all of them. I knew that I was going to be here for a few hours, so why not give the little munchkins a treat. Plus, they got to meet Lara Croft, which was a win-win in my book.

I hurried up the stairs to get ready for the kids, but when I approached my door, it was already opened about an inch. Damn it! I crouched down under the window and put my back against the wall. As quietly as

264

I could, I took a couple of loaded magazines and clicked them into my Glocks. Silently working the slide, I chambered a round on each pistol. I was grateful for this morning's foresight, or I would have had some useless weapons.

Both guns drawn, I pushed open the door with my left hand. The lights in the apartment were out, so I switched my sight to the thermal spectrum and peered inside. Scanning the room, I saw no signs of heat patterns, so I crept through the doorway. Once inside, I saw that my place was trashed.

There was so much debris strewn across the floor, that I couldn't continue moving around using my thermal vision. Checking for heat one last time, and finding none, I stood up and flipped on my lights…holy crap.

I holstered my guns and surveyed the destruction in silence. Everything in the living room, kitchen, and dining room had been ransacked. My couch cushions were cut open and stuffing was everywhere. The computer was smashed and its storage device stolen. Overturned tables and chairs were tossed in random places. I walked into the kitchen, and my feet crunched over broken glass plates. The refrigerator door was torn from its hinges, and all the cabinets were emptied. Their contents were strewn all across the tile floor.

Moving into the living room, I saw that all the Halloween candy was torn open and flung everywhere. Now *that* pissed me off. I might as well have bought that cheap, nasty, bubble gum that looses its flavor after five seconds.

I moved on into the bedroom and found that my mattress was ripped to shreds. The clothes in my closet were torn from their racks and thrown all over the room. Shit, they'd even cut up my shoes. The bathroom hadn't escaped their wrath. My mirror was shattered, the shower head was broken, even the lid to the toilet tank was smashed and water was all over the floor.

Furious, I sat down on what was left of my mattress. If nothing else, I was glad I'd taken my handguns with me today, otherwise, they'd might have stolen them. At least now, I could use them to protect myself, which it was beginning to look like I might have to do at any time. However, I didn't think the guns were the reason they'd broken into the apartment. So, what the hell could they have been searching for, that would require this level of destruction?

Before I could give that thought any serious consideration, I heard a noise from the front of the apartment near the door. I sprang off the bed and drew both my weapons. Rushing to the wall near the bedroom door, I leaned my head out to have a look. There were three trick-or-treaters standing in my doorway. The children were around six to ten years old, and were dressed in various Halloween costumes. There were two boys, and one little girl. The Internet told me that the younger boy was dressed as Captain Jack Sparrow, and the older was the adventurer Nathan Drake, from the *Uncharted* movie. The little girl must have liked Disney, because she was dressed as Elsa, from *Frozen*.

I holstered my guns and went out to meet them. The moment they saw me, I was greeted with shocked faces and several exclamations along the lines of, "Look Sue! It's Lara Croft!" and "Wow, It is!"

They stared at me, mouths open, as I walked to the door. When I reached them, I spoke using my Lara voice. "Hello Jack, Nathan, and Elsa, how are you tonight, better than me I do suppose."

The older boy spoke first, and he tried to exhibit the swagger of Nathan Drake. "Well Lara, it looks like you've had some thieves raid your home. We could team up and hunt them, if you like."

"Yarr! That's right, we'll make 'em walk the plank!" said the younger boy as he brandished a small plastic sword.

The little girl screwed up her face into a scowl and said, "I'll turn them into ice cubes if I catch them!"

I smiled at each of them in turn as I said, "Yes, the ruffians have truly trashed my flat, but the real tragedy is they destroyed all the treats I had planned to distribute."

Their faces fell, and they turned to leave, but I stopped them. "Wait a tick. If you have your phones, I can give you a few pounds to buy your own candy later."

They all spun around, and began to dig in their pockets, retrieving their cell phones. As they held them up, I leaned over and passed my phone over them. As I was finishing up giving the kids their Halloween treat, Viktor's data device that I wore around my neck shifted and gave me an itch. The kids thanked me profusely, and ran toward the next apartment. Absentmindedly, I scratched at my neck as I shut the door and turned off my outside light. That way no other young visitors would show up looking for candy.

Still adjusting the annoying data drive, I turned around and viewed the mass destruction of my apartment. Then it clicked, I was *wearing* what they were looking for, Viktor's research. There must have been a surveillance camera in the old satellite building where Viktor had left it for me that night. I took a moment to realize how lucky I'd been. I needed to get this information to Elizabeth as soon as possible. After all, it was her father's research, so she should have it. Unless…

I realized something. There was no physical proof that this Elizabeth woman was actually Viktor's daughter. I mean, she had just shown up with a few pieces of inside information, and made that claim. In fact, she had come here with Adam, just in time to get me to join the NSA. Wow, how could I have missed that? That was all way too convenient, what a fool I'd been.

Except, what if she *was* Viktor's daughter? I shouted, "Shit!" at no one in particular and kicked at some of the trash on the floor in frustration. How the hell was I supposed to know for sure? There was so much at stake. As I thought this, I noticed that one of the cups we used for coffee last night, lay broken on the floor. I bent over and picked it up, turning it over in my hand. It suddenly entered my mind that I could run a DNA test on the cup if it contained enough genetic material.

Stunned, I looked at the cup and just blinked for a second. This wasn't the first time this had happened. Back in Russia, my training had been cut short by Stepan, who had forced the team to send me out in the field. There could be hundreds of things I was capable of doing that I simply wasn't aware of yet. I had even found other skills like this by having a need to perform some task, and my mind responding with the needed knowledge.

The cup had some dried coffee in the bottom that was a light tan in color. That meant it was either mine, or Elizabeth's, but who's? Oh well, only one way to find out. I ran my thumb all around the rim of the cup to gather as much of the DNA as possible. Somehow, I could tell that I'd gotten enough and that the test had begun.

Once I had the results for Elizabeth's DNA, I'd need some of Viktor's to match against hers. My thought was, that since he was a scientist, he might have had some DNA tests run on himself at sometime in his career. I could elicit Athena's help to search for that data.

As I waited for the results, a horrible thought crossed my mind. Eliza is almost as good at disguises as I am, and she had fooled me big time back in Russia, by imitating one of my squad mates. What if Adam was working with Eliza to capture me? What would the DNA test even show for an android?

A couple of minutes later, the test finished and I had what I thought were Elizabeth's DNA markers. To see what a test would look like on an android, I licked my thumb to get a sample and began a test on myself. A few minutes later, the results came back, but they looked nothing like a human's. The graph was different in most every way. That told me that at least I had another human's results, and not Eliza's. I let out a huge sigh of relief.

Wanting to be thorough, I started searching around in the debris for Adam's coffee cup. However, after a few minutes, I abandoned the search. I couldn't find it anywhere in all the mess. Okay, what to do next?

I could contact Athena, and begin the search for Viktor's DNA results, but my apartment wasn't safe anymore. The people that had trashed it could show back up at anytime. FlexJen wasn't safe. They'd planted a bomb on my car while it was parked outside there. There was no time to find another place to stay, I was supposed to contact Adam later tonight and go with him to the NSA office. I couldn't head over to any of my friend's homes. There was no way I was going to involve them. Besides, they'd all be at Sloss tonight.

Now there was an idea. I could go to Sloss, find some quiet, secluded place, and interfuse from there. If I was able to find a set of DNA results for Viktor, and they showed that Elizabeth was related to him, I'd go with Adam at the end of the night. However, if Elizabeth wasn't Viktor's daughter, I could disappear from Sloss and go into hiding from this Adam and his female accomplice. Yeah, that just might work.

My stomach growled, and I realized that with the distraction of the break in, I hadn't eaten any dinner tonight. Looking around, I wondered if there was anything left that might be edible. While digging through the rubble, my phone rang. I checked it and saw that it was Felix, so I answered.

"Hey Felix, what's up?" I asked.

"Anna, I'm so glad I was able to reach you. Have you left for Sloss yet?"

He sounded worried, and that made *me* worried. "No, I'm still here at my apartment. Why, what's going on?"

"Thank goodness," he took a calming breath, "See, I wanted tonight to be special for everyone, you know, for all the hard work you've all done. So I reserved us a table in the main room at Sloss and had all these decorations I wanted to put up just for us."

"Wow, that's so considerate of you, Felix," I said, while wanting him to get to the point.

"Thanks, but uh, this is kind of embarrassing," he paused to catch his breath again, "I've gotten everything in the car, but it was a lot more difficult than I'd expected."

Wow, how much stuff had he bought? I was beginning to think Felix had an impulse-purchasing problem.

The desperation crept back into his voice as he said, "I guess, I'll just get to the point. Would you mind riding with me to Sloss and helping me unload all this stuff? I don't think I can unload and setup all this before David and Kimber get there without some help."

I frowned. Not because I didn't want to help him, but because he hadn't thought this through. "Felix, I'd love to help, but I don't live near Sloss. Depending on where you are, it might take you longer to come get me than just asking someone there for help."

His voice cracked, like he was on the verge of panic, "You live out in Hoover right? My house is near there and I can just swing by and pick you up. Please Anna, can you lend me a hand?"

Although I thought he was becoming worked up over something trivial, I caved. "Sure Felix, I can help. Do you have my address?"

After I agreed, he became much calmer. "Thank you *so* much, Anna. Yeah, I have all three of you in my phone. Just in case I needed to reach you for a work question. I should be there in around fifteen minutes. Thanks again!"

He hung up before I could say anything else, and I chuckled to myself. I wasn't laughing at Felix. It was the situations I always seamed to find myself in that made me smile. Here I was, standing in the middle of my trashed apartment, about to join up with the NSA, running for my life from KGB agents, and what was I about to do? Why, I was going to a Halloween party to help decorate while dressed as Lara Croft, of course! Now that made *perfect* sense.

I shook my head in disbelief, but I realized that even after all that had happened, I was still looking forward to the party. After all, this could be the last time I saw my friends from work.

My stomach growled again, begging me to eat something, and I began rummaging around in the floor of the kitchen trying to find something to appease it. After five minutes, all I'd managed to find was one bottle of SmartWater and three vitamins. Luckily for me, I didn't need much to keep me going.

I sat down on what was left of a couch cushion and opened up the warm water. As I downed the vitamins and polished off my drink, I planned the rest of the night in my mind. If everything went well, this day could still be a good one. By the end of the night, I would know for sure that Elizabeth was Viktor's daughter and have a great going away party with my friends. I felt like tonight could be one of the best evenings I'd had in a long time.

Chapter 29

I finished my *meal* and decided to wait outside for Felix. Sitting around in my destroyed apartment was turning my mood sour, and I didn't want to carry all that emotional baggage to the Halloween party.

As I stood outside in the crisp fall air, clearing my mind, several more kids and even a few adults noticed my outfit. They called out words of praise for my efforts, and I waved back thanking them. It was funny how small things like that could improve your mood.

A few minutes later, I saw Felix zoom up in his immaculate Honda Element. He was in such a hurry, that he was sounding his horn to move the kids out of his way. I decided to head down the stairs, before he drove up them to get me.

Jumping in the front seat, I almost didn't have time to close the door behind me before Felix was rolling again. I turned to him as I buckled my seatbelt, and his eyes darted over to me. "Hey Anna, I, uh, just wanted to say thanks again for doing me this favor."

I'd never seen him this edgy before. "Sure, not a problem Felix. Say, is everything alright?"

He glanced back at me and showed his slickest smile. "Sure, sure, I'm just afraid we won't have everything ready in time."

He motioned toward the back of the van and I turned to look. It was packed. Every bit of space that wasn't occupied by his wheelchair lift device, had boxes, blankets, and buckets stacked to the ceiling. The only way he could see behind him was his special rearview camera that was displaying its image on a screen in the center console.

I turned back toward him and exclaimed, "Damn Felix, how much stuff did you buy for this party?"

He grinned sheepishly and said, "Sometimes I go overboard, but it's just because I want everyone to have a good time."

I put my hand on his arm and said, "You know it's appreciated, but we don't need all that stuff to enjoy each other's company. Everyone being together is what makes something like this special."

A melancholy expression crossed his face as he said, "Yeah, I know."

His mood flipped, and he was upbeat again. "Hey, have you ever been to Sloss before, even for like a normal visit?"

I shook my head. "No, I've read about it online, and watched some holographic tours, but I've never been in person."

"Oh, it's great fun," he paused and glanced over at me, "but I don't suppose you had many places like Sloss where you're from, you know, Russia."

"Parks like it no, but facilities still in use like it, we had a few," I said.

He was quiet for a minute, and then said, "You haven't ever talked about Russia, or your past much. How was it over there? How did you come to immigrate here?"

What? How did we get to this topic? "It was, and still is, cold over there," I quipped, "and it's a different world compared to America."

He smiled at my joke, and said, "Yeah, I'll bet," another pause, "so, how hard was it to get a visa when you immigrated?"

This was damned peculiar. Felix had never been this pushy about my past. Sure, he'd shared the story about how he had been paralyzed with me, but he volunteered that, I hadn't dug it out of him. Maybe he was just trying to make small talk until we got to Sloss.

"It was a bit of a run through a minefield to get here, but luckily I made it, and still in one piece," I replied.

He nodded as we made our way through the heavy downtown traffic. I saw him start to ask another question, and cut him off. "Hey, is that Sloss over there?"

I pointed to a glowing area a couple of blocks from us. Before he could answer, I heard the heavy, rhythmic thump of powerful subwoofers. "Yep, there she is," he said.

We were still half a block away, but traffic was at a crawl as we approached the twin searchlights set up outside. The music grew in volume until I could make out more than just the bass line. Sloss was rocking out to *Dead Man's Party* by *Oingo Boingo*, a late eighties band that had Danny Elfman as a member. I mean, this place was jumping. It was completely different than I'd expected from all my online research.

According to the web, Sloss Furnaces was a smelting plant built in the late 1800's, when the production of pig iron began to grow exponentially in the young city of Birmingham. It was constructed on a huge, fifty-acre site, and occupies most of that land. During the next hundred years, Sloss was expanded. It helped supply iron and steel for America's war effort in the early 1900's, and enjoyed great prosperity through the middle of that century.

After its prime, Sloss, with its two four hundred ton blast furnaces and forty other buildings, was named a national historic landmark. It allows visitors to go on tours, either guided or alone, and holds various social events like weddings and corporate gatherings. The Halloween event was the most popular. It could be because of the numerous ghost stories surrounding the workers that were killed on the premises. Having a job where you handled glowing, red-hot molten iron before the time of OSHA was a risky proposition.

Another reason might be the way Sloss looked when it was dressed up for Halloween. The rusty-red brick structures were inter-connected by hundreds of cast iron pipes, all of them in various diameters. The pipes twisted and turned all over the buildings, like veins and arteries circling a huge heart. A DJ blasted his bass-heavy music, providing the *Wha-Whomp, Wha-Whomp*, sound of the heart's beat. While the revelers, dressed in their outlandish costumes, were the life's blood of Sloss. They coursed and surged through its chambers, relentlessly pushed on by the music.

The tallest structure at the site was the enormous pale-white water tower, which looked down over the pulsing organ from over three hundred feet in the air. If you viewed it from just the right angle, the lights and shadows played across it to form the visage of a grimacing human face. Like a masked, morbid surgeon, that loomed over the whole scene, ready to slice free their pulsing prize. The *face* sat on top of its long, lanky supports, which from below appeared to be arms. Arms that were reaching out to take the now freed heart as it choked and sputtered to a permanent stop.

The place gave me the damn creeps.

As enthralled as I was by the sights of Sloss, I noticed that Felix was taking a right turn away from the front entrance. "Hey, I thought this was the way in over here."

He smiled at me and said, "Yeah, that's the main entrance, but thanks to this," he tapped on the side of his wheelchair, "I get a special parking spot on the back side of the park. It's even closer to our reserved table."

"Oh, okay," I said and went back to gawking at all the spooky sights outside my window.

Felix drove further and further around the site, until the lighting became more infrequent, and the music grew distant. Finally, I noticed that we had reached a dark secluded area at the back of the park.

We turned toward a small gravel covered parking lot. In the lot stood regularly spaced massive concrete columns, which supported an elevated railway. I imagined it must have been used to move the ore around the factory. The Element's tires crunched and slid slightly as we turned into the small parking area. Just two other cars were parked here, and they were about fifty feet ahead. The drivers had positioned them on each side of where Felix was headed, pointing in at a forty-five degree angle. Both vehicles were white four-door sedans.

Felix pulled up near the other cars, put the Honda in park, and killed his lights. When he did, the lights on the other two cars flared to life, their beams meeting at the front of the Element. Not understanding, I turned toward Felix. He was squinting while his eyes adjusted to the glaring headlights, and even though it was cool in the Honda, sweat covered his face. I knew he could see me looking at him, but he refused to turn toward me. He behaved as if I didn't exist, and sat motionless, hands on top of his steering wheel. Oh, no...damn it all to hell.

Chapter 30

Not knowing what else to do, I was about to yank the door open and run for my life, when *they* moved out from behind the gray pillars. Two androids like the one I'd fought that night on the interstate, stood on each side of the Element, staying just inside the shadows. However, this time instead of a suit, these two were wearing what looked like a full set of body armor, complete with a grenade belt. To go with their black, military spec armor, they brandished fully automatic AK-47 rifles.

I was certain that I couldn't out maneuver two rifle-wielding, super bots, but it got worse. A sudden motion came from behind me, and I whirled about in my seat to face this immediate threat. Yet, all I was able to do was freeze as I came face to face with the barrel of a pistol. One of those damn androids had been hidden under all of Felix's crap the whole trip here. Except this one was different. He had an eye patch over his left eye, and the combat helmet he wore sat crookedly on his head. I realized it must have been the one I'd fought that night during the monsoon.

"Damn Patches, you're looking rough," I said.

"EEESCRRSHBRPERERERRBPBRPEEE!"

Whatever repairs had been made to him, hadn't improved his conversational skills.

277

Before Patches and I could do anymore catching up, a woman called out to me from somewhere in the shadows, "Slowly, and I mean, very, very, slowly, open the door and get out of the car. You have three seconds, or we will open fire and kill you both."

I knew that voice, and I knew she'd follow through on her threat and not think twice about it. Of course, if I got out, she might just shoot me for fun anyway. Oh well, it wasn't as if I had many options. I shouted back, "All right, don't shoot. I'm getting out."

Reaching over, I opened the door and began to ease myself out of the car. As I did, I bent low, so that for about two seconds I was out of their line of sight. I used this time to reach back and unfasten Viktor's data drive from around my neck. Having nowhere else to put it, I let it fall between my breasts and land in the bottom of my bra. I would have to hope that I wasn't searched thoroughly enough to find it.

"Put your hands over your head, Now!" the woman screamed.

I followed her instructions, as Patches opened his door and tried to exit the Honda. I glanced back at him, and saw that he was having trouble getting out of the van. It was obvious that something was wrong with his sense of balance, but he was able to struggle his way out of the Element's door. He steadied himself and leveled his gun at the back of my head. It made me wonder if a bullet fired from a pistol would penetrate my dense, metal skull. I decided finding that out, would be a last ditch effort on my part.

"Walk forward and stand in front of your car," came the voice from the darkness.

I moved slowly from the side, toward the front of the Element and into the brilliance of the crisscrossing headlights.

The voice called out again, "Come closer and let him get behind you."

I followed her instructions once again.

"There, stop right there," she said.

As I stood there in the light, Patches lumbered behind me, and the other two moved from their original positions to flank me on each side. I thought this was a tactical error, since if they had to fire, they could wind up hitting each other, but then I remembered whom I was dealing with. She didn't care if they destroyed themselves, not in the least.

After she felt that I was neutralized, Eliza emerged from the darkness in between the two sedans. She was dressed in a black leather body suit that clung to her like a coat of paint, and the front was unzipped about an inch below where her cleavage ended. For some reason, Eliza had changed her hairstyle to a fiery-red, short bob with a small curl at the end. After a moment of thought, I realized it was close to the style that *I* normally wore.

She began walking up to me, savoring every step. The stiletto heels of her black leather boots sank between the loose pieces of gravel, but it didn't make her stride look awkward. It only made her hips sway left and right even more than usual, which bounced her Makarov pistol about violently.

Eliza walked right up into my face and studied me for a good minute. Finally, she said, "What the fuck are you wearing?"

Something in the back of my mind told me not to, but I couldn't help myself. "Look who's talking. Hey, don't you have a john that's due for his spanking right about now?"

Her left hand shot up almost too fast for me to see and she grabbed my ponytail. Yanking my head back as far as it would go, she put her lips up to my ear. "Shut the fuck up before I shoot you and your four-wheeled boss over there."

I didn't reply. It would have been hard to speak anyway with my neck stretched so far. I heard her fumbling around for something, and then she placed something that felt like a gun against my head.

"You think you're so damn clever. That you can just do anything you want, with no repercussions. Don't you? Don't you!" she screamed into my ear.

I thought I might have pushed her too far this time. I tried to talk, but it came out as garbled nonsense.

"Well, I guess now you know that you can't," she said and pulled the trigger.

A pain shot through my scalp as the projectile tore its way through my skin. I realized I wasn't dead when the headache came over me. It hurt like hell and I could only dampen it down to a dull throb.

Eliza released my hair and my head snapped forward. I fought off waves of dizziness and nausea as I lifted my gaze to stare at her. Her smirk was unnerving, "There, that little pill will make sure you don't make any unapproved calls."

It took me a second to realize what she'd said, but when I did, panic flooded over me. I tried everything, Internet, GPS, even my compass. It was all disabled. Eliza had cut me off from the outside world. I couldn't connect to anything or anyone, and it was terrifying.

Seeing my expression, she erupted into one of her psychotic laughs. She ended it suddenly, and leaned into my face. "Now, let's find out what else you have," she purred in a way that set me on edge.

With her eyes locked with mine, she ran her hands over my body, searching me for weapons. She found my phone, and crushed it in front of me, letting the pieces fall to the ground. Confiscating my Glocks, she tossed them over near the sedans. Then, Eliza got personal. She began searching places that would have made a TSA agent blush. Unfortunately, my worst fear came true. She found Viktor's research.

As she pulled the drive out of my cleavage, her reaction was sickening. "Well, well, no wonder we couldn't find it at your apartment. You were wearing it around like a high school girl wears a promise ring."

Furious, I moved toward her, but the guards stepped closer and aimed their rifles at my head. This elicited another wicked laugh from her, as she pocketed the drive into a small pouch on her belt.

"Now dear sister, turn around, put your hands behind your back, and lean over the hood of the car," she said.

I eyed her suspiciously, and didn't move. In response, she pulled her Makarov, pointing it at my forehead. "Do you have *any* idea how much I want to kill you? Just give me a damn excuse!"

That much was true. She must have strict orders from Entsky to bring me back alive, or she would have finished me already. I had no choice, and followed her commands.

As I bent over the hood of the Element, I glanced up and saw Felix looking at me through the windshield. His face was pale, and he looked horrified. I shouldn't have said anything, but I had to know. "Why, Felix?"

At first, he simply stared at me, as if he couldn't believe what was happening. Then, he inched his left hand off the steering wheel and lowered the window on his door. His voice sounded heartbroken. "That woman contacted me several weeks ago and asked me a bunch of questions about you. At first, I wouldn't tell her anything, even when she offered to pay for the information."

He swallowed hard, and continued. "But, then a couple of the proposals that I'd been counting on to keep FlexJen solvent, fell through. I..I was going to lose the company if I didn't come up with the money. The banks wouldn't lend it to me, they said I was already overextended and wouldn't help."

"I was out of options," he sighed, "They...they told me you were a fugitive and that you would only be deported."

He couldn't look me in the eyes anymore, and dropped his head. "She offered me enough money to keep my business afloat for a whole year, and…I took it. I'm sorry. My god, I'm so sorry, Anna." he whispered.

When he looked back to me, his eyes were brimming with tears. I was desperate to help him, but I wasn't sure how. At least I could absolve him.

"It's okay Felix. You didn't know. Eliza has fooled a lot of people with her sweet words and promises."

The expression on his face brightened slightly, and I forced a look of determination onto mine. With confidence I didn't actually have, I lowered my voice to a whisper and said, "What we need to do now, is focus on getting out of here. You have to do exactly what I say and don't question me. After she takes me off your car and becomes distracted, I want you to inch your way backward and get out of here."

He was about to speak, but I cut him off. "No, promise me you will do it, Felix."

He nodded, and I smiled back at him. Lying, I said, "Everything's going to be fine."

The guards that had been on each side of me had approached while I spoke with Felix. Now, one of them put their weapon right against the side of my head, while the other pushed me forward and pulled on my arms. I realized they were going to bind my hands together, making me helpless. I was out of time, but still outnumbered by too many enemies. Then, I had an idea.

I forced myself to concentrate, expanding the size of my wrists and hands as much as I could. It wasn't going to be much, those parts of my body weren't as malleable as others, but I had to try something.

One of the androids pulled my hands together, crossing them at my wrists and I heard the sound of a zip tie being pulled. The hard plastic bit into my flesh, as my tormentor pulled it tight. Painful throbbing in my hands told me that he'd cut off my circulation.

Sounds of crunching gravel came from behind me, then someone grabbed my ponytail yet again, and snatched me off the car. I gritted my teeth as they whirled me around, spinning me so hard that I lost my balance and fell on my rear.

Looking up, Eliza stood over me. She was in full *gloat mode*.

"What? Did you wonder why your *friend* betrayed you? I'll tell you why, money! He sold you like a steer at auction, like an old dress on eBay, like a busted up, used car!" she said.

I tried to stand, and fell again, on purpose. I was inching back away from Felix, hoping he could drive away without Eliza noticing. Maybe I could make my way to the huge support column ten or so feet behind me. I shouldn't have worried. Eliza rushed at me and grabbed my shirt with both hands. She lifted me up to my feet, then drove me backwards into the column, slamming my back and head against the concrete structure.

My vision blurred, and I saw double for what felt like forever. Meanwhile, Eliza kept ranting, which was exactly what I wanted.

"Is this why you're better than me, because you can give a shit about these worthless meat sacks? Tell me, what good did that do you? Did they hide you from me? Help you escape from me perhaps?" she asked.

As my vision cleared, she grabbed my chin with her right hand, while holding me in place with her left. Her grip was like a vise as she forced me to meet her rage-filled stare. Spit flew from her mouth as she emphasized each word. "No! They...sold...you...to...me!"

"You...You'll never be able to understand, and that's why I feel sorry for you," I said.

She let go of my face and before I could even react, punched me in the stomach. The blow was so hard, that I doubled over and fell to my knees. I couldn't breathe, but I could vomit.

She squatted down to my level and whispered while I retched. "Don't you dare ever *feel* anything for me except hate. Because that is all I feel for you."

When I could breathe again, I spat a few times and looked up. In my peripheral vision, I saw Felix easing his Honda back away from the sedans. He only made it about a foot, before he was betrayed by the sound of crunching gravel.

I knew Eliza had heard him when her expression changed. She looked at me and grinned that evil, psychotic smile that I knew all too well. As she started to rise, I whispered, "Please, no," to her. She just looked down at me and placed her hand on her chest in feigned offense.

Her words dripped with poisoned honey as she said, "Mister Jennings, don't rush off without the rest of your payment."

As she stood, Patches came and took up a vigil at my side. She shot a look at the other two androids, and they turned and walked toward the sedans. Opening the driver's doors they got in and cranked them up. Since I hadn't heard her give them any commands, I figured she must have a type of mental link with them. I also noticed that she'd just cut her advantage down by half.

As she walked toward Felix, his eyes grew wide and he looked over to me for help. Struggling, I got to my feet and leaned against the concrete pillar as if I was still out of commission. What I was actually doing, was reducing the size of my wrists and hands in an attempt to slip them free.

I covertly checked my guard to see if he was paying attention to me, and he was. However, I was on the side with his blind eye, so I had that going for me. I pulled and twisted my hands, desperate to free them, but that bastard had pulled the zip tie so tight, that all I'd accomplished was restoring my blood flow.

Eliza had reached Felix by now and I could hear her talking with him, "It wouldn't be right if I didn't live up to my end of the bargain Mister

Jennings. Now would it?"

"Th…that's all right. We're even," I heard Felix stammer.

"No, no, no, I insist," Eliza said as she produced a white envelope from somewhere I couldn't see, "I have to maintain my reputation. After all, what's a woman once she's sullied her reputation?"

Damn it, I couldn't get my hands free. I twisted and pulled, wrenched and jerked. I was working them back and forth so furiously, that my arms began to sweat.

"You may leave now Mister Jennings, our transaction is concluded," I heard her say.

Felix looked at me one last time, and mouthed the words, 'I'm sorry'. Then he looked down and checked his console, preparing to back up.

What happened next, was slowed down due to my combat reflexes. Eliza turned to me and winked, as her right hand dropped to her Makarov. She turned back to Felix, while drawing her pistol and pointing it at the side of his head.

I pulled my hands as hard as I could, not caring anymore if Patches saw me. Thanks to the sweat running down my arms, my hands finally slipped free from the damned zip tie…right as Eliza fired her gun, point blank at Felix.

His head snapped to the side and blood sprayed the inside of the car. The car that he'd always kept so immaculate. Felix sank down in his seat, unmoving. I heard myself scream as she pulled the trigger again, pumping another round into his already dead body.

He must have released the brake, because in the silence that followed, the Honda inched backwards in a lazy arc across the crunching gravel. After a moment, it bumped into one of the support columns and came to rest.

I kept my hands hidden behind my back as Eliza turned around toward me. "Now, are you ready to go?"

My face contorted into a snarl as I growled, "Oh, yeah. I'm fucking ready."

Chapter 31

As Eliza looked at me, I snapped my hand out, grabbing at the waist of my guard. Because of his bad eye, he didn't see me move until I already had my fingers through two of the safety pin rings protruding from the tops of his grenades. I pulled the rings free and flicked them at his face. "Think fast Patches!"

While he dropped his weapon and moved for the grenades, I sprinted toward the two sedans. Out of the corner of my eye, I saw that Eliza was drawing her Makarov. As she leveled the pistol at me and pulled the trigger, I dove forward, going into a roll. I came out of it right beside my Glock pistols, grabbing one in each hand.

I pointed the one in my right hand back toward Eliza and fired blindly, forcing her to seek cover and stop shooting at me for the time being. With my left, I aimed at the android in the far sedan as he moved to exit the car. My barrage of bullets convinced him to stay put for now.

In that moment, I ran forward between the two sedans, and kicked the now opening driver's side door of the one nearest me. It slammed into the android trying to exit his vehicle. The door hit him with such force, that he was knocked horizontal across the front seat, with his legs dangling outside the car.

Still running forward, I risked a glance back over my shoulder. The sight of Patches still struggling to get the grenades off his belt was encouraging. He groped at them desperately as he screamed.

"EEESCRRSHBRPERERERRBPBRPEEE!"

"EEESCRRSHBRPERERERRBPBRPEEE!"

Just as I thought he wasn't going to make it in time, he got the grenades loose and flung them in the direction of Felix's Honda…which was where Eliza had taken cover from my gunfire.

"You stupid fuck!" she screamed and bolted away from the van. She had gotten a couple of steps, when the grenades exploded. The concussive blast knocked her about fifteen feet through the air, where she landed face first onto the gravel. Even at my distance, it staggered me, and I stumbled before regaining my stride. I bolted around the corner of a nearby building, looking for somewhere to catch my breath.

Finding an open door in the side of the three-story building, I headed inside. It was dark, and I had to pick my way through the various pieces of debris scattered across the floor. I made my way over to a window that faced the parking lot. Placing my back against the wall, I peeked out to access how much damage I'd caused.

Eliza had picked herself up off the ground and from what I could see, had only suffered superficial abrasions. She was stomping toward Patches, who still lay on the ground.

He managed to sit up as she reached him, and emit his eerie cry.

"EEESCRRSHBRPERERERRBPBRPEEE…"

She held her hand up to silence him. "I knew I shouldn't have tried to repair you. Even before Anna kicked your ass, you were nothing but a fuck up."

Eliza pointed her pistol at his head, and fired three rounds into him before he could even screech in protest.

"There, at least I don't have to hear that god awful sound again," she said as his body lay twitching on the ground.

She turned to the other two androids, which had gotten out of the cars and looked uninjured. Without speaking, she pointed in a couple of directions, and the androids headed off to begin their search. Before Eliza could join them, the gas tank on the Element exploded, sending a fireball into the night sky. She shielded her eyes and face, but the explosion was more of a light and sound show than anything dangerous.

As the burning car died down some, she called out to me, "How does it feel Anna? How does it feel to know that you failed again, and because of you, another person is dead?" She looked over her shoulder at the burning hulk and continued her taunts, "Not only dead, but pretty much well done by now. Oh what am I thinking, it doesn't even get to you anymore. You know, cause it's happened so often. Hey, that makes you more like me than ever!" Her maniacal laugh echoed off the old deserted buildings as she ran into the darkness. The hunt was on.

I pretended to myself that Eliza's words didn't hurt, but I couldn't fool my own conscious. Shaking my head, I realized this was exactly what she wanted. I had to get moving, and find a place to examine my head. If I managed to undo what Eliza had done, I could call for help. Because even though I'd just seen a colossal sound and light show, I was sure it hadn't been enough to be seen or heard over the Halloween party. I could still hear it from out here.

Turning away from the window, I moved deeper into the building. Behind an enormous, rusted generator, I found a flight of rickety stairs leading to the second floor. Leaping over the railing that was intended to keep guests out, I picked my way up the derelict steps. This level of the building had a much more oppressive atmosphere than the first. There was a musty, neglected smell, mixed with the overpowering odor of machine grease. It was also much darker, which made the pits formed by sections of collapsed floor a challenge to navigate.

Gingerly, I made my way around the gaps in the floor and found a spot near the stairs up to the third level. It was dark and secluded, with no windows visible. Sitting down on the grimy hardwood, I began to feel around on my head. I easily found the entry wound, where my hair was matted with blood, but it took me longer to find the device Eliza had shot into me. Right under the base of my ponytail, there was a capsule-shaped lump about the size of a multivitamin. I wasn't sure if it was what she'd intended, but my evil sister had lodged the device where it would be difficult to extract. I'd have to undo my ponytail and then make an incision in my scalp to rid myself of the damned thing. Just unwrapping my hair would take several minutes. Minutes I realized I didn't have, as I heard soft footsteps on the level below me.

Time to get moving. I stood and tiptoed toward the stairs up to the third level, but the deteriorating floor betrayed me. A few feet from the base of the stairs, there was a loud crack as the ancient wood splintered under my foot. The footsteps below stopped for a moment, then accelerated toward my location. Stealth be damned, I bolted for the stairs.

It had been a good choice, as a hail of bullets splintered the boards where I had made the noise. They followed right behind me as I reached the stairwell. It was in worse shape than the first, but I didn't have time to be picky. I chose the best pathway up that I could see, and made it to the third floor without falling through the rotten wood.

I could hear my pursuer climbing up to the second floor, so I didn't have much time. Looking around, this area was completely open space with a few required support columns to hold up the ceiling. The corners had large unopened crates, probably containing long forgotten smelting equipment. I noticed the hardwood flooring was in worse shape than that on the second level. There were several holes in the twenty-foot high ceiling and rain had rotted much of the hardwood, while weakening the rest. Running along the ceiling, there were thick iron beams, woven together in a complex pattern of squares. Long chains that almost reached the ground hung from various places along the beams. The half-inch thick chains were mounted to an elaborate track system that had wheels on each side of the beams. I tested one of them and saw that they could be rolled to different areas of the large open space. From the size of them, I guessed they were used to move large machinery around.

Hearing the footsteps grow nearer, I saw that some of the cast iron beams angled down and exited through a set of fifteen-foot wide wooden doors. The doors were open, but I couldn't see what was beyond them. I decided it was too risky, and looked for a place to hide. I pulled as many of the chains around myself as I could, and readied my Glocks. Whoever came up the stairs, was going to get a nasty surprise.

I listened as the *clomp…clomp* of footsteps drew ever closer. I wiped the sweat off my forehead, *clomp…clomp*. Holding my breath, I took aim at the top of the stairs, *clomp…clomp*, and then…silence. They'd stopped, but why? They must suspect a trap and…

My thought was interrupted when an AK-47 popped up above the stairs and opened fire. I bent low and gathered as many of the chains in front of me as I could, trying to protect myself. The android rushed up the stairs a second later, still firing the rifle without any clear target. Now that I could see him, I returned fire, and he zeroed in on my location as we rained bullets down on each other. Luckily, I had the advantage of cover, so none of his found their mark. The android had no cover, and even through his constant stream of bullets, I managed to tag him once in the left forearm and once again in the left thigh.

The cacophony of gunfire ceased as we both emptied our magazines. For a heartbeat, we stared at each other. Then, he made a move to reload his weapon, and I sprang forward, dragging a few of the heavy chains with me. As he locked the fresh magazine in place, I slammed the chains into his upper body screaming, "Too slow, Lefty!"

The impact staggered him and he dropped the AK-47. It bounced back down the stairs, coming to rest on the second floor of the building. He came at me fast, trying to grapple me around my neck. Still holding the chains, I swung the ends of them up, deflecting his attack and keeping him at a distance. He began to circle me, and I moved with him, keeping the dangling chains between us. I sized him up, noticing that he was favoring his right side because of the gunshot wounds.

Stepping back, I lured him more toward the center of the room. I knew that his comrades would be on their way, so I had to end this fight in a hurry. I weighed the chain in my hands, and getting a good feel for how it moved, began to slowly whirl it around in front of myself.

The android didn't attack. He just circled. His plan was to wait for the reinforcements to arrive, something I couldn't allow. I lowered the spinning chains and turned slightly toward the large open doorway. "Well, if you don't want to dance, I'll go get myself another partner."

That did the trick, he rushed at me to prevent my escape, and I snapped the chains back into position. As I lashed out, he blocked the one coming from the right, but his left arm was too slow to prevent my off hand attack. The heavy iron links slammed into the side of his face with a loud crack, and the stunned android staggered back.

I pressed my advantage, and swinging my chain in a slower, looping arc, caught him at the base of his neck. As it wrapped itself around his throat, I launched the other with the same goal, except this time I was aiming for his chest. Before he could raise his arms, the second chain had wrapped around him twice, and pinned both his arms to his sides.

I wasn't sure that these androids needed to breathe the way I did, but since they were made by the same team of scientists, I felt the odds were in my favor.

Proving me correct, the android began to make quiet choking sounds as the makeshift noose finished closing off his windpipe. I almost felt a twinge of guilt as I swung toward him on another one of the chains and stomped on the floor underneath him. There was a loud crunching sound and the rotted floorboards splintered and fell to the level below.

My momentum carried me over the large hole I'd just created in the floor. When I landed on the other side, I looked back to see Lefty jerking and convulsing as he swung over the open pit. I turned away from the gruesome sight and moved toward the open wooden door leading outside.

After taking a few steps, I heard someone charging up the stairs to the third floor. Out of options, I took several long strides to get up my speed and leapt for a chain. Grabbing hold, I rocketed toward the open doorway. I'd cleared it by maybe five feet when another hail of automatic gunfire ricocheted behind me. To my relief, the track was still in one piece and took me around the corner to the left, away from the swarm of angry bullets.

Holding on with both hands, I flew through the night air about a hundred feet off the ground. If I hadn't been running for my life, it might have actually been fun.

As the track straightened and headed for a nearby building, my luck ran out. The large, red brick workshop had a set of doors just like the ones I'd made my daring escape through, but these were closed tight. Not only that, but they looked nice and solid, unlike some of the wooden floors I'd encountered. I had about three seconds to figure out something, or I was going to splat like a bug on a windshield when I hit those doors.

I glanced around, desperate to find a way out of my predicament, and I noticed that there was an android about two seconds behind me. He was holding on with only one hand as he tried to aim his AK-47 at me with the other. The android realized it was a lost cause since we were both swinging so erratically, and he didn't waste the ammo trying to hit me.

I was about two seconds from being flattened, when I saw a series of pipes running between two different buildings. They were about ten feet wide and twenty feet below my rail. I'd have to time this just right. In this case, being an android paid off, and I ran the calculations in my head. Point four seconds later, I let go of my chain and landed in a crouch on top of the largest pipe.

Knowing company was right behind me, I stood and ran toward the nearest building. The music from the Halloween party was growing louder as I neared where the pipes curved around the outside of the workshop. I took the corner as fast as I dared and shielded my head with my hands as more bullets plinked and bounced all around me.

Slamming my back against the wall, I dropped the empty magazines from my Glocks and jammed my last two spares into place. I hit the slide release on both guns, and leaned around the corner firing with both hands as the android charged toward me.

I knew I hit him in the chest a couple of times as he returned fire, but I also knew he had on a bullet proof vest. My aim would have to be perfect, if I wanted to take him down with my guns. He was approaching too quickly, and I had to abandon my corner. I fired a few more rounds in his direction, and bolted further down the pipes.

After about fifty feet, I reached the end of the road. The pipes I was currently on entered the side of a building with no extra room around them. Searching around, I saw another set down and to my right, about fifteen feet away. Backing up a step or two, I readied myself to jump. However, right before I leapt, my left foot fell through a weakened section of pipe and trapped my leg up to the knee.

I pulled and yanked, but my boot was caught on the jagged edges of the opening. Cursing, I drew my pistols and aimed them at the approaching android. In response, he leveled his rifle. We both opened fire at the same time.

I focused in on his upper neck, above the protection of his vest. With lead flying all around me, my concentration paid off as I hit him once, then twice near the throat. After the second shot, he staggered and almost fell. I thought he was finished, but with a dogged determination, he charged at me and dove.

I had let my guard down for just that brief second, and it cost me. The android landed between my legs, leading with the butt of his AK-47. It caught me square in the jaw, and if my foot hadn't been stuck, I would have fallen off the pipe. As it was, I fell flat on my back, and he straddled me, slamming the rifle into my face again.

He would have killed me if his blows had been full strength, but the wounds I'd given him were taking their toll. The android began to slow, and I could feel that thick, silvery fluid that they used for blood dripping from his neck onto my chest.

As he raised the rifle for a third strike, I made an exaggerated motion with my left hand, bringing my pistol up to aim at him. He turned and knocked it free of my grasp with his rifle, and it bounced off the pipe to the ground below.

He never saw my right, as I brought it up under the bottom of his vest. When he felt the barrel sticking him in the stomach, his eyes snapped to mine, full of realization. I emptied my last five hollow points into him, and his eyes went dark. He slumped forward, trapping me under his weight for a moment as more of the silver goo burbled out onto my neck.

"Fuck that's nasty!" I said to no one in particular as I rolled him to the side.

He fell off the pipe, and slammed into the ground with a *Whumph.*

With the immediate threat eliminated, I was able to loosen the laces on my boot and work my foot free of the collapsed pipe. Digging my boot out of the hole, I slipped it back onto my foot, and began to lace it back into place.

I hadn't seen Eliza in a while, and was beginning to wonder where she was hiding. Then I realized that I was in a terrible tactical position. My guns were now gone, and hers weren't. What I should do was run, and get as far away from this place as possible. However, I wasn't going to do that. Eliza still had the data drive containing Viktor's research, and I was *not* going to let her keep it.

A new song began blasting from the Halloween party nearby, and I knew how to draw her out. I would find the party and make it appear as if I was planning my escape. Once Eliza saw that, she'd come to me. Involving a crowd of innocent people in my plan gave me a knot in my stomach. I certainly didn't want to get anyone hurt, but I was confident that even Eliza wasn't crazy enough to open fire on hundreds of random people. Was she?

Chapter 32

As I ran down the pipe, the music from the party continued to get louder, and the surrounding area grew brighter. I must be getting close to the party now. In front of me, the pipes split into two directions, one circling back the way I'd came, the other entering an enormous brick and wood structure under a dirty, partially open window. I ran in that direction, hoping I could get through the window and check out the building.

When I reached the old rusty window, I grasped the framing and pulled, but the metal hinges had rusted in their current position and wouldn't budge. I began working on prying it open, and it took several stressful minutes before I'd widened it enough for me to fit through. I scampered inside and dropped back down to the pipes below.

As I entered the building, I was stunned. I knew I should keep moving, but I had to look around for just a moment at the sights and sounds all around me.

The building I'd entered was rectangular and roughly half the size of a football field. One of its short sides had no wall at all, and was entirely open to the outside lot. That must have been how they were able to get the mammoth crane inside. It was the size of several tour busses, and almost reached up to the pipe where I was standing, over fifty feet in the air. It sat along one of the long sides of the stadium, somewhat rusty and unused. Yes, I said stadium. Because whatever this building had been used for in the past, loading freight cars or storing dinosaurs, this was where the Halloween party was going down tonight.

The open side held all the partygoers, over six hundred by my guess. Near the back of that area, sat tables where people were enjoying their dinner. As you moved into the building, the tables disappeared, changing the space into a huge open dance floor that ran all the way to the stage. There were about a hundred dancers, waving their glow sticks and generally enjoying themselves. I couldn't blame them, it was good music. Along with the DJ I'd heard earlier, Sloss had gotten a live band for tonight. I didn't know who they were, but they were currently performing a techno dance song, and they were nailing it.

The pipe I stood on ran all the way to the other side of the building, right over the elevated wooden stage where the band was performing. It continued on, through the wall, but it also was about twenty feet above the enormous crane. I could run across, make a leap to the crane, and climb my way down to the dance floor below.

Looking around for Eliza and seeing her nowhere, I took off at a trot toward the other side of the building. I paused again over the stage, allowing her time to find me, when I noticed a smoky haze had gathered in this area. At first, I was worried that my crazy sister had set the place on fire, but my nose soon told me that this wasn't *that* kind of smoke. I looked down as the band kicked into another song, and that was when I heard the shot.

Reflexively, I ducked at the noise and a searing pain burned my left shoulder. I knew the shot hadn't come from in front of me, so I tumbled to the side, rotating around to face the other direction. As I did, two more shots whizzed by my head and legs, giving me an idea where the shooter was.

I came out of my roll, into a crouch and scanned the area above me. Hidden in the shadows further back behind the stage, Eliza sat on an iron beam supporting the buildings roofing. She was looking at her Makarov, and I could see its breech was open, indicating her magazine was empty. She felt around on her belt, and grabbed a new one. I was a sitting duck.

As she loaded and readied her pistol, I hatched a crazy plan. Eliza leveled the gun at me right as I jumped toward her. She paused as I flew through the air, thinking I'd just jumped down to the stage, but she was wrong. I wasn't that desperate, at least not yet. My target was the large suspended lighting fixture that hung under her perch.

Landing on the eight-foot circular dome, I grabbed at the cabling that held the light to the beam. The whole fixture began to swing like an out of balance load of laundry, and I could only hope that the cable was sturdy enough to hold me. I looked up to where Eliza had been and saw that she was leaning over the edge, preparing to fire. I rocked the fixture back and forth, moving my body in random directions to throw off her aim. Bullets hit all around me, and I jerked the lighting fixture's cable violently, making it sway even more.

She rapid-fired her pistol out of frustration, and soon I heard the satisfying clicking sound of a hammer falling with no ammunition to strike. I waited for her to pull out an AK-47 or a grenade, but she apparently didn't have any with her. Eliza had run out of options. No ammunition, and no way to climb down where I was without me pummeling her unconscious before she reached me. I couldn't help myself.

"Great shooting Sis, you actually managed to graze me when my back was turned. Maybe you shouldn't have counted on your tin soldiers to do all your dirty work. You're starting to lose a step," I said.

Putting my finger to my mouth as if I was thinking, I continued. "Or maybe you're just too afraid to face me after I kicked your ass the last time. Yeah, I bet that's it. Man, if Stepan could see you now, he'd…"

I didn't get to finish. My intention had been to taunt her into climbing down so I could take her out on the cable, but my plan worked too well. Eliza's face contorted into a snarl and she hurled herself at me.

"You bitch! I'll kill you!" she screamed.

My eyes widened in panic, because I was sure she'd break the fixture away from the ceiling beam once she landed. Out of pure reflex, I sidestepped her lunge, and she adjusted in mid flight. Grabbing the cable with her right hand, she swung around on it and kicked me in the side.

The light fixture rocked like a toy ship in a tidal wave as I fell toward the edge. Metal screeched, and I heard something give way. I managed to wrap my legs around the dancing cable as it whipped forward, lengthening and dropping the both of us about ten feet before it caught and held fast. Eliza's grip was broken on the cable and she was thrown to the base of the fixture. Meanwhile, I bounced up several feet and slammed back down on it, smacking my head against the hard metal.

Sparks spewed from the halogen light as it ruptured. The band stopped playing, and the crowd below us began shouting. Dazed, I turned my head and looked down to see hundreds of people staring up at us as we swung over the stage.

I regained my wits just in time to see Eliza charging forward. I pulled my legs up to my chest as she threw herself on top of me. Her hands wrapped around my neck and it was like I was caught in a vise.

She began lifting my head and slamming it back down against the fixture. Eyes wild with hate, she kept screaming, "Shut up! Shut up! Why the fuck does he want you back? Why?"

I clawed at her hands with my fingers, but I couldn't get a grip on them. Darkness filled the edges of my vision and bright light flashed across my sight each time she smashed my head back down. I realized she wasn't going to stop. Eliza was going to kill me unless I did something. Panic set in and I thrashed about like a fish out of water. In a last ditch effort, I kicked out with both feet using all my remaining strength.

Her fingernails dug deep gouges in my neck as I flung her off me. My vision cleared in time to see her stumble backwards. I'd kicked her back, just as the fixture was swinging in the other direction. Her feet tangled in the cable, and she fell. Bouncing once on her side, she rolled and grabbed at the metal, but it was too smooth. Her fingernails made that horrible chalkboard squealing sound, and she slid over the side.

Her scream echoed throughout the now quiet stadium, ending with a resounding metallic crash.

My god, I'd killed her. I stumbled to my feet, and holding onto the cable, looked over the edge. Eliza was sprawled in the ruins of a drum set, and she wasn't moving.

I had to sit down. This wasn't what I'd wanted. What was I supposed to do now? Yes, she was one evil bitch, but I'd always thought there was some chance I might connect with her. Fix her. Now all that was…

Without warning, the fixture broke loose from the ceiling. I rode the lighting canister down, as it plummeted toward the stage. There was a strange feeling of weightlessness, which came to an abrupt end when the light and I crashed into an electronic keyboard.

For what felt like forever, I couldn't breathe. I figured that it must be because I was dead, and didn't need to breathe anymore. When my chest convulsed, and air filled my lungs, I realized that somehow, I was alive.

I eased myself into a sitting position, and then pulled myself up to stand. I moved my limbs around, and by some miracle, I hadn't broken any of them. My entire nervous system made it feel like my body was on fire, but I was hoping that would pass. Looking around, I saw that the band had fled the stage, and I stood alone among the rubble of my crash site. I'd landed near the left side of the stage, and I soon realized that the entire crowd was staring at me. Their expressions were full of awe, and they silently waited, unsure of what was happening.

A rustling came from near center stage, and to my surprise, I saw Eliza stand up as well. The sight filled me with various conflicting emotions that I didn't have time to process. She soon noticed me as well, and we locked stares with each other. Slowly, we moved out of the rubble and oriented ourselves to what was happening.

The crowd began to murmur among themselves, trying to make sense of what they saw.

"Well that one's Lara Croft, but who's the other one?"

"Did you see the way they fell? That was the best stunt I've ever seen!"

"What the hell is Black Widow doing fighting with Lara Croft?"

"Best, party, EVER!"

Stacks of amplified speakers that were about the size of tractor-trailers spit static and crackled to life. From each side of the stage, a preprogrammed announcement came thundering out. "Good evening, we hope everyone is enjoying the entertainment at Sloss Furnaces tonight. You know, just because the band has taken a break, doesn't mean you have to stop dancing. Let's keep this party rocking. Everyone get on the dance floor!"

The voice cut out, and techno music blared out of the speakers. The beat was so fast that at first, I thought a software glitch had altered the song's speed. Upon hearing the music, the crowd cheered and began to chant. Some of them were yelling, "Lara! Lara! Lara!" while others screamed, "Widow! Widow! Widow!"

A male voice in the song shouted over the beat, "Mortal Kombat!"

It finally dawned on me that the crowd thought we were fighting as part of the evening's entertainment, and they were rooting for their favorite. Costumed guests surged forward and gathered around the base of the stage, trying to get the best view they could for the upcoming fight scene.

Eliza and I stalked around, sizing each other up. I noticed she was dragging her left leg just a bit, and thought maybe her hip had been injured in the fall. At the same time, I hoped she didn't notice the pain I was in from my messed up nervous system.

When she spoke to me, she used a different voice. It was higher pitched, and she really poured on the Russian accent. Her words were picked up by one of the microphones still standing all around the stage. The music even automatically lowered in volume, so the crowd could hear her better. "I'm impressed. You actually tried to kill me. You failed like always, but you tried. Way to grow some balls."

"Ooooooooo!" echoed through the stadium as half the crowd appreciated Eliza's mocking.

Ah, she must somehow know this Black Widow character, and was playing her role so her cover wasn't blown, nice thinking.

I replied in my Lara voice, "You've got it wrong, Love. I was just trying to defend myself. If I'd tried to kill you, you wouldn't be standing there looking like a stretch of bad tarmac. You'd be dead."

"Ooooooooo!" came from what must have been my supporters.

"Why don't you save yourself a public humiliation and just come with me. You know, like a good girl," she said.

"Widow! Widow! Widow!"

"Why don't you give me the data drive, and walk away before I have to *really* hurt you," I said.

"Lara! Lara! Lara!"

Eliza reached into a pouch on her belt, and fished out the drive. She held it up for me to see and said, "You want this little thing? Why it's so flimsy, I could break it with just two fingers."

She flexed her hand and the drive bent in the middle. I lost it. Grabbing the closest thing I saw, a cherry red Gibson guitar, I charged toward her.

303

"Give me that data you demented dipshit!" I screamed.

"Lara! Lara! Lara!"

She dropped the drive back in her belt pouch and grabbed her own guitar, a baby blue Fender, and raised it defensively. Her trademark psychotic laugh blasted from the speakers as she blocked my overhead smash.

"Not on your life, you chertovski suka!" she said.

"Widow! Widow! Widow!"

Eliza had just insulted me in Russian. She *was* pissed. The collision of our guitars knocked us apart a few feet, and we began circling each other. I swung for her midsection, but she parried and pushed me out of position. Coming back around, she was able to clip my side before I could leap back. The blow wasn't hard, but my messed up nervous system translated the hit to a feeling of burning fire all down that side of my body. I grimaced and went for an overhead smash. When she blocked, I let go of my guitar and it flew behind me. Dropping into a kneeling position, I punched her in the left hip as hard as possible. Eliza fell backwards, landing on her rear, but holding her guitar in front of herself.

I stood and walked back to retrieve my Gibson. Eliza scooted back and used her Fender to stand. I could tell her left leg was on the verge of total failure. This fight was almost over.

I circled her slowly, and she backed up more to keep some distance between us. Once I had her standing where I wanted, I rushed her. Charging her left flank, I swung my guitar in low, forcing her to reach down and parry my attack. Our guitars collided and blew apart, showering us with colorful splinters and coiled steel wires. Eliza was so off balance from my attack, she couldn't see the next one coming. I dropped the shattered neck of my guitar and grabbed the microphone stand that was off to my left. Using it like a baseball bat, I swung it down toward the back of her head. The heavy base connected with her skull and a loud *crack* rang out. The base flew off the stand, broken by the impact. Eliza straightened, her eyes unfocused, and I swept the metal rod around, aiming for her wounded hip. My improvised weapon made contact right at her hip joint, and she collapsed in a heap.

The crowd went wild and chanted my characters name. "Lara! Lara! Lara!"

I turned and threw the microphone stand down on the stage behind me and looked back to Eliza. She had managed to get into a sitting position, feet out in front of her. I spoke to her softly, so the crowd couldn't hear, and this time, I used my own voice.

"Now, give me Viktor's drive so I can leave," I said.

She sneered at me and softly said, "Come and get it, if you're not afraid."

I took a step closer to her, and she shifted her weight. I sighed and said, "Eliza, you and Stepan could go about your lives, doing whatever the hell you wanted, and I'd never bother either of you. If you'd just let me live in peace."

"I'll never stop coming for you, this I swear." She tried to laugh that insane laugh of hers, but it stuck in her throat and she could only cough.

"I'm coming for the data drive, are you going to make me kill you?" I asked as I approached her.

She put her head down and said, "No, no...I'm going to kill you first."

Something about the way she said it made me freeze in my tracks, but it was too late. She adjusted her right leg, and the heel of her boot flew at me. The attack was so absurd, it caught me by complete surprise, and I couldn't get out of the way. The projectile wasn't large, only the size of a thick pencil, but it had serious speed behind it. It struck me in my right thigh, just below my shorts, and sank in far enough to hit my femur.

Searing hot pain so intense that I almost blacked out flooded my system. Through tear-blurred eyes, I saw her getting her other leg into position to fire the killing blow. If Eliza's left leg hadn't been defective, she would have already hit me right in the chest and made good on her statement. Luckily, it took her an extra second to aim, and by then, I had recovered enough to avoid the projectile. Right as she fired, I dropped to the stage floor, and it sailed harmlessly above me.

"Widow! Widow! Widow!" came from the frenzied crowd.

As I lay on the stage trying to dampen the pain in my thigh, Eliza struggled to her feet and began to limp over to me. I was in bad shape, but I couldn't let her know that.

I sat up and set my face with an angry scowl. "That's right, come on over so I can finish you off!"

She paused and weighed her options. "No, I think not. I have the data, and you have only minutes to live. I'll watch you die from my venom at a distance."

My mouth dropped open, and she smirked, "After all, it can get a little messy."

With that, she turned and shuffled off the stage.

The crowd waved glow sticks and chanted her name as she left. Without looking back, she flipped them the bird, which only made them chant more.

After she left, I began examining my wound, wondering if she had been bluffing about the poison. With her, I couldn't take the chance. I'd have to remove the spike here and now just to be safe.

Looking at my thigh, I saw that her heel had sunk all the way under my skin. Pressing around the wound, I could see the tip of it through the dime-sized hold it had made. This was going to suck.

Pressing down around the entry wound, I exposed as much of the spike as possible. A sharp pain went through my thigh, as I spread the opening to reach in and grab the end of the metal rod. Taking a few deep breaths, I pulled.

A fiery agony raced through my entire leg causing me to let out a scream. The sticky red spike slid out of my thigh, and the pain began to ease. Holding it up to have a look, I saw that it was solid with no compartment to hold any kind of poison.

The crowd gathered around the stage had gone silent, watching my makeshift surgery. Staying in character, I announced, "That was one black widow that didn't have any venom."

I shrugged and tossed the small metal rod over my shoulder and it clinked across the stage. The stunned crowd erupted into cheers.

Getting to my feet, I looked around for Eliza, but she was gone. The crowd was still cheering, so I waved to them and moved to leave the stage. I didn't want to be around when Sloss security arrived and figured out all this wasn't part of the show. Walking toward stage left, I fumed in frustration. Like a fool, I'd lost Viktor's data to Eliza, and to top it off, I lost Eliza.

Hearing several people running toward where I stood in the wings, I knew it was time to leave. Silently cursing myself, I slipped into the deep shadows and pondered my next move.

Chapter 33

Slipping away from the stage area, I headed for a bathroom to clean up and gather my thoughts. I found one, and washed the blood off myself. Luckily for me, the bleeding from my thigh wasn't that bad, and I was able to tie my socks together, using them as a makeshift bandage.

While cleaning up, I ran through all my options and came up with a course of action. Since I still couldn't contact anyone, thanks to Eliza, I decided to head back to my apartment and work on removing the signal blocker in my head. Either I would be able to remove it and call Adam, or he would show up there if I didn't contact him tonight like I'd agreed. Either way, I could then get help in finding her and getting Viktor's data back.

The first thing I had to do was get a ride home. Eliza had smashed my phone, so I would have to find an ATM and get some actual money to use for payment. Leaving the bathroom, I walked by the dance floor on my way to the entrance gate of Sloss.

I stuck to the shadows and out of sight. The last thing I wanted was to be seen by someone in the crowd and have them notice that my wounds were actually real. The task turned out to be easier than I thought, most of them were still talking with each other and using their cell phones, so I just walked right past.

Nearing the main gate, I located an ATM sitting back in the corner, away from everything. There was only one security guy at the gate, and I made it past him without a hassle.

I walked over to the machine, and it appeared to be functioning. It had a hologram playing of a person passing a phone over the input device, but since mine was broken into pieces, I selected the 'cash withdrawal' option. The ATM thought about this for a moment, and then asked to scan my retina. I held still and allowed it, and after a few more seconds, I had access to my account. Withdrawing a couple hundred dollars, I headed toward the parking area to catch a ride.

Once I arrived there, I saw several cabs were waiting for fares, probably to take guests home that drank a bit too much. It took me a few tries to find one that could accept cash, but once I did, I hopped in and we were off without delay.

The cabbie wasn't as friendly as Paul, and to be honest, I wasn't in much of a talking mood anyway. I sat in silence, berating myself for losing the data drive with Viktor's research. I was certain Stepan wouldn't be able to get past the encryption, but that didn't matter. Until it was recovered, I couldn't pass it on to Elizabeth, who was its rightful owner. I smiled knowing that once I was able to contact the NSA, I would have plenty of help retrieving the drive. They would want her to have that data as much as I did.

I paid the cabbie as he pulled up outside my apartment. He thanked me and left as I climbed the stairs up to my door. Pushing it open, I flipped on the lights, revealing the mess that Eliza and her goons had made. A sight that just pissed me off all over again.

Sighing, I made my way toward the bathroom. All I wanted was to get this thing out of my head, and call Adam. While he was on his way, I could take a shower and change. Then we could work on tracking Eliza down. There was no telling where she could be by now.

As I walked into the bedroom, I flipped on the lights and couldn't believe my eyes.

Eliza sat on my bed, leaning her back against my headboard. She'd changed out of her painted on leather look and was wearing loose fitting combat fatigues and boots.

"Took you long enough to get here," she said.

I instantly went into a fighting stance, but she held up her hand. "No, there's not going to be any of that. You're going to come with me, and you're going to do it right now."

"Why wouldn't I just kick your teeth in and take back Viktor's research?" I asked.

Her twisted grin grew until it reached from one side of her face to the other. "Because, if you don't, it will go quite badly for your friend Zory."

"Who's that?" I bluffed.

She scoffed and pulled out her phone. When she hit play, a hologram appeared floating a few inches above the phone's surface. It was Zory. He sat alone in a featureless gray room. His hands had been bound behind his back, and his face was bruised and swollen.

He spat, and spoke to the camera. "They're making me record this, Anna. I'm supposed to convince you to come back, but you know you shouldn't. They're just going to kill me as soon as they get you back, so stay safe, wherever you are," he coughed and spat again, "Don't come back for me, Angel, it's not worth it."

As his image faded out, all my anger and hatred focused on Eliza. I moved forward, intending to end this here and now.

She shook her head. "You don't want to do that. I'm supposed to contact Stepan every so often and check in. If I don't, well you know what would happen to your buddy, right?"

I stood there, clenching and unclenching my fists. I felt so damn powerless.

"There, you see, you *can* be trained," she said.

"Zory is right. If I did come back, you heartless bastards would just kill him anyway." I spat.

Eliza's smile somehow widened, then surprisingly, disappeared all together. "No, we wouldn't. Stepan tells me that we would keep him around, so that you would stay obedient. He thinks it would be a valuable incentive."

Stepan had me figured. I'd do anything to protect Zory. He had saved my life several times over, and I would do the same for him. Besides, as long as he was alive, I could work on a plan to get us both out of there.

"How the hell do I know you won't just kill me if I go with you, Eliza?" I asked.

A frown found its way to her face. "Because Stepan has ordered me to deliver you alive. He knows I've found you and that you are relatively unharmed."

"What, did you send him a report?" I asked.

"Not really. Here take a look." She tapped in a few more commands on her phone, and then held it out for me to see. Eliza had pulled up a website called YouTube. It was a place where anyone could upload videos that they wanted other people to view. On her screen, was a listing of at least a hundred videos, and they were all on the Sloss Halloween party.

I looked back to her, and she said, "That's right, our fight has gone viral. It looks like a shit ton of people recorded our stage show and uploaded it to the web. Matter of fact, it's on track to be the most retweeted topic in the history of Twitter."

"So Stepan saw this, and knew you'd found me, and that I was alive.

Amazing," I said.

"Not so much. All the intelligence agencies are notified anytime something hits the web like this," she said.

I smirked and said, "This must be so horrible for you. Knowing I'm so close, and you can't touch me."

She sighed and looked thoughtful. "Oh, don't worry about me, I'll figure something out. Now stop stalling and let's go."

"I haven't said I was going anywhere," I growled.

"Look, I'm tired of playing. If you don't get your ass in gear, I'm going to contact Stepan and tell him to kill Zory right now," her evil grin returned, "Plus, I'll have him kill the rest of your buddies from that dump where you work. What were their names…"

"You fucking leave David and Kimber alone!" I yelled at her.

Ignoring me, she continued, "yeah, David and Kimber, that's them. So let's go, no more talk, right now."

We stared at each other, both of us trying to decide what the other was capable of doing. I knew she'd won. I had to agree to her demands. She was well aware that I wouldn't risk my friends.

Resigned to what I knew I had to do, I said, "Alright, I'll go with you. But I swear, if you hurt any of my friends, I'll kill you and Stepan both. Report *that* to him."

Her face-encompassing grin returned. "Now that's a good girl. See, all this can be accomplished easily. You just needed the right incentive. Now stand still and let me search you."

She slid herself off the bed, still favoring her bad hip and hobbled over to me. The first thing she checked for was the signal-blocking device. Once she was sure it was still in place, she patted me down. Satisfied, she said, "Okay, let's go."

"Wait, at least let me change my appearance back and put on something warmer," I said.

She leaned against the doorway and said, "Oh all right, but don't leave my sight...and be quick about it. We have a plane to catch."

I would have given anything to wipe that smirk off her face, but for now, I had to play along. Moreover, there was a positive side. I'd be able to stay close to the data drive, making it easier to recover when the time came...and it *would* come.

"You know what, I knew you'd surrender and come with me," she said.

I ignored her and continued dressing.

"You would do anything for those weaklings, those fragile humans. The sad thing is, you are superior to them in every way, and what do you do? You waste your time trying to *be* one of them...and the pathetic thing is, you will never fit in with them!" Her eyes were wild and with some effort, she stood up and walked over next to me.

"Do you think if they found out what you are, they'd protect you? Welcome you? No, you'd be turned over to their government for research and development. Treated just like a piece of property, a tool for them to use however they saw fit," she said.

That was enough. Straightening up from changing my shoes, I met her demented gaze and said, "How the hell would you know anything about them? Eliza, your mind is broken and you can't comprehend the good things about being human, being a person, not just a machine. Yes, we are stronger, faster, and better at most things, but they are complex in ways you'll never understand."

Pointing my finger at her, I continued, "All you do is try to kill them, rule over them. You don't try to understand them, live with them. Listen to me, I know you feel some sort of loyalty to Stepan, but he's using you the same way you just talked about. You know it's true."

Eliza lowered her head for a moment, and then looked back up to me. Her fevered, psychotic expression was gone, and in its place was one I couldn't entirely read...consideration, perhaps even doubt? Seeing this as a chance that I might not ever get again, I softened my tone.

"Eliza, let us return to Russia, but when we get there, we will follow a different path. Instead of you turning me over to Stepan, and both of us being forced to serve him, instead, work with *me*. Help me free Zory, and in turn, ourselves from Entsky and Ice Castle. Afterwards, we can return here to America. I have friends that we can call on, that will protect us from him," I said.

She didn't reply, and I thought that I might have found a way to reach her. "Look deep within yourself, and you'll see that I'm right. Find it in your heart to listen to me, to your sister. I know you're worth saving."

She looked at me for sometime, and with the passing of each second, my hope grew that I'd actually broken through to her at last.

Finally, she turned her back to me and said, "If you're done, let's go... before I decide to kill you for making me wait."

Her words hurt more than any blow she'd given me all night.

We walked out of my bedroom toward the front door. My eyes brimmed with tears because I knew that had been my last chance. Despite all Viktor's wishes, and even mine, I couldn't save her, couldn't reach her. If I was ever going to be free of this life of hatred and pain, my path was clear. I now knew that I was going to have to kill Eliza.